Midnight Fire Media presents

NIGHT ON EARTH
BY
AMOS KEPPLER

A London Story

Midnight Fire Media

http://midnight-fire.net/mfm
For more about Night on Earth:
http://midnight-fire.net/noe

E-Mail:
ak@midnight-fire.net
manofhood@yahoo.com

Cover, text, design, art, premedia and photos Amos Keppler

ISBN 978-82-91693-07-1

a few years from now…

CHAPTER ONE

The rain poured. The water was hot before it hit the ground. The droplets jumped hissing back up in the air. Water flowed into the sewers. Steam drifted as thick and high as the buildings from the ground up. The ground had yet to cool from the white-hot day. This flood, after a dry and glowing hot sunny day shouldn't be a surprise to anybody living here. This happened often in London during the summer. Rain poured and ten minutes later the streets were just as dry as before the rain.

It was December…

Christmas trees were clearly visible in Camden High Street this evening. Christmas decorations did dominate the store windows.

The man stumbling from Camden Town Underground station turned soaking wet in an instant. He didn't seem to notice, but kept moving forward. Every time one of his feet touched the ground, he revealed how unsteady he was. To the few who bothered to take a closer look at him, he seemed to have trouble with his vision as well. He ran into poles and corners. Something was clearly wrong with him. The eyes had a strange, rigid quality and his entire behavior was… weird. People hurried on, not revealing even the slightest willingness to help him.

He stumbled across the road. It seemed like a miracle that he wasn't run down. Angry horns were muted in the torrential rain. People couldn't fathom how he could avoid reacting to his surroundings, to its obvious dangers, but his face remained stoic, and he kept stumbling forward, as if there was no other course of action available. It dawned on those who followed his plight with a certain, indifferent interest that he followed a kind of pre-programmed route. It seemed to be a somewhat correct conclusion, because he was evidently on his way to the Inn called the Green Rose not that far ahead. Perhaps it was luck that his walk led him to the door and not on a collision course with the wall, but he managed (somehow) to push down the handle, and stumble through the opening revealing itself. He practically fell inside, fell from the quiet rain, to the lively noise within the four moist walls.

Very few of the guests noticed every time the door opened and closed. The noise level in the bar wasn't necessarily that loud, but still loud enough to suppress most other sounds. The door opened and closed. People might see it, but no one heard it. People arrived and left all the time. Nothing strange about that, nothing strange at all.

Water flowed from the newly arrived. It vaporized quickly, almost before reaching the floor, and added to the steam and mist already present in the room, from sweat and heat and empty glasses.

Barkeeps, women and men, were busy behind the counter. The night was unusually busy. They moved constantly and hardly even slowed down. There was a certain energy here, one who might also be present in other places, but not to this degree and intensity.

One of the first things a newcomer would spot would be the *damaged* TV above the bar, black and broken and still smoking. People looked at it, looked a lot… before looking away.

– It was attacked during the news earlier tonight, an eager beaver explained repeatedly to all newcomers that happened to end up by his side. – The news got to be too much for the poor guy, I guess. Not so strange that. No one watches or listens to the news anymore.

– It's unusually crowded here tonight, a woman remarked. – I've never before seen it so crowded.

– People get an ever stronger need to celebrate, the man who enjoyed speaking to newcomers about damaged TVs remarked. – It's getting crazier and crazier out there, so it stands to reason that places such as this mirror that… right?

His voice fell to be almost subdued at the end of the sentence, drowning in the buzz.

The man who had stumbled through the rain kept stumbling across the floor.

– He stares at you, Claudette Francis said to the owner, Evan Shelby.

– Not really, Shelby said lightly. – It just looks that way.

Claudette nodded. He was right. She and Shelby stood behind the bar and the man was heading for the bar, his muddy eyes hardly focusing on anything. Claudette shrugged, and then she turned fully towards Shelby, turned to him with her revealing clothes and demeanor. He looked at her, but not with the interest, the desire she wanted, desired. She smiled at him, but he didn't return her smile, her inviting smile.

– Everything seems to be falling apart out there, she said helplessly. – The world is turning more dangerous every day.

– Old allegiances crumble, he nodded. – The new are more informal.

– A girl can go far to secure her future these days, she said softly.

The newcomer asked for a glass of beer, sniveling to a point of being almost unintelligible. After waiting impatiently for it he emptied the entire pint in one big gulp. He immediately asked for another. The maid serving him caught a glimpse of his eyes and shuddered. There wasn't… anything in there.

The man brought two full pints from the bar and found himself an empty table, incredibly empty, in the crowded room. It didn't seem to dawn on him that many of the guests didn't have a table and could easily have sat down there, if they had wanted to.

Four guys at the neighboring table, involved in an intense poker game scowled at him. One froze and was about to rise when another stopped him.

– Not yet, he hissed. – Remember, we're new here. Let it sink in…

And it did sink in, in other people present in the Green Rose, and the talk wandered across the room.

– They had their own tables at Uniforms and Arms, an old sailor whispered to his companion. – But someone blew the place to smithereens. It left them in a rather foul mood. And the rumors are flying. People say they deliberately chose this place as their new haunt, since many of those present here tonight quite conceivably could be the perps.

When looking at the four those rumors looked very conceivable. And the music being played here didn't exactly make them any friendlier. It was a rare mix of pagan music and modern rock, called Mystical Rrock, the new underground fave of the twenty-first century. Not their type of music. Absolutely not.

The stumbling man sat there and stared deep into the second glass, long after he had emptied it. In a way they couldn't explain he became a kind of variation in their conversation. A conversation that wasn't really that deep. But now even the most innocent word took on a different, sinister meaning.

Claudette put a hand on the man's shoulder. He shook and his eyes burned her. She froze. Didn't dare do anything else.

– Can I help you with anything, sir? She wondered, attempting to speak kindly.

He turned his attention back to his glass. She heard him mumble something. Was it anything like: «I can't be helped»?

A young couple sat face to face. The girl was pregnant. They held hands and warmed each other with their eyes.

– I wonder what his problem is, the boy said curiously.

– It's big, no matter what it is, the girl emphasized.

They rocked with the beat, the music giving relief, but it also made sure they didn't forget.

– He's like a smooth surface, the girl said wondering and frightened. –

His eyes don't mirror his soul, but ours.

– So deep.

The boy was unable to emphasize the humor he wanted in his voice and demeanor. And she couldn't either, when she smacked his fingers.

Needles of rain kept passing the windows, kept hitting the nascent sea on the ground. It fell straight down. There wasn't even a breath of wind outside that could make the droplets deviate from their course.

– I wonder how high the UV-reading truly was today, the girl said distantly.

– High, the boy grunted. – We can say that for sure.

– I mean… it would be great to hear the correct numbers, hear the truth for once.

– It's the same as with the dam, he said sarcastically. – *Officially,* we'll never hear anything except that it will be able to take the pressure of any given amount of water pushing at it, at any time. The number of cancer cases will never rise, and it isn't proven that cow disease can be transferred to people…

The biggest man at the poker table swore. He had lost an important game. The other players were used to him winning, and smiled scornfully behind their masks.

The stumbling man belched, prolonged and thoroughly, uninhibited and unlimited. The four players raised more than one brow. The man rose and stumbled on unsteady feet towards the toilets. There was something pathetic and strangely threatening about him at the same time. The players exchanged glances.

– Perhaps he won't be back, one said.

– Perhaps not, another said, both with reluctance and expectation in his voice.

The entrance door opened and closed briefly again, way too briefly.

– Damn, the man dealing the round said. – More worthless lowlife. If at least some of them had drowned tonight, I would be happy.

The man, not less unsteady, returned from his expedition to the toilets, and dumped down on the same chair at the empty table. The four card players raised more eyebrows, but remained in their chairs. They couldn't avoid hearing the snickering in the room, knowing fully well it was at their expense.

The entrance door opened again, and this time it stayed open for quite some time. The four grinned widely. Six people entered the room. The leader towered above everybody, but all of the six filled the doorway well when they walked through it. Two of them were women, and they hardly seemed much smaller.

Claudette fearfully accepted their coats. They didn't seem to care about either her or the surroundings, and for once she didn't mind. The last thing she wanted was attention from these people. She almost felt sorry for the lone man at the table. Almost.

The leader seemed to take in the situation with a single glance. He led his entourage directly to the two tables, exchanging brief nods with the card players, until he slowly and deliberately turned to the lone man at the neighbor table.

– I'm gonna explain something to you now, he said, as if he was talking to a child. – Listen carefully, because I won't repeat it

The lone man at the table just kept staring at his glass and his beer, seemingly not hearing anything.

– We're ten people who have reserved these tables to drink and to play. Five on each table, get it?

– As far as I know there isn't… table reservation in this place.

The man hadn't looked up or moved, and at first no one nearby could be certain that he had actually spoken. Not until they saw the large man's reaction.

– You don't *get it*. These tables belong to *us*.

The stumbling man began moving his hand over the table and under it as well, looking under it, before looking up with a silly grin, with eyes with the same empty expression. It looked like there was no one home, no one at all.

– *What?* The large man exclaimed impatiently.

– I don't see any… brand, the man with the muddy eyes said in exalted triumph, – any proof of… ownership.

– You're retarded, ain't ya? The large man nodded. – Well, you should know I've never cared much for those shitheads.

The people in the room waited for, anticipated the explosion, and knew they would be rewarded.

– There's no table reservation.

They all turned, changed their perspective. Shelby, the owner suddenly stood close to the table, without anyone actually seeing him go there.

– First come, first served, that's the «rule». But there are empty chairs here, to be filled, if there are no objections.

– There are many, the large man spat. – By damn!

Uncertainty gnawed at him, and he signaled to the nine in his entourage that they should keep their calm.

– I've heard about you, Shelby, he said. – Heard your name whispered in fear. It's said it's very dangerous to cross you.

Shelby stood there, clearly waiting. People held their breath.

– You don't take shit from anybody… I can respect that.

And thus, it ended, with no one losing face. People let out their breath. The buzz returned.

– You can take the extra chairs, Shelby said gracefully. – No one else seems to want them…

All ten of them were able to sit around the other table, tight, but not too tight.

One of the ten, one of the women hit the table with a fist.

– This place is dark as a crypt, she cried.

It was dark, unusually so, compared to other establishments. All lamps shone with muted light, and there weren't that many of them. The room was filled with shadows.

– I enjoy the dark, Shelby said, – and I own the place. The guests enjoy it as well. But I see no reason not to be accommodating in this matter. CLAUDETTE!

– Yes, Boss? She spoke sweetly, moved sweetly, very accommodating.

– Put one bright bulb in the lamp above this table.

– At once, Boss! She grinned. – Right away, Boss!

Eagerness mixed with uncertainty burned within her, as it always did in Evan Shelby's presence. She rushed into the kitchen, knowing well she had always been able to handle men like Shelby, fully aware that she was unable to handle him. Shelby's presence… unnerved her.

The swing doors closed behind her. She stared at him through the small, round glasses in the doors, did it for a second or two, looking at his eyes, half turned away from her, before pulling back, heading for the drawers in the darker parts of the room.

– You look shitty as hell.

She shook, jumpy as hell. Her cousin appeared from the shadows.

– I can't help it, she said angrily. – He… *spooks* me, *okay*. I swear he has those eyes on me even when he's looking away.

Shelby turned away from the ten on the cramped table, and turned towards the man who seemed unsteady, even when sitting.

– If we can help you with anything, don't hesitate to tell us, he said pleasantly.

– You can't! There was an abrupt snarl. – Stay away from me.

Claudette returned with the bulb and changed it with smooth, sensual moves. Her entire female form was well displayed, both to Shelby and all others. The eight men didn't attempt anything, didn't even look at her with more than a passing glance. Their leader evidently had total control over them.

And Shelby controlled him, controlled the thug controlling the thugs. Claudette looked at him with eyes filled with desire and admiration.

She returned to her chore as waitress. The Inn sort of calmed down. The potential for trouble had passed, at least momentarily, and people turned their attention to other things.

– No game tonight, the leader said, deadly calm, to his compatriots.

– Patience, patience, one of the women stated with a pointed glance.

It turned quiet. Perhaps not in sound, but the high energy buzz clearly faded. But in the quiet darkness people talked and lived on. In the other, even darker room, a boy walked out on the dance floor, and began doing «Kacha», a special form of nature dance and gymnastics that had been popular for a while now. Several others joined in. And then, after a few minutes, when the music changed, the dance erupted in savage moves. Even during the calmer parts of the music, the dance remained intense and wild. The mystery Rrock and the dance kept going throughout the night, both loud and quiet.

The world is full of contradictions, Evan Shelby thought.

He registered that the stumbling man visited the toilet many times during the time he was a guest of the house. Evidently to throw up. Sharp eyes easily saw the vomit at the corner of the mouth.

The frustrated poker players didn't enjoy the drunk sitting close to them. They didn't enjoy it at all. He smiled and laughed and made a number of hiccups a minute, slurped and cried, and evidently had no control whatsoever over himself. They took every move and sound coming from him as a personal insult. Shelby exhibited an ugly grin. He almost had to admire their constraint.

Almost.

They left the place early, with a demeanor colder than ice, anything but overtly snarling. The time hadn't even passed midnight when a waitress passed them their coats.

– Thank you for visiting The Green Rose, she said politely, sweetly. – Please come again soon.

They didn't take that in a very positive way either.

It was hard to tell if the waitress actually meant it, if she was a dumb goose or one with a very fine-tuned irony.

People made bets about it, as they easily did on such matters these days.

A while later the stumbling drunk broke down in laughter.

– «Thank you for visiting The Green Rose», he cackled. – «Please come again soon». HE HE

He buried his face in shaking hands and he sat like that for a long time. This time, when rising and heading for the toilet, he didn't manage more than a few steps before throwing up. He vomited over two married couples eating. One of the women rose and punched him so hard that he flew across the room and turned over several tables on his journey.

The guests laughed themselves silly. Including those he had landed on.

– We'll make more food, for free, Shelby said hastily, before the discontent spread.

– C'mon, do you want some more?

The woman snarled and posed in a defensive position.

– Damn bitch, the man's mouth hissed hatefully. The rest of his face didn't rid itself of the dull look. – Damn you all!

– Beware! A man jumped angrily to his feet.

The drunk took a stab at him, but missed by a mile. His coordination wasn't better than it had been. He struck nothing but air and fell, and hit the floor hard.

– I curse you all, he mumbled, as he crawled on the floor. – *Curse* you…

He pulled himself up on the chair and once again dived deeply into the swimming pool of a glass. Suddenly, without notice, he seemed to have forgotten everything that had happened.

– One free drink to all, the owner cried, once again rising to the challenge of strategically calming the guests. – Kindly remain in your chairs, and we will serve you all.

The guests also seemed to have delegated the memory of the drunken man's hatred a few minutes before to the depth of their mind. Bar guests behaved strangely sometimes.

It turned out to be a bizarre night for the people visiting the Green Rose. And the lone man caused most of it. There were episodes. People kept changing their opinion of him. They didn't know whether or not they should dislike the man, pity him, laugh or cry. Help him, or fear and hate this eerie creature of a human being.

– … remember…an old song, he hummed. – «Feel the glow, the glow we all must feel»… and it scares the shit out of me.

No one was able to tell how many glasses, beer, wine and liquor he had been drinking. They knew it was a lot, bordering on the improbable, and that it returned the same way it had come a few minutes after he had drunk it. He hadn't eaten any food, not the tiniest piece.

He was pale. Everybody had pale skin these days, caused by lack of sunrays, but he was *pale*. He looked so bad that they found it remarkable that he was able to stand. There wasn't anything wrong with his strength, though, only his coordination.

Everything about him seemed wrong… or different, in a way they were nowhere close to explaining, far less put into words.

Some remained in their chairs, silent and brooding, while others used the occasion to let go. They felt the special mood and responded accordingly.

This place had always been something special, at least since Shelby had taken over. But tonight, the stranger spiced it all further. *The Stranger…* not only in the sense that none of them had met him before, but an understanding of the word going way beyond that.

A pack of youths danced to the beat. Supple young limbs threw themselves into the laughter and play. They didn't just use the dance floor, but also the space between the tables. Everywhere between the floor and the ceiling. The rain kept pouring outside and the water formed a river in the streets. A river turning into a sea. Inside the Green Rose the water constantly vaporizing from the floor didn't put any damper on the mood, the exuberant mood.

They smilingly surrounded the lone man's table. Usually, they would leave such a downtrodden man in peace, but they had so much fun now that they were ready to take on hopeless causes. A girl reached for him with two open palms. He jumped up and pushed her, pushed her hard away. So hard that the others just about managed to catch her before she hit the bar. Shelby was there in an instant and grabbed the raised arm.

– Hey, man, pull yourself together.

The stumbling drunk stood there, momentarily frozen. Then he struck the open, offered hand. He backed off from Shelby, backed towards the entrance with a snarl. The entrance door opened and closed with a loud crack. He had vanished in an instant, as if he had never been there at all.

– Good riddance, Claudette sniffed indignant.

Shelby held his tongue. His face had taken on a distant quality not totally unlike that of the stranger. He had his entire attention directed at the door. And beyond… at the wet, dark streets outside. At the needles of rain stabbing everybody stupid enough to expose themselves to them. He felt them, as if he personally felt them hit his body.

They all heard the rain. They could no longer avoid hearing it.

– The dam must have broken, a man said fearfully. – This can't be just rain. It just can't.

The rain poured down. Tonight was one, continuous shower. People finding themselves outside looked at each other, in loss of words. The dirty, lukewarm water bathed them. The dirt covered everything, most noticeably the flickering round, orange traffic lights. This was certainly not a night where the ground dried. Instead, there was no ground anymore, only the vast sea-like river drowning the city.

The man stumbling out of the Green Rose, pressed a hand at his mouth and was soaking wet after just a few steps, as the ruthless forces of nature assaulted him. Perhaps he registered this deep within himself, but nothing suggested that he did, and he continued his blind walk. The thoughts racing through his mind hardly reached any rational level. They were merely random pieces in a puzzle without meaning.

He was freezing, freezing violently in the heat of the night. Nightmarish images chased away any heat he might have felt. Where had he been today? He couldn't tell. What had he done? Where did he just come from? Where he had lived all nights before this remained unknown. Did he know… who he was? He knew he couldn't even start to reply to that question. He knew he ran from something. From what he couldn't say. A white glowing ice-cold rage, both known and unknown rose from his depths, making him straighten and remove his hand from his mouth.

The pain came first. Then the violent, all-consuming nausea. He was forced to crouch so much that his hair almost touched the ground. He wondered about how he was able to stay on his feet, didn't wonder about anything anymore, merely took steps one by one, until he reached a dark alley. A large, endless gap swallowing him whole.

A beast swallowed him whole and raw, but it wasn't that beast that was growing. He was, until he had grown so large that he *became* the monster. Everything turned black and he saw existence with absolute clarity. He felt like he ran through the pitch-black hole. It happened so slow, so slow. A wall, he had to find a wall, something to lean on. He had to stop, breathe out, breathe in. It was so hard to breathe. Vomit flowed from his mouth like a geyser. Another round of vomit. He couldn't understand how there could be more left down there, all the times he had emptied himself. The hollow room in his stomach hurt so much that he felt there was nothing but bowels left down there, and now everything returned topside with a vengeance. He crouched, but didn't fall. The body felt powerless and powerful at the same time. The ears listened and they didn't listen. Did he hear steps? The ears that listened heard steps. A pack of monsters slipped close to him, surrounded him. He had been aware that they were hunting him, but the paralyzing indifference dominated his being.

– Look at this SICK bastard.

They blinded him with flashlights, a sun in his face. He didn't really see anything but shadows, shadows with horns and claws.

– One will hardly encounter anything more sickening, another confirmed. – I've never done so.

– By damn. And such trash is supposed to belong to the human race.

He was grabbed hard around his arms and pulled up. The first strike hit deep within the sore, empty stomach. Many fists followed that first. They threw him through the air. His head hit a brick wall. He hit the ground hard. They began kicking him. Everything hurt, in a distant, horrible way. He registered no surprise in himself because of what happened with him. Only the pain was real, was true.

They lifted him up by the hair and held him up by it. Experts like them knew well how much people could take before they stopped feeling the pain. Except they were wrong. There wasn't one pain, but one with many different points, dull edges beating endlessly within. They didn't understand shit, Satan's pigs… roasted pigs, he, he. He had feared for a while now, that he was on the verge of insanity. He remembered that, registered it dully, like he registered everything else. He had stopped caring.

– Hold him.

A knee struck his crotch. Another in a long row.

– Damn, the guy must be a blood donor. He's hardly bleeding.

– Everything is diluted. He's drowning in alcohol.

He heard the grin more than he saw it.

– The red color is virtually gone.

The laughter was hard and rough. Someone would perhaps call it ruthless and terrifying, but not he who knew well what was truly ruthless and terrifying. They didn't. Not yet.

– Let's put an end to this wreck.

– No! A sharp commando voice. – Let him serve as a warning, a harsh lesson.

Experts, no doubt. They didn't break a single bone in his body, even during the final, prolonged beating. The white light grew, until the black glow was the only thing he «saw». He saw nothing. Nothing but horns and pointed tails. Everything turned to shadows once more. Steps grew distant. He knew they were, even though he heard nothing.

The last of them released him, let go of his hair. He fell far, and landed on the hard ground a thousand meters below. His head hit the tarmac. He felt it like he landed on a field of soft feathers. The wreck of a human being remained where it had landed, unmovable.

CHAPTER TWO

Water flowed, passed by ever faster.

The darkness still smothered Sheila Watts like a blanket when she stepped out of Camden Town underground station. The Tube, the Underground ran during the night now, and had done so for some months, something that in a backwards kind of way was connected to the fact that the city council, a few years earlier had voted to cut the power to the streetlights.

This was a dangerous area. It had been that way for a long time, but it had deteriorated further the last few years.

The Tube ran in the night… if there were trains at all. Delays were frequent. No train and tube company operating on British soil had ever been on time, and that record hadn't improved any lately.

Sheila was quite pleased by the delay just now, though, the boring, one-hour delay. Disappointment reigned in her when she reached street level, and rain still flooded air and ground. The fact that she had forgotten her umbrella in her office didn't really register. Nobody could be that stupid… right? She had waited the entire time during the boring ride, and hoped for the rain to stop. But no such luck.

She had shown her badge and the doors to the station hadn't been closed between each departure and arrival, as was usually the case. But finally fed up with waiting for nice weather she had left. The guard had gratefully closed the doors, feeling a bit safer, a bit more protected against the sinister people passing by and staring a lot in the process.

She ran the last stretch to the Camden police headquarters. The run to her apartment would have taken twice as long and made her soaking wet. Just before arriving she slowed down, walked very slowly the last few steps. She had heard about coppers that had been shot, shot with a hail of bullets, because they had approached a given station at high speed. And if she had charged through the door, then one or several people inside definitely would have filled her with lead. So, she calmly, with shaking hands pushed down the handle and opened the door. In the hall inside waited a control post protected by bulletproof glass. There were no people outside or just inside of it, but if there had been they tended to be very, very… jumpy. She walked to the glass, the wall, slowly, without making any sudden moves.

No people, nothing alive visible anywhere, only an optical «eye», and the hole in the wall working as the computer's second control mechanism.

And there was also a third, a number of surveillance cameras behind the glass filming visitors from every possible angle. Nothing was apparently left to chance here. She caught herself smiling acridly.

– WELCOME TO THE CAMDEN TOWN POLICE HEADQUARTERS, the computer greeted her in a very, very friendly tone of voice. – PLEASE INFORM US OF NAME, NUMBER AND BIOGRAPHICAL DATA, AND STAND READY FOR IDENTIFICATION.

– Watts, Sheila, xYz15336835, Inspector, Special Forces, Scotland Yard.

A broad laser beam lit her right eye. She felt a slight pain when the epidermal layer of the skin on the finger she pushed into the hole was peeled off. It lasted a good while before she heard a click, and a part of the glass slid aside, just enough for a human being to pass through.

– YOU ARE CLEARED, the computer enlightened her, fairly unnecessary. – PLEASE PROCEED TO THE NEAREST DOOR, WHERE A CONSTABLE WILL WAIT FOR YOU.

It was remarkable how much like a person it sounded. If the clearance had failed or if there had been a civilian guest, it would, in the same nice tone, have asked that someone to wait.

She opened the door and stepped inside. And stopped again. It was sufficient with one single observation and not necessarily any outstanding logical abilities to know that something extraordinary was taking place here.

Every man and woman she could see, uniformed or not, had their guns drawn and their attention was exclusively on her. Except for the occasional glance at the darker corners of the room. They all stared very hard at those corners. The mood was very strange.

– Are you carrying arms, Inspector? The man closest to her asked, showing unusual aggression.

– Of course, I do, she snapped. All policemen and women in this country carried arms in this time and age, even those not on duty. – *What's going on here?*

She just boiled with irritation. They all heard that.

– We have a possible infiltrator on the premises, Inspector, another man replied hoarsely.

She stared at him, very impatient, very cross. He was sweating.

– A body has… vanished.

– A *body?* Do you mean a *dead* body? What has happened here? Did it suddenly decide to *walk* off?

The Sergeant was sweating even harder. He was visibly relieved when

the door to an office opened, and a man stuck his head outside.
– Sheila, in here, that someone cried.
After considering the invitation for a moment, she decided to accept it. It was simply way too tempting to refuse.
Gordon Tyler was, as usual, impeccably dressed. In a suit, complete with a tie, white shirt and black shoes. Usually, he radiated a high level of self-confidence. And he had that armor on now, as well, but now she saw clear cracks in it. Her interest was further piqued. She smiled sweetly to him as she followed him into the office. He closed the door and pulled out a chair to her. She self-consciously touched her long blonde hair, wet now, darker now, wet like her clothes. Only the coat had kept her from being soaked. She put it over another chair. Water practically flowed down on the carpet and formed a wet spot. He looked at it, clearly not approving. She saw it and threw her head back in irritation. A movement, an instinct that not all the civilized domestication could hold back.
– You come from headquarters?
She nodded, fulfilled his reluctant prayer. It was true. She did come from headquarters. But not on the errand he expected.
– I have a story you most certainly will enjoy. He smiled charmingly.
– I can believe that. She returned the smile. – Can I safely assume it has something to do with the runaway dead body?
He caught the irony and wasn't suspicious.
– It goes like this, he began, both nervous and expectant, both dramatic and businesslike. – We found a body, badly mangled, on patrol earlier tonight. A male, somewhere in his thirties, with old clothes, easily torn. He had been kicked and beaten repeatedly. Yes, yes, I know what you're thinking. A routine matter, just another bum knocked around by some hoodlums, another sheet in the paper trail.
– But… He led his fingertips together and looked conspiratorially at Sheila. – Certain irregularities were present very early on and were confirmed later. You see, we actually managed to do a cursory examination before…
– Okay. He coughed. – Only the facts, isn't that what we're taught?
– Point 1: He didn't die of the kicking or beating. None of the injuries were even close to being dangerous, not each one and not together, far less lethal. They were made by experts to look bad and cause pain… the highest possible pain.
He looked poised at her.
– Point 2: He stank of vomit and alcohol. We asked around and discovered that he had lived his final hours at the Green Rose Inn. We

have countless witnesses visiting the place tonight who can testify that he drank sufficient quantities to die many times. But we hardly found a trace of alcohol in the only blood test we managed to get. That, too, is consistent with what the witnesses told us. He threw up everything right after he had ingested it. The beer, the wine, the liquor. He drank everything and threw up everything…

– A wealthy drinker for sure… Watts noted.

– He paid for himself, without breaking a stride, Tyler said. – But he still walked around like a beggar. A fact bringing us to Point 3: He paid for himself with one of those nameless credit card accounts.

Sheila nodded. He belonged to one of the highest circuits in town, «The Untouchables».

– We didn't find it on him. – Tyler shrugged. – Who knows, perhaps he flushed it down the toilet.

He rose and signed for her to follow him. There was clearly more. She followed him willingly. There was something here, something, something big. Also one or more details he was unwilling to explain or hesitated to explain.

He took her to his computer on the other desk. After waiting until she sat still in his chair, he punched some keys on the keyboard and started the recorded video. He had evidently prepared himself well.

Images of a man in a chair appeared on the large monitor. The room's interior could be seen in the background. Watts recognized it. It was inside the Green Rose.

– Evan Shelby, the owner. Another weird guy.

The Inspector looked dutifully at the recording.

– … paid with money at first. After a while he produced the card.

Shelby's voice. She looked closer at him, at the face on the screen. She didn't really see much.

– The first few hours he was pretty calm. Then others also began hassling him. Eventually he turned ever more… aggressive and aggravated towards virtually everyone present.

Tyler encircled Shelby, preparing the decisive blow.

– You, too, then?

– No, not me, Shelby replied distantly.

The interrogation kept going for a while after that, but it had really ended there and then. Tyler turned off the computer.

– I've interrogated a lot of «tough» guys. He shook his head. – Some crumbles fast, others deny their guilt fervently. This guy is different. He seems completely indifferent and he also, incidentally, has a tight as a vice alibi...

Tyler pulled himself together, plowed his fingers through his hair.

– No matter, the body… yes, he was dead. I personally confirmed that fact. There were no signs of life. The deceased was brought here and carried down to the Cooler, to our resident Doctor Frankenstein, the coroner, old Miller, old and frail, but damn good. He reacted strangely, as well, though. I've never seen his hands shake before. He still made a thorough examination of the body and ended up as I did, with the same, final result.

She wondered what he held back, what triumph card he waved before her eyes. Something valid that she both wanted and didn't want to know about. He kept grinning conspiratorially at her. The good mood seemed clearly forced to her, as expected. He was a climber, a mask, a pretender, and their mask was never true.

– This is how it goes… He rubbed a finger back and forth on his upper lip. – We had left the body on the autopsy table. There were quite a few bodies on the tables that night, but I was impatient and told Miller to start on this one immediately. The guys left us. I also left the room for a few minutes to get some much-needed coffee. You know how boring this stuff is. I had planned to return after a while, when the good doctor had worked on it and hopefully would have something substantial to tell me. I was at the top of the stairs when I heard his scream. And it was very clear and loud, almost as if he stood right beside me. An insane scream it was, so loud and distorted that I didn't realize who it was and where it came from at first. It took me at least a few moments to realize it came from below. It wasn't that hard to put two and two together. I rushed down and found Miller on the floor. He was still screaming, but was so hoarse by now that there wasn't that much of a sound left. He went into cardiac arrest as I looked at him, and started to whisper, even more insanely the moment he stopped screaming. There was nothing intelligible to get from him, no matter how much I tried. Some connections, his version of the… the incident. Not more than that. I didn't get a change to speak much with him, before they took him away, rushed him to the hospital. I'm told he's alive, but still in critical condition.

– He had taken a trip to the john, he told me. His bladder, as usual. When he returned… the body was missing. Poor Miller. He was even paler than usual. During his many years of service, he has experienced a lot, but never has a body risen from the table and run off before.

Tyler hit his thigh. Sheila covered her mouth. This was indeed a hysterically funny image.

She found his extremely shifting moods, from fear to horror-mixed joy ever more suspicious, though.

– Too bad it wasn't just another bum, he complained, momentarily failing in his performance, once more chasing his hand through the unusually unkempt hair. – I suppose his card can be stolen or lost, but… I shudder at the very thought of all the paperwork ahead of me, and what am I supposed to *write?* Especially about…

He looked uncertain at her.

She was convinced he was still playacting. She wasn't stupid enough to believe otherwise. He only pretended to be her confidant. It hardly even irritated her that much. She would hold out more, much more, to find out what he was hiding.

He was about to spill his guts, to reveal it all. She didn't doubt that. Or he wouldn't have walked so far out on thin ice, as he had. She was, after all, his immediate superior right now, the person he believed decided Heaven and Earth as far as he was concerned. And if she got him to reveal the final piquant detail, that would actually be a correct assumption.

She had stumbled over something big, something dangerous. Something…

A constable stuck his head into the room. He seemed worried, very worried.

– Yes? Tyler barked, uncharacteristically.

– Superintendent Emerson is here, sir, the constable said, in something resembling a whisper.

Watts was close to paralyzed. She hadn't even begun to imagine this case's significance.

Tyler threw daggers of accusation at her. He was unable to hide himself anymore.

– I'm not here in any official capacity, Gordon, she said softly, not without a certain scorn, able to hide her disappointment. – What did you want to tell me?

– Nothing. He closed himself off like a 200 tons vault. – Nothing important.

– Did you take pictures?

– Yes, we took pictures, of course we did. Even though they weren't much use, so badly beaten the asshole was. I would say I have nothing more to say to you on this matter…

– What do you think happened, Gordon? Sarcasm played in her smile, in both their smiles.

– That isn't difficult to guess, he shrugged. – Someone from the inside, here at the station, must have taken the guy, stolen him, so to speak. I have no idea why. Frankly, it doesn't interest me much. Perhaps the thief's god commanded him to do it. Perhaps his dog did. Perhaps a friend of the body recognized it… in spite of the mutilation, and didn't want him to be cut up. Things like that happen all the time.

He met Watts' scorching eyes and added quickly, almost involuntarily, something, a slip of the tongue, or deliberate misleading information.

– Perhaps he recognized a mole…

– A *mole?* Did you see it?

– No, nothing like that. I just mention it like an example. For all I know a dead grandfather commanded him to steal the body. People are so crazy these days that I won't rule out anything.

– Isn't it a bit strange, that in a room filled with stiffs, the thief steals the most interesting item?

She could no longer hold back the sarcasm.

– That should be all, I would think.

He rose. She had already done so.

– May I take a look at the pictures?

– Of course. Shall we go?

He held open the door to her.

She went through the pile of electronic images. When finished she went through them again. And again. And slowly, slowly… she felt something, something strange, wonderful and terrifying. They pulled her, pulled at her, deeply disturbing as they were, without her being able to tell why. She had seen many like these, many similar, but none quite like them. Something… Perhaps not the images themselves, but something beyond them, beyond immediate understanding. She just couldn't put her finger at what eluded her, why she felt drawn to them.

Something…

She had left the well-lit offices and wandered aimlessly through the night. That which stretched out endlessly before her.

It had stopped raining. The only sound she sensed from the silence, from the background noise, was that of the water flowing and playing in the streets. What moved in the city this night did so without giving away any sound. Not so different from when Sheila had been a child, only even more careful, controlled. Something happened around her, but not when she listened. They were so tuned to her movements that they moved when she moved, stopped the moment she stopped. When she stopped to look at the sky, perhaps they did as well.

She looked at the sky. There was no rain, but the sky was blacker than ever.

Usually, she walked straight to her apartment, and in a relaxed manner, but not tonight. Something moved within her, also moving, also present in the wisps of air surrounding her, in the dark alleys she passed on her way. And something that resembled fear stirred her insides, the hidden path to her inner self. A close to ghostly and ghastly challenge she met with trembling legs.

There was no direction to her walk, no aim except for the final goal, her apartment. Nothing to listen to but the night's rhythm, street down and street up. She might have done something similar before, but not like now, not like this.

The Green Rose appeared in her expanded vision. She passed the building at a distance, but closer than she had intended. The place was closed now, contrary to common practice. It usually closed just before the first line of light lit the east. She had observed that, during many a night, as she had returned home from work. Now the building towered above her, just as threatening as everyone else in the area. All the houses here were quite low, usually two or three floors tops, but for some reason she never felt it like that. Tonight, less than ever.

She spotted the old, abandoned construction site she measured to be about fifty steps away. Approaching it she counted her steps, and ended up at fifty-two, as she stopped in front of its torn down gate. The unfinished building, at the center of the property, had stood there half complete for ages, and would surely remain so, into the distant future, until it crumbled under its own weight.

There would be a long way to walk around it. She hesitated briefly, before entering the premises, starting on the crossing.

Campfires oozed and fizzled in several places. Her nose could still separate the natural smoke from the poisonous pollution. The smoke surrounded her on all sides. The scent of burned meat tore at her nostrils. She heard them run on all her sides. Run in position.

She raced along the edge of her own direction with both fast and firm steps. She wasn't hiding.

The creatures closing in on her didn't care, though. They allowed no one on their territory. Many had gained that insight in a very brutal manner.

Tiny two-legged rats playing hunters raced towards her from all sides. Quiet, unseen, but it did them no good against her. She heard them. She saw them. And at the last part of the distance, they had to expose themselves, in the light of the burning, abandoned fires, and they became her targets, not the other way around. She almost waited until it was too late. In a single, fluid move her hands chased under her coat and brought forth the twelve-gouge shotgun. She never went anywhere without it, not even in the brighter parts of town, and this was nothing like that.

She fired a shot over the head of the closest pack.

– FREEZE! She shouted.

She turned around, one single time. Everybody froze.

She looked down, met the glass hard children's eyes. The oldest of the dirty, skinny creatures were not more than ten years old.

– It's the Copper, she heard from within the crowd.

– The crazy bitch, she heard from the opposite side.

Watts ignored the sound of the smacking lips and concentrated on those with even harder eyes, those who stood out from the crowd.

– I lived here, she said aloud. – Long before you little brats were born.

She had played here, before everything in hell went to hell. The neighborhood kids had adopted it as their home, their darkness, their fortress. They had feared the big black that seemed to surround them, reach for them, even from afar. But it was home, and it was theirs. Sheila had always felt the fear and belonging every time she had passed the place, long after she left, a long time after she had escaped. She had convinced herself that a child's fear of the darkness had dissipated as she had grown big and strong, but now she realized that it, in many ways, had grown. Hadn't she and the other kids, the pre-rats, taken on the fear, unblemished and wild?

– You're not *wanted* here, a girl warned her. – What do you want?

– I'm looking for a man, Sheila cried. – A stranger, with disfigured face, who died nearby tonight. I want answers, and then I'll leave.

The sweet, sweet ogres exchanged glances, before once more turning to the giant in their midst.

– We did see a stranger lurking around here…

– He was good, another acknowledged. – We had a hard time discovering him, even knowing there was someone here at all.

– … but his face was quite okay, and he was certainly not dead.

– He hadn't croaked. A toothless grin. – But he moved like a ghost. See?

Watts pulled a smile. She would have cried if she hadn't been so hardened.

She didn't say: «I'm leaving now». She just left, continued on her way. The pack hesitated a bit, before splitting up, granting her passage. The passage was not wide, but more than wide enough. She didn't feel threatened.

Sheila Watts heard the sound of her own steps, but not theirs. Still, when she turned around, and looked behind her, the midgets were gone. It didn't worry her. No rats or ogres, big or small, worried her. Only after she had left the endless construction site, and re-entered the streets, she felt truly unsafe. She had put her shotgun inside the coat again, but knew precisely where it was. Her fingers knew where it was, knew how the cold and hot metal felt on the skin.

Something… had invaded her. As if someone had split her open with a sharp tool, not the body, not the physical, but something far more fundamental. Her feverish reason translated that into a horrible mirage, a skull dancing in the air ahead of her. Not only a skull, but one with hair, skin and color intact. A head but still a skull. An insane walking dead traversing the streets in Camden Town, on holiday from the river Styx' most frothing currents. It was the images Tyler had shown her, added something to make it even more terrifying.

Little two-legged rats ran through the back alleys. She didn't care about them. Someone ran on the roofs. She didn't hear that, not with her ears, but with a sense infinitely more far-reaching. Such a strange thing. This strange path she had never known, that a part of her had always known.

No people heard the steps on the roofs, not even those who lived in the buildings.

A prolonged, horrible and distorted yell rose from between the houses. Sheila started running instantly, without thinking about it, without thinking. Thoughts raced through her mind. She didn't know for sure, couldn't decide whether or not the person screaming was the victim or the attacker, he, she or *it*. The sound seemed to come from all sides simultaneously, impossible to localize. She leapt around, ran back and forth, until breathing became more than labored, and she was so exhausted that she could hardly stand. She neither heard nor saw anything more.

She stared at her hand, at her Heckler & Koch revolver. She couldn't recall having drawn it. The free hand pushed hard at her knee. She stood there, heaving for breath, crouching in an impossible position. Her head and eyes constantly moving. Her head, eyes, head and body seemingly not belonging to her anymore, but to an independent, unknown entity. She wouldn't have admitted it to anybody, but she breathed hard through her nose, sniffed in the air, and the scent of her prey burned in her nostrils. The prey she hunted, the hunter hunting her. Nothing. Nothing but air even more perverted than all other air in this town.

The gun was gone again, inside her coat, accompanied by its brothers and sisters. In spite of this she felt the pressure on her palm, on her fingers crouching around the handle. The images depicting the face, distorted, insane. Feet directed her towards her the home. Solid door there, few windows, four walls, safe.

Things happened in the dark. Both the worst and the best. Sheila could easily see herself through the eyes of whomever it was that ran on the rooftops. So insignificant and defenseless she was down here, such a tasty snack.

She pulled herself together the instant after the thought had appeared and turned solid. Her face twisted in anger. She wasn't a rat, running through the maze, crouched and fearful.

A fence towered above her. Anything could hide on the other side, the side she couldn't see. But she doubted that, straightened herself, proceeding huskily. The fence reached far ahead of her. She kept glancing to all sides, even down and up. Her life could depend on such a routine. She couldn't hold herself back. Like a child knowing it could be smart to fear the dark.

The entire street, indeed the entire block, was either in ruins or awaited demolition. And the ruins seemed ancient, as if the process had started thousands of years ago. The construction worksite on the other side of the long fence was lit by a dirty, almost useless lamp. The powerful floodlights didn't seem blinding, not in any way. But it did keep her from seeing what happened in the shadows.

She moved forward step by step, and on the boarding she couldn't see through, her shadow did the same. The floodlights were finally behind her, and she got her shadow in front of her. It wasn't until she had walked to the end of the street that she discovered another shadow… following hers. But when she turned abruptly, turned in a whirl of fear, rage and movement, she saw nothing there. She glanced at the workers, those working the giant machines and those outside them, crouched and broken. No help there, even if she would need it, even if she would want it. She raised a fist. What was it with her? This neighborhood was tough, and it had been tough for a long time. If anyone was assaulted, released their death cry, so what? It was nothing new. She could take care of herself. She always had.

They had cleaned up here, tonight, the clean up crew, part of the Metropolitan Police. That kind of surprised her. They usually did nothing with this area except ignoring it.

The signs were clear, though: Few people outside. Few or no one standing around rusty oil barrels to warm food, an act many in the neighborhood usually took part in. Virtually no one here had resources to cover the sky-high electricity prices.

People knew of her here, knew who and what she was. They scowled at her, but kept their distance. They didn't dare do anything else. Their previous attempt at attacking her was a year ago. She felt secure in the certainty that it wouldn't happen again.

A neighborhood of Dirty had found another barrel and lit it up. Watts felt its fire burn the hair of her skin, in spite of the distance. In the hot summer heat, the Dirty gathered tight around the barrel and the fire devoured them. Watts passed the alley, making sure she walked with normal speed, showing no interest whatsoever.

She shook and stopped for a moment. She could hardly believe it, but just then she actually felt a cold trickle down her spine. And it didn't resemble anything she had experienced before. She felt it, like something purely physical. A spike, one of ice, something she had never seen, but if anyone had asked her, she could have made a detailed description of it. A knife rubbing at her spine and paralyzing her body. There was nothing solid in any of it. Nothing she could point at. The neighborhood looked exactly like it always had to her. But in all ways that counted… it had changed, changed to the point where it was totally different from what it had been just last night. The stink of fear had always been here, but now there was a presence in every corner and edge of the eye.

The shadows… huge, threatening, rushed by in the eternal night. But these she could see, touch, like something tangible. What she most of all wanted to catch, grab was hardly something visible. Not like anything but flashes and glimpses on the edge of the eyes. A mirage, a demon, heartbeat and noise in the background. A sense deeper than any streets, brick and mortar or any modern gods like Mammon or Jahve. The certainty that the hunt was on, and she was its *prey*.

She reached her neighborhood, what was supposed to be her territory, but that was nothing but polished rock. The line she crossed wasn't visible, the changes almost imperceptible at first. The buildings were visibly improving in quality for each step she took forward. Another difference was more striking, though. There wasn't a soul present in the streets. No one moved outside here, if they knew what was good for them. Nothing moved here that she could see or hear. Not even her. No matter how much she strived, she couldn't hear herself breathe or see the tiniest bit of herself. Arms, legs reached out in the darkness. Nothing. She smelled what her eyes and ears didn't sense, sensed the scent of fear in her mouth. Reason told her that it was impossible. No one had such sharp senses. No one growing up in the city, the Stone Desert, the Gray Fog. It had to be something else, a sense based on observation and experience. No matter what it was…

There was something out there... Something…

Closing in on her… playing with her, as spittle flowed from its snout… She turned around her own axis in a constant move. Something… It could just as well pretend to be a draft in the night. She wondered if It hunted on the ground or from the air, and realized it didn't matter. She was convinced now. Something hunted her.

A SOUND. A heel scratching dead rock. Another distorted and horrible yell, different this time, expressing bottomless rage and hatred. Sheila suddenly realized she stood with her back pushed at a wall. Both hands tightened painfully around the revolver. She looked above, to all sides, all angles, even down (there were no manholes nearby). She was also tempted to look *behind* her. A horrible pathological thought she was hardly able to resist. She stood tight to a wall, not to a human, not to *It*. The bricks were cold. Not warm, moist and alive, no illusion, no monster threatening to devour her.

She stared hard into the darkness. Nothing there, other than Darkness. She directed her entire attention at it. If one or more attackers had come at her from the sides, she wouldn't have discovered them. Not if they stood right beside her. A foot appeared from the shadows. Then a head. Then a body. And she felt totally absent from her body. She recognized Evan Shelby instantly.

– Is everything all right?

She thought his voice sounded strangely normal.

Everything looked suddenly perfectly normal to her.

She straightened, put her gun away and smiled a bit. If anything was strange it had to be her, with the wild eyes, and her back to the wall in an empty street.

– Everything is all right, she replied, suddenly very relaxed, already breathing normally, only marginally wondering how she could calm down so quickly.

– Want some company? He offered. – I'm going your way.

She was grateful for his discretion. He hadn't said: «Let me take you home». She made no protests and allowed him to take her arm. They walked quietly away from there. She looked up at him. He was half a head taller than she was. That, too, felt unusual. He seemed calm and composed to her. She still sensed something… haunting in his being. It worried her, but it was also a feeling she could identify with. She reminded herself that he had an alibi for the murder. All the employees and many of the guests had independently of each other claimed that he was in the bar all night, all the time, until the police had shown up.

An alibi didn't have to mean shit, of course. She had heard rumors, a hardly audible whisper, about the new, emerging cults. About how one single charismatic leader could make his or her subjects do anything, execute without hesitation the most heinous act. Then the leader, with the alibi, would be the true killer, and they who did thc act itself nothing more than a knife, an axe or any other weapon.

The establishment's propaganda machine produced such rumors on an assembly line, though, about those living on the edge of society perpetrating the most horrible acts. There was nothing solid, no conviction worth believing, in a world of ghosts and shadows.

She remained on guard the entire, uneventful trip to her front door.

– Thank you, she said simply, and then cheerfully: – Thank you for not mentioning how dangerous it is for me to walk alone outdoors at night.

– I think you're among those who have no need for such an advice. He exposed his teeth in a quick smile. – You're well aware of the maxim that no matter how big a bite you have, there are those who have bigger.

She laughed, couldn't help it, as she turned to open the door. She punched in the code. It didn't matter whether or not he or anybody else saw which buttons she punched. The codes changed every time they were used. One for each apartment. Here and on every door to the apartment.

The machine spat out a piece of paper with the new code. She would now have five minutes to memorize or copy the new numbers before the paper self-combusted.

– This seems a bit too much sometimes. She laughed nervously. – There are limits to how safe one can be, right. I mean… I've heard stories about what has happened to people who have lost the code…

She wanted to ask him in, but when she turned around, he was gone, vanished into the dark gray twilight. She shivered a bit and hurried inside. The door closed behind her, and she could relax, relax more. Out there, in his company, she had forgotten herself, thrown all caution to the wind.

One level up, her level. Another door, one door for every floor. Through it, to another door, to her door, and finally, she could enter her own soft darkness, collecting the final code. She walked to a table, writing down the newly collected codes on a single piece of paper and put it in the right pocket of her coat, and then she discarded the notes in a metal bowl, one already filled with ashes. Shortly after that the first scent of burned paper filled the air. She opened the door to the refrigerator and grabbed a bottle of water. She drank directly from it, greedily, emptied everything in the bottle and sent it down her dry throat. And it did feel like water just then, delicious, life-giving water.

The clothes dropped on the floor behind her, across the living room, to the bedroom. She removed her last remaining clothes and crawled into the bed. Eyes closed the moment her head touched the pillow. Before her inner eye she once more saw the façade of the Green Rose, the heavy, black curtains, the dark fabric taking the form of people levitating in the air. Everything seemed unreal, and she realized that, even though she wasn't sleeping, she was deep within the Dream. She had imagined she was very, very awake after what had happened, but she dropped right down on the bed and fell asleep.

She slept - and dreamed.

CHAPTER THREE

The windows in the conference center weren't big. The word «big» didn't suffice when directing one's eyes at the enormous glass plates, the even taller walls. That which seemed to grow together, not to anything even remotely resembling a building. But a *complex*. And this was merely this single room, the auditorium. The Center itself reached across many similar complexes, a huge overbuilt area with countless levels. Each level could consist of offices, minor halls, or quite simply entire streets. And almost everything was open air, at least up to the curved ceiling, stretching into the heavens, far up in the coal black atmosphere. Down, down in the auditorium was the center stage. Long rows with padded chairs rose from there. From every single chair there was an enviable view. The entrepreneurs behind this project had spared no expenses.

The December sun, pale and gray, shone from a yellow and gray sky. The sunshine wasn't prevented by clouds to reach the stone desert called London, but by the thick layers of dust hovering above the city. And there wasn't the slightest draft in the air that could even begin to remove it. Many days of constant rain had had no visible effect. Solid, thick, dark windows made sure nothing but light was let into the Center, and hardly that. No lethal rays. Those who wished it, though, had a nice view over the area once called Docklands, an infamous idea that had turned into a mire of half completed prestige projects. These days the area had many names, changing from where in the pyramid a given person came from, and most of them were less than flattering.

Boys and girls, dressed in tight white fabric, danced on the main stage.

In the orchestra pit beneath the stage the orchestra played the classical music piece exactly as it had been played for two hundred and fifty years. The dance was stiff, mechanical, hardly leaving room for improvisation. The boys' hair was short and well done. The girls' long hair sat in a top. If it had been free, one would have seen it was all the same length. When feet were raised it happened at exactly the same moment. When hands met above heads, there was no noticeable deviation. There was hardly a movement not planned, diverting from the formation. The entertainment was done like the rest of the tedious arrangement, like a preaching, spotless, blameless and repetitive.

Like seeing a gathering of assembly lines, everything, Sheila Watts thought. Stiff, mechanical, effective… *so fucking boring.*

Sheila wasn't on the list of invited guests. She was present in her function as a public servant, standing straight, dressed in full uniform. From her spot she had a great view from the upper levels. Her task, responsibility, was to have the overall supervision with the considerable police force present and also the general security during the arrangement. To fall asleep here wasn't just very possible but probable. Even though they weren't visible everywhere, police constables and security forces *crowded* the place. No one uninvited and/or not thoroughly checked in advance was let through a radius of one kilometer around the complex. Including photographers, technicians, personnel and journalists. So, she could just as well have slept soundly in a bed. But she was also responsible for the guards' behavior and appearance. If one was seen intoxicated or with a single blemish on their uniform, she would be held accountable.

Just to be let inside these walls was seen as a great honor and opportunity. Watts curled her lips ironically. It was about displaying excitement as well. If it happened in a correct manner and the right people noticed it, the opportunities could open up for the lucky guy or gal. Or the abyss could swallow the unlucky that had been noticed in an unfavorable way. The people here worked their ass off, and were only occasionally picked for greater tasks. But they didn't dare anything but to keep toiling under the strict, strict regime. There was always an alternative, one far worse. Things could always be worse.

The cute teenagers danced to two pieces. One more or less modern as well. It could have come to something, Sheila reflected, if it hadn't been so rigid, and planned. The pop music like music had only been accepted as a part of the program because it didn't really make sense to open a place intended for the future with music passé several hundred years ago.

The music rose in the air, fading slowly. The girls curtseyed and the boys bowed deeply. Polite applause flowed towards the stage from the entire local part of the complex.

– They're so *cute,* an elderly lady said excitedly to her companion.

The kids curtseyed and bowed all the way, while leaving the stage.

Time passed while people took a breather and relaxed. They were served sandwiches and cocktails. Rotating lights and exciting rhythms kept the mood going.

A lone woman stepped out on the stage. Sheila knew her. It was Wynette Richards, the TV-hostess. They had been in the same class at school and still had a kind of contact.

Wynette was met by excited applause. She excited the audience' mood further by repeatedly raising and lowering her arms.

Aside from her TV-presence, she worked as a hostess on occasions such as these. And she was extremely good at what she did. She thanked for the applause by smiling widely and waving to her people. It flashed in diamond rings and golden earrings. The brown hair was lightly curled and pulled back, most of it falling behind her shoulders. She wore a smart business suit with a skirt, the fashion statement these days.

She began her well-prepared speech speaking in a clear, pleasant voice. Sheila didn't give a fuck about what was being said, and heard only a few sentences here and there.

– … the hunters are dying off, their crumbling influence disappearing. They've been few for a long time now, and their numbers are ever decreasing in our ordered, organized society. Through the last ten thousand years humanity has undergone a remarkable development from Stone Age level to our modern civilization. Slowly, but surely, we've taken control over our life and improved it generation by generation. The hunters were necessary once, to assure food, assure survival. Now, in the modern world, we've built a system, a web, to care for people's needs. The way I see it this is a natural development as we grow up as a species…

Shelia heard a growing buzz, shaking her head, uncertain if it originated from outside or inside her.

– … problems, but we're solving them. We're getting ever better at protecting ourselves from nature's wiles. Yes, we're rising above them. They grow insignificant. I'm fairly certain you are as excited today, as I am, when you're present during the opening of this new step in our civilization. Ladies and Gentlemen… I give you the… Thatcher Center.

The applause and cries rose towards the ceiling. Wynette kept smiling while ending her well-prepared speech.

– Together with key stations on the Underground it was built and refurbished with one particular purpose in mind. A lot of the work is now completed, and as the system becomes fully operational ever more people will move around town *without going outside*. We'll be able to shop without a single drop of rain falling on us. And the Sun that has turned into such a bother won't bother us anymore. We won't need to take any shit from anyone or anything from this moment on.

– … All this… the progress we've made the last few years, points to one thing: The future and a completely new way of life.

The gathering rose and applauded enthusiastically. The séance went on for minutes with loud noise, until Miss Richards left the podium. Watts turned her back to it all and left the position she had assigned herself.

– Take over here, she ordered her closest subordinate, as she passed him. – If necessary, I can be contacted in the dressing room area.

Just the VIP's had their own dressing rooms. She certainly hadn't. He stared at her. She knew he wanted to ask her what dressing room she was going to visit, but he didn't dare. She kept walking down the hallway, whistling a brittle tune. Available privileges should be used. She had learned that early on. In all these dark nights one had to take what was possible in this world.

As the person with the overall responsibility for security she had access everywhere, except to the dressing rooms. Not even during an emergency. An iron circle of personal bodyguards guarded people with that kind of status. They blocked access to everyone who didn't belong.

– I'm here to meet Wynette Richards, she said formally when halting in front of the gate with the snapping guards.

– You're not on the list, the female sentry said deliberately suspicious and patronizing, without bothering to check her list.

Sheila stood her ground and knew she couldn't do that for very long without paying for it.

Wynette stuck her head out and waved.

– Sheila, step inside, so nice of you to come.

The two-legged dogs stepped aside, suddenly very respectful. Neither Sheila nor Wynette dignified them with their attention.

Watts stepped into the luxurious room while constantly wondering what she was actually doing here. She didn't really doubt what she was actually doing here, but clung to doubt and felt like a wet cloth in an agitator, wondering if there was more a perverted instinct than a conscious purpose that had led her here, where she didn't really wanted to be.

She strived hard to mask how uncomfortable she was.

Wynette closed the door behind them. She opened the Champagne that had been cooling and poured two glasses.

– They *love* me, she exclaimed, red-cheeked, with eyes shining in excitement. – People love me. And do you know why? Because I tell them exactly what they want to hear.

– I should be grateful then, Watts commented sweet and sour, – that you recommended me to watch over your precious hide.

The Champagne flowed from the expensive glass and into her mouth, while it bubbled down her throat, and very, very pleasantly in her stomach.

– You accepted.

The cheerfulness evaporated as she raised a brow. The words were served with the Champagne and a cheerful irony.

– One doesn't reject an official request, Watts returned. – One isn't that stupid.

Wynette poured more Champagne. Sheila felt how the precious fluid bubbled even stronger in her stomach. She had already said more than she should have, but this had been a long time in coming.

– Why do you stay on the nightshift? You can't have enjoyed more than two hours sleep this morning, tops. One sees such things, my dear.

– I… enjoy the nightshift, Sheila replied. – And I dream a lot within brief moments. I've never needed much sleep.

– One thing you should do immediately, Wynette kept going, – is to move out of that hole you call an apartment. The hole in that horrible ghetto. You don't know what's best for you, honey.

– You know I can't afford to move, the other said meekly.

– You know or should know that I can help you with all of it. Wynette spoke with certainty and conviction. – As I've told you several times you have infinite possibilities. Infinite. If you would just let me help you with the first crucial steps. I am, as you know, not an insignificant power in this town, and I can give your career quite a boost. Until you find out what's good for you… and then we can both help each other. Doesn't that sound very nice?

Sheila had heard enough, she felt, more than enough. She held back the irritation and the smoldering rage, but her eyes turned roguish. In the shadowy room her mouth formed a twisted smile.

– While we're speaking about Power, Wynette, dear heart… I know you're familiar with the extended authority of police officers…

– Of course! A shrug.

– … but I'm not sure you've considered the ramifications. I can, for instance, arrest whomever I want, whenever I want, without any formal charge or reason. This includes those who are to a certain degree «protected». That's one reason you guys are also protected from us coppers. I can arrest you this moment or any time I choose, and no one will be able to help you. Hell, we both know no one will show any interest in you or your fate after something like that. They'll just find themselves another doll, a new and exciting toy… without caring which garbage can the old happened to be dumped in. I can handcuff you, but I know you're so sweet that you'll come voluntarily, isn't that right, *Miss Richards?*

At the sight of the swinging handcuffs Wynette turned visibly pale.

– Very funny, she joked meekly and bravely. – Great playacting. You should really do television.

Both started laughing. Sheila dried her tears. But she didn't truly laugh.

– People do disappear, she said solemnly. – And are never seen again. You should look into that.

– Surely, you're joking some more, Wynette said incredulous – I would vanish without a trace five minutes after my first inquiry.

Sheila's burning irritation didn't go away and she… this was one of the times she was afraid of herself… had a burning need to see how the handcuffs looked around Wynette's thin and lovely wrists.

The telephone rang.

They both looked up and straightened from their rather strained positions. Wynette replied.

– It's for you.

Watts took the phone, and it was as if the surroundings changed, melted away, around her, until she returned to the streets, to the violence and death, that had never truly left her. She sank deep into a chair.

The chopper flew her across town, and just before the sun, with its lethal rays, had set, she once more found herself in Camden Town. Transported, transformed, from one hell to another.

The chopper landed in the middle of Camden High Street and stopped all motorized traffic there. Children dressed in shreds gathered around the machine before it had landed. There had been begging children in Camden for as long as Sheila could remember, but their number had increased heavily just the last year. The approaching constables brushed them aside, as they also expertly and brutally took care of obstinate drivers who couldn't or wouldn't move their cars. Watts was surrounded, guarded and escorted away and through the streets. People's whisper reached her ears, in spite of the loud noise.

That wasn't unusual. But something was different now. The envy and hatred in voices and eyes and bodies had gained a scornful quality.

– *One of THEM got it this time...*

– *A lucky stiff took good care of the copper. The stiff and the rats, by damn...*

– *He, he...*

The body, what was left of it had been thrown on top of a heap of black garbage bags. Torn legs and arms had been thrown all over the place and were more or less scraped clean. The upper body, its remains, was in a similar condition. The head... the head was strangely untouched. Sheila would later recall her thoughts from that moment. What was... wrong with the head, making the rats leaving it alone? What had led them to lose their appetite, so to speak?

The head, but also some part of the neck and back, and the chest. Most of the ribs were bare.

– It is one of us. Sergeant James Tramer covered his mouth with a tissue and mumbled more than spoke. – So far there has been no positive identification, but we found the badge.

– What about the ID?

– We... didn't find it. We believe it has been... devoured. It must have been.

– Devoured?

– Yeah, came the hoarse reply. – It's gone. Devoured.

– You're not saying that the rats ate the tasty plastic card and let the head be? That *is* what you're trying to tell me, Sergeant?

– That's correct, Inspector, Tramer replied nervous and cowed.

He pushed the tissue even harder at his lips.

Roderick Carpenter, Scotland Yard's newly appointed coroner, Frank Miller's successor, danced around what was the remains of a human being like a moth around the fire. He didn't fly into it, but it was a close call. There always had been, as long as Sheila had known him. Perhaps that's why she so enjoyed his company, even liked him. He was even closer to the edge than she was.

«Stare into the Abyss, and it stares back at you».

– One doesn't see many like these, does one? One could hear the unconditional excitement in his voice. – A true beauty.

The majority of the constables and brass had long since pulled away in contempt. They stared at him with anger in their eyes. He basically ignored them.

He was, at first glance, what some people would call a «nice young man». Nice features, dark hair, reaching to the shoulders. Unfortunately, it kept covering his eyes and he had to keep brushing it back up with his hands. Blood and tissue remains were stuck in the beautiful mane. The policemen and women could no longer even bear to stare at him. All of them had pulled back. Only Sheila remained and looked attentive at him.

– If I'm allowed to guess, and I am… He grinned widely and winked to her. – I'll conclude, at least preliminarily, that he has lain here since the previous night.

– Rod, why did the rats leave the head intact? She asked softly. – Were they… interrupted?

– Perhaps they just didn't like the guy's face? I can understand that. It doesn't have to be anything wrong, you know.

With the same sweet smile Sheila drew her gun and pushed the barrel at his larynx.

– We don't share your love of death, Rod, she snarled. – We're interested in completely different things. *Now?*

She removed the gun. He led a hand to the throat and rubbed it, holding up the other hand as a peace gesture.

– The rats weren't distracted, interrupted in their task. The remains of this piece of art are way too cleaned for that. As stated, they didn't like the guy's face, at least not its *flesh*. What do I know about rats' appreciation of beauty?

He crouched over the body and kept working with it, while the others hurried on, concentrated on other things. They heard him mumble to himself.

– I don't love Death. It's just that I have a job that's boring me to death. We should all be allowed to do things to brighten our lives, right?

– One thing is certain, a constable exclaimed, with a muffled voice that had to give voice to something. – It isn't the rats that have torn off the arms and legs.

Carpenter raised his head and brightened visibly.

– A thinking young man. What a revelation.

– C'mon, Watts challenged him. – What about guessing some more? How big was the guy doing this?

– Big! Carpenter once again swept a hand through his hair. Those who studied the move could have sworn there were bowels there. – His arm would have to be thick as a thigh, and he would have to have a short forehead and have hair all over his body, a chest like two bruisers…

– You're describing a Gorilla. Sheila enlightened the unenlightened, as she cocked her gun.

He wasn't certain she wouldn't pull the trigger. She saw it in his eyes. A fact she found pleasing and almost exciting.

– Well, as you know, there are stories of people who have made similar miracles, he said quickly. – During moments of extreme rage or under the influence of certain illegal substances. Very skilled masters of martial arts might be able to loosen the arms, but hardly tear them off, as has been done here. Sorry, even guesswork, imagination, is insufficient in this matter.

- Rod Carpenter doesn't have a clue, Sheila said. – That's something I thought I would never see.

And everybody looked at him, and the fear in their eyes came to overshadow that of the disgust.

His eyes, when studying the carcass, were filled with love.

CHAPTER FOUR

The Sun disappeared behind the buildings in the west, and the red western sky slowly turned gray and black. The day didn't last long, only one third of twenty-four hours, at London's latitude, now, in the middle of the dark season. And the soup of poison in the air made it all the darker.

It was now, the streets, close to empty in daylight, were filled with people. Nobody went voluntarily outside in daylight anymore. Ever fewer, even when forced, exposed themselves to the Sun's ever-deadlier rays. No matter how much the public or private media assured people it was safe, that the radiation was well within «acceptable limits».

Claudette stood outside when Evan Shelby walked down the stairs to the bar. He led the glass in his hand to his lips and drank it empty, sucked every drop into his mouth, down his throat. He put the glass on the bar before walking to the door and letting Claudette in.

– You're early, he remarked.

– I wanted to come earlier today, wanted to help out, she said seductively and coquettishly.

She didn't hide her intentions.

He smiled with slightly twisted features where he stood with his face in shadow, forcing himself to hold back. It was mandatory, really, weak as he had always been for well-grown and well-developed women like… the one before him… and Sheila Watts.

Besides, with his experience he had few problems looking straight through her.

– You're starting the day with a Bloody Mary. I saw you, you know.

She pulled close to him, rubbing her delightful curves against him as she walked inside, and smiled a confident, conspiratorial smile.

– That's okay by me. I've heard it's supposed to be healthy, too. One drink each day stimulates the blood. One lives longer.

She stood with her back to him, still performing for him, and didn't notice his extra wide smile.

– It pleases me that you're here…

– Oh? She lit up.

– I'm going out, he told her, not without a certain scornful joy. – It's such a fine evening for a walk. You can begin the evening preparations while I'm gone.

He could picture her and hear her, way beyond the first corner, sense her rage and frustration. It… pleased him.

She didn't wait long after he was gone to pull her cell phone from her pocket. It took several seconds of punching numbers before she realized there was nothing happening on the display. She had forgotten to turn it on. She did so, feverishly, punching the numbers again. The response in the other end was practically instantaneous.

– He needs further encouragement, she said.

Silence still reigned in the streets. Many, and especially those who would make their mark on the night, had only recently awakened. Camden High Street. He walked through it, keeping his nostrils closed with his fingers. The stench, the exhaust stench, always bad, reached another level tonight. And the areas off High Street were just as deadly, in… other ways. And still people celebrated, as if no tomorrow would come. And it wouldn't, of course. He grinned, a very bitter grin.

His very sensitive sense of smell was almost overwhelmed, overloaded by the exhaust. Just one breath made him dizzy. The late afternoon traffic, people moving as slow as snails, moved even slower today. People were sweating hard in their sardine cans, their coffins, on their way back to their slightly bigger coffins, searching desperately for a home.

Shelby did not set course for the bigger market further down High Street tonight. Instead, he dived into Inverness Street. The smaller, common market had been moved ever deeper into the street the last few years. That small move improved the air quality from horrible to bearable. Fruit and food were covered by plastic. Shelby kept coughing, and irritation and anger boiled within him.

The man he had come here to meet, appearing from behind a stall, was some piece of work. Franzz Herbert looked like a stereotype of an African

American gangster in an American early nineteen seventies' movie. A man with light brown skin and with a (to put it mildly) colorful dress code. A long coat, a flowered shirt and a hat covered by a lot of fake flowers. He wanted to be seen, to be noticed.

Four giant bruisers surrounded him. They were his shadows in his shadow.

Shelby wasn't intimidated, and he knew Herbert knew that.

– Shelby, *my man,* what brings you here tonight?

He raised his hands in greeting, but lowered them again when Shelby made no sign of returning the gesture.

– The same as always, Herbert… goods and good conversation. One should never underestimate the value of an inspiring conversation. And you're such a stimulating man to talk to.

Herbert laughed. His teeth were white, and he practically used every opportunity to showcase them. He was quite the cheerful guy.

– I can safely say, he said, – that I can provide both, though you must, as usual, provide your own transport for the one.

– As I prefer it, Shelby nodded. – Any particular problems since the last time?

– The major decision-makers in our corner of the world are too busy making the wheels turn to trouble the smaller fish, Herbert grinned. – I, and others in my position, have their half-hearted blessing to run our own tasks.

– But there is rivalry, the other pointed out, – also within a given *firm*. Aren't you worried your strong arms will just take over the business?

– Not at all. It was said lightly, easygoing. The rows of teeth showed even better. – A certain type of humans may be useful, but still can't put two and two together and have five. The strength of these four is that they know that.

His expression turned solemn as he continued.

– You, my friend, are a far greater enigma. It's interesting what you said about rivalry. Particularly since I've hardly had trouble since we began our little partnership… We both know that competition is fierce. Small and large distributors are devoured and removed from the map every day and night. The fact that you've survived for so long does arouse my curiosity. It's a work of art, in my opinion, and you have my admiration and respect. My problem is that I haven't managed to find out how, not with all my contacts and skill…

– I have my methods. Besides, it isn't your problem.

The interruption was abrupt and didn't invite further scrutiny. «Smiling

Franzz» kept displaying his impressive rows of teeth.

– Please don't take it in a wrong way, he assured the other with just the right tone of regret in his voice. His four giant friends kept looking straight ahead, as they had done all the time. – But you should consider giving me a few pointers here. The reason I chose to expand upon our conversation tonight is that I'm a nice guy, and that contrary to during our previous meetings you've been very communicative, yes, straight out philosophical. Has anything happened that I should know about?

– No, not really, Shelby responded with a slight, almost invisible frown. – I wouldn't let it *worry* me… if I were you.

– I see, Smiling Franzz saw. – Shall we get back to business then?

– Same time, same place.

Shelby discontinued the conversation while turning around and leaving them.

– Okay, the smiling one cried to his back. – No problem.

They kept an eye on him until he disappeared between the stalls. They expected him to appear on the other side, but he didn't. Herbert gave his four shadows the signal and they moved. He waited, not certain why he had sent them off. Perhaps because they shouldn't sense the sneaking fear he felt, only at the very thought of Evan Shelby. He didn't expect them to be able to trace the man, and as expected, ten minutes later they returned, without even catching a glimpse of Shelby. The man - Herbert used the word loosely - had vanished in the dark and the night. Franzz nodded controlled, poised to his companions.

– We're dealing with a very dangerous individual here, he emphasized. – That's an advantage, in the short run. It isn't our problem yet, but it might be.

He heard them from far away, in spite of the noise. His senses approached their potential tonight. He still understood so little about himself. His inner self, still the Other, whispered and roared in his mind, very noisily, aggressively, perhaps cautiously.

The number of cars decreased. The streets were slowly filled with people. Some streets, at least. The temperature dropped only a few notches compared to what it had been during the day. Not sizzling anymore, but hot - and desert dry. The night before rainwater had flooded the streets. Now, there was no longer any sign of the many hours of torrential rain. The occasional enormous downpours didn't help much to improve the drinking water situation either. The groundwater had dropped so much the last few years that it would take months of continuous rain to restore it above critical level.

And it had to be cleaned ten to fifteen times to even be used to wash clothes.

A lone trumpet sounded above the quiet noise. Long, grueling tones. Heat burned in the air, seemed to burn in the very air. Evan remained cold in spite of this. He was always cold.

He wandered the foreign streets and sensed, more than sensed the pull, as he always did. Feet ruled themselves, ruled him. He let it happen. The air still quivered after today's heat. But the cold growing in the day was far more pronounced. And in the night, a heat closed in, hotter than anything that could ever be measured. Evan Shelby smelled the fundamental imbalance. He saw, heard and smelled it, more than sensing it. It screamed at him, was thrown as a tsunami at the rocks, distant, torn rocks. So strange he had never noticed it… before, even though it had always been obvious, to him more than others. He had allowed himself to be distracted, like most others.

The long, wailing tones flowed from the lone trumpet. It poured it, like a lake that would never run empty. Evan couldn't decide from which direction the music came from.

A man stood on a corner, shouting, shouting words making repeated shivers run down Evan's spine.

– IN THIS… LABYRINTH of ORDER OUT OF BALANCE, there is HARDLY ANYTHING BUT The Gray Fog, the dead stone destroying EVERYTHING, around us, SMOTHERING, INFINITE AND ETERNAL

His voice rose and fell, fell and rose, died and lived, as people ran past him, terrified by a dread they couldn't name.

Sounds, images Evan knew weren't real penetrated his conscious mind. Unwanted memories. A set of keyboards, pianos, synthesizers, organs. Fingers playing live music. Music reaching out, in space, in time, in the world. He shook his head, clearing it, wondering why this came to him now, at this particular moment in his life.

Lights. Blinking. Red and blue. Aggravated, stinging like wasps. A closed place. Closed to trespassers. But there were a lot of curios people staring, outside the yellow ribbon, there always were. He kept to the shadows, like he always did, but he saw her. She was crouched above something, probably the dead body. A man, the coroner, Rod Carpenter, jumped up and down by her side. She turned her head and spoke sharply to him. That was when she visibly wondered. She straightened and looked past the spectators and into the darkness. Evan swore quietly. She had spotted him. Their eyes met. Her eyes, they were green. Huge, and open to the world, in spite of everything. She had learned the rules of the game, but hadn't yet accepted them.

He pulled sideways away from there. It happened fast, but he thought he moved unbelievably slow. She followed him with her eyes all the time, even though there was no way she could actually see him, as if the crowd and even buildings between them didn't matter. He pulled back, completely into the darkness. It once more surrounded him. He turned abruptly then, and left the place in a swift and even walk. Through streets more dark than bright. He was grateful for that, at least.

Quiet streets, talking streets. Noisy streets, silent streets. All lamps shone bright in his face. He preferred the shadows, the cool and the hot. The silent noise didn't go away. Here between rocks formed and polished, the quiet darkness was always filtrated, indistinct against all the sounds in the background.

An invisible light split from the others, stronger than them all put together.

He speeded up, not quite agreeing with himself how to react. So, he sat course for the inn without setting course for the inn. He would reach home quickly enough.

Home… he tasted the word. Yes, it was a home like most homes, both sanctuary and prison.

After moving in circles for a while, he sat down on a staircase, in the shadowland, in the street adjacent to The Green Rose. He could see it without anyone there being able to see him. They used to arrive at this hour, the first guests. He was there to see them arrive and to see them leave. To study them with his predator eyes…

A lamp lit the stairs in the adjacent entrance, in the periphery of his vision. Moths whirled around it, and it generated a pale and gray light. As it had done in another place, an eternity ago.

His vision cleared abruptly once again, his body softened and hardened simultaneously. The surroundings, even the deepest dark, appeared distinct. He had been inattentive. Just a tiny moment, but that could cost him, he knew that.

He directed his attention, fairly uninterested, at the two men filling his vision. A mild irritation seemed to rub at the inside of his frontal lobe. A light wind before his eyes, not anything worse than that. Just now it was enough.

– We represent… interests in the freight business, one of the men opened by saying.

He went right to it, cut to the chase. That was always something.

– They're willing to be very generous, if you will change your mind and join their cooperative. The other joined in, clinically, automatically. – Their generosity goes so far that they're willing to give you one, final chance.

– My reply is the same as before, Shelby replied politely. – Thanks, but no thanks.

– Our employers are getting mighty tired of that negative attitude, the first man said, clearly content. – They've sent us to give you a powerful incentive. So, you'll more easily listen to our employers, look at it all from their point of view, so to speak…

Shelby rose, took one head in each hand, and smashed them together. It happened so fast, like lightning, like shadow. They hadn't caught more than a shadow of his movement. Both fell like empty sacks on the sidewalk.

Sheila turned the corner and stopped. She and he stared at each other across a deep divide, one that couldn't be crossed by two small steps.

She approached, apprehensive and infinitely curious.

– You made mincemeat of them, she said weakly.

– They didn't expect the unexpected, he said, serious minded, guarded. – I had it easy.

– It happened so fast, so… beyond easy.

He knew that. If he had known she would be there, watching, like he should have, he would have slowed it down a bit.

– What are your plans for the rest of the evening? He heard himself say.

– Plans…? A momentary disorientation before she replied patronizingly. – Oh, I had planned on going home, relax, get some hard needed sleep.

– You seem awake enough, he declared teasingly. – More than able to follow me in my dark walk across town.

His dark walk across town… She frowned.

– I didn't follow you! She denied infuriated. – I most certainly didn't. I was on my way to you to ask you a few questions.

– I can show you the town. He had to smile, unable to hold it in check anymore. – And you can ask me about anything you may desire.

– Show me the town? What a strange thing to say. Especially since I've grown up in this town and you haven't.

Then she smiled as well. She waved her hand, moved her head, signed for him to come with her.

– I must take a shower, she declared decisively. – And change clothes. After I've done that, barring unforeseen circumstances, I'm free for the evening, free to do whatever I may… desire.

He reached her quickly, walking by her side. The stink of her mild perfume tore in his nostrils. He hated it when there was no wind. She smiled uncertain at him. He returned the smile. Like a mirror in a dark hallway.

– … *quiet,* she said, as if she completed a sentence begun in her mind. She studied his face. – I mean, there are always tiny ogres here, or little rats, as they're also called. They're either begging, or lurking in the shadows. I've grown skilled in *hearing* them eventually, but tonight they're just not here.

– Wise little ogres know to respect their bigger cousins, he said simply.

They reached her building, her house, her fortress, her home without interruptions of any kind.

Home… The word would always carry a strange connotation for him.

She punched in the security code. The door slid open. She collected the note, with the code, almost like an afterthought. The street was silent, so silent. She looked swiftly back at him, as if to assure herself he was still there.

– I can wait out here, he said quickly. – It's okay.

– No, it isn't okay, she said decisively. – Come in.

She punched in the security code to the apartment. Another door slid open. She collected another note, another code. Many lamps lit the bright colored walls in the hall, and he was glad when they walked inside the apartment and she only lit one single lamp there.

– I like it a bit murky, she said, both thoughtful and with a distinct challenge in her voice.

She wrote down the newly collected codes on a single piece of paper and put it in the right pocket of her coat, and then she discarded the notes in the metal bowl.

– That's okay, he said dryly. – You've perhaps heard the affectionate name on my place? *The Sleeper Awakens.*

– What a strange comparison. She laughed thrillingly, before her eyes grew intense. – But I imagine I know what it means… The fire is brighter in the dark, right? *Right?*

He wanted desperately to confirm her question, her plea, but he hesitated. She spotted the emotions mirrored in his face and their contact was strengthened, not weakened.

– I don't know, he finally said. – Perhaps it's only a matter of survival?

– At any cost? She breathed.

– No, he replied sharply. – No… not at any cost.

Now he returned her stare, and his intensity was many times stronger than hers. Her face took on a strong red color before she caught herself.

– I'm taking a shower, she said meekly. – Make yourself at home.

She turned and walked towards the bathroom. But just as she reached it her hand froze on the door's handle, and she turned half back.

– The night is something tangible, almost alive, isn't it?

– Yes, it is, he said hoarsely.

– And we're desired by the night, she said.

And her words echoed inside like soft thunder.

She slipped into the bathroom, and closed the door behind her.

The first self-combusting paper went up in flames.

He looked at himself in the mirror, at the strained smile slowly fading.

Water from the shower roared in his ears, but he didn't hear it. He came to be wandering restlessly back and forth in the apartment, looking numerous times through the window, down on the street. A habit he had acquired. People rushed back and forth outside. They usually did. This neighborhood was seen as relatively safe, but was close enough to the slum to keep people from relaxing. They never relaxed.

He sat down in a chair, relaxing. He often did. Even when he didn't. He had to. His eyes followed the shadows moving on the walls. Aside from that he sat close to unmoving.

The past… Only rarely and unusually did he allow himself to think about it. But the weird thing about memories was that they often returned uninvited, impossible to hold back. The apartment, the surroundings, the situation, the here and now faded, at least briefly. The breaks in routine came only in flashes, but they were long enough, strong enough to hurt.

The room had been bigger, and with far more people, celebrating youths, hungry for life.

He rose and headed for the door. Sheila strolled from the bathroom, wearing a huge towel around her body, covering her breasts and the body to her thighs.

– This was a mistake, he said curtly. – At best a bad idea. What questions did you want to ask me?

– Questions? She looked blank at him, before grinning and brightening. – Oh, you mean the *questions?* I'll get them answered sooner or later, no sweat. In case you're wondering, I can divulge that I did indeed follow you, did stalk you in the night… You're supposed to show me the town and tell me immaculate secrets. Do you know what? I can hardly wait.

– You enjoy playing with fire, don't you?

– Yes, she whispered. – *Yes.*

Voice rose and almost turned normal when she continued.

– I like you. You're an interesting man, and I would love to get to know you better.

He remained in place.

She shook her head and hurried into the bedroom. He heard her pulling out drawers and open closet doors.

– You don't need to go, she assured him, while striving to keep an even and fairly normal tone. – I'm a big girl and can take being burned.

She shouted loud enough to wake the dead. He sensed that he was wakened, slowly, painfully, irrevocably.

She slid out from the bedroom dressed in a short, dark skirt, a black dungaree jacket, and a thin, tight T-shirt with very visible nipples. Slowly and soundlessly fire lit his eyes.

It seemed like an eternity passed before he once again heard the sounds of engines and whistles outside. She looked expectantly at him, but also with a glimpse of irony. He liked that.

He held the door open for her. When she passed him she said jokingly:

– What big teeth you have, grandmother.

– To better smile at you, child, the wolf grinned.

CHAPTER FIVE

They took the underground to Leicester Square. It went straight there, without them needing to change lines anywhere.

The underground... indistinct objects flickering by her and the vision itself began flickering. And what she saw with her inner vision grew as images she could see and touch. She stumbled and had to support herself on Shelby. It was pleasant, but perhaps that was exactly the reason she didn't enjoy it. Memories were what came to her. Memories that had always been buried beneath the surface. Strong, powerful, in spite of that. She walked... was led by her mother inside a train. The train rushed into the black tunnel... So strange. She rode the underground every day, back and forth, back and forth, to nowhere. What made her think about this now? It wasn't Evan she saw through the shimmering windows of the train rushing by in the opposite direction in the black, black tunnel. It was a woman, a face uncannily familiar. A sight so memorable that she could never forget it.

Busy Leicester Square, pulsing Leicester Square… The area from Trafalgar Square to Oxford Street had for a long time been a part of London's exhibition, the way the city displayed itself to the world, and that was to an extent still true. The world's nomads, and those who wanted variety in life, still sought here. And there were still a few tourists, totally unable to register the special mood they according to rumors had come here to experience. During recent years the authorities had sought even harder than usual to increase the ordinary tourism and remove the… unofficial, more colorful regulars flooding the streets. The fact that traditional tourism had pretty much collapsed didn't exactly make this course of action less weird.

Those who arrived in town these nights came here to stay. For as bad as things were here, they were far worse most other places. What official media called riff raff and even worse euphemisms were kept off the streets by large forces of patrolling guards, but as always, such actions only made the unwanted gather elsewhere, in official and unofficial places.

There were people in the streets, even fairly many, but they constantly looked around and moved their eyes, on the lookout for scouts and uniforms and heavy boots. There were only remnants left of the mood Sheila remembered from her childhood.

– Why did you move here? She asked the man by her side.

– I used to like this town, he said to the air.

They walked towards Covent Garden, through brick-covered alleys just as lit as the christmas trees they passed. All stores they passed had trees, but there were almost no people inside.

– The christmas celebration is going down the tubes, she said cheerfully.

– Everything does, he said, shaking his head, returning her crazy grin.
– Both good and bad things in the world are sucked into an irresistible, inevitable maelstrom.

They left the well-lit alley. They reached an area that was almost an exact copy of the one they left.

He shook his head, shook his head again, and far more determined this time.

– Everything looks the same these days, he stated. – This place used to be called The Market. But it was far more than that. There was street performance and theater here. Everybody who wanted to do so could perform. The performers encouraged participation among the audience, and their calls were often heeded. The result could be quite spectacular, a wild, wild release before dawn.

She looked at him. Both irritation and longing were clearly present in his voice.

– That's so beautiful and poetic, she said quietly, with just a slight, slight irony in her voice.

Suddenly she swallowed hard and wanted to take his hand.

This notion, this unbearable need was counteracted by the certainty that everything they did was filmed. Every move, every smile was caught by the security cameras in place everywhere. Most people knew of, couldn't avoid knowing of the extensive surveillance on «sensitive» places all over London and everywhere these days.

But she knew more, a lot more, of what was hidden, what was worse.

She sensed he led them to a less trafficked, less lit street, and she couldn't decide how much to tell him. This area was filled with cameras, much more so than other places, as it often was on «tainted» places.

They walked, and walked through many a tainted street.

Then he stopped, finally in a broad, lit street, in front of the entrance to First Bite, a well-known restaurant, with the stamp of approval from the authorities. He led her inside. They strolled through the first room without anybody noticing them, at least none that Sheila noticed. Her eyes resting on Shelby grew even more scrutinizing.

– This isn't exactly your style, now, is it? She couldn't stop herself.

– Appearances are deceiving… He evidently had a hard time holding back himself.

Their eyes met, in mutual cheerfulness and something resembling understanding.

What am I doing here? She wondered.

His eyes. His eyes…

They burned, burned like ice.

– Where are you taking me? She asked weakly, completely missing her usual power.

– Down, down below, he grinned.

They walked down the stairs to the toilets.

– I can see that, thank you, she snorted angrily.

He laughed. The sound sounded strange to them both.

The toilets were close to the stairs. They passed them and continued further in, into a corridor quickly turning darker. A corridor without end. They kept walking. What was this? A corridor without end, beneath a well reputed restaurant, with a cellar without boundaries. Sheila felt certain they had walked at least a minute before she glimpsed a brightening in the dark ahead of her, a door lit by invisible lights. She wasn't truly certain it was there until Evan stopped her from walking into it. He knocked on it. An intricate signal no one could copy by chance. She heard an angry voice call out in a foreign language, so foreign she had never heard it before, never anything like it. Evan replied in the same language. The door slid open.

So dark… even darker than the long passageway outside. She corrected herself instantly, strangled the sickening sense of fear and need to be protected, and stubbornly raised her head.

The journey continued, deeper in and down, and the darkness surrounded her ever tighter. They possibly passed through several doors. Sheila couldn't decide if they did. Her feet touched the ground. Hands stretched out to the side touched nothing, nothing but empty air. She didn't see anything but the black void, and had to support herself on Evan. And there were sounds and hisses in the black void making her shiver and shake. She pulled close to he who led her, led the poor blind girl. There were warnings, *snarls* coming from him, directed not at her, but at the darkness, and even though they scared her, they were also kind of comforting. *He* didn't have trouble seeing.

Light increased slowly in strength, so slowly at first that she hardly noticed. As if it was far away. And it was. They walked until her feet were sore, of all the walking, her throat was sore, of all the heavy breathing. Suddenly he stopped, stopped her. She stood at the top of a staircase. She swayed and would have fallen if he hadn't caught her, held her. A long staircase, not steep. From the top there was a nice view to the large room below. The light flowed from there, muted between all the shadows. She heard music. It rose towards them as they descended the stairs. Not music she had heard before. Mystical sounds, guitars, drums, keyboards. She felt as if she had never truly heard music… until this moment.

– A place like this… in this place? She exclaimed incredulous.

– You won't complain over the neighborhood, will you, my dear? He kept a straight face. – It's way beyond average, in my opinion.

The place wasn't filled with guests. Not even all the tables were taken. Just about right, Sheila thought.

She had always found packed places way too noisy.

– What do you think? He wondered. – It's not too late to turn around.

– Why? She said, she challenged him, teasingly.

She took his arm, and he took hers. She walked at Evan Shelby's side, down the old staircase, into the mist and the shadows.

Her skin pricked, caused by the intense looks directed at her. She heard voices, picked them up from the air itself. They whispered about the forbidden, and she discovered she was listening.

They sat down by an empty round table, with a nice view of the bar.

– Are you expecting… guests? She nodded towards the two empty chairs.

– Perhaps, he replied noncommittal.

She listened, and she observed. There was a strange… symmetry here. She watched as people moved, as she always did, and these people moved... differently, at least some of them did.

– Something to drink? The waiter had slipped close to the table so suddenly that Sheila almost shook.

– A Bloody Mary for me, please, Evan said, with a distinct, ironic humor she didn't understand.

Probably a private memory or a joke he shared with the waiter. There seemed to be a certain familiarity between the two of them.

– Just Club Soda for me, thank you, she said cheerfully.

She observed as the waiter left them. Yes, he slipped, slid more than walked.

– That guy is good, she commented. – He moves very fast, but still has no problems with balancing his tray.

Evan didn't comment on her comment. It was as if he hadn't heard her.

The service was impeccable. The glasses, unusually large, were put on the table uncannily fast, without delay. Another waiter, clearly one with more authority, brought them. Sheila noted that the guy had actually begun his journey from the bar before the other guy had reached him. They hadn't spoken, and she hadn't seen any signs or anything. Some fairly sophisticated signaling system had to be at work here. Not so surprising perhaps, at a classy joint like this.

– We haven't seen you in a while, Mister Shelby, the headwaiter said politely.

– It has been a while. Shelby nodded.

– May I be allowed to give you a special greeting, tell you how good it is to have you back?

– It's good to be back.

The waiter pulled back discreetly. Actually so discreetly, so quietly that Sheila didn't notice, until she looked up, and the guy had vanished.

– Cheers, Evan lifted his glass.

After a brief hesitation, unnoticeable, she hoped, she lifted her glass to his. Glasses met and parted. They drank.

She noticed he sipped the drink a bit before drinking. An act of caution? She did as well. There was no *wrong* taste.

He drank fast. When he had emptied his glass, she still had half left, and he had a strange look she couldn't read.

He looked at her. Waited.

– A strange place, this, she said after a while. – And people have studied me since we arrived. Not us, me!

– You're a new fish. They're always the object of some attention.
– The elite are frequenting this place…?
– A minor part of it. He shrugged. – A minor part of other social elements.
– I spotted a policeman I had never imagined would be caught in a place like this… One learns new things every day, huh?
– I'm not so sure bringing you here was the right decision. It may have put you in danger, in more ways than one.
– I can take care of myself, thank you, she stated, and a trace of pride fried her synapses, over the fact that she hadn't felt any form of anger over his words.
But the words, and the way he said them, made a familiar trickle race down her spine. She didn't see him as a person who made claims lightly, and he didn't need to be overly worried about his own safety. She vividly recalled how easy he had handled the two thugs.
He nodded, more confirming something to himself than agreeing to her statement.
Something kept bugging her. It circled on the edge of her consciousness. Something about the way he had said «neighborhood» and «turn», but she couldn't grab hold of it.
No matter, time didn't just fly, but rushed by in his company. He looked like or at least resembled «the perfect gentleman», «the attentive and considerate companion», a role he played close to perfection the way she - and she suspected - he defined it. Thoughts raced and didn't stick, and the pulse beat in her jugular. She leaned forward, across the table, and didn't even notice, didn't notice time flying away.
– … so Wynette and I studied archeology. I've always had this interest for old things, for the past, before all this existed…
She indicated a wide range with her hand, a range obviously extending beyond what they could see and their immediate surroundings. She felt it… so real… felt the city, the world, what she described in words. She laughed embarrassed and pulled back in her chair.
But the feeling persisted. Lights flashed in the mist. Mist pulsed in shadow. And then she saw the woman on the dance floor. A lone woman, a bombshell with smooth, fair hair. One she hadn't seen before, hadn't seen arrive to this place of mist and shadow. She was baffled and didn't understand how she could have missed her, how anyone could have. Evan seemed totally indifferent. He behaved as if he hadn't seen her, but how could he have avoided it, when every man and woman in the room watched her as if hypnotized? There were many people on the dance floor,

but Sheila saw no one but her.

Sheila blinked. She was back at the table, with Evan Shelby. One storm within a storm.

– Your true interest is for the passing of time, its alterations, the future, he said.

– You may be right, she said, and shook imperceptibly. – Far into the future, when all this is dust. It's the ultimate form for curiosity.

The conversation eventually turned to more conventional subjects, to the degree this was even possible between the two of them. But she didn't forget, and neither did he, she was quite certain of that.

Then, between one moment and the next, he turned and looked around. This was so sudden, and so unusual for him that she was almost shocked, and led to her doing it as well. She hadn't seen him do it, not once, during the entire evening.

The woman was no longer on the dance floor. No other place in the room either. She had… vanished.

He sat still for a moment, before smiling roguishly.

– So why are you in the police? He wondered.

She bowed her head in an almost imperceptible nod, before raising it.

– You know what they say about connections and lineage. She was unable to keep the hollow quality from her voice. – It has been like that for a long time, and today it's even truer than ever. People like me either become a cop or become their prey. Beyond that the alternatives are rather… l-limited.

Both she and Wynette had early on learned to use of themselves and their looks to achieve advantages.

– I'm sorry, he said. – I regret I've opened old wounds.

– You say such funny things. She rolled her hands into fists under the table. – What is there to regret? It isn't your fault.

You're involved, she thought. One way or another you're connected to all of it.

She laughed a bit, with a forced smile, clutching his hand.

– I don't know what's wrong with me. She choked. – I'm not usually this up and down, not bipolar or anything.

– It doesn't bother me, he assured her. – Besides, I've heard it's supposed to be a sign of a wide array of emotions. I like that.

She wanted to say more then, open up. Her lips parted several times, but she was unable to get anything out.

A man approached them, openly. She recognized Lloyd Emerson, a section chief, a Superintendent in the Metropolitan Police. His eyes stared through her. His smile stayed smooth. He looked terrifyingly pleasant on the surface.

– Nice to see you, Evan, he greeted. – What brings you here tonight, business or pleasure?

– Nothing but pleasure tonight. Lloyd. Evan smiled, just as pleasantly.

– And what about you, Inspector? Emerson turned his head slightly as he sat down. – Are you enjoying yourself?

– I am indeed, sir, she replied. – This is an enjoyable place. I like the venue, and I like its situation.

– I do as well, he pondered, – it's perfect for so many things.

– Sit down, Lloyd, Shelby offered.

Emerson curled his brows a bit… just a bit.

– Do you know what, Evan? I have, for some time, now, wanted to meet you, meet you face to face.

– I'm fully aware of this fact, Lloyd, was the very happy reply. – I can only offer my regrets. I've quite simply been way too busy lately to be available to you.

Sheila breathed deeply. She managed to do so slowly, while striving to decide which of the two men was the most dangerous.

The conversation continued in more conventional ways. No statements had much depth, even if there were a lot of implications, hidden and fully open. Sheila was convinced she heard thunder beneath the music and the humming, but couldn't tell whether or not it was real, or if it rose from the reptile part of her brain. A warning of a coming danger.

Both men seemed very polite and forthcoming, too much for comfort. Their cold stares flared more than once. Aside from that, there was very little implying anything other than that two old acquaintances had a nice conversation in order to get to know each other better. This was, in a fundamental sort of way, also what happened, but not exactly how it seemed.

After a prolonged exchange of pleasantries, the conversation was discontinued. Emerson rose with the nice smile in place.

– I'm glad we had this talk…

– I am, too, Shelby agreed.

– And Watts… you and I must have a talk in my office soon.

– Of course, sir.

He had already turned and gone.

She waited a bit before speaking, venom in her eyes and voice.

– It's said a word from Lloyd can make or unmake a person, she said dryly. – And very few can challenge him or would want to do so. He's a true untouchable.

– I don't believe anyone is, Evan said lightly.

– I noticed, she countered.

She closed and opened her eyes once.

A hand rested on her shoulder, in an almost comforting touch. Her eyes widened when she realized that Evan still sat at the opposite side of the table, rigid and guarded.

– *Did that naughty man bother you, sweetheart?*

A hand touched her cheek. Silky voice, silky skin.

The woman walked to Evan's side, though not too close.

It was *her*.

– He didn't bother me, Sheila emphasized. – Didn't bother me at all.

– What a sweet girl you've found yourself, Evan. The woman laughed, and even the laughter sounded like a song. – Introduce us, darling.

– Sheila, this is Sheba, he said, very, very nice. – Sheba, this is Sheila.

Sheila wanted to giggle, perhaps precisely because the situation didn't invite to it.

– Such a She-Demon, Sheba almost whispered. – She's so sweet that I want to sink my teeth into her.

– The Queen of Sheba, Sheila let out, – will perhaps learn I'm not that tasty.

– On the contrary, my dear, Sheba laughed. – I think I might for once be pleasantly surprised.

– What the fuck are you doing here, Sheba? Evan exclaimed, so uncharacteristically, as Sheila knew him that it made her blink.

– The same as you, precious, Sheba laughed, just as excitedly. – Seeking new friends and checking up on the old.

– *See you later, both of you.*

A breath and a whirlwind, and she was gone.

Her dialect, impossible to place. Especially the word «precious». Frost haunted Sheila suddenly and painfully, and it certainly didn't go away when she looked up and met Evan's eyes.

– So, which one is the most dangerous? He asked her lightly.

He grabbed her hand and squeezed, perhaps without realizing the brutality in his action. Perhaps he realized it in full.

– Answer me!

– It hurts, she whimpered. – It hurts so much.

– *Who?*

– Both…

He squeezed harder.

– She is. SHE IS!

He released her hand, released it abruptly, and pushed her away.

– I shouldn't have brought you here, he mumbled. It didn't seem like he sat there completely by himself, as if there was someone there, close to him. – Both the black and white shadows follow us wherever we go. The insane world reaches everywhere. Locked doors are not keeping anybody or anything out. Even a fool should know that…

She sat there, sunken, downtrodden, filled with despair and terror.

Something awakened in her, abruptly, shocking. Fear had come first, then the terror. The… other followed in its footsteps.

Impulsively, in sudden, shocking feral movement she grabbed his hand.

– Listen to me, she said low and growling. – Whatever happens, whatever happens to me, you did the right thing bringing me here. Do you hear me? Do you hear my *call?*

He sat there, not moving.

– What I will do now, what I will do is dance, yes, I will. Come… come…

He lifted his head, his eyes. They came alive. She saw it. She felt the tingling inside like a roar.

– I want to dance, she repeated, she encouraged him. – If not anytime or anywhere else, then only tonight, only here. Dance with me.

She stood in front of him, throwing off her jacket. He saw her jugular vein beat below the twinkling eyes.

They whirled out on the dance floor. He let himself be whirled, replying to her euphoric desperation. A desperation that had been hiding beneath a thin layer, since he had first seen her.

– … live, she whispered close to him, incredibly enough audible in the noise.

– *That's right,* he returned the whisper. – *Let go*.

– You, too, you, too, she said, with her eyes half closed.

She doesn't know what she's asking.

He turned her around, without letting her that far away. She gasped in joy. He knew what she went through, now. The same liberation he had undergone ages ago.

They passed by the table where Lloyd Emerson sat. Evan bent forward and whispered something in her ear. She threw her head back and laughed out aloud. Emerson reddened.

– I'm about to lose control, huh? She sniffed a bit.

– That's not a wrong observation, he nodded.

– Do you know what? The thick lips curled. – I *love* it!

Smoke similar to mist drifted everywhere. In this place, so equal and unequal to the world outside. Sheila, dancing close to Evan, only had eyes for him. But in tiny glimpses, a face here, a voice there, she sensed her surroundings, and enjoyed them to the fullest. She saw and heard a lot that she would have pondered a lot, if she had bothered. People stretched on the chairs with red cloth, with gray cloth, together and alone, and they spilled wine, while others sat straight on their chairs, engaged in deep conversation. The controlled and the unrestrained seemed to exist side by side. Human beings and ghosts danced in the mist. Several times Sheila had to convince herself her senses played tricks on her. Everything was so… intense. She hardly noticed the torrential rain and the thunder as they left the establishment and laughingly ran through the already flooded streets. And the hot air in the Underground dried them faster then the best hairdryer.

They sat tight as the train raged through dark tunnels. The coach was crowded, but Sheila didn't care, and in tiny glimpses she imagined that everyone… vanished, quit simply faded away and that they were alone. It didn't matter anyway. She rested her head against his shoulder.

– I've enjoyed myself immensely tonight, Shelby, thank you very much, she said saucily, dreamingly. – I haven't slept for ages. In spite of that I'm more awake than I can ever remember. But there's… more. A cold wind cuts through me, through the fire. It's like a rollercoaster of emotions… indescribable… different from anything I've ever experienced. It makes me very vulnerable, does it not?

It surprised her how she could trust him so. She wasn't usually so open. Hell, she used to be *closed!* He had trusted her, shown her trust when letting her through the backdoor of First Bite, but it went deeper than that. She couldn't tell why, but she trusted him. So much that only a minor part of her suspected that he, with a rare skill, had manipulated her.

The storm had already eased up when they stepped out on Camden High Street. Lightning and thunder were content by flashing and rolling in the distance.

– Your place, she said, before he managed to say anything. – I've always wanted to see it from the inside.

They chose to walk through the front door to The Green Rose. After two steps or so inside people noticed them and recognized them, and they stared.

The time they spent downstairs, on the dance floor, seemed timeless.

– A watch shows so very, very little, doesn't it? She pondered.

– There's nothing there worth knowing. He nodded.

Sheila recalled that he had showed her the guestrooms on the ground floor. The upper floor was in its entirety made by him, for him, and whatever he wanted to do there. It was a world on its own. She recalled the walk up the stairs, of feet on the steps. Or rather the sense of steps pushing against her feet. Everything seemed strange, so very, very strange.

There was a thick and heavy door at the top of the stairs. She remembered that vividly. He put three keys in different keyholes and unlocked it. Pushed the heavy door open with his fingertips. Sheila stepped into a long and broad hall, one of shadows and flickering lights, candlelights, tall, black candlelights. The entire upper floor had been made into a single apartment. She rubbed fingers on thick windows, solid walls. The place… opened up to her, as she walked around wide-eyed.

Objects revealed themselves to her, as her eyes got used to the modest lighting. An… exhibition of another world.

She stopped in front of a golden piece. Her lips forming an o, and she could hardly breathe.

– Tuth Ankh Amon's gold mask, she yelped. – It's… genuine?

– It became available last year, he said dryly. – I couldn't let it go. It's safer here than any other place, anyway.

– There's so much interesting stuff from the Dynasty period, she said. – But this…

They remained on that spot for a while.

– The Egyptians, he began, emphasizing his words. – They were obsessed by the thought of immortality, of eternal youth.

– And you accused me of being overly taken by the past, she said stunned.

– Technically speaking I didn't, he hawked. – I merely proposed an alternative interpretation to yours.

– You sly scoundrel! She returned his grin.

The question had to be… how sly was he?

White and black curtains, like sheets, blew in the draft, the wind pulling through the room, not merely covering the windows, but also hanging from the ceiling all over the floor. They flickered like the candles, like the shadows, turning white, turning shadow. The room changed before her eyes every time she blinked.

There was a bit of furniture here and there, a few chairs and tables. It was really one, huge room, except for the hardly noticeable closed off square at the center. All thoughts faded. That included superfluous thought as well. The place spoke, spoke silently to her. She listened to the music from below, so distant that one could hardly sense the rhythm in the floor. She swayed by that distant music, distant rhythm with half closed eyes, half outstretched arms.

– So, where's the bed? She asked, half invitingly, half jokingly. – You must sleep somewhere.

He pointed without pointing. She followed his eyes to the small room at the center. She discovered a door. He walked ahead without doing any attempt at touching or kissing her. She followed him inside, and hardly sensed the door closing behind them. He lit a single candle. The bed, a single mattress without blanket was placed in the middle. That was all.

– Jeez, I didn't know you had financial problems, she said lightly, in an attempt to break the heavy spell in the air.

At this place, and between the two of them. Not solemnity exactly, but a soberness he always wore like a blanket.

– I prefer simplicity, he explained to her. – The world is hard and ruthless, and comfort distracts you from what you need to do to survive.

– I understand, Evan, she said quietly, didn't want to look at him at first.

She met his eyes, stood still for a moment, before loosening her jacket from her shoulders and letting it slide down on the floor behind her. Conscious thought faded and it didn't really bother her. She knew what she did here, what happened here.

He pulled her tight, an act making her sigh through the open mouth. She looked at him with both an eager and drowsy look, a dreaming quality he could hardly name. He wondered how much of what he saw was a result of his own hunger. He managed to kiss her somewhat controlled, ever harder, more violent. When he put his arms around her, he felt her full lips push back at his, and then move over his face and neck.

– It feels so good when you're holding me. She smiled content.

They kissed harder. Evan sensed his control slip, the control he might have over himself, slip away like water on ice. He pushed her clothes off her shoulder. His mouth seemed to move of its own accord down the woman's cheek and to the side of the neck. His eyes remained open, locking on to the broad mirror on the wall. He rubbed wet lips over that soft naked shoulder. It boiled and pounded there. He desperately attempted to stay away from the neck and the major vein pulsing hot and hard. His head turned. He sensed the roar even stronger inside now, sensed how his fangs grew, saw it in the mirror. Long, pointed fangs. His eyes seemed to change, his face twist, into something different from how he perceived himself. He saw the Stranger in the mirror, and it felt infinitely attractive.

To Sheila it seemed like the beeping tone came from far away. A breath of wind seemed to surround her. She opened her eyes and couldn't see Shelby. He had stood close, holding around her. She turned around her own axis a single time. He was no longer in the room. She bent down and reached mechanically for the cell phone inside her jacket. Her finger pushed the reply button, even though she couldn't imagine how she could do that, in the daze she found herself.

She said her name, didn't say more, just listened.

Outside the door everything remained quiet and dark.

– Evan…? She said to the open door. – I must go. Another policeman has been murdered.

She pulled towards the door, to the stairs, stopped a moment with a hand on the handle. Smiled, a bit pale and hot both.

– I've enjoyed myself. I want to do it again. And continue where we left off…

In spite of the last sentence coming out a bit less savvy than intended she couldn't believe her own courage.

Perhaps she saw a movement in there, in the shadows, perhaps not, though she didn't expect a reply. She slipped through the door and hurried down the stairs. Confused, scared… interested.

He saw her turn and wave as she crossed the sidewalk. There was no way she could have seen him. He stood several steps away from the window, well into the shadows. The need, the hunger in his stomach had turned tangible by now and his mouth dry. What a fool he had been by letting her go. He was angry with himself. She would have been just one of many, and she represented a clear and present danger to him. Sheba would have told him he would never learn, and perhaps she was right.

He heard soft steps behind him, and turned abruptly. He had been lax - again.

– The door was open. Claudette froze under his feral stare.

– So, you entered, he said softly. – In spite of me telling you repeatedly that you are not wanted here.

– You let *her* in, she spat in inflamed jealousy.

She had unbuttoned her blouse, almost completely exposing her breasts. The initial worry delegated to a deeper part of her, she turned brave.

– I had almost convinced myself you were gay, she exclaimed. – But I saw you with her, and observed very little of your usual restraint. But I keep wondering about you, my boy. Why a goddamn copper, and why bother to cross the river for the goodies?

She sounded almost aggressive and clearly aggrieved. And so

transparent. He smiled.

– So, you feel I shouldn't hunt beyond the confines of my territory?

– Why should you? She pushed her arms together behind her back and let him see, so confident, in herself, in her femininity and her seductive power. – I'm better than her in everything that matters.

She made a pirouette, wriggling her butt in slow, sensuous moves.

– It hasn't occurred to you that there is a reason I chose a copper?

He headed for the door. Her eyes revealed her sudden confusion and uncertainty, until he closed the door and locked it. He returned to her, and her confidence returned with him.

She started breathing faster, feeling it, feeling her pulse beat harder and faster. She knew she was attractive and not just because of her looks. But because she loved it, and it showed, in her eyes, in every move she made. There could be a number of reasons why men held back. Sometimes even she had to endure hesitation, that's all. Patience always paid off. She felt the sweet pain below and welcomed it.

– I'm skilled in business, as well. Her eyes dwelled on him. – You know that.

She kicked off her shoes and leaned invitingly against the wall. Her eager eyes revealed how much she wanted him to hurry. The need grew so strong she feared he would dominate her, instead of the other way around. She had wanted him for a long time. Nothing wrong with that, as long as she got it out of her system.

His face twisted into a slanted smile. It remained hidden in the shadows, but she felt her blood leave her face, and the first sting of true fear. Suddenly everything changed, and she didn't understand what had happened.

– I don't know what's worse, he said conversely. – Your pathetic attempts to «catch» me… or the stupid shadow fighting your brothers and cousins do. No matter, it's not very sexy, not very sexy at all. And irritating, not the least irritating.

She could hardly think anymore.

– What's wrong with you? She choked. – Why do you talk this way? You don't need to do that. I'll be good. Please be good to me. I promise I'll be good, I promise. And obedient, very obedient. You can do exactly what you want with me.

He took that one step out of the shadows.

– Don't TOUCH me! She suddenly howled.

She wanted to run, wanted so badly to run away from him, as far away as possible. But his eyes, growing bigger and bigger, and fear of the consequences of defying him, stopped her.

– But don't you know, dear Claudette, he sang from the hidden mouth, – that you must be very careful with what you want, because you most certainly will get it?

He took one more step forward, out of the shadows, into the light. She saw his face, saw all of it and screamed insanely. He welcomed the pulsing rage. Perhaps it was harder to hold onto rage than to hold it back, he mused. But not this time. He welcomed the irresistible hunger, used it, the Hunger, when he easily, effortlessly stopped her useless escape attempt. His hands caught her and held her. He ignored her screaming, her antics to a point where he hardly heard it, using his left hand to tear off her collar, tear the blouse completely off her shoulder. The fangs grew to a point where they pushed against his lower lip. He opened his mouth wide. He bent down and bit through her skin, her soft skin. Her entire body turned rigid, before softening. The scream faded. The blood filled his mouth. He drank deep, swallowed the sweet blood, sucking it right out of her.

CHAPTER SIX

They wanted to pick her up in a chopper this time, too, but she refused. Islington Green was north of Angel Station, just three stops from Camden Town. It took her ten minutes.

They had been very thorough this time, placed blockades and checkpoints tight as sand. She didn't have to show her card more than once, but passed at least ten checkpoints before reaching the center, the center of the storm.

She sensed something uncanny, something threatening in the air. Uncanny, because the torn body in uniform didn't create such a stir within her. But the mood among the present policemen and women was approaching dangerous and ugly. Powerful flashes flashed. From the police photographers and from the journalists behind the blockades. Watts shook off the sound of discord, as she often did.

It was no problem for her to recognize people tonight. They came out of the woodwork tonight, that's for sure. Influential people, in and out of the force, and they didn't look happy. That in itself wasn't strange. Influential people were always upset when something, no matter what, threatened their position, threatened the status quo. This was different. She spotted people… that didn't belong. The sense of an uncanny, alien presence didn't go away.

She recognized Gordon Tyler and caught herself wondering about what he, he, too, was doing here. Unimportant, in itself. Just another confirmation of the stirring in her guts.

Not one person, she thought. Not necessarily. Not here. The big picture, the puzzle lacked pieces… or it had too many of them… Because the weave was largely unknown?

Gordon wasn't impeccably attired either. She noted, as an afterthought, small cracks here and there, in a seemingly impeccable façade.

She spotted Rod Carpenter dance around the body. Now and then he bent down and made a closer inspection. No façade there. If there had ever been one, something in his past cracked it wide open. He didn't pretend, didn't bow down for anybody.

Eyes followed her, some friendly, many hostile, most indifferent. She ignored them all and walked straight to Rod. He greeted her with his usual death grin.

– It's still here, all of it, or almost all. They haven't found one of the arms yet. One advantage is that no rats have served themselves this time. Probably because this place is fairly high up. Above the raging streams, huh, Sheila?

Cold, so cold. Far beneath the deepest marrow. The big, black deep closed itself around her, like when she was a little girl. What she had felt reach for her so long, no matter where she went.

– Too hot for four-legged rats, she said pointedly, and it felt good.

– Ooooh, won't you repeat that one a little bit louder, he laughed joyfully.

She looked around in the mist at those studying her, watching her every move, all her movements and decisions, as if it was all a test.

She stared down at the remains of a human being, the decorations forming an intricate pattern on the ground.

– He's angry, she said. – This isn't a game to lure us astray.

The powerful male body had quite simply been torn apart. Small pieces had been spread outwards. The arm and the legs, found quite a distance off, had been placed nicely on a plastic cloth, breaking the impression of a complete, disordered savagery. The torso had been split in two. No pattern, only insanity. Or the most insane rage she had ever encountered. A shapeless creature that murdered and mutilated.

– My claim is that it is our gorilla, Rod told her helpful, very helpful.

– Ninety-nine percent, pure gold, ninety-six percent liquor, would you know more?

– How can you be so sure? She wondered slowly. – Except for him… for the obvious common factors, the mutilation and that both were cops…

Very few had seen the other cadaver. Aside from that there was no lack of people who wanted to copy that success. But no matter, Sheila knew, and there was no doubt in her, that… this, and that in Camden Town had been done by the same person.

– From now on no constables, no higher or lower servicemen or women, go anywhere alone, she said, first distantly, then louder, sharper. – Not anywhere. Not a single step in the streets, on duty or as a civilian. Not to the john, not to a party, not in bed without looking under the bed first. No one goes anywhere, without reporting it, reporting it and being given explicit permission from his or her immediate superior.

Independently of her words they would all take their own precautions, safeguard themselves. These were flock animals, most of them. And they would gather against those who would threaten them. Fear gathered them. They usually had good protection against outside threats, though not against this nightly predator hunting its prey among the lords of the jungle. A shadow without blood, invulnerable, invisible. A creature without face, body, soul.

– No ID here either, Sergeant James Tramer reported formally.

… or blood. Sheila froze all the way down to her feet. Where had all the blood gone? She bent down and studied the ground. A few drops here and there, if one looked closely, nothing more. Not much. She studied the wounds. Almost nothing there either. Not liquid, not hardened. The body hadn't lost much heat, and that and the rest was displayed to those who could see. A hunter. Whoever had done this deed and the one the night before, was proud of it.

Watts pondered the issue. Was there really any motive here, except for the murder itself?

When she strolled over to Tyler, she didn't bother hiding her intentions. She wasn't geared for such nonsense anymore. At least not now.

– So nice to see you, Gordon, she began happily. – Are you here in an official capacity?

– What do you mean? He asked suspicious and clearly nervous.

– Not much, really. You're far away from home, that's all. Three stops on the underground…

– I'm an observer in connection with another case.

– What case? She asked sharply.

– Another case, he stressed and rebuffed her.

– Your tie is skewed, she told him sarcastically, and left him.

She left the crime scene, with the scent of blood and thunder in her nose. On her way off she passed Rod and exchanged some random words with him.

– I want a full report in an hour, she snapped.

– Your word is my command. He bowed. – O'Daughter of Midnight Fire.

She didn't know whether or not she should shoot him or laugh. What was the matter with her? It had been going on for a while this, long before she first met Shelby. Was she finally… fed up?

Rod hadn't done anything but telling her the place of their upcoming meeting, and he had done a great job at it, done it in such a way that the audience would have trouble understanding where it would take place.

Less than an hour later, they sat in a corner in the depths of the restaurant Thames Wide. Sheila stared at the painting on the wall above Rod. *Daughter of Midnight Fire,* William Carter Lafyette's infamous rendition of Stacy Larkin. This was a copy, of course, but it didn't seem to have lost anything of the original's… bite.

He had painted a witch in moonlight. She stood by a campfire. The moonlight and the light from the fire danced across her face, her incredible face. Demonic, terrifying and irresistible simultaneously. And the fire wasn't contained to the campfire, but danced in the air, like small tongues encircling her. Eyes burning and stinging.

The painting was on the wall other places in London as well, so even if they had known that Rod had meant the painting, they couldn't know where, what special meaning this place had to them both.

For her inner eye, she pictured how it looked outside the restaurant.

Thames River passed by, with its black water and ever-wider run. Embankment had long since been flooded. Pumps worked full time. It had no discernible effect. Land dry for so long, drowned in water. There was no moon, were no stars. Lights from the city no longer reached the clouds, but stopped in the thick layers of smog hanging over everything. It sucked up most of the light, hardly reflected it at all. Black water flowed in dark waters.

Not far from here was one of the many homes of the Parker family, sone of the most powerful people in today's reality. Sheila saw the lights from it, heard the sounds and shouts from one of their parties, smelled the spiced food, heard the meeting of glasses, the loud voices and shouts, the upper class doing their thing.

– Okay, Hercule Poirot of the morgue, she began mockingly, – what do you have for me tonight?

– You're reducing yourself to the use of flattery, he remarked. – The tracking dog must be eager, even more eager than she usually is, to taste blood today.

– The body was empty of blood, she prompted him.

– Not empty. He plowed fingers through his hair. – And I can't be absolutely certain before I've made a thorough examination, but yes… The body hadn't been moved, and extremely small amounts of blood remained in the lower levels of the body. So, I must assume that having his blood removed killed him, and then he got his limbs torn off. Our dear gorilla seems to have been almost coherent as he committed his crime.

She cleared her throat, issued a warning.

– What I don't get, don't get at all is the apparent need at the top to put a lid on a lot of this. He chased both hands through the hair. – It makes me downright nervous, you know.

– I understand what you mean.

She patted his hand.

He didn't react to it in any way she could discern.

And that made her nervous.

– The first body had a bite between the neck and the shoulder, right in the jugular vein. He kept going, kept moving his eyes, his flickering eyes. – Skin was so swollen that I didn't see it at first, but eventually it was hard to avoid, as it was with number two, when I knew what to look for. Are you, by the way, aware that blood related diseases are the cause of ever more deaths in this our proud town?

– I didn't know that. She shook her head.

– It's true. We coroners get to see a lot of information that never sees the light of day. Bureaucrats are a strange lot. They're scared shitless when it comes to sharing available information, but they never get rid of anything. Everything can be found if one knows where to dig. Public records, not made public are a virtual plethora of hidden facts. Records showing just about anything. The increase in all type of diseases, for instance, infertility, the return of tuberculosis, weakened immune defense and so on. A common cold can kill a person today.

– One may wonder what's next, she wondered, lost in thought.

– That one is easy. He spoke with even more of his usual flair. – People are cracking up, ever more often and with more pronounced results. And it's not hard to know why. Push down a lid on a boiling kettle, and the pressure just keeps increasing.

– «Madness is a healthy reaction to an insane society», she quoted.

– You know what it is about, he grinned. – I knew you would.

She pondered, pondered a lot, in the following hours. Perhaps too much. Because, in the hours after that, she had an infinitely long time to think.

The night screamed at her. She wandered aimlessly through the streets. There was nothing there, nothing to latch on to. So, she walked, and kept walking.

Empty hospital halls, a dark silence cutting to the marrow. There were no creatures there, except some rats, running back and forth between the rooms.

A newly renovated hospital, and it looked like the pits. This, in spite of it being one of the less rundown hospitals in the city.

The man in bed, alone in the naked room, looked so weak and worn that it was easy to imagine he didn't exist. She carefully sat down on the bed where Doctor Frank Miller rested. There was just about sufficient light for her to see the wrinkled face. She heard on what went for breathing in his case that he was awake.

– I just need you to confirm something for me, she said quietly, a bit less considerate than intended. – You just need to nod.

The face before her twisted further. The chinks he had in the place of eyes, opened and closed painfully.

– The beaten up body was drained of blood?

A nod, hardly noticeable.

– Very… little… blood. She hardly heard the brittle whisper. – He was dead.

Watts nodded to herself.

– So, he died of the blood loss, she said, lost in thought. – But a large number of attackers beat him up, right?

– He was dead, the old man mumbled.

– I understand, she said, suddenly impatient. – But who could have taken him from the morgue, and why?

She *shook* then, abruptly, violently. Miller sat up. He grabbed her around both her wrists, with an iron grip. She saw… she saw the image reflected in his eyes and froze.

– You don't *understand,* he hissed. She moaned in pain, helpless in the paralyzing grip. – He was dead before he was beaten, long before. And he was stone cold, and he wasn't taken. I saw him, I saw him, I SAW him rise from the autopsy table and walk away, and the eyes were dead, and the man was dead.

A freezing wind blew through Sheila Watts. Miller released his grip on her and fell back on the bed, Rigid eyes, rigid body, no breathing, no blood, nothing. She remained on the edge of the bed, totally paralyzed.

In his eyes, in the mirror of the soul… what had she *seen?* She couldn't move, not a single, tiny muscle. Like a mouse stuck in the claws of a big, bad cat, just before the playful kitten sank his teeth into your soft flesh. She had never felt like that before, so utterly helpless, so fearful. She didn't dare move her head, didn't wish to know if anybody watched her from deep within the pitch-black shadows.

So short a time. A few minutes since she had stepped into the room. Merely ticks of moments since she had felt Frank Miller's ice-cold skin against her own. And all her notions, illusions, about life, about her faith in herself, had vanished down the tubes, had been pulled down into the deepest abyss.

A line of light in the east. She had no idea how long she had been sitting like this, a child, terrified by her parents' stories about the dark. The room, she could see all of it clearly. Every single corner, under the beds, behind the curtains. She heard the sound of many feet closing in on her in the hall. The physician and his team, nurses and guards on their morning round. Sheila rose on stiff legs and hurried clumsily to the closets. She hid in the biggest and deepest, crouched in the darkness.

She heard them talk, out there, in the light. It didn't really concern her what they were talking about, but she still listened. She imagined they stopped by the bed where the dead lay, without knowing for certain.

– … must have been breathing his last early in the night… Damn, without an alarm it's impossible to tell the exact time these days.

– You know, a nurse giggled nervously. – He doesn't look so bad. I think he looked far worse while he was still breathing.

One of the others swore.

– What the fuck…?

– The guy is still warm.

– That's so gross. Is nothing normal these days?

Sheila didn't recall much after that.

She had heard it, heard the breathing behind her, and sensed it against her neck skin. The shaking increased and she pushed her knees tighter at her head. Eyes stared at nothing.

Perhaps someone heard her moaning. Perhaps the cleaning crew found her. And someone pulled her out of the closet.

– Poor girl, one said, quite compassionate. – Completely catatonic. She must have escaped from confinement and seen the old man croak.

Shaking hands fumbled in the pocket and after long seconds finally found the ID.

They stared at her, incredulous.

– What happened here, Inspector? She heard, just as far away the voice of the young physician.

She was unable to reply. No matter how much she tried she couldn't voice her terror. Finally, she managed a nod, and a semblance of a smile.

Perhaps. She could never decide for herself whether or not this little event, replaying itself in her head, had actually happened.

It seemed so real. As it did when they dragged her screaming and howling, and totally hysterical down to the basement, to the confinement area below the morgue, where the hopelessly insane lived.

She sat in her office in the New Scotland Yard building, blinking, blinking, blinking, and it didn't seem real, not real at all, and she couldn't convince herself that it was. The new New Scotland Yard. A top modern refurbished building, once again restored to dignity and honor, one of the most visible buildings in Central London. Strong electric lighting, well equipped, with no expenses spared. Only the best was good enough for London's finest. A lot of space for everybody. A lot of people, also close to her. She stared at herself in the mirror. Saw herself, saw her own walk through dark morning streets. A walk through insanity. She had stared at herself for a long time. At this point it was probably a matter of hours. The messy hair, the transfixed face, the wild eyes. Hands that wouldn't stop shaking. She clutched one in the other. Rubbing them hard against her cheek, in an attempt to rub off the runaway lipstick.

Nothing of it useful, nothing at all. She remained twisted and inside/out. Rinsed, washed and spin dried. Rinsed through and through.

She wished she had never gone to the hospital, that she had stayed at home, watched a movie, gone to bed, thrown all curiosity overboard.

– I need sleep, she said aloud.

Back to the apartment. The dark shadowy rooms and what waited there. She screamed sharply and stared blindly at her hand. She had bit it.

The handle was pushed down. She saw it move. The door opened towards her. She watched it move. Sergeant Tramer stuck his head inside.

– Did you say anything? He wondered, carefully curious.

– No, nothing, she replied emptily. – Nothing important.

– You don't look so good. He pushed his entire, considerable frame inside the room. – You should get yourself some sleep. After the meeting with the Super, that is.

– What's up? Irritation suddenly boiled within her, even though it in her ears sounded strangely tame. Not even that she could do right. – Why didn't he use the chain of command?

– I really don't know, Tramer merely shrugged. – I guess it's a matter of some haste. Not so strange these days, really.

She didn't comment on that. She should have and could have. Her vocal cords worked. Everything worked. She just couldn't make it work.

– He's in one of the *special* rooms. If you'll follow me, madam…

His sudden use of formality made her react somehow. She followed him, like an automaton. Shadows whirled in the air before her eyes, through many dark hallways. The church bells, they beat twelve times. The time was still not more than nine in the morning. The frost stuck inside her. She thought about Miller. He had died like he had lived, paralyzed by fear.

Tramer led her to one of the soundproof and secure rooms, one that Watts hadn't known the whereabouts of. The Sergeant left her outside the door. Seconds passed by, humming and ticking, like a bomb. She was about to open it, when it was opened from inside. Superintendent Lloyd Emerson sat behind a desk in the deep part of the room.

– Ah, Inspector, good of you to join me. Please come in.

She stepped inside. Emerson pushed a hidden button somewhere, and the door closed behind her.

She stopped in front of the desk, before his sticking eyes. Could he see through her façade of defiance, into the place where there was nothing but jelly, a dry twig that would break by the slightest wind? She had been to the bathroom on her way here, or at least she believed she had, possibly making herself a bit more presentable, but it did no good. How strange. As late as yesterday she would have burned with the desire to challenge him, his authority.

– I've called you here in connection with the two… murders of our colleagues, Malone and Allen…

Was there a bit of hesitation in his voice? If there was it was certainly a first.

– He's throwing leads left and right, sir. We'll catch him soon.

She assured him.

– It's just a matter of time.

– That's not *good enough*. He threw a large, brown envelope on the desk.
– This was delivered to my home, to the *main door,* sometime during the last twenty-four hours.

Watts kept quiet. She knew how tight security was at his home, and feeling a little better, she knew why he had made this a priority. Fingers reached for the envelope, opened it and emptied the content on the desk. Quite an unremarkable and limited content, really. Two ID's and a sheet of paper with two brief messages.

– The content isn't scrutinized, he pointed out sharply. – Very few have seen it.

She took one of the ID cards between two fingers and held it up. A message, a very clear message, had been scribbled on the smooth plastic surface. Frenetically, wildly, uncontrollably. But not very hard to read. One said:

ONE OF TEN

The other said:

TWO OF TEN

And the messages on the sheet, also quite brief, and not very difficult to interpret, at least not in a literally way. Here the writing was meticulously correct. Letters were beautifully written and almost every word started with a large letter.

«I Have *Become Death, the Destroyer of Worlds.*

And further down on the page:

«...And They Were Given Power...
To Kill with Sword and with Famine
And with Pestilence and by the Wild
Beasts of the Earth...

The writer had used a feather pen and the ink he had used... was blood.

Watts once again felt the cold shudder all over her body. The blood was almost incidental, really, compared to the words and the resonance they created in her. And the experience didn't feel as potent as before. This was more physical, something she could relate to.

– So... what's your opinion?

Emerson asked her.

– The upper text is from the Bhagavad Gita, sir, she said distantly. – The lower from Revelations in the christian bible. It's about the final days, when the four horsemen of the Apocalypse are ravaging civilization...

He waved her off.

– There's a system to the madness, sir, she insisted.

He moved behind her, with his hands on his back. She felt his ruthless scrutiny as something solid stabbing her body.

– Malone and Allen belonged to a group within our special forces, he informed her.

It ruffled her feathers instantly.

– And I wasn't informed? She flared. – The leader of the investigation has been kept from crucial information. What is this... sir?

– The group led by Joseph Colton, Emerson said.

Cat got her tongue.

– Colton is and has been an important asset to us. He's good at rooting out whatever that needs to be rooted out. We believe a new group of revolutionaries is behind the recent events, one able and willing to use harsher means.

– There are no revolutionary groups in this country… sir, she said with a notable chill in her voice.

– Policemen from all over the world come here to study our methods. He ignored her. – Someone wants to demoralize our proud force, the best force in the world. That won't happen. A mad dog, lurking around in the dark won't ridicule us.

She noticed that his cheeks actually had a slight reddish quality, and the cold and the heat flowed through her veins simultaneously.

– Colton takes over the investigation, Emerson continued, suddenly very relaxed. – You will assist him to the best of your ability, Watts.

– No way! She snapped, and no longer cared that she revealed her anger. – I demand that you undo your decision.

He smiled dryly and confidently, patronizingly to her.

– You will be serving under Colton from now on. He searched through the papers on his desk and handed her a sheet of paper. – He and his associates are waiting for you in Cafeteria Five, where no one will be disturbing you. Your orders are to report to him without delay.

She looked at the paper, looked at it with impunity. An official transfer order with a lot of stamps and signatures. She crumpled it in her hand to a hard ball, and threw it in the wastebasket.

– I will find «the mad dog», she snapped, – and I'm going to get him.

– Good luck, Inspector, Emerson said formally.

– You won't be throwing me away like garbage, once you're through with me, like you've done with so many others, she challenged him and wondered if it was right to throw all caution to the wind.

– That would be all, Inspector.

Yes, to the wind! Where it belonged. It felt good. She had been *stupid* to let fear, and fear of the dark, rule her. The world was hard and ruthless and nothing more.

She headed for the door. It opened itself to her. Emerson hadn't mentioned anything about Miller and the vanished body, and she had no intention of doing so. That was one advantage in her favor. She intended to find far more.

Miller had lived and died like most people, in fear and reserve.

Dark corridors dominated these clandestine parts of the building. Bright day and daylight hardly reached them. Several bulbs were missing in the ceiling. Those that weren't flickered constantly because of the faulty electricity supply. In the twilight outside everything was dry, desert dry. Ash rained down from the sky, and covered everything.

This was a part of the building that didn't exist officially. A place where windows weren't washed.

Light, a line under a door. The door slid open, and the strong light blinded her. Through tears she recognized Joseph Colton. He took her in the arm, and led her away.

He squeezed her arm, hard and ruthlessly. She shook herself loose in one single move. A cold smile flared around his mouth.

– Welcome, Inspector, he greeted her heartily. – Time flies, doesn't it? Glad you could come.

– Glad to be here, she replied aloud.

A choir of rough laughter replied to her.

– Let me introduce you to my Sergeants, Colton said, keeping the friendly tone.

The room, the room of possibilities cleared to her outer vision. Suddenly she was surrounded by a luxury she had trouble imagining.

Half of the space consisted of a well-equipped gym. The other half was covered by one, perhaps two living rooms, so overwhelmingly equipped that merely the sight of it would have stunned one of The Dirty.

They gathered around a billiards table. The lamp hanging low above the green felt cast shadows over the upper half of their faces. Everything done in her honor. Just for her.

For them. Just for them.

How stupid were they really? How stupid did they believe she was?

Lines in the air, of dust radiated in light. She concentrated on remembering as much as possible about these faces appearing before her. She knew of Kathy Williams, well enough to know what hid beneath the woman's classy exterior. Colton told her the names belonging to each and every face, and she remembered them. Tiberius Shaw, Anthony Johnson, Dominic Colby, Warren Ferrie, Sturgis Hunt Harding, Dilys Hoover, eight in all, including Colton. They had been ten and their wrath drifted in the air.

– I don't know… Dilys Hoover pulled a face and looked patronizing at the newcomer. – She doesn't look like much…

– Let's not judge prematurely, Sturgis Hunt Brading grinned. – Let her have her chance to shine.

Watts shrugged, conveying irritation and indifference, compromising nothing under their uncompromising stare. Colton turned to her, just as indifferent.

– As you know we were somewhat reduced in number recently, he said cheerfully. – I lost my old Inspector. He evidently didn't have what it takes. Not the other pussy either. We're running a rough ride here. Not everybody can keep up.

– That won't be a problem for me, she heard herself say. – What about you?

More rough laughter. No respect, only scorn.

– I'm quite convinced you'll fit in well among us, Colton told her. – I knew you belonged with us the first time I saw you.

That stunned her.

She remained when they left, shivering inside. She feared she would start shaking. Was it like this to them as well, so filled with hatred, fear and rage that there was hardly room for anything else?

– C'mon, the huge, rough Sturgis Hunt Brading called to her. – We've got a job to do.

– And we do it well, Kathy Williams grinned. – No one fucks with us.

Watts breathed in the smoky air, breathed silently, silently hissing. Those who waited for her were eight of the toughest, roughest and most brutal servicemen in the entire force. She had always detested their methods and detested them personally even more.

And now - she was one of them.

CHAPTER SEVEN

A weak line of light fading. Eyes opening slowly. A heavy mist of sleep vanished in seconds.

He rested unmovable on his back, more than sensing the bed against his skin. Very little light drifted in from the outside. None of it burned in the room. He studied the details in the ceiling. They were different every time he awakened. When he lifted his head, his vision worked to perfection wherever he directed his eyes. He still felt wonder how well his vision, all his senses worked. He heard sounds far away in the night, but no one close. Sounds, smells, an infinite number of other impressions close and far, nuances he still had problems accepting actually existed.

Evan slipped out of the bed. One moment he rested unmovable. The other he stood straight on his feet. He still felt wonder concerning how effortlessly he moved.

Without turning on any lights he opened the heavy door to the outer hall. He sensed the city and the street's sounds even easier. How the afternoon traffic crawled, as it usually did along Camden High Street. An ongoing, buzzing roar he rarely avoided. He heard the engine, its discord and explosion of fuel. All the sounds of the city gathered in his thoughts, gathered forever. A background noise dulling his senses, reducing colors and nuances to something gray, dirty.

He lit a few of the tall, black candles he had placed randomly in the large, open room. He didn't need them to see, but he enjoyed the glow. It enhanced the already special mood. There were also candelabra. Five candles together creating a stronger glow. The black and white curtains around the room, made the room seem smaller… and infinitely large.

What he a very long time ago had called the creative glow inside felt stronger now than it had in a very long time. He had even pulled his old keyboards from the closet and played a bit in the hour preceding dawn. This entire place had been turned upside/down and inside/out, and it had happened so quickly, so unexpected. He had changed and the place with him. His cave, his nest, from where he looked at the world had become something completely different. He recalled the icy waters he had walked as the child. Transparent ice, looking black, deep water, black water. To stare directly at the ice was to stare at nothing. Eternity waited down there, and you raced across the ice, balancing on a razor's edge.

And he wondered when he had stopped seeking uncertain ground.

He dressed slowly, almost subconsciously. His eyes touched the closet with the heavy door by the stairs, but he didn't stop there, as he usually did. He walked down the stairs to the bar, as he always did. Nobody waited for him tonight. Not guests. Not others. Hidden or openly. It didn't worry him. Guests would arrive when he opened, the desperate, restless, and lost, strangers, but not strangers to madness.

He left his home through the main entrance, quiet and calm, as quiet and unnoticeable as he always returned. Slipped into the darkness, gray and black. He enjoyed the night. He could sense it move, sense the overwhelming scents from the crowds. This was the time of the day when people thought they were safe, while ever more of them turned into hardly more than faces in the windows later in the evening, surrounded by the dark, victims of their own paralyzing fear.

The old construction site rested there, dark and quiet, truly dark and quiet, but not abandoned. Shelby smelled and heard the little rats when he passed the buildings in there, without spotting them. They hid themselves. Very sensible, knowing what lurked and hunted in this stone desert.

A few blocks later he reached another highly trafficked area, with cars and people. Moderate compared with High Street. Better.

The buzz increased in his ears, turned to a roar. He knew he could mute it, control it. For a while. He chose not to do that.

A rush of wind, of smell and blood. He sensed it awaken, everything he had struggled to keep in check, everything he now released. Was this the hunter awakening in the human being? Were they one and the same?

A man walked a bit ahead of him and had done so for a while. A tall and fairly well-built guy, fairly ordinary. One who hardly turned his head when he continued on his predestined course. The easiest form of prey: One who didn't realize he was one.

Not in bright day, and certainly not in the dark night.

They moved along what Shelby remembered as the northern corner of Regent Park, but that had long since been transformed into an area with an endless row of fashionable apartment buildings.

But the shadows spread here as well, stretching long and deep. Inevitably. Ten years ago, the city's elite had seen this as a promising area. Now, hardly more than the illusion of former glory remained. The downfall had come quickly. One or two years after completion, and no one wanted to buy or rent apartments here. No video surveillance had been set up. Broken lightbulbs were rarely supplanted in the blindingly bright streetlights. Ever more «unwanted» elements moved in. In the apartments, and in the streets outside. Shelby smelled a minor group of Dirty around a burning oil barrel only a few blocks away. He pushed the memory caused by the smell from his consciousness. Instinct, a hardly conscious act. He was close now. Thoughts faded, until just a few, random remained, as the hunter slipped close to the prey.

So close… distance, all measure turned meaningless. Evan sensed the scent of the man in his nostrils, the taste of him in his saliva, saliva flowing through his mouth. Red became the only color he could see. He sensed the trembling in the man, the desperate need to *live,* in spite of the city's horrible surroundings, destroying the human spirit. *But not mine. Never more! Come what may.*

A darkness between two streetlights, a step to the side, into another world. He attacked the prey, caught up to him like an intangible ghost. This time Shelby didn't allow the victim to release a single sound. He cast a spell, darkened, brightened, intoxicated the mind of the man he grabbed, which paralyzed body he held easily. He tore aside collar and clothes, and bit through thin, unresisting skin. Blood filled his mouth and was sucked into him at a rushing speed.

(White light) A place behind his eyes, outside, inside itself, a waterfall of light and dark. The roar turned deafening. He managed to stop before it turned overwhelming. The taste, the smell strengthened and refreshed his entire being. Through blood, through life, he strengthened, fed every single corner of himself.

He let the limp body slide down on the sidewalk. The man's pulse was uneven, but strong. He would probably survive.

Shelby slid further through the darkness. Black eyes glimmered in the shadows. He imagined he could see the moon again, that the thick layer of poison and dust didn't cover everything.

WIDE AWAKE

Drumbeat, heartbeat, storm drum, who could know the difference?

He could, as he continued further into Regent Park. Not only as it was, but also as it had been and as it would be. Not the slightest nuance felt strange to him now. The pressure from butterfly wings thousands of miles off, the sound of a pin hitting a carpet in High Street. It had been such a long time since he had fed so often… that he had almost forgotten how it felt. Now, he remembered. A second, an eternity later.

The number of trees in the park had increased dramatically. They stood tight, now, almost like in a forest. He had seen them grow, seen the green grass grow tall and yellow. The park hadn't been maintained for many years. The zoo was quiet, all its cages empty. Cages and bars were half turned over. Growth penetrated floors and ceilings. Doors slammed in the wind. There was no wind. The animals had either been eaten or they had escaped. The wilderness erupted in the stone desert's midst, and no one did anything about it. A strangely pleasing sensation rushed through him.

Back in Camden Town. He had no idea how long time had passed, and he didn't care. He had to go home and burn the clothes, but there was no rush. People in the streets didn't really see him, didn't see the shadow in their midst.

He stood on the threshold of a bright-lit street filled with people. Without conscious thought he sought into a dark alley. He had no problem seeing in there, in the pitch-black others would see. His hand seemed to reach out by itself, grab a gutter, and test it. A moment it and the air around shook. Then Shelby climbed up the wall, in a flow instead of in a series of pulls. An ape climbing a tree, a black panther lurking in impenetrable darkness. A few seconds and he had reached the roof.

The roof stretched out in all directions. He was above it, not below. The stars were there, beyond the thick, poisonous layer of clouds and smoke. He would have known, even if he hadn't seen them. He felt ecstasy… And then he felt the frost down his spine, of a presence beyond any description. He had sensed *it* ever stronger lately. And he wondered how long he had slept, how long he had had his head stuck in the sand. Now, he turned more and more into a hawk flying in the dark, and it was no unpleasant feeling.

He had stopped on the edge of the roof and looked down on one of the places The Dirty lived. The police swarmed like ants down there. Not exactly an unusual sight. Raids happened several times a week in these places. Tonight, routine had been thrown out the window, though. The police officers took their time tonight, looking downright skittish, both in eyes and movements. Very uncharacteristic, compared to how they usually behaved when they raided a neighborhood of Dirty.

– An impressive sight, isn't it?

He didn't turn, didn't need to. He knew precisely where she stood.

– What do you mean? He turned.

– Look at them down there, Sheba said. – How they play their games and pretend they have power, that they have the slightest idea of what it is.

– Why do you come here, now? He raised his voice. – Now, when you've left me in peace for so long?

– Long? She smiled in patronizing intensity. – It was only yesterday to me.

She measured him, all the time with the patronizing, speculative smile in place.

– And you shouldn't flatter yourself. The world isn't that big anymore. It's no coincidence that we met here, that we're both in London at this point in time.

– The world has turned infinitely big again, he corrected her, – as it was long ago.

They held each other's eyes. The lights from below and the smoke from the put-out fires drifted and flashed between them.

– It isn't just like everything is falling apart now, he said. – Everything is dissolving.

– I've seen this happen many times before. She shrugged.

– It's different this time, Evan insisted.

Her eyes glowed dangerously. A glow seemingly surrounding him, and he had trouble shaking it off, in spite of him having fed extensively lately. He could never hide anything from her. She did this to test and irritate him.

– Don't you feel that much better, now, when you're about to cross the line again?

– Yes, he replied hoarsely.
– Don't you feel better than you've ever done?
– *Yes!*
A breath of wind and she was gone.
He grabbed his neck. It hurt, after all this time. *Phantom pains*. She could still hurt him.
Smoke and fire flowed as one. They always did. One always hid where the other was strongest.
He studied Colton's elite force in action. All the officers, the seven sergeants, the new Inspector - easily recognizable framed by the bright hair. In the street, in every apartment.
The wings of the night reached out, cut through the darkness, at the figures down there, out there, in there.
Water, overheated, steaming, gushed from broken tubes. The humid heat here mixed with the dry heat elsewhere in the city. Watts coughed in a scarf and attempted to breathe through it. And in that moment, she sensed the violent frost down her spine, to a degree she had never before even approached.
Uncertainty and paralysis burned within her, and she hated it. She hated everything she saw here, and she despised herself. She was so unused to this, to have so little control. Her body felt damp all over, as if she hadn't showered for days. She found herself in an «apartment» with two constables, saw herself in a dirty, broken mirror. Greasy, unmade hair, swollen eyes, swollen skin. The eyes staring back at her seemed twisted, alien.
The two constables interrogated a dirty man in rags. The same monotone questions were asked time and time again. Did he know anything? Had he seen anything? Had he heard anything? Did he have any ideas? Did he know about others who might know anything? Every new question was followed by a slap, or a strike or a kick. His family and the other families they shared these rooms with stared in apathy at it all with their backs pushed against the walls, waiting for their turn. The man squeaked as he brought forth his denials and apologies. The servile, pathetic attitude made Sheila furious. In an explosion she turned abruptly, and waved the officers off. She grabbed the man's collar, and lifted him up from the floor, pushed him at the wall. He was light, as if he wasn't anything but the rags he wore.
A rush of hot wind, the familiar pressure at the eyelids. A tiny moment she feared the pressure inside would tear her apart. And the fear she carried, that she couldn't name. She hated it, almost as she would a

person. She exposed her teeth to the man she had in her grip, in her power, and she knew the smile scared him, and it pleased her. Deep inside his eyes she saw her own fangs flash.

– You're not stupid, she said kindly, terrifyingly. – You *know* we won't leave here without answers. So why not give them to me, now, instead of later!

It wasn't a question, but an order, a royal command. She smiled.

His lower lip and his entire jaw shook. Eyes rolled in their sockets. First one, then the other. He looked to his left. A tiny boy stepped forward, frozen, looking at his feet. The begging, servile looks of them all washed over her like dirty, lukewarm water, making her sick. She ignored them. Her hands simply loosened the grip they had around the man's collar, and he fell to the floor, unresisting. She turned towards the boy, and reached out with a hand, making four fingers push like feathers under his jaw. A mother looked in a motherly way at her son.

Standard police training.

– I s-saw It fly over the r-roof…

– It? Watts' lips narrowed slightly.

– Yes, by damn, he exclaimed, with maturity far beyond his years. – Not a human being, Mistress, I swear. The wind, Mistress. The fire, the rain, the Earth itself, in the form of a man, a huge man, a horrible Beast.

– Hecate - the Moon Goddess, Mistress, a woman said solemnly, – returned to wreck vengeance upon the injustice that was visited upon her by the Romans two thousand years ago.

– A Demon that has come to punish us for our sins, another cried at the ceiling, his arms raised above his head.

Several others echoed their agreement.

– AYE

– That will be quite enough, thank you, the policewoman snapped. She momentarily lost control over herself, so easy, so fearsome. Then cold and hot again, to the boy: – You'll come with me.

This police operation ended, as all police operations did. The Dirty had already begun the cleaning up detail, those who hadn't been taken into the dark cars.

Cell by cell back at the headquarters had been filled. The prisoners were pushed at smooth walls, at doors and bars.

Watts stood at Colton's side. They honored the interrogations with their presence. The sounds stemming from routine punishment resulting from lacking or unsatisfactory replies echoed in the room, in all the rooms in the building. Screams of despair stemming from physical pain and deeply rooted mental anguish.

– Someone always knows something. Colton chuckled. – Including those who don't know they know. Find enough small pieces, and we'll find those who are behind the subversion. The group we're hunting isn't stupid. They have realized that to achieve anything in life one must use fear, intimidation and terror as a weapon. And to undermine Law and Order one needs to attack symbols of authority. But… they're amateurs. They will fail.

She felt bound, hands and feet. He touched her around the jaw with a hand that felt enormous. She felt bundled together, like wet paper.

– You've shown yourself to be quite useful, he acknowledged. – As I knew you would.

He removed his hand. She more than sensed he wasn't interested in her as other than a henchman. At least not in any way he would risk anything for. He had cut his hair short. It made him look even more brutal, but he didn't even approach the cliché of a thug. She knew that. He was on his way up, sharp, dangerous, and with a brutality always tempered by a conscious, deliberate and cognitive mind. He had a wife and children, a social position. To not ruin his social respectability, he took no chances in any area, beyond the confines of his job requirement. Especially not now, when they all had a much higher public profile than they usually had.

Sometimes, like now, he studied her with a special look, the same expression she remembered from their first meeting. The same way she saw herself; like a bird in a cage. She recalled her earliest thoughts about it, how she had visualized the cage as heavy and true. There was a certain safety in there, she had thought. Because it also contributed to keep dangers out. But now she realized he just waited to gain access to the cage… or for her to stick her neck out.

The Kacha dancers threw themselves on the floor in the deepest deep of the Green Rose. The Mystical Rock flowed from the very air itself. The mood in the inn was savage and strange. Every step in here, every sip of fluid, every intake of substances, every bit of food, was enjoyed with a feverish intensity. Every move, every single act, seemed to be inspired by the fact that it could be the last time.

The outer room didn't sound that muted. The lights didn't glow that dark. Watts sat in the bar with the others… her hunting buddies and partners. People sat along the entire bar register and drank. Sheila did, as well. Just beer, but it gave her a pleasant sensation and a warm weight in the stomach. Lights and colors dissolved, and everything became meaningless. Shelby had put up a new TV on the shelf above all the bottles. It buzzed on, and no one watched, and no one listened. *Cold.* She touched her arms. They were truly covered in fabric and not bare. It just felt that way.

There was a hole in the wall of sound. At least for a brief, extended moment. Or did the long row by the bar quite simply speak lower? Whatever, suddenly one heard the TV loud and clear.

– *And then we have today's UV reading.* A smiling and masterful meteoroliar «reported» that every day, as if that, too, was a matter outside human control. – *We're on our way down, the third day in a row. Prognoses show that we'll keep falling the next few days... Pressure on the Dam is, as usual, well within safety limits... In more good news collected air samples still show a stable...*

A full glass, leaving a trail of beer in the air, crashed into the TV. The explosion was unexpectedly powerful, and black smoke flowed into the locale. A burned piece landed in a huge man's glass, and he swore loud.

– HEY! He cried. – Who threw the glass?

Scornful comments hit him, hit him hard, and he had huge problems explaining that the reason he had spoken up, was that a piece of burned glass had landed in his beer, and that that was the reason for... He ended the hopeless attempt by meekly pointing out that a guy at least should be able to enjoy his beer in peace. No matter what might otherwise be wrong with the world.

A few started coughing and left the room. Most remained, being well used to breathing smoke and dust.

Sturgis Hunt Brading used the opportunity to push himself between Dilys and Sheila.

– What do you say, girls? Time to rent a room and get on with it?

– Get lost! Dilys replied icily.

Sheila didn't say anything.

– What do you say, sweetie?

He concentrated fully on Sheila, as had been the purpose of his advances from the start.

– I've never had the habit of taking drunks seriously, she commented.

Dilys followed the exchange with keen interest. Sheila felt the eyes of all her colleagues on her. They witnessed the brief display of teeth, the predator smile. She felt the flare of cold and heat, ice and fire inside. She wanted so much to show them her gratitude, tell them how pleased she was because they gave her the chance to express it. The eyes almost glowed in love when she turned to Brading. She threw the beer in his face. Before he managed to lift his hands in defense, she pushed her free hand into his abdomen. He fell off the chair, and hit the floor with a roaring crack. She rose calmly and kicked him in the chest. He yelped in pain. She charged and kicked him again. And again and again.

He crouched by her feet. The last kick had hit him on the cheek and made blood gush from his mouth. She pulled back, breathing hard, feeling the air move down her throat.

– A beer, she spat.

With insane eyes she sat on her stool and rubbed saliva from her jaw.

She swallowed the beer in huge turns, in an attempt to overwhelm the bitter taste of dust and shit. After a moment of pondering, she walked to the table where Colton sat. He sat with his back to her. She put a hand on his shoulder. He turned on the chair and looked at her.

– I want to thank you, she said. – You helped me get rid of an irritating itch I couldn't reach.

– You proved you belonged with us, he said. – I always thought so. Sit!

Brading's empty chair awaited her. She sat down on it while making sure she smiled seductively to Colton. He didn't take his cold eyes off her.

Shelby entered the room, whistling and walking in a very relaxed manner. He carried a brand-new TV. The cheerful whistling took on an even more expressive nature. He put the TV down on the bar.

– Excuse me. He smiled apologetically to those who had to move their glasses.

He pulled out the plug from the socket and moved the vanquished furniture from the shelf to the bar. Still whistling he supplanted it with the shiny, new TV. He pushed the on button, and it was on. Just like that. Then he returned to the dark dance hall where people writhed, danced and lived.

– He does it on purpose, the guy who had thrown the glass mumbled, looking despairingly into his new, half empty glass.

Laughter, Rough, scornful, warm.

– Go to him, Colton told her. – He knows something. Find out what.

Her eyes sought Evan, his back, as he vanished from sight. She made no protests. Every time Colton gave her an order, she felt a little less worthless.

Brading shook his head and fought himself up. He stumbled towards the toilets. She walked right behind him, indifferent. He showed no signs of having noticed her.

She considered going to the toilet and fix her herself a bit, filled with contradicting emotions. She wanted to look good for Shelby, but then she would also serve Colton's purpose.

No, she shook her head vehemently. Not Colton's, but her own.

In a near dream state, she flowed through the swing doors, through night, through mist. Her eyes and she, the entire her, as well, quickly, uncannily fast got used to the darkness in there. She spotted Shelby's dark curls. A waitress passed a bit in front of her. Sheila, in her dream, noted things about her, vague thoughts, impressions. The girl seemed very pale and tightly woven. She, who had looked so spirited the night before.

Sheila forgot about her, rocking lazily to the music. Shelby sat in the deepest part of the room with a pack of young boys and girls, deep into the shadows. She reached out to him with her hand, so far away, so intimately close.

– Dance?

She couldn't tell if he heard her voice, her husky voice. He heard the invitation, her siren cry, leading him out on stormy seas.

And she heard his.

He rose, accepted her hand. Not long after that, a blink of an eternity later, they danced, danced tight. And she forgot Colton, forgot everything. She remembered the melody, the melody starting slowly and slowly increasing the pace, the beat. The organ music, the naked voice, from another time, haunted them. Their eyes met and mixed.

The rough current leads us away.

We dream of fire, as the night turns cold.

She rested her head on his shoulder, while they writhed close, rubbed themselves against each other like two snakes, warm-blooded wherever they writhed. Feverish, indistinct thoughts mixed with the music, the lyrics, the song she wasn't certain she heard right.

The man is dead
A walking dead
A ghost breathing
The wind brings
Fake rot and all bad things
The child is dying
Breath by breath
The man is dead

Time. A river sleek as soap. Many years felt like yesterday.

They whirled round and round and round. She expected dizziness to come, to overwhelm her, but it didn't.

Feet trampled on the floor. She heard no feet trampling on the floor. All moves changed to pulls and pushes, in accordance to the raw, rhythmic music.

– *Kill,* she mumbled, as if in trance. – *Kill, kill, kill…*

She pushed her lips against his, held around his neck, in glowing passion.

The totally senseless dance ended. A calmer rhythm returned for a few seconds, until the music… ended.

She knew her greasy hair was wet with sweat. That she had color in her cheeks, that her breasts were more than half revealed, and that she looked better than ever. She breathed and walked on air by his side, back to the dark stall. Shocked, she didn't dare meet his eyes at first. Shameless as she was, she had considered squeezing her breasts a bit, to make them swell… but it hadn't been necessary. She felt them push at the fabric of her blouse, swollen and with hard nipples, one of the nipples resting outside, clearly visible. When they sat down, she kept her eyes lowered. Out of breath she raised them and was held by his dark, direct stare.

– What can I get you?

– Scotch, she replied hoarsely. – Aqua Vita.

– Ah, he sighed longingly. – The Water of Life.

– Yes, she said. – Just like wine and blood together once upon a time was called the blood of the gods.

What was the matter with her? Did she attempt to… seduce him? If she wanted to behave like a tramp, why don't do it with one of her superiors, to help her career?

She recognized the waitress and recalled her name from the reports. Wasn't it Claudette? Yes, Claudette. The girl returned quickly with their drinks. A large Glenmorangie Whiskey to Sheila and in Evan's case - a considerable supply of Bloody Mary. She drank fast, but he finished his well before her. Not so strange that, naturally, since her drink was much stronger than his. She giggled, without really knowing why.

Claudette brought him an entire bottle.

That's better, Sheila thought meekly.

She noticed that the girl had a scarf around her neck. It fit her, in a way. But in another it looked totally wrong.

Then Sheila forgot everything but the moment, what was right ahead of her.

– Cheers, Evan said, clearly relaxed, studying her with hunger in his eyes.

But still there were strange notions and thoughts distracting her. She imagined that she saw and heard Sturgis Hunt Brading while he bent over a sink in the toilet and mumbled curses.

That fucking bitch. She's gonna get it!

And she tasted blood as it flowed from his veins, tasted the iron, the sweet, sweet iron in her mouth. She shook as Evan pulled her to him, and she wondered if he had given her of his drink. She couldn't say for certain. Not that, or if there was a guarded look in his eyes. He rubbed a hand at her neck and pushed the fabric aside. Her entire body softened, and she pulled close to him.

The mood in the room changed, as if by magic. Watts blinked. Shelby had vanished before her eyes. Had she just imagined he was there? She had stood up, without really registering when it happened. She stood there, with the gun in her hand. Someone had turned off the music. She advanced through the crowd, the suddenly so silent guests, crossing the boundaries to the outer room. Her eyes were instantly pulled to the bar. A man hung over it and crowed insanely. Watts discovered that she froze constantly down her spine. Constantly.

– BLOOD, BILE AND GUTS! Froth covered his lips and the eyes glowed in something beyond any description. – E-eyes…

– He was like this when he left the lavatories, the man standing by his side explained helpfully, relaxed, not registering his own, wide-open eyes.

– I s-saw him… I SAW HIM NOT

The frothing man kept at it, while supporting himself on the bar. He seemed more like a little boy than a large hundred kilos man.

Colton and the others appeared by her side. She nodded to them. They nodded to her. Eyes didn't really seek out the toilet. The bodies did, gliding silently, unnoticed across the floor. Silence reigned in the entire building now. The guests should have heard the nine move, but they didn't hear a sound, except for the now so distant traffic outside. Colton's men and women cooperated to reach the toilet the fastest they could, and it was as if they, and Sheila as well, never had done anything else.

Tiberius Shaw threw himself into the well-lit room. Possibly with slightly less peace of mind than he usually exhibited during operations coincidentally similar to this. Didn't his hands whiten, Sheila wondered, clutching the sawed off, twelve shot automatic shotgun? Didn't his back tighten a bit too much?

Nothing seen, nothing heard. Time buzzed, but they couldn't see it, couldn't hear it. Five seconds later they were all inside. In an effective, ruthless progression they checked stalls, corners and ceiling. Nothing.

– Here, Kathy Williams said muted.

On the dry enamel, at the back of a sink, near the door, they found a few drops of fresh blood.

But otherwise, in a typical well-used toilet, they found nothing alarming.

– Where did your friend run off? Colton asked.
– He sat there, right beside me, Watts replied distantly.
Then they shook by the noise of a flushing closet. Not here. They exchanged looks. In the other room.
A woman raised terrified her hands above her head when she got eight heavy weapons directed at her.
– I haven't done anything, she gasped. – Please…
– You haven't heard anything, Ferrie barked.
– Nothing, she assured them. – Nothing at all.
– He asked you a question, dear, Watts sighed, slightly annoyed. – What we want to know is how long you've been here, and if you've heard anything *suspicious*.
– T-ten minutes, was the reply, just as frightened, timid. – Nothing… I haven't heard *anything*.
Watts didn't listen. She had already taken her attention away from the younger woman. What iced and burned within her suddenly burned that much stronger. This was the first time she was clearly close to the murderer. She didn't need to convince herself of that fact. Eyes sought and were pulled away. To the side, backwards. There, on the floor, in the corridor, four steps away, the ruby drops began. Now, when she had spotted them, they formed a clear trail towards the backdoor. She was unable to utter a word, a single sound. The brain worked, in a way. The body moved where the eyes rested, and restlessly sought, and her fellow artisans followed in her tracks. It wasn't the first time she had seen blood, far from it. The blood in itself meant little, compared to the impression overwhelming her senses. She had never before felt such horror. It didn't help that she had seven of the most dangerous people in existence at her side when she rushed at the exit. It didn't help at all.
Colton kicked open the door, kicked it right off the hinges, in a single rough energy output. She threw herself through the opening…
And stopped cold. The gun and the hands holding it, in a painful, shaking grip, was slowly lowered.
Right there, at the center of their view, where the lights from the street, from the cars, reached the deepest part of the alley, Sturgis Hunt Brading, what was left of him, hung, nailed to the wall. His belly and large parts of his chest were missing. His guts had been torn out. Most of it was unevenly distributed on the ground, including something… resembling… half his heart. They looked feverishly, moved on stiff legs, with stiff limbs, during the first, initial seconds, for the other half, in vain.
On the wall above the body, the mutilated corpse, there were two words,

scribed in blood:

ABNEY PARKer

Watts frowned. One of the others, she believed it was Dilys, finally managed to open her mouth, and say something.

– Who the hell is Abney Parker?

CHAPTER EIGHT

They were shaken to their bones. Stoic masks revealed little, but she spotted it easily. In the dirty yellow office light, they were gray around the edges.

They sat behind their well-fitted desks. She sat behind hers. Her new desk, in her new, co-opted office. She turned an ID-card in her hand, caressing it between her fingers. In a very predictable move, someone had written a note on it, a note in blood.

THREE OF TEN

– C'mon, she said cheerfully, – you must know *something* about our dear Abney Parker?

– You better shut your fucking mouth! Kathy Williams snarled at her. – Before I shut it.

Everybody stared hateful at her.

She ignored them, and concentrated instead on what displayed itself before her on the table. Somebody had forced Roderick to formulate a written report. In several copies, she assumed. She turned the pages. Sentences and words blurred. The inevitable result of the fact that she hadn't slept for days started to become apparent. She felt dead tired, but not sleepy. Eyes didn't close, no way. Heavy weights pulled the lids down, but no way. Everything entered her mind undistorted. So much, that she couldn't fathom how she could still see.

The essence of his report, written in his ironic tone, was that there was no substantial difference between this murder, this cadaver, and the two preceding it. «The tapping of blood was completed when the hundred and ten kilos Brading was nailed to the wall. That and the mutilations were done by raw strength. We're dealing with the gorilla - again».

In other words, the murderer had beaten large nails into a solid brick wall… with his hands. She rubbed her temples. A circus performer, she thought. Circus performers had done similar stuff, so-called strong men that, by long-term exercise and pure willpower, could perform seemingly impossible acts.

– … mutilations
– What was that, Watts? Colton asked sharply.
– He… or she… performs ritual mutilations, she said excitedly. – I should have seen it earlier. It's common to mutilate an enemy. At least it was common among primitive people. The underlying reasons could be many, but basically it concerned killing the Enemy as thoroughly as physically and spiritually possible. To make the enemy weaker and oneself stronger.

Colton didn't comment on it. He left it to Dilys.

– So what? She made a face.

Watts studied Colton more closely. Even he showed certain signs of *stress*. In spite of the hair being short, it seemed unkempt. The tie was skewed. He hadn't changed clothes the entire evening. She suspected strongly that he had started to smell.

– It might be important, she insisted. – Information is power, right?

Not long afterwards they were called to Superintendent Emerson's office. The door was sealed behind them, according to procedure. The office was strategically placed at the center of the building. Many a practical joker claimed Emerson had an insane fear of being *recorded*. Sheila didn't doubt that.

He showed, contrary to Colton, obvious signs of being stressed, and it was so out of character that it led to Sheila beginning to think in earnest, to reason her way through the maze of confused imagery. Her condition no longer impeded on her thought processes, but improved them. She started smiling. And once again she turned warm and cold simultaneously.

– I'm not pleased, Lloyd Emerson sniffed. – Not pleased at all. You're supposed to be the elite, the best of the best. And what happens? A simple investigation of terrorists, high profile terrorists and you botch it. What's your specialty, dish washing?

Froth, yes, froth flowed from his mouth. What a fabulous sight. One Sheila never had believed she would see. The Super stood there, an image of palatable wrath. And the feared special unit looked like wet dogs. Their weakness was exposed, and her strength increased.

– We have access to genetic material, sir, she said, very correct. – That should give us a fairly good idea of who the perpetrator is.

– I don't give a shit what methods you're using. I want results, do you hear me, incompetent FOOLS!

She refrained from mentioning that they should have received the results from the lab by now.

He probably knew already. He had to know. And he hadn't said anything, hadn't even implied it.

Something… went down. Something big. She had suspected that for a while, suspected that, too. Now, they had convinced her. This wasn't about a few killed coppers or even a reaction to the fact that someone dared to attack the special unit… No, this was about far more.

– The terrorists do ritualistic mutilations, sir. Colton cleared his throat after a noticeable pause. She stared hard at him. He ignored her. She refrained from speaking. – They're copying many primitive tribes where mutilations were common. They want to *crush* the enemy, sir.

Something passed between the two men, an understanding… Then Emerson shook his head, rejecting it all.

– So what? He puffed.

Anthony Johnson hid a smile behind the hand covering his mouth.

– The case has become clearer since the last incident, sir, Sheila remarked. – We were so close we could map the entire scenario. The first two times we were faced with two classic cases of affect killings. That's obviously not the case this time. The victim was drained of blood, nailed to the wall, and then mutilated. All this was done by a single person. By a man, about six feet, strong, he must be incredibly big and muscular. He might be irrational and show signs of savagery on occasions… But during the few minutes it took him to kill and place his trophy… That was an act made by an extremely rational mind. We can classify him as a kind of terrorist, sir, if we want to, but I personally would call this an *act of vengeance*.

She smiled to them, an ice-cold smile.

– There is little doubt concerning whom he wants to get even with, don't you agree?

– Fabulous, *Inspector* Watts. Kathy Williams applauded. – An excellent lecture. The best shit I've heard for quite a while. Understanding is certainly important, but little, impudent girl, you know very well that our enemies are under every manhole, in every sewer in this town… Understanding will only take you so far, while information… information is power!

– An excellent analysis, Sheila, Joseph Colton said kindly. – Your analytic abilities contribute, as expected, positively to the group. You can't tell us the most important, though, what we need to know to find the bastard.

– I know where we can find him, Sheila said sweetly. – He told us that. He wants us to come and play with him.

They stared at her. She waited. Enjoyed the situation. Let them suffer.

Let them feel the terror in their bones.

– I call the court's attention to exhibit A. She walked to the desk and grabbed the case file.

She found a photograph, and held it up.

– Beautifully composed, she stated with a gallows humor worrying them.

She trembled inside. In fear, danger, excitement, joy.

The photograph showed the body nailed to the wall and the blood writing above.

ABNEY PARKer

– Abney Park Cemetery, she enlightened them. – The last two letters, written with ordinary red color are there just to confuse, a joke on his part.

– A… joke? An uncertain flash appeared in Colton's eyes.

– Where the hell is this place? Shaw wondered. – I've never heard about it.

– It's an ancient, beyond downtrodden, overgrown cemetery in Hackney, Sheila replied willingly. – Quite a few dignitaries and infamous people from the nineteenth and early twentieth century have been wormfood there.

She stared defiant at them.

– So, what do you say? Who can refuse such an elegant invitation? I certainly cannot.

– Why didn't you tell us this before? Colton raged. All pretence had vanished in him. *He can't handle this.* – You went outside the chain of command.

– That's right. The Superintendent turned to her with a grave expression in his face. – What do you have to say for yourself, Watts?

– I had every intention of sharing this with my superior, sir, she said innocently. – But I didn't make it before we were called here. I hope you'll accept my sincere apology.

– I guess we can all accept that, he nodded and looked at the others.

They nodded and shrugged while looking anywhere but at him.

– I'm not convinced this is genuine, Colton spat. – You can go there with a unit, and take a look.

– You've lost it, she scorned him. – You no longer dare look beneath the biggest manholes.

– You twisted cunt…

– That's enough, Emerson interrupted them. – You will all go. This moment.

Decline hidden in gray fog, even more of it. Emerson's face faded in the colorless surroundings.

The cemetery and the surrounding area - Stoke Newington - were in Hackney police borough. They didn't pay a visit to the headquarters there, not to any station, but went straight for High Street. Anthony Johnson parked under a broken streetlight not far from the post office. All of them left the vehicle armed to their fangs.

It was just the eight of them, plus two young recruits. The major units were held back. Sheila hadn't objected to that. So dangerous - and insane - she more and more suspected their opponent was, it could have been a massacre. And he hunted them, no one else. Perhaps he wouldn't have shown if they hadn't come alone. They had a better chance of catching him this way, with a small, no less dangerous unit. So insane she suspected herself of being.

She asked herself if the others had any idea how dangerous he truly was, if she had. They all had experience from the rough, hard streets... This was different. Something beyond their realm of experience. Something... She told herself that this person was just a man. Out here, cut off from the police fortress' relative safety, she wasn't sure. She occasionally felt the fear, just as much as displayed by the two greenies. They had been brought as bait, and had no idea what was going on. She did.

They stood in front of the main gate and looked inside. The derelict building to the left. To the right further inside, through the wild growth, they could just about make out the ruins of a church. A road led into the forest, and faded a distance into the gathering darkness. The bad light from the street didn't reach very far.

Sheila attempted to remember an old melody that had always made her feel good, brought forth her devil-may-care attitude, but it was no use. Everything was quiet here. She couldn't hear a single, identifiable sound, no matter how hard she tried. Even the sound of their feet on the gravel sounded muted, dead. There were no sounds here, as if all life had gone.

Or fled.

Or perhaps it was more like life had faded away and rotted a long time ago.

The paths crisscrossed all over the green area. Joseph Colton led his pack on its walk, tight together, through the bewitched forest. In several places the forest was so tangled that what had been broad roads were blocked. There were paths, though, remnants of what had been. Almost all the gothic gravestones had been covered by green, moss and branches, with juicy green leaves. The more human-like sculptures seemed almost alive. And the same, abruptly, did the forest. Mist and shadows danced in

the air without anybody being able to decide upon the shadows' origins.
– Jeez. Dominic crossed himself, and what was worse: He didn't care if the others saw it.
– What an excellent choice for a meeting…
Watts was struck by the quiver in her own voice.
She didn't have to spell out whom it benefited.
One thing was certain: A traditional guerilla group had no advantages in this place.
He attempts to terrorize us, and he's doing it.
In her thoughts she fired her gun at the invincible shadow - and it just kept coming at her, inevitably.
The ten of them used an hour to familiarize themselves with the surroundings and thoroughly search it. They searched the derelict church, searching through everything, turning every leaf. And they didn't find the slightest sign that anybody had walked here in a very long time, far less earlier this evening.
– We do it like we planned, Colton said low and enraged. – Whether there are one or several mad dogs, we'll take them all down. God have mercy on anyone falling asleep on duty tonight. I sure won't have.
Nervous laughter. They found it completely improbable that anyone could fall asleep in this place.
There was no way they could cover the entire area. They split in groups of two, and walked to the spots they had worked out in advance. Everybody knew where everybody was. Each group carried a two-way radio. Everybody could listen and everybody could talk.
Watts stood with Tiberius Shaw at the northern wall. They stood with their backs to it, at a place where there were several steps to the bushes on both sides. Restless eyes moved from side to side in the ghostlike terrain. And they caught each other in looking behind them. A supple person could easily attack them from behind. Sheila knew of people who were able to put a noose around people's neck from far away. A noose at the end of a long stick, for instance, used with great skill, and the victim died without a sound.
Most people would be defenseless under such an attack.
Shaw was known to be both skilled and calm under pressure, and that impression he had also given her during the brief time she had known him. She had been surprised they had given her him as a partner. If she was expandable, why don't give her Hoover or Colby? Perhaps they had realized how good she was at this, and that she could be useful a little while longer?

Or perhaps they saw him as just as expandable.
They circled and constantly changed their position, but never came closer to each other than about ten steps.
– Are you positive you don't want a «cannon»? he re-offered.
He sure had enough of them. One shotgun on each hip, and one in his hands. She shook her head.
- I have my own, thank you, she grinned, brushing aside her coat. – Just in case.
No wind, no sounds. Quiet. She saw the shadows and the white shadows sweep his face as he moved. His eyes seemed so big, so aware, that she wondered if he had taken something.
– My senses are so sharp, she confided in him. – I never thought I could see the world like this.
– I know what you mean, he said, unexpectedly openly.
She spotted something in his eyes, something she could, if she wanted to, take as more than superficial interest.
Something…
Colton's voice shook them through the radio.
– *Is everybody in place? Parker? Lowell?*
– We're there, sir. They heard Parker's characteristic brittle voice.
– Everything is okay, Lowell confirmed.
– Hoover? Colby? Colton kept going.
– Everything is calm, Colby replied.
– Boring as death, Hoover remarked. – It's about time we end this.
– Shaw? Watts?
– Until death keeps us apart, Mein Fuhrer, Sheila blew flippantly.
– Nothing unusual to report, Shaw reported dryly.
They finally heard Williams call Johnson and Ferrie. Everything was okay.
Sheila looked at her watch. Just past midnight.
– The Hour of the Dead, Shaw said frostily. – As it was known in the old times.
The ten repeated the security procedure at uneven times. There could be two minutes since the last check, or merely ten seconds. Any of them could start it, at any time.
– A method as fullproof as it can possibly be. Shaw shook his head. – There isn't any fullproof method, of course.
– Of course. Sheila nodded.
– The cobra is out there, with its fangs, Shaw kept at it. – We have willingly displayed ourselves, to make it stick its head out… so we can

chop it off.

– Checking, Williams' voice echoed through the electronic system once again.

The time was almost one.

The Hour of the Dead was truly Dead. Even Sheila despaired. She could hardly recall her confidence an hour earlier.

– Moonlight and coke, they heard a tired and even more irritated Dilys.

– Hope springs eternal.

Dominic made those very telling noises with his lips.

Shaw looked down. He exposed his self-consciousness and didn't want to look at his partner. *The tough guy is sweet.*

– Johnson reporting in.

– And Ferrie. Still at large.

Cheerfulness, variety, creativity from these guys? She smiled to herself. They had to be bored to death. She hardly listened while the others reported in, when she yawned and looked at her watch… When she froze. She could hardly concentrate sufficiently to raise the radio to her mouth and speak, was hardly able to hear herself speak. There was this foggy sound she shouldn't really be able to make any sense of. But she did. She heard everything. What had she said, what words? Something about how fragile the illusion was.

It was quiet. No wind. Not in the entire city of London. Not by the Dam. Not by the coast or further in. In spite of this…

She sensed the wind. She felt it grab her greasy hair. It whistled in her armpits, through the air vents and deep in her dark passages.

Hadn't Dilys' voice instead of being tired and irritated sounded weak and timid? And Dominic's an excited tone, full of expectation. Had it truly been Dominic?

– I want to go home and sleep, Lowell complained.

– We should all go to sleep, Parker chanted.

He was the last. If it had been Parker that… Or Lowell. Was anyone truly… anyone? How could she *know?* During the course of the next second she covered the distance to Shaw and grabbed him, made sure that he… He didn't turn to smoke in her hands or was torn apart in front of her eyes. She put a finger on his lips and drew her gun. She started to walk and signed for him to follow.

She walked stealthily through the jungle, through the wilderness, and hoped she did it so quiet that Death wouldn't hear them - and understand. Hardly more than the toes touched the ground, made it even softer. They hunted in the forest, very quiet, very fast, bordering on the impossible.

– Johnson, Ferrie? Sounded Colton's voice, worried, insisting.

Damn!

– Present.

– Present.

Sheila increased her speed. She ran. Branches rushed by.

– Colby, Hoover?

There was no reply. The heart jumped a beat or two…

– COLBY, HOOVER?

– *Hide and seek, one hides, one is found. Two hide, two are found. I can hear you, I can smell you, I am a transformed God on a mission of vengeance among humans.*

Blood… Blood cooled in her veins. Not to water… to ice crystals, blocking all movement, all life. This was what wasn't Colby's voice displayed in full. Not a voice from the grave, but from the river Styx' frothing rapids.

DilysandDominichungnudefromropesonthesouthernchurchwall. Everything happened so fast, now, when it finally happened, as they should have expected. Everything seemed to… gather, to focus. She felt strength and a quickening beyond anything she had previously felt, as if pure energy had been injected right into her muscles. Adrenalin, Endorphin, and also something else… indescribable. One look at the two unmoving bodies was enough. Dead. Dead as doornails. *He was here*. She held her revolver out from her body, clutched it in both her hands while she turned. Shaw stood there with his shotgun, ready for anything. There was nothing to direct a weapon at. No movements, no sound. She heard Colton and the others from far away. She registered Colton, Williams, Johnson and Ferrie break out of the jungle, out of the buzzing, living jungle. Ropes were cut, or released somewhere. Two empty shells fell to the ground. And broke. The front, from the neck to the groin, broke, and everything inside fell out.

Sheila saw how Johnson crouched and threw up. Her attention and will were elsewhere, anywhere but here. Eyes chased the line of the bushes, the underbrush, as fast as her heartbeat. She concentrated on seeing past, beyond lit and smooth surfaces, into the shadows. In the smoke and fog beneath the illusions she glimpsed afacewildandhorrifying. She fired. One shot, two, she had no idea how many. No gorilla. The face, the demon mask disappeared. A horrible scream sounded through the jungle and stone desert, the moonless, starless night. It thundered when they all fired their weapons, at the scream, at the fog, at the smoke. Forest and gravestones were shot to pieces. They advanced forward in one raging wave, so fast that they normally would have feared it happened too fast, too careless. If they had been in their right mind. They threw themselves into the fog, into the smoke beneath the illusion - and stopped, and remained frozen in their tracks.

They stared. On the wet ground two ponds of blood flowed and pulsed, flowed together to one, at least half a step across. It seemed to *grow* as they stood there and stared.

Parker and Lowell almost crashed into them. Their eyes were wide and their mouths open, and they looked very young.

– We're gonna find him, Colton snarled convincingly. – It shouldn't be necessary, but if so, we split up in two teams and comb every single spot of this fucking place.

Sheila had already followed the blood tracks… to their end. A broad trail quickly narrowing. Eight, nine steps from the pond… it ended. It vanished. A few, huge drops at the end, that's all. And then nothing.

They found normal footprints a bit beyond the blood, and then they disappeared as well.

Eight began the search. An hour later the number had grown to several hundred. All members of London's special forces. No one was let through the iron perimeter raised around the area. A journalist who attempted to climb the fence to the park was shot dead on sight and then his body was thrown back into the street right in front of his stunned colleagues.

Watts paced impatiently back and forth by the bodies already before Roderick Carpenter had managed to touch them. Colton stood at the opposite side. His facial skin seemed gray in the yellow light. Not all the pretence in the world could hide the fact that he was badly shaken. Sheila couldn't fault him for that.

Roderick held up the two ID cards. Sheila had already looked at them. There had been no surprises there. They actually looked surprisingly normal. Two normal ID cards. The writing on them was practically identical to previous messages.

FOUR OF TWELVE

And:

FIVE OF TWELVE

– You guys are so lucky, Roderick complained heartfelt. – He truly tries hard when it comes to you, when he's executing his production. But everything is the same old shit when I arrive. He doesn't give a fuck about me.

Abney Park Cemetery was searched from the east, north, west and south. All vegetation was scorched with huge flamethrowers. The smoke further darkened the London skies. The demolition of the church was completed, until there no longer remained a single stone to turn. All the hassle, insanity, frustration about to explode, in vain. The search yielded no tangible results.

They were brought back to the headquarters. Led back, taken, almost like prisoners. Sheila sat by the window, and stared blindly out at the streets racing by. Stared at those who stumbled to their daily chores, where they earned their daily thin, tasteless bread. The first poor suckers had already started on their hard road to hardship and despair. She saw their sunken, twisted faces. Eyes closed. It was no use. She still saw them, saw everything. Eyes opened.

– He can bleed, she insisted. – He is vulnerable. We can take him.

– He should have been *stone cold* the way he bled.

The beyond insane lurked very close to the surface in Anthony Johnson's dull eyes.

Eyes closed. She leaned her head back, until it rested somewhat, on the hopelessly low seat top. The world flickered and passed by. She didn't register any of it. She couldn't.

The next turn of events she recalled happened in Superintendent Emerson's office.

– You're all off the case, he stated in a tone more than indicating he wouldn't accept any voice of protest. The six in front of him were hardly able to stand on their feet. – From this moment on, more competent people will take over.

Sheila knew well what that entailed. This, this case had now been upgraded from being a police matter to a national security issue. Those who handled such matters weren't exactly nameless. They had many names. Among the few and many who knew of their existence, they were known as «The Faceless». They operated in the shadows, in people's dark corners, in the rusty paths of modern life, and they made Colton's pack of thugs look like a kindergarten.

– I hit him, she heard herself say. – We're closing in on him as he's closing in on us. We're the only ones who can take him out.

– Yes! Shaw exclaimed. – Yes, by damn!

– That will be all, Emerson said in a crushing blow. – Watts returns to normal service. The rest of you will from this moment on never go anywhere alone, not even to the john without being accompanied by a platoon of guardians. The slightest break from this will result in extensive reprisals. Ladies, gentlemen…

He nodded, rejecting them. His voice had hardly deviated from the evenness cutting into them. He seemed far more dangerous now than during the explosive rage they had witnessed earlier.

And they, that much more like wet dogs.

– Out of the q-question, Johnson stuttered. – He will come for us, no matter where you hide us.

– Good! Emerson grinned ruthlessly.

Sheila had never seen him like this before. She had seen a lot of him, but never so hard, so totally ruthless. She wanted to freeze, but was too tired to even do that.

She crouched in the seat. The underground, the coach where she crouched raged on. She no longer cared about the countless delays.

The street, quiet. Many cars in Camden High street already. Not so many yet, that it interrupted the general flow. Quiet, in spite of the noise from the countless engines, a part of the background noise. London always hummed. She had grown up here and sensed the silence right there in a heavily trafficked street.

She walked right to her apartment. She imagined that her shotgun and her revolver were in place inside her jacket. Perhaps they were. Perhaps not. She just couldn't tell. What use had it? A sound reached her from behind. She turned, turned swiftly, and the Heckler & Koch was locked in her hands. There was nothing there. No humans. Nothing alive.

An idea had struck her. A thought. She had asked for Parker and Lowell before leaving the station. No one had seen them. Could it really be that simple? Was the fact that the two last letters in the blood writing had been spelled with small letters a double misdirection? But why? She was uncertain whether or not she wanted to find out, if she wanted to know. Uncertainty and a nagging fear haunted her and made her run the last stretch to the apartment.

She had her fingers on the number plate before halting, before everything in her grinded to a halt.

The fingers didn't move. She stopped breathing. That fucking code. She had been given the latest numbers, but now… she couldn't remember them.

She fumbled in her right pocket. Nothing. Damn, she always put that fucking piece of paper there. Always.

Suddenly she stood with her back to the door, completely beside herself. She had her gun in her hands. Hands shook so hard that she distraught fired a bullet. The bullet whined through the street, hitting the tarmac, the bricks and walls, before whistling into the night, the black, black night.

Panicked, sissy girl.

Pathetic, sissy girl.

– Pathetic, sissy girl, she sniveled.

She had repeated it inside until she managed to form the words with her mouth, like she had done as a little girl in this area of town.

The rage that had always sustained her, pushed the fear back to a level she could handle. A hand reached for the number plate, fumbled for the numbers. She didn't look at it. Fingers pushed buttons. She had her eyes locked forward. And to the side, totheside.

The door slid open, and she slipped inside. No one inside. Good. Relief haunted her, haunted her like fear. She kicked the door close. Eyes moved to all sides, as she ascended the stairs. She pushed the code to the apartment with steady fingers.

The door slid close behind her. Arms fell down her sides, weak and shaking. The gun slipped out of her weak hand. She fumbled some more in her right pocket, and there she felt it, the paper with the now, useless numbers. Laughter rose from her sore, sore throat. She stood a while before the big entrance mirror. She had heard them whisper behind her back at the headquarters. Oh, how she had heard them. They had looked at her. The rumors went about her future, her career, about how it had reached a dead end.

Something had closed in on her the last few nights, sneaking up on her. It had begun no more than fifty hours ago. Something, fate or something else, had pointed at her. *Something*. Burned her, marked her. A shadow on the wall no one truly noticed until it struck. A creature without face, body, soul and blood. She pulled her feet across the floor, into the living room, until she stopped, face to face with Death.

Parker and Lowell, in a manner that looked like a piece of art had been nailed to the ceiling. In the close to brilliant position he had placed them, they looked almost alive. But they had broken eyes, and were dead, dead. Dead!

She carefully reached for them, fearful they would dissolve before her eyes or that they would dive like birds of prey to attack her. Fearful about everything. Terrified to destroy the perfect art.

They hung there, nude, and there was hardly a mark on their body, except for the two tiny punctuation marks between their neck and shoulder. They had their ID cards hanging from their necks.

SIX OF THIRTEEN

was written on one of the cards.

SEVEN OF THIRTEEN

on the other.

She just lay down, right there on the floor. The way she crouched still on her side, it looked like she was sleeping. She remained there with open eyes, staring blind eyes.

So peaceful. If she just lay here, relaxing, he would surely come and fetch her, Death. She was already dead. If someone came and checked on her, they would find no pulse, no heartbeat, not find the slightest brain activity. She was convinced that no matter who would come, would come only to draw her form on the floor, draw her with a piece of chalk, and that would be the only thing of her that remained.

She fought herself up, slowly, painfully. She couldn't tell if she was breathing, but at least she moved.

What made a human take a step forward? What made it keep moving, keep breathing?

An oblong, blue sign penetrated her vision.

CAMDEN TOWN STATION

She couldn't recall leaving the apartment. Everything just slipped away in the fog, the gray fog.

The gate was closed. There was no train arriving in ten minutes yet. To be better safe than sorry she also checked the other gate around the corner. That was closed as well. She walked the few steps back on unsteady legs. For some mysterious reason it was always the western gate that was opened at night. Well, High Street had more traffic. More lights, less shadow. Sheila didn't care about that. She didn't care about anything.

Wynette Richards lived in a luxurious apartment complex in Docklands, right by the newly opened Thatcher Center. Sheila had been there only once before, during the moving in party in the enormous wall to wall apartment. She asked herself, wondered why she sought there, now, but didn't bother to reply.

The train had coaches with huge windows of bulletproof glass. It raged pleasantly forward, above the persistently rising coastline.

The pumps worked tirelessly. It was no use. Gas flames fired often from the overextended machinery. Fired from several spots. Also close to the central complex. No matter how modern everything was supposed to be.

Everybody that wanted to matter in this stone desert lived here.

People lived here. They worked here. It was said that many of the children had never even visited London's older parts. The inferno surrounded Sheila, bathing her in its heat.

She easily passed the outer perimeters. Her ID opened most doors. She reached one of the gates in the outer inner ring, protecting all the luxury within. There was only one single man behind the counter. She knew such a sparse presence of guards was an illusion, that the place crawled with surveillance cameras, that something resembling an army was ready to act at any time. At most a minute off, perhaps only ten seconds. Behind the nearest wall.

She felt so much lighter, now, having left the heavy shotgun in her… what had been her apartment.

Sheila walked to the counter, facing the guard.

– Miss Richards is expecting me. She leaned over the counter and smiled to him.

She had fixed herself ever so little with a pocket mirror, fixed the worst. More than presentable to him. She was willing to bet he preferred sluts. And bet was just what she did.

– That isn't very likely, now, is it? He said, very patronizing.

– I called in advance and told her I was coming, she insisted. – Call her, and she will confirm it.

– We protect the neighborhood here, he said, bathing in his perceived superiority, his power. – And you should be aware of one thing, sweetie: That includes untimely interruptions.

– You're so loyal, so tough, sir, she purred, she suddenly purred, hardly able to believe herself, believe her shameful behavior. – I like that in a man.

She gave him her most seductive smile. Perhaps a bit too wide, the way the canines showed.

– What do you mean? He said suspiciously.

– Such a becoming modesty, she overdid it. – I get all giddy. But you think I'm sweet, don't you? You just said so… You want to see? I know you want to. You want to touch? Yes, I know you'll want to comfort a poor girl in need…

– I want much more than that, he said, suddenly quite brusque. – Come here!

An order, a command she couldn't resist. Her mouth, her full lips made a face he didn't see. She didn't even need to move on to her «silly blonde» performance. She had shown great skill, great skill in the game.

She slipped inside the small, open cubicle, close to him.

– On the floor, he ordered harshly.

She felt an increasing, dull worry, telling her she had possibly underestimated him.

– Why? She grinned. – Are you shy?

He reached for her. She slipped away. He caught her and pushed her back, until she had her butt pushed at the desk.

– Bitch, he breathed. – Indecent slut. Your tiny badge won't protect you here.

She feared he was right. This place was way beyond her sphere of influence.

He tore open her blouse, and tore the skirt halfway up her thighs. It didn't matter. She kept staring dully straight ahead. They were well-used clothes. He spotted the Heckler & Koch, but it didn't seem to impress him. Of course. it didn't. She was pretty sure he had access to far bigger firearms.

She spotted Wynette appearing from the elevator. Relief flooded her mind. She freed herself by a slight twist of the body and by applying pressure on a point on the man's wrist. After a second or two she once again stood in front of the counter. She made no attempt to cover herself. No matter how hard she tried she couldn't close her eyes, and was also unable to open them more than halfway. She imagined, more than experienced that Wynette embraced her and kissed her on both cheeks.

– Uh, Miss Richards… It originated nervously from the deep well the cubicle had become.

Both women turned to him with their most radiant smile in place.

– That will be all, Wentworth, Wynette said cheerfully. – We won't need you anymore. Thank you for looking after her for me.

– I forgot, didn't I? Sheila shook her head in wonder. – So thoughtless of me. Yes, thank you very much, sir. We will remember you…

They laughed, and left him, arm in arm.

The small, closed-in compartment moved across the rails, heading for the inner circles of wealth and power.

The lights flickered and failed for a moment.

– FUCK! The director promised me he would get it fixed. He swore.

A system long since stretched beyond the limits, was stretched once again. It flashed in shadows and lights all over the enormous complex. She managed to blink, and what she saw was eternity. And in the bad light Wynette's face looked like a demon mask, with long, bloody fangs.

The visions faded, but Sheila kept her eyes wide open after that.

Wynette studied her with keen interest.

– I've moved out of the apartment, 'Nettie, Sheila finally said in a low voice, averting her eyes. – It would be great if I could crash here. And sleep. I need to sleep.

Wynette's smile was filled with ambiguity. Sheila had been prepared for that, and held herself back, kept holding herself back.

She imagined she heard music, but she didn't care. Her vision, her senses hardly received anything from the surroundings. Wynette led her, led her away, led her astray, and she let herself be. She stumbled forward until she reached a bed, and fell headlong into it. Everything turned quiet. And if there was noise anywhere, she didn't hear it. All output was closed off. Quiet, but not peaceful. Fear followed her into sleep and dream. Fear and He, the Beast. Impressions faded quickly in the silken blackness, and sleep held a conditional peace. That was the only thing she held on to: The certainty that he hunted her. She slept the sleep of the dead.

CHAPTER NINE

Something was awakening. Something he had thought had died a human lifetime ago. He was impatient, irritable. *Good.* Something stirred within him, an expectation of something new and different. Like long ago. Longing hadn't been buried in him then, but been a potent lifeforce within him. He realized, shocked, how predictable and routine-dominated he had allowed his life to become.

He appeared early at his appointment. The exhaust tore into his nostrils worse than ever, but affected him less. Even before he turned left and dived into Inverness Street, before he reached the actual market, he knew with a certainty he didn't question that something was *wrong*. He knew the smell of fear. An aroma he knew more than well. Before he truly realized it he walked between the stands, between salesmen and customers. He walked in their midst. Their fear and blood resembled a song in his heart.

– Goods are late tonight? he commented, lacing a slight question mark to his words, turned to one of the salesmen.

– They are a bit late, the man behind the counter confirmed nervously.

– I've heard certain rumors that the cargo will encounter problems tonight, Shelby said abruptly, as he stared at the man.

– There are rumors, the salesman replied, cautiously, very cautious.

Evan could have pushed him harder, pushed all the scared rabbits here that much harder, but there was no need. He knew, to the point of not needing any final conformation. And there was no time.

The train… He needed to go north, stood there undecided a few seconds. He considered using the train, but realized, without really considering it that it would be too slow, much too slow. There was no time.

When he rapidly walked around the corner it seemed, to those who watched him like he was running… in a strange, effective way. He thought about taking the train again, a stray thought quickly forgotten. By then he had already passed the underground station, and seconds after that also the railway station, making good time, more than good time northeast, along Camden Road. He didn't care if anyone spotted him. They didn't for long. Just long enough for him to smell their fear. They didn't see a human being running, but a non-dead that to their eyes floated above the street, without actually touching the ground. He ran faster than he had ever done before and didn't feel the slightest fatigue. Past underground stations, through streets. He sensed the hunger, the ever-present Hunger like a heartbeat. Already a long time ago he had learned the threshold for when it would turn unbearable. Flashes of memories from another time still caused an unpleasant tingling in him. He wasn't certain he would call it pain.

He had learned this route and others by heart, instinctively. Because he had expected as a certainty that he would one night need the knowledge. It hadn't exactly been the most difficult of predictions.

At Tottenham Hale he spotted a busload full of armed police officers. He had no doubt their destination was the same as his.

He rushed up Forest Road, a path between huge, open water reservoirs, all filled to the brink, with content stinking to the point that even people with defunct city nose, usually unable to smell even the heaviest of pollution, had to notice. To the south smoke rose from the overtaxed purifier plants. Evan resisted the temptation to cover his nose. He hardly did anything to keep out horrible smells. To the east the late afternoon traffic moved at a snail's pace on the M11 linkroad. Entire streets and parks had been sacrificed to complete this road. To the west there were rows and rows of old and new industrial parks, spewing more poisons and destroying ever more of the last remaining green areas.

The poison had been present for a long time, now, but never so extensive.

He had no clear sense of how long he had run. Only that he moved faster by far, than any ordinary human was capable of. It had never really occurred to him to test the boundaries of his endurance, and he didn't now. When he reached Epping Forest, he breathed slightly harder, but felt nothing even approaching exhaustion.

Much had changed, been razed since his first visit to London many years earlier. Razed here, too. The southern part of Epping Forest was practically gone. The only remaining green was the golf course. Only when reaching the Essex border there was a number of trees resembling a forest, when he had completed a route encompassing major parts of northeastern London.

The forest had been diminished, but he still sensed its smell, its deep.

And the stink of weapons, of fired guns.

And blood. The taste of copper and iron, the revenant of dawn lingered in the poisonous air.

The true dawn waited hours, years off.

He stood still, listening from the deepest shadows.

Herbert was still here. The deliverymen were still here. The supplies, too. Shelby's supplies. Shelby started moving around, checking out the area. He stopped counting the number of constables fairly soon, seeing no point in continuing beyond fifty or so. Undetected, like a shadow he moved around, forming an image of the logistics involved in his head. «Smiling Franzz» with subordinates and Shelby's own men, and the suppliers, had made their stand somewhat in the center of it all, left with very little room for maneuvering, surrounded by several anthills of cops.

«Smiling Franzz» yet smiled, in a strained way when Shelby reached him. The wounded man sat with his back to a tree. Evan whistled the signal. Both Franzz, and Connors, Shelby's second in command lifted their hands.

– It's him, Connors said.

Evan Shelby appeared in the brighter shadows, a legend, a myth, lethal and true.

– We don't have much time. He knelt down by Herbert, towering above him.

– The pigs ambushed us. Herbert strained to speak. – They waited until we had gathered together before striking. Fortunately, they were stupid enough to call for our surrender before firing. They got many of us, but we got many more of them. After that they have concentrated on keeping us here, which is sufficient, from their point of view. I think they've called half of the London police force and «volunteers» here since then, and more are arriving by the minute.

Shelby nodded to himself. He hadn't been mistaken about the wounded man when meeting him five years earlier. To «Smiling Franzz» the phrase «no retreat, no surrender» was more than a mere phrase. No matter the cost.

– Make yourself ready to leave this hole, Shelby told them, a bit preoccupied. – Leave the supplies. Looks like I have to take a loss tonight.

– That's mighty generous of you, Captain, Smiling Franzz nodded. – It might still not be sufficient to get us out of this rathole, though. But you got in, so you will probably get back out, too. I presume we will see your mysterious, invisible sentries in action tonight? If they're half as good as you I think we may have a fighting chance…

– The action, Shelby nodded, conceded, – but not much more.

He smiled in a way that left all the tough men and women close to speechless.

A breath of wind stood there, before moving on. He was gone.

– We just had the honor of meeting quite a dangerous man, Smiling Franzz stated quite solemnly.

And he smiled. Pain cut into his face as he fought himself up along the tree, but eventually he was back on his feet, and not unsteady at all. For the first time in years, he got back his faith in the human willpower, what it was able to withstand and endure.

– When it happens, it will happen fast, he said. – Be ready.

Evan sensed the crawling under the skin, sensed the Hunger move and scream. He slipped through the bright darkness. That was how he saw it, anyway. He was perfectly aware that others did not, even though he sometimes had to remind himself of that fact. While they could mistake lurkers for bushes he saw them, sensed the veins pulse under their shadow skin.

Bodies looked like mounds where they lay stinking on the ground. They remained where they had fallen. Dead bodies, dead blood. He wrinkled his nose in involuntary disgust, registering details without really wanting to. He saw the bodies clearly. None wore uniforms. This was an unofficial operation, a method used when somebody high in the hierarchy wanted something done. No matter the clothing they stank of Copper a long way off. He had never had any trouble smelling this particular type of human. Leftover weapons, dark metal flashed there, on the ground.

There was a low roar, a sound he knew the others present couldn't hear. He saw all the people crouching there in the dark. Seconds passed, as he sneaked around, back and forth, while seeking the best possible position. He saw them well enough and also knew they had no chance of seeing him.

– Fuck, I must pee so B-BAD!

The whisper and the subsequent gloating laughter, shockingly enough, sounded like thunder in his ears. He smelled fear and hatred. Quite a number of the policemen and women were clearly shaken, unused as they were to any kind of forceful resistance. It had lasted far longer than they had expected and turned into a kind of trench war. But one Herbert's people were doomed to loose, if something unexpected didn't happen, something changing the odds dramatically. Evan smiled, an expression of his he knew was terrifying.

The young recruit's shyness and uncertainty led him to the bushes, where his older colleagues couldn't see him. Evan enhanced the mist surrounding his mind, and slipped quickly, silently behind him. Fangs grew. He sensed it more than actually physically noticing it, as if it was actually something foreign, and not a part of him.

Fangs bit into soft flesh. The boy had his eyes closed while life was sucked out of him. When Evan released the limp body, he sensed he had sucked so much that it would probably mean death. He found nothing in himself being sorry.

He was in no hurry when searching the dying boy's pockets. No one approached. No one had noticed any well-founded reason for the fear they felt crawling under their skin. It just was there, a presence in their midst.

The ID-card was hidden inside a sewn, closed pocket below the heart. Evan felt its texture, its familiarity under his sensitive fingers. He ripped it out, quickly writing a message in blood, using the boy's index finger:

one of many

In one powerful move, he pulled the head off the body. He put the head on the ground a few steps away and placed the card on the pale forehead. Half distracted, half sharp he kept moving, and he continued his Journey.

He erupted from the bushes, and fired at everybody even remotely close. Only the few being hit the last managed to pull their weapon's trigger, just before they, too, fell. Seven died in a heartbeat, before they had realized they were being attacked. More charged forward and closed in on him from all sides. Loud, enraged cries sounded from their mouths. They shot wildly at the indistinct figure fading into the shadows. He was hit and snarled at them. Pain overwhelmed him for a second or two. Another bullet hit him. He hated every time it happened. Then he was clear, and their rounds hit only the bushes and the grass, and their comrades.

– Where did he GO? A man shouted. – We had him. What *happened?* Where did he go?

Evan ran as he reloaded, ran through the night, and when next time he shot at them it was from a completely different angle. Bullets hit them from behind. He howled at them as he fired. They screamed in surprise and fear. They were like statues, staring at each other's dead eyes. Less than ten seconds more, and he fired from yet another position.

– How many ARE THERE? A powerful voice shouted. – We fucking cleared this area. Didn't I TELL you to take care of stragglers? Didn't I…

Everybody stared in horror at him, at the Inspector, at his throat, at the blood gushing from his torn throat.

Afterwards they weren't sure of what they had seen.

– I *saw* it, one insisted. – A pale faced *demon* appearing behind the Inspector, ripping his throat.

– It was only the light, another insisted. – Only a trick of the light.

They convinced themselves, to the depth of their heart. The situation had abruptly, horribly been turned completely around, in their disfavor. They saw no enemies, had no idea how many hostiles there were, knew only they were fired at from all sides, and fear blocked all their higher brain functions. Everybody pulled back. It started as a kind of organized withdrawal, but had soon broken into a totally chaotic run. Nobody cared about the wounded anymore. There were bodies, bleeding and stinking bodies and bloody weapons everywhere. Evan emptied clips and discarded the guns, picking up new ones as he advanced, as he chased panicked-stricken rabbits on their return south. The majority of the hundred-man force ran. And they didn't stop. More than one were run down by cars. Some ran straight at the cars. All caution thrown to the wind.

There was no escape. No matter where they ran the enemy was *there*. Even though people eventually stopped firing at them. At that time, they were hardly more than pale ghosts of their former so bragging and brutal selves. Most of them would remain in the force, but they would never, from tonight on, be fit for anything but paperwork.

The creature attacked a wounded, female cop. She tried, in nameless fear, to raise her weapon. He took it from her weak hand and lifted her up. He drained her of blood as he ran. Emptied her… of every single drop. World turned indistinct, the surroundings crystal clear. For the first time he experienced, fully conscious, when a victim expired while he was still sucking blood. He felt something that both was and wasn't matter flow into his being. He slowed down until standing still. The last wounds closed. He was aware of every bit of skin stretching and mending. As the pain stung and died in him. The living and recently dead in the entire park… he felt them, felt life beat his skin and death knock his door. He felt EVERYTHING

Wide-open senses stirred, and sensed the surroundings anew. Never more the same way. His. Hers.

He let her slip from his grip, down on the ground. Her broken heart had stopped beating. She still heaved for breath in small, short gasps, but no air came. With her eyes, now so full of life she begged him. Now, when her life was about to fade, she fought for it. He might still save her.

Perhaps. He couldn't make himself try.

A sound far behind him, a whisper in dead leaves, in juicy leaves. He had been sharp, and then let himself be distracted for a fraction of a second. He turned abruptly and Sheba stopped, not more than ten steps, a toe away.

– Stay away from me, he snarled.

For the first time he spoke to her with a voice containing not the smallest brush of fear. She laughed throatily.

– What a great carnage, she applauded. – How unlike you.

She picked up a huge patrolman moaning in nameless fear, and bit him. When he died her eyes turned clear as glass. She threw him away with a contemptuous outcry.

– HAH! She held Evan's eyes with her own. – Just a snack, but a tasty one.

She walked around and picked up the wounded, one by one. He imitated her with a feverish unrest ruling both his body and soul.

When the last laid still on the ground she had emptied five and he three. He still saw hunger in her eyes, while it clearly burned less intense in his own.

– Just twenty, she teased, tortured him. – All that ruckus and only twenty dead. If I didn't know better, I would think you aimed badly on purpose.

– The purpose was served, he said roughly. – I saw no reason to stress the point.

– Evan, dear Evan, she smiled. – You still have a bit to go, but not far. Just a little longer, now, and you will join me, without reservations.

She turned her back to him and departed, walked away, slowly enough for him to actually observe it. To him it made her no less disturbing. He never turned his back to her, if he could avoid it.

He remained there, for a while, before breaking the light paralysis, and headed back to Herbert and the rest. They didn't have much time. He tore off his clothes while running, scratching off the clotted blood. Another half a minute passed while he circled in the place where he had left a bag of clothes, similar to the bloody he had thrown away. He was ready to go home.

\\\\\\\\\\\\\\\\\\\\V//////////////////////

She dreamt. Insane images of carnal desire. Warm skin on warm skin. Impressions of a woman with long, fair hair hunting in empty streets. Carcasses floating everywhere. Floating in dirty water, floating in the stream, wherever it led. Those without flesh on their bones rose and walked. The others dissolved and their remains flowed with the river.

Silence descended first on her in the spacious room. She noticed that first of all. Cautious eyes opened. The room, this room alone, as big as her entire apartment, revealed itself to her. She brushed the silk sheet aside and stepped out of the bed, her first, hesitant steps. The huge wall-to-wall mirror exposed her nudity. Somebody had undressed her. She had a nice view of her dirty, disheveled body, the bloated face, the naked expression.

She stumbled to the shower/bathtub. Weak fingers turned on the water, to the point of it being a waterfall. She didn't plug the hole, but the water level kept rising. The soap flowed over the edge and out on the floor. She soaped herself in thoroughly and enthusiastically. Shit floated off with the water and soap. She felt as if she was floating off, but didn't care. It lasted long and well until she sat by the breakfast table with Wynette.

Wynette had dinner, but had good-natured joined Sheila. Male and female servants moved discretely back and forth between the table and kitchen. The kitchen was far away, and nothing there disturbed anything here. Luxury was everywhere in this place. Sheila knew she looked around her with wet, shiny eyes. What had happened to her, what she had lived through… everything seemed so meaningless, now.

– I must say you showed great initiative confronted with the… grouchy guard this morning. Wynette cheerfully swallowed a piece of smoked salmon. – I've already secured the somewhat indiscreet recording, of course. Not that there's such a big chance of it turning up in any wrong places, but why risk it?

In spite of the dull expression in huge, insane eyes they kept staring at Sheila from the mirrors, wherever she turned under the unruly hair.

– No, why indeed…

Sheila sipped more wine. It didn't help any, really. The alcohol seemed to evaporate within her, and in no way calmed her wretched nerves.

Wynette kept ranting. Sheila listened, while a pleasant paralysis spread to her limbs.

She heard music from somewhere. Piano/Keyboard music, mixed with drums, sounds and guitars. It flowed from speakers built into the walls, but it seemed like it originated from the very walls themselves. She heard the music, not with her ears, but with her body and mind.

– Sounds familiar, right? Wynette's half smile turned playful, triumphant.

Sheila nodded.

– I've heard it before, but can't place it. Sheila shook her head in wonder. – It's something rare, unusual, I'm certain of that much.

Wynette nodded. An entire wall vanished, and a Vid-screen appeared.

Not the modern 3D holovids, but still-photos and reels from the previous century. A face, a man. Sheila sensed her facial skin prickle and burn.

– Yes, this is James Evan Shelby, rock musician, idol of millions, in the nineteen seventies… It's remarkable, isn't it, the similarity, I mean with his grandchild?

– Remarkable, Sheila replied preoccupied.

There was a buzz in her ears, sparks before her eyes. Sharp smells and scents floated in the air, danced on the tongue. And no matter how one could describe the deeper, less obvious senses, and what they told her, it would remain insufficient.

– Have you checked him up? She asked, just as distant, through bubbles, through soap. – Had me followed?

– I tried, Wynette admitted willingly. – But the people I hired to keep track of you met with, how to put it… unfortunate accidents. So, I needed to make use of more indirect methods. As you know I have an extensive web of contacts at my disposal… and you haven't exactly kept a low profile lately.

– The last two days, Sheila remarked.

– What?

– Only the last two days. Before that I was no one.

– Isn't it about time you stopped underestimating yourself, now, honey? Wynette kept a slightly challenging tone. – I've always said you've got potential. You just haven't been willing to develop it yet.

– Yes…

Sheila was ashamed. She was so very ashamed, and Wynette didn't help her, made it deliberately that much harder for her to proceed.

– Your offer, Sheila choked. – Your standing offer… I've decided to accept it.

– Excellent, Wynette exclaimed, unable to contain herself any longer. – Absolutely excellent.

She jumped to her feet and started pacing around the room, full of energy.

– Don't worry. I've planned everything, down to the smallest detail. There are so many ways we can utilize you and your talents. I have lots of ideas.

Numb. She drifted away where she sat, so receptive.

She drifted with the wind. Rested in bed. Slept some more.

When she woke up, she knew it was night again. There were no windows in her room, she just knew. She bathed and washed some more. Dried herself with huge towels, in the storm created by large and pleasant fans.

The mirror, large and deep, showed all of her. Pale, very pale skin. It had never been touched by the sun. People gobbled vitamin D like crazy these days. Not everybody was lucky enough to have access to the life-saving pills. She had been lucky.

She knew of people, even some with a bit of income, where the word «skinny» gained a new significance. She wasn't skinny, couldn't even be called thin, but had well-developed muscles and forms. Through sheer willpower, she had pulled herself out of the slum, through more of the same, she had kept herself away from it.

The dark bags below her eyes from the last, few days hadn't vanished, but shrunk significantly during the day.

She combed her hair. Clean, blonde locks changed her looks completely. It seemed completely changed from two days ago, and she couldn't tell whether or not that was her imagination speaking. Not that it mattered. Something in her eyes, in the very way she moved and breathed, meant far more. She had changed.

Wynette's servants had found clothes for her. They didn't look that bad. Quite different from her usual attire, but okay. Not too glaring. She dressed in slow, deliberate moves.

Another mirror. The clothes hid more than they revealed of her body. They suggested and pointed, more than revealing it.

She knew well how to apply make-up. This was more advanced, more stylish than she usually did, but the Metropolitan Police held courses in applying makeup as well, in addition to many other things concerning correct behavior and display. To burn with a weak flame, to hide herself, her true self wasn't anything new to her.

Wynette met her in the hall, scrutinizing her.

– Not bad, she said thoughtfully. – Not bad at all. Just a few improvements here and there, and we'll be ready.

– Ready, Sheila intoned.

– But it will have to wait. You see, we have a guest…

– A… guest?

Sheila scolded herself because she hadn't noticed the increased security in the apartment. She should have seen it immediately. The guest's guards weren't dressed any different from Wynette's discrete gorillas, but… the eyes, the movements clearly differed from them.

– A very important guest, Wynette eagerly assured. – *Discrete* is the key word here. I know how good you can be at it, if you want to. It isn't directly tied to the more… public part of our setup, even though it can give us definite advantages at a later time…

He stood by the window, looked through it, into the eternal night. They stopped a few steps away, and waited respectfully. He looked up and smiled to them with his dazzling eyes.

– Mr. Parker, say hello to Sheila Watts.

– Johnston Parker, he said charmingly, and gave her his hand. – Nice to meet you, Sheila, I've heard *so* much about you.

– Likewise…

She took his hand. It almost drowned in his big.

He had «heard about» her through archives and files. She had heard about him and had heard him through official media several times a day. Not so strange perhaps, since he was heir to one of the city's last dynasties. He was one of the true «untouchables», those nobody dared to fuck with. Their spider's web reached across the city like a suffocating blanket. No one escaped their vengeance, their wrath.

And through rumors and stories shared among police officers, she knew he was just as little a typical rich guy or rich man's son, as Joseph Colton was a typical bully.

His intense stare made her dizzy, and she sensed she was blushing, helplessly.

– I've got a problem, Sheila, he said.

– A problem I can help you with… Johnston?

– I would like to think so. He released her hands and started pacing around the room, incredibly enough, a bit anxious. – You were on my list of possible candidates even before I heard about Wynette's inspired plan. Clever, skilled and discreet. You're not afraid of speaking your mind, and that has given you some trouble through the years. But you also respect the chain of command and hierarchies. And now you show initiative, revealing ambitions. I, for one am convinced you're the ideal choice, and I don't need to convince anybody.

He paced some more. Hands remained on his back. Most people moved their hands when speaking. He didn't. He was very controlled.

She waited patiently.

– To tell you the truth, he continued, – I've tried all conventional methods at my disposal, and as you know, they're considerable. In forty-eight hours, they haven't turned up one single lead. In forty-eight hours, they're usually capable of finding whatever they might be looking for. The Holy Grail, the eye of the needle and so on, but in this case, they're coming up short. It's time to try unconventional methods.

He looked pointedly at Sheila. She waited, knew that even if everything didn't always come to those who waited, it would in this case.

– My brother… is missing, he said, clearly uncomfortable. – He vanished during a party three days ago and hasn't been seen since. I want him found dead or alive, no matter the condition he might be in. Do you understand, Sheila?

– I understand, she said, soft spoken, but clear.

– Nothing must come out, but except from this one limitation, you've got free hands. Whatever you want of personnel, permissions, privileges, you'll have them. Do you get what I'm saying?

She nodded, didn't trust her voice. The buzz deep in her auditory channels became a roar. Free hands. It meant something quite different here, compared to what it had meant other places, in most of the Earth's earlier ages. It did indeed mean what it said. He had given her a permission to do whatever she felt necessary, at her discretion, no matter the reason, a blank canvas, in which she could paint her acts, to go where she wanted, to injure, kill… With a wave of a wand, he had given her more power than Lloyd Emerson and the Prefect (that figurehead) and the clandestine services, everybody, including himself. And only he could lift it.

So incredible - and horrible - had the social-political situation become in the city of London, well into the twenty-first century.

Wynette looked at her. The uncertainty, the prevalent fear, had returned to her eyes. *Good!*

Sheila turned her attention to Parker, her entire attention.

– Tell me everything you know, she encouraged him.

– I've already done that. He smiled softly. – Perhaps you know more than me already… Constable Parker and his death *may* have something to do with it, even though I doubt it. He's just a distant relative, from an insignificant part of the family.

– *When* did you last see your brother?

He frowned, as if being caught in being imprecise was below his dignity. He truly believed what the media reported about «the new royalty».

She did, too, though. She had seen too much of the results of what their reign led to, to not believe.

– We held a party on the family estate, an extended party.

She knew what it meant. Contrary to a closed party, there would be invited a few, selected people from the level below the top of the pyramid.

– He had a few tramps in tow, but this isn't unusual. I didn't know them, but that isn't unusual either. He left us early, which is very common. We had our usual quarrels, both earlier in the day and during the evening.

Their quarrels were, to put it mildly, no secret. They had been the commoners' pleasure for years.

– I control the family fortune, he stated, matter of fact, before she came to ask about it. – I will inherit his modest part of it, if he should be gone. This isn't about money.

The audience ended, ended well. He left, but it was they who were sent away. They followed him to the entrance.

– Then we agree, Sheila? He took her hands again.

– I report to you only, to you personally, Sheila said. – I keep you informed. If something decisive occurs, I contact you instantly, no matter where any of us are, no matter the time.

– You should really consider a career as a «detective», he said cheerfully. – You've got a talent for this… But I knew that before I spoke to you. I know you're the right one for the task.

She didn't start shaking until after the door had closed behind him. In fear and expectation. She made sure she didn't expose herself to Wynette.

– He's interested in you, the black woman stated dreamingly.

– Not in my body, Sheila shrugged, very deliberate. – He wants my talent as creative bloodhound.

She led on back into the living room, and she was the one finding the glasses and the bottle of wine. She opened the screw easily, contrary to her earlier clumsiness in that regard. She waited a minute or two, allowing the wine to breathe, before filling the glasses. She handed one to Wynette. Wynette accepted it, hesitatingly, half fearful, half ecstatic.

– A toast, Sheila said. – To our cooperation. May it be long and productive.

Half an hour ago, it would have been Wynette who would have said that. And it would have been little doubt as to who was the dominating partner… as little as now.

Wynette toasted with lowered eyes. They drank. Sheila sensed the red fluid flow down her throat. Tasty, delicious. The scent enhanced the taste, the sense of taste. She had never been conscious of that fact before. What else had she missed? Wynette walked back and forth long after her friend had sat down on the comfortable couch.

– I would give anything to be able to do a piece on this. But the first thing a good reporter learns is restraint. There are quite simply events not suited for publication.

She smiled and joked, and behaved just as exited as before, but still, where it counted, far more restrained. The respect and the almost doglike admiration showed every time her eyes touched Sheila Watts. The scale had fallen permanently down on one side.

So fast things can turn around, Sheila thought. Again.

She had truly experienced quite a few twists and turns on this rollercoaster ride the last few days.

Back to the city. Back and forth, and not as far. The four grim faces on loan from Johnston Parker had waited for her outside the apartment, and followed her from then on. From this moment on, they would never lose sight of her. She had to admit she felt both unnerved and comfortable in their company. Her life hadn't exactly been the storybook image of safety. Not for as long as she could remember.

Everything had been turned around at the police station as well. The grapevine had already told of her new stature. Everybody wanted to greet her, but didn't dare. She had always been seen as dangerous, and now she had the Power to back it up. And they hesitated when it came to shake her hand, fearing the four sharks would bite it off (that thought, in particular, made her smile big). All four fangs were visible.

Her office hadn't changed. It still said «Inspector Watts» on the door. Meaningless. That, too. Her title meant even less now than it had done.

Emerson didn't even show his face. She sighed and removed her feet from the desk. Keeping them there had mostly been in his honor. He hated any disorder, hated even its slightest implication of it.

She moved among them, as one of «the Faceless», totally in the open. They didn't have a handle on them. She confused them, scared them further. They didn't know why she had achieved her newfound stature, what her mission was, if she had any, if it mattered. She was. More than that they didn't need to know.

It intoxicated her, and she couldn't hold back the triumphant smile when she stared down everyone she met.

She stood in front of the «reception» desk by the entrance and smiled pleasantly to the sergeant there.

– Where are Colton and the surviving members of his group? She wondered.

– They're incarcerated in the D-block, he yelped. There was no hesitation in him, he knew his duty, the very dutybound man he was. – They're heavily guarded. No one has attempted to break through that circle of protective detail.

– He will come, she said, half turned away from the man behind the counter, more to herself. – He will wait a while, for the strongest possible effect, and then strike.

The fact that the monster out there had more than implied that she, too, had made it to his list was one she had buried deep within herself.

She gave the sergeant a patronizing pat on his cheek, and left him, followed by her pack of wolves. The fear she encouraged, the one she had chosen to represent had already gained a mythic imprint in people's consciousness, in the present day neo-feudal society. The very thought made excitement boil within her.

The street outside. She started automatically to wear her street smarts, listened, looked, sensed to the utmost of her capabilities, stretched and softened stiff limbs and muscles, reprimanded herself because she hadn't worn them inside, but it had been too tempting, too intoxicating to, for once throw caution to the wind.

He, her employer, hadn't said anything about how or whether she should make a list of her various priorities, but had rather implied it was advantageous that she stuck her head out. So, she intended to do just that. What had been Wynette's idea now fit her plans in excellent ways.

She visited the estate the brothers shared. Nobody asked for her ID. Guards greeted her at the gate, and she was brought the long way to the castle in an old Rolls Royce. They didn't make cars like that anymore. Livery dressed servants greeted her in the hall. Nobody paid attention to her four shadows. They moved so much in tune with whatever were the surroundings that she felt she had to occasionally look for them to be sure they were still close (they always were). She asked herself if they had sacrificed all their humanity to become living - or dead - shadows.

She sensed their presence. She realized she would have sensed if they weren't there. They were her kin, her brothers and sisters in the night.

But she never took their presence, their protection for granted, like Johnston Parker and his kind probably did.

She was shown photos from the party. Another pile of electronic images, displayed on a large monitor. Deep, life-like images, giving the viewer the impression of being there. The latest technology, the second latest technology, before the final pretence of innovation had vanished from society like smoke.

The images flowed together, into a blur, as much as she allowed them to. Her sharp eyes didn't ever give her any rest. She always expected the unexpected, a teaching, a wisdom beaten into her from early childhood.

And the reward came, as it almost always did, in the form of the harsh burn between the eyes. What she looked for was something that didn't fit, or didn't really fail to arouse her awareness.

The images turned truly alive to her. She saw Charles «Carl» Parker posing, for her, no matter how he looked on the surface, a haunted man.

The way she saw it he deteriorated as much in these surroundings as his brother thrived. She saw them together. The faces didn't separate them, but body language did. To Watts, as detective and hunter, body language was far more important than appearances. Humanity had «forgotten» this language through thousands of years of civilization and domestication, but to one who was able to understand and even speak its thousands of nuances and expressions, it spoke volumes. Through those thousands of minor, subconscious movements, alone and in an infinite number of combinations. Now, more than ever, since most people no longer recognized its significance.

She watched herself in the mirror, her front, but also all possible sides simultaneously, the crouched body that most civilized humans didn't notice, but to her stood out like a sore thumb.

The party had, as usual, many distinguished guests, practically all who could crawl and walk in London's upper classes and what remained of European nobility. She recognized the majority, of course, they weren't exactly unknown quantities. Emerson had honored the host with his presence. The cute bitches - not two, but four - constantly competing for Carl's attention had figured in the gossip columns lately.

But the one who truly caught Sheila's attention remained in the background, in hiding, in the shadows. She was never seen close to Carl. There was no direct contact between them, none revealed on the photos. None of the images of her were sharp, were in focus. But Sheila recognized her. She recognized the walk, the moves, the shadow of a smile in the unmovable face.

Sheba.

CHAPTER TEN

There seemed to be cameras everywhere, wherever she turned. And that «suspicion» turned out to be absolutely right. She occasionally glimpsed Wynette and other details in the ruckus surrounding her, but most of the time everything just seemed to be in a total confusion of random movement and individuals. Wynette found sense in it, though, and even thrived.

The street behind the illusion, the reality behind the illusion was still there, but muted. Sheila's senses didn't work properly. She didn't even complain when one of the makeup girls rushed to her and started powdering her.

– The cameraman and light man agree that you need powder, the woman explained, like the most natural case in the world.

Was there an implied regret in her voice?

My imagination, my wishful thinking, Sheila decided.

She glanced at the monitor. It showed a long, empty street, but it was truly crawling with people… behind the camera. Sheila felt a prevalent desire to giggle. Humor mixed with hysteria, she gathered.

The camera turned. She stood with Wynette in something resembling a dark, sleazy alley. So much for realistic background reporting…

Wynette stood turned away from her, towards the camera, speaking into the microphone.

– … we're here with Sheila Watts, the leader of the investigation into a string of murders of police officers shaking our fair city recently.

She turned towards Sheila in a dramatic fashion.

– Inspector Watts, what led you here tonight?

– We received a tip, Sheila revealed, – about a nude man lying unmoving on the roof nearby.

– Is it a copper?

– That I can neither confirm nor deny at the moment. We don't even know if the tip is good. It might be a joke, or the guy may have stood up on his feet and gone home…

– But you're checking all tips, and the murderer is viewed as *extremely* dangerous, isn't that right?

– That's correct. That's why we're also responding swiftly and decisively to every tip, as if they're genuine, appreciating everything, all reports on strange occurrences fitting the profile, no matter how seemingly inconsequential.

– And this report… fits the profile?
– Absolutely. The murderer has undressed several of his victims.
– So he… prefers them nude, then?

Watts felt the well-known sting of anger and wondered what she would reply to the «question», what would happen in the next moment. Fortunately, she didn't have to, saved by the bell, as she was.

A woman ran from an old house. She waved her arms in distress, clearly in bad shape, out of breath after just a short run. Constables ensnared her well before she reached Watts.

– My husband, she gasped. – My husband, he…

With a sudden pale color in her face, she fainted on the spot. Eyes rolled in her head, and she turned limp in the constable's arms. A camera showed everything closeup.

Watts drew her weapon. All the officers, too. A gasp, a thrill shot through the audience. Watts stormed the house, followed by a pack of press and police.

A man froze straight there in the first stairs when having a load of guns directed at himself.

– … upstairs, he pushed from his frozen mouth. – He's on the r-roof.

She pushed him aside and chased further upstairs. Torn wallpaper was torn some more as the force fought itself upwards. Fortunately, this was an ordinary, old-fashioned two-story London building. It didn't take them many seconds to reach the roof. Watts kicked in the door, kicked it off the hinges, jumping out on the roof. A flat roof with the traditional fake chimneys, many houses tight together. Small sheds everywhere. Thank god for the pollution. If not, it would have been row upon row of drying clothes here.

The members of the attack force placed themselves in groups of four, back-to-back, moving slowly through the uneven and not very visible terrain.

– This is just the way he likes it, she warned them. – We can't see much. He has full overview. Shape up, boys and girls.

She could feel the hatred and bloodthirst burn in them. As in young hunters, right before they made their first kill.

And she could smell her four shadows. They were always close. Even in the most illuminated parts of town people didn't spot them, but they were always there. She saw them. And when she didn't, she sensed them. As with seeing one's own shadow one had to turn the head slightly, to see them, but she had a lot of experience doing that.

The nude guy lay flat on a lower roof… on a mattress? a bit away. He didn't seem to be harmed in any way, but she couldn't decide whether or not he was breathing. She recalled Colby and Hoover's torn bodies. They, too, had looked okay the second before they had fallen apart.

Suddenly, movement, a whispering wind from behind. Sheila lifted her hand calmly, calmingly. One could say a lot about the London police, but they were very astute when it came to receiving signs from superiors.

One of the shadows stood there, holding a man in an unbreakable grip. The guy didn't look harmed in any way, but he stayed sort of calm in the other man's grip. Sheila nodded. The shadow released the guy.

– So, the Metropolitan Police have finally decided to act, he said sourly. – It's about time, even though this is to exaggerate everything slightly. The fellow is nuts, but he is, after all just one man.

– I'm not exactly following you, sir. You better explain yourself mister…

– Glass, Harvey Glass. The case here, my friends is that one of my neighbors has been sunbathing for three whole days, now, threatening to gun down anybody getting close… but if you're not here because of that…

His eyes widened.

– You're here because of…

Sheila pulled down the two officers closest to her. A bullet whistled over their heads. The guy in question was no longer relaxing on the mattress. She caught a glimpse of him as he ran behind a chimney.

– I WANT TO SUNBATHE, he cried hysterically, – I WANT TO!

She turned towards the other tenant.

– What's his name?

– Harry, something, Glass replied, suddenly fairly indifferent. – I can't recall the last name. We don't necessarily frequent closely with all the neighbors, evidently a very sensible decision…

– HARRY, Sheila called, – may I call you Harry?

– I WANT TO SUNBATHE, he cried hysterically, – I WANT TO!

– You can't do that, Sheila cried back. – You're scaring people and causing a disturbance in your good neighborhood with such an erratic behavior. We must ask you to come down this minute.

– I WANT TO SUNBATHE, he cried hysterically, – I WANT TO!

This time he fired a shot. And not long after that another one. The bullets went off in two way-different directions. The sound of the second drowned in the murderous salvo from the police force. Bullets flew and ricocheted in every direction. There was a scream of pain and they heard, as incredible as it sounded, the dump sound of a body hitting the concrete.

Silence, abrupt and shocking reigned. Watts ordered people forward. It took four, perhaps six seconds until they convinced themselves there was no more danger. Harry lay stretched out on the concrete, bleeding from a wound in the side. Except for that he seemed, incredibly enough, quite okay.

Wynette Richards pushed the microphone at his face as they put him on a stretcher and carried him down and off.

– I want to sunbathe, he complained. – Why can't I sunbathe?

The camera was turned towards Sheila.

– What happened up there, Inspector Watts? Wynette asked lightly.

– The Metropolitan Police stopped a threat to public safety and morale. Sheila smiled all over her face, evidently about to break into overwhelming cheerfulness. – No officers or constables were injured.

– What about the perpetrator?

– Oh, he will probably survive the minor gunshot. The sunburn is more in doubt, though…

Wynette turned towards the camera, looking directly into the lens. The operator zoomed in on her face.

– In the dark shadow of a greater threat another danger to public health and life, as we know it is averted. This is Wynette Richards for Thames Television.

Fade to black.

+++++++++++

– This was great! Wynette chuckled. – It fit perfectly. We couldn't have done better if we had planned it. You're now positively established in the public consciousness, and we can move on to the heavier stuff.

– Hurray! Sheila toasted with her and drank the light, bubbling fluid.

– The next step must by necessity be something less spectacular, Wynette continued eagerly, – but much closer to true journalism. Me, you, a photographer, and your four invisible friends. Perhaps we should pray we don't see too much of them?

– That makes sense, Sheila nodded.

She stood by the window in the apartment and stared at the ocean of buildings and smog, lit by electrical fire-protuberances shooting from the ground and leaking pipes. They occasionally swept close enough to a building for people inside to feel the emanated heat.

The three of them met Rod as scheduled the next evening, in the twilight. After a night with sleep, without any recollection of having dreamt, Sheila used the day to go through old archives. Old images, photographs, not 3D, but they were clear enough. Documentation in databases about this and the previous century would have to be called phenomenal. Both in central, public records and public private collections there was more information than ever before recorded in human history. One single disk had a virtually infinite storage capacity. Even though the former dynamic part of the computer industry had also collapsed lately, the production itself hadn't stopped. The innovative part had vanished. Nothing new was invented, but parts were yet produced locally. The London government had imported an entire production factory a while ago.

Sheila didn't have to do a search on James Evan Shelby. Wynette had gathered and systemized it for her. James Evan Shelby, Linea Shelby, Evan Shelby. Linea, mother. Father unknown. Fingerprints, retina scans, DNA registering. Evan was/had been a British citizen. She looked at the old images from the rock concerts again. The «day to day» pictures from a life in the public eye. She heard the music, and it haunted her.

Rod stood hidden in a narrow alley in Kensington High Street. This neighborhood had also seen better days. Here, too, the housing projects reached into the former park area. Hyde Park had been reduced to a bed of flowers somewhere in the jungle of new, more or less completed housing projects. The buildings reached to such a degree into the clouds, the soup of «air» that they imagined they were on Mars… if Mars had had buildings. So very far away from London, the city Sheila had grown up in.

She still heard the music. Did she just imagine it… or did she truly hear it? She heard something, she always did, a lamentation rising from the glowing sewer below streets filled with glowing red and gray light. So much stronger now.

– Where are we going? she asked Rod after feet had turned sore and patience run thin, *and* Wynette's photographer had been told to temporarily put his recording on hold.

– There's a house here, Rod enlightened her, in the very minor suggestive way in which he was an expert.

– Oh, a HOUSE! You're such a genius…

– I've worked hard for this information, so I feel you should show a little appreciation.

– Okay, Rod, she said sourly. – I promise you I'll show my devoted appreciation.

– Your friend has a house here, he said willingly. – Not the friend giving you your latest assignment, but the friend, the brother he asked you to find. It's weird, though. As I understand it, the owner hasn't visited the apartment for days, and he used to live there.

Sheila nodded to herself. They would probably not find anything, especially since the Faceless had visited the place. But it was always useful to visit the home of a person to find out more about her or him, create an impression of that person.

One impression, cut off from all the others, all the others dancing in the shadows, on the edge of consciousness.

The door hadn't been broken, but outright *removed.* Strange. The Faceless usually executed a certain restraint, discretion. Not that this case wasn't special, but that could be said about any case they were given. If it, in truth was seen as a special case, even compared to other special cases even Sheila's unique imagination couldn't reveal what the reason for it was. Thoughts scrambled through her head. They were actually whizzing and dancing like hell, in the narrow pathways of her mind. But whatever was… buzzing didn't see fit to express itself.

All other entrances in the street had their door in place. This didn't have any.

Rod stepped inside. Sheila swiftly pulled him back out. First, they heard the sound of one person cocking a weapon, then a score of others.

– We're from the police, she told them, incredibly relaxed. – Put down your weapons and come out.

She pushed the hand with her ID into the doorway, exposing herself. Miraculously enough she didn't get it shot off. In the deafening silence she hardly heard the camera rolling. They didn't use speech to speak in there, but evidently hand signals. She heard steps, and people appeared, empty handed. People from the more secure and prestige-filled areas of the town, and they looked totally bonkers.

She could have called in an entire team of interrogators. That would have been the normal thing to do. Boiled the young, up and coming society leaders, reduced them to songbirds, sucking every bit of information out of them. That would have been the correct procedure, in a case like this, where all consideration had been thrown out the window and the fact that they were all members of influential families meant zip, nada. But she dropped it. Not because of the families, but because she had lost faith in the London police' well-proven interrogation methods.

She grinned like a skull (a trick she had learned at a young age), and the sons and daughters of the city's queens and kings pulled away from her.

The apartment didn't show obvious signs of having been searched, of burglary. Only people with an eye for such things would discover the minor signs.

As with the outer door the door to the apartment was also missing. The

Faceless had most certainly paid the place a visit, but they hadn't done this. No way! They didn't use exaggerated methods needlessly. They were shadows. As opposed to Colton's group their «reputation» depended on them not being seen.

The entire place appeared as a study in contradictions. No cups or plates on the table or in the washing machine. The bed had been used. The computer was on, and the monitor showed television programs. There was no displayed food.

– We replaced the doors the first times it happened, one of the tenants stuttered. – We set up new surveillance equipment. It was n-no use. Doors and equipment just kept disappearing. Yesterday we posted guards. They disappeared and later showed up at the hospital in a confused state. Most of us moved. Being fed up the remaining people have since then done guard duty personally. Fifteen at day, fifteen at night. If the guy had entered through the door, he would have been reduced to chopped liver. He didn't, honest, or we would have seen him… right? But we still heard the TV from the apartment, heard it turning itself on and off. Nobody went inside to check if there was anyone there, but…

Or something, Watts thought.

Rod pulled her aside, outside the range of the camera and its microphones. He was unusually meek, and didn't she spot a worried flash in his eyes?

– I took a look at the doorframes, he said hesitatingly. – Without me giving you an expert statement in such a matter I would say the door was… torn off the hinges.

She hadn't considered that until now, hadn't realized what it signified.

– Our Gorilla? She whispered.

He nodded.

The connection between what had seemed like two different cases, chains of incidents became even stronger. It trickled even stronger down her spine.

– He didn't kill the guards, she said.

– He doesn't kill the guards standing in his way, but is systematically killing a group of police officers. He could easily have sneaked past the guards and entered the apartment without them having any chance of discovering him, but he's attacking them, bringing them with him, and then letting them go again.

Rod nodded for the third time.

– Did the guards bleed? She asked aloud.

– W-what? One of the young tenants lifted his head in confusion.

– Did the guards bleed when they were found?
– I can confirm that, he said, even more worried. – From small bites on the neck. This, more than anything made us freak out. The guy is obviously not well, and we decided to blow his head off, as soon as he showed it… but he never did. We haven't seen a piece of him, head or other.
Watts looked at Rod again. This time he didn't nod.
The hospital was nearby, the same hospital. Sheila would have recognized it blindfolded. The old stink of disinfections and sweat, and rotting death in the nostrils made her almost freak out completely. The old, vibrant fear made her wretch. Remember.
They walked straight to the reception desk. Watts showed her ID. The guy behind the counter sat with a cigarette stump in his mouth while tapping the keyboard and the ash fell to the floor.
– They're dead, he said. – All three.
– All three? Watts frowned. – That can't be right. We were told they only had minor injuries. May I speak with the physician treating them, please?
– She's gone home, the living dead man behind the counter shrugged.
– The address, Sheila growled.
She got it.
So, they went ahead again. She would later look back at this night as a long row of seemingly unrelated events, flashes in eternity, like a dream, inevitably real.
The female chief physician lived by the St. Paul's Cathedral. It didn't have the glow of light of the old days, but the neighborhood hadn't fallen out of favor like so many others and was still seen as one of the more fashionable in town. They walked through the long subway, to the street on the other side of the block. This particular subway didn't go under the streets as most did, but under houses and buildings. Bigger, broader, longer. Quite a few electrical lights, but badly lit. The light seemed to fade, in a way. Sounds were enhanced, but they, too, faded in deep corners and shadows. Watts realized she was imagining all this. It didn't make her feel any better.
None had torn off the door to this entrance. It was there, closed and locked. Watts rang the bell, while making sure her face and badge were revealed to the video camera on the wall.
No reply. She pushed the button again. Still nothing.
She made a small, close to imperceptible sign with the hand and stepped aside. The four shadows rushed forward. Suddenly, they just appeared in front of the door. Like one being they kicked it, kicked it in. It flew off the

hinges and was trashed against the stairs inside. Another door gone, one more of many.

- I wonder what's wrong with quite simply opening closed or unlocking locked doors these days, Rod grinned.

The shadows vanished into the building. Watts turned to Wynette, Rod and the photographer.

– You wait here, she commanded. – We'll fetch you.

They didn't dare voice a protest. Sheila saw something reflected in their eyes. She wondered what they might have seen in her eyes making them look this naked.

Then she, too, disappeared into the building.

The four cleaned the way for her, she knew that. But didn't allow, wouldn't allow it to influence, dull her senses.

The stairs seemed perfectly normal. Everything seemed completely normal. The walls, too. The door to the apartment stood open, now, but hadn't before the four had passed here. One of them carefully announced himself. Not to her eyes, but through a familiar sound he, they had used before. If she was wrong and it wasn't him, but a stranger, a threat, she would be in lethal danger, because she hesitated blowing off that person's head.

The physician lay on the floor in the living room, lifeless. Sheila touched the skin on her neck, feeling for a pulse. Dead. Cold. She had been dead for quite some time. Sheila shuddered inevitably when she saw the characteristic bite marks on the neck. But here there was no mutilation, no sinister messages, only quiet, sudden death.

– Okay, show yourselves, she spoke up, irritated, as she rose to her full length. – I'm not used to having a conversation through my subconscious.

One of them placed himself in one of the paler shadows, clearly visible to her.

– Are you sure? He asked.

– I want to hear your ideas, she said, very decisive, while doing her best to hide how the flat, lack-of-emotion voice distracted her.

– Are you sure? A female this time, stepping forward the moment she spoke, as the other faded back into the deep shadows.

Sheila pushed the fingertips at her temples. This was stupid. The room was well lit, wasn't it? More than well enough for her to see them easily, wherever in the room they might be.

– See? It was simple. You were right when you said you needed a bit of practice, though.

The female laughed, laughed a chuckling, non-existing laughter.

– This isn't unfamiliar to us, another said. She could see them all, now.
– And the reason for you not saying anything is, if I can be so bold?
This time there was no oral reply. She replied to herself.
– Because it didn't concern you before…
Perhaps she heard the soundless sound behind her. Perhaps she saw something in the four's eyes. She turned swiftly, twisted her body around so fast that it hurt.
The woman, the physician, she who had been dead there, on the floor, moved forward in a sort of freaky, rocking way, so fast she seemed indistinct. In spite of this Sheila saw her face clearly, saw the large, cold, inhuman, dead eyes. One of the four, the man who had spoken last, moved in, in front of the physician, attacked her. She brushed him aside, as if he was nothing but air. She hadn't been able to grab him, but merely the fact that she had managed to achieve contact, body to body, suggested a lot. Sheila couldn't take her eyes off the face, and to say that the sight of it made a chill trickle down her spine seemed hopelessly inadequate.
Five weapons were fired simultaneously. The figure before them was hit and thrown at the wall under the massive deluge, dissolving against it. All five kept firing into the smoking, disintegrating body. Firing pins clicked against five empty chambers. Finally, the cadaver stopped moving.
The five remained frozen for a considerable amount of time. The man had a scratch in his clothes. A bit deeper and the scratch would no longer have been a scratch. The five didn't look at each other, didn't open their mouths for anything but breathing. They conversed without words.
The panic and the shock went deep in them all, and it was very, very visible. Suddenly she saw them as human beings and not mannequins.
– This world is seen as a brick, right? she breathed. – Something tangible. More so, than ever before during history. Everything not easily quantifiable and measurable doesn't exist. But we all know that this is a thoroughly wrong view…
She… had them, now. Sudden and unexpected they belonged to her, and not their employer.
The world had turned upside down again. The world had been thrown a monkey wrench - again.
And when they returned to the street, walked silently and quickly down the stairs, the walls no longer resembled walls.
She realized that Rod and Wynette had obeyed her orders and stayed outside the building. How unlike them. Something… happened. She drew her gun under the coat, instinctively, close to completely unaware. She saw them stand under the streetlight outside. She stepped outside. There

was no one else nearby. She saw one of the four move on the edge of her vision. The camera recorded everything. Wynette spoke uninterrupted.

– … Inspector Watts is appearing from the building where the shots were fired. She has no visible wounds.

The four weren't filmed, weren't mentioned. Occasionally Sheila wondered if they registered on film at all. They spread in the terrain surrounding her, once again becoming a part of the scenery.

But not to her. Never again. She knew them. They knew her.

She sought out Rod with her eyes. He realized immediately that something was off with her. But not what. Not anymore. She signaled. The camera was turned off. The microphone was turned off. She sought close to him, a bit away from the others.

– Marks after bites, she said. – Otherwise, she was… undamaged.

– Let me take a look…

She stopped him with a look.

– She was dead, cold and dead. We had determined that… when she rose and attacked us. We shot her to pieces. The entire her seemed to… to collapse into nothing.

– That's unbelievable, he said thunderstruck.

– You should have seen her face, she said.

They were given no time to elaborate, share their thoughts more than that. Her trigger-finger had itched for a long time, and she hadn't put away the gun again under the coat. Perhaps that's why she managed to pull it out and fire one single shot before they were over her. The bullet tore into one of the attackers. One of her rigid, deadly hands destroyed a face, one foot broke a kneecap, before she was beaten senseless in their grip.

Everything turned foggy. She felt a strange indifference, even when she sensed the rope tightening around her wrists, arms and ankles. Her four protectors lay dead in the street, skin split from neck to pelvis. And the attackers were… other Faceless. Thoughts raged through her mind. *Power struggle*. They had lost face. She had taken over a task they saw as theirs, that they to this point had had a single right to, without their approval. Or this group wasn't a part of Parker's sphere of influence. Or something had happened, something making them flip completely.

They hadn't killed them all yet. She wondered why not, as they were taken away, like meat to the butcher shop. They hadn't tied her legs tight. She could walk, but hardly more than that. They hadn't bothered tying the others. She didn't know whether or not she should be flattered. They had killed their former colleagues without hesitation, without mercy. She felt hatred, wrath, murder lust, easily recognizing it was in vain. They had tied her hard and effective. She had no chance of freeing herself. And what if she, against all odds should accomplish that? She didn't care about counting them. They were all around her.

– You want me to give in, assholes, she mumbled, – to beg for mercy, but I never will.

They heard her, she knew that. They showed it, without word, without expression. They kept up their task.

The assembly reached a well-lit, open area. A fence, a steel fence, between the street and the sidewalk. There were no other humans close, but they were close enough to see what was going on and the rumors would fly, and everybody would hear. The two women were thrown over the thick metal bar. Sheila felt how they loosened her bonds, to refit them, to tie her hands to the bar. Wynette's, too, were tied in the same way. The clothes they might have around their hips were torn off. Sheila only thought, the only thought with a kind of sense dawned at the sight of Wynette's brown butt, pointing up… how silly it all was. When she felt a hand roam between her thighs, within her. With a total lack of emotion. It was merely a means to an end. And this cold, more than anything made her howl in fear. And they would come and come, until she was reduced to an empty shell. Then they would finally slit her throat, give her peace…

She sensed a draft, a pull in the air.

She turned her head, looking behind her.

And she saw Sheba, in a whirl of movement and blood. A face, rigid, inhuman. A paralyzing cold beyond mere fear. The Faceless seemed just as indifferent, while reacting as they would against any opponent, any threat. Five of them had already succumbed, dead or dying on the ground. The remaining did their very best, but didn't stand a snowball's chance in hell. Sheba held one, like a scarecrow in the wind, her mouth buried in his throat, while breaking another's neck like a twig. Those were the last two. The scarecrow, drained of blood died with a long, tortured whimper. She took another round, lifted up those still alive, sank her teeth into them, drained them of blood, letting go of their empty husks. She had wounds, but they seemed completely superficial.

The four of them embraced her, free of their bonds, gasping in relief and gratitude… when they sensed the pull of the creature, the black hole by their side, and they turned to her, and they were nothing more.

Everything turned indistinct for Sheila after that. She remembered standing before Sheba with her friends, making several attempts at expressing their gratitude verbally, but that the mouth, the larynx had ceased working, everything had ceased working. They fell on their knees before the woman towering over them.

– I was tempted to let them keep it up for a while, to enhance your coming Wrath, but I wanted you fairly unspoiled. It's better this way.

Sheila sensed a hand grab her jaw, sensed more than experienced that it was pulled up. She met a pair of eyes and she drowned in them.

Sheba grabbed a single rope and tied nooses around the four's necks. They stood on their feet, now. Sheba pulled in the rope, their chain, and they followed her like eager dogs. Sheila was aware of the rope tearing into the skin, but in… a numb way. She was able to see, to think, but everything felt very, very far away, and Sheba felt close, close, close. It dawned on Sheila that they were walking, were moving, but they could just as well float. For all she knew Sheba might pull them through the air like a cluster of balloons. They had no direction on their own, but had to follow wherever she chose to take them. Her presence alone made them tiny. They felt a sickening gratitude towards her.

Like a dog towards a master.

Shiny, shiny walls met them somewhere, new materials, shiny floor. In spite of this, the palace-like building they were taken to gave them a powerful impression of *age*. Egypt, it reminded of a reconstruction of ancient Egypt.

– That's right, Sheba told her. – But this isn't reconstruction. This is the way it was. Not completely, of course. Even my memory has its limits. But it is the real thing.

4000 years. Sheila felt a strong urge to talk. Mouth moved, but there was no sound.

– Hush, child. Sheba put a finger on her lips. – Everything will be clear to you. Soon.

Sheila fought to express her worry, but the only expression was a wide smile covering her face, spittle flowing from her mouth, her tongue hanging out.

They were led into the bedroom. A room not comparable to the hall outside, but with a size fully comparable with ordinary halls. Oil lamps oozed and burned, illuminated corners, casting long shadows.

– Yes, Sheba breathed like a storm. – This is a home equal to my home in the ancient south, but it lacks life, it lacks servants, the splendor of the Pharaoh's court. Humans today are rude and uncultivated, lacking respect for their betters. So, what I'm going to do is elevate you in life, give you the gift of Eternity. You will become the first in my court. And you will scour this land for me, help me recreate my homeland in full, by this new

Nile.

Sheila almost saw it, saw the Queen of New Egypt on her throne, and saw the whirl of people in her court, her warriors scouring the night.

Sheba placed them in each their bed. In the room there were exactly four beds. Huge, more like a room in itself than a modern bed, huts, with walls covered in pale silk, curtains blowing in the wind. On the wall, over the middle pillow was attached to the concrete a chain with a collar. She put the collar around their neck, a golden collar, with ancient Egyptian inscriptions.

– This is your room, she declared. – This is your playground as you grow to adulthood. You're all such beautiful children. It's been a while now, since I last gave birth, since I shared my gift. It's about time. We will take our time, as I teach you the mysteries of the world, as you listen, as you learn, grow eager in your Hunger for life and knowledge.

She chose the photographer first. Sheila realized she didn't even know his name. Wynette hadn't cared about presenting him. Sheila hadn't cared about being presented to him.

The paralysis let go of them. They could think once more. And with thought returned the paralyzing fear. They would have known what Sheba was, even if they hadn't seen it with their own eyes.

– Stay away from me. He attempted to pull back and pulled in the chain.

In vain, Sheila thought, Sheila sang.

Sheba slapped him, snarling, overwhelmingly superior.

– Don't worry, she whispered. – We've got time. You will eventually learn respect, learn how to live, how to live in my service. Poor little boy. So obstinate, so helpless.

Voice seemed to soften again, until it once more moved inside them, inside him. He froze, turning rigid and still. She petted his cheek. He stared blindly at her. Sheila shook. She couldn't stop shaking, still able to think, thinking too much. Either Sheba couldn't hold them in her grip indefinitely, or she chose not to.

She wants to show us, show us her Power. Let us See.

Show that resistance was futile.

– I'm thirsty, the man, the putty doll she formed in her hands whispered.

– Certainly not, she chuckled. – You still don't have the faintest idea what true thirst, what Hunger is, but soon, very soon it will be the only thing on your mind. It will dominate your thoughts, your every waking moment.

And Sheila was unable to look away. She Saw. Saw the figure bend down, shred the shirt covering the fairly muscular body, saw the fangs in the rigid face grow long and sharp. She heard the silent snarl when the creature sank those fangs into the skin in the transition between the neck and shoulder, when two lines of blood flowed down the man's tight back, heard the sucking sound when Sheba drank.

She didn't drink long or much, but took her time doing it. A pair of predator eyes twinkled and burned, even more so than before. She released him, released his body. He fell moaning on the bed, writhing in pain and ecstasy. Sheba patted him passionately on the back.

– Don't be afraid, she assured him, soothed him. – There's nothing to be afraid of and soon you won't have to be afraid of anything. These are merely the initial preparations. We'll have joy together, all of us, as soon as you're ready. The waiting, the eternal waiting will be over and only Joy will remain.

None of the others managed to move. Not a muscle, not a finger or a brow. Wynette whimpered a bit when Sheba approached, that was all.

– Now, who will be the next to receive my gift, my dark gift?

Sheila started breathing faster. She couldn't help it, couldn't keep herself from wagging her tail when Sheba closed in on her.

– Yes, I know you're impatient, little friend. You can sense your blood move and saliva flow in your mouth, can you not?

– Yes, SSSSSSheba, please, Sheba.

The human female pulled her chain. If she did so to get closer to Sheba or in a useless attempt to escape, she couldn't say. Laughing in triumph and joy Sheba put an index finger on the skin by the collar, moving it until the nail halted by the huge pulsing vein.

Sheila fought, fought against the force ravaging her, but she shrank to something very small under the predatory onslaught, faded until there was nothing left.

– Yes, I know you're desperately struggling to resist, my precious. It's futile, you know that, but you keep resisting. You're strong. Your little friend there is a cute pet, but she's weak. But, you, dear child are a Hunter. You will serve me well.

Sheila knew she had to get free, get away from the demon closing in on her. There had to be a way, a chance, if she just could have some more time.

Time. Time is up. Time is

She met the intense eyes for just a moment, before lowering hers, sighing heavily, turning her head sideways, exposing herself, baring her neck. Clothes were torn apart. And then, then she felt the sharp pain in her neck, the pain that in an instant turned to a sweet, sweet itch. She cried out, short and sharp, turning rigid, then softening. The shaking stopped, and she fell into a deep, black hole inside. The desperate resistance turned to eager submission. She fell on the bed with a smile on her lips.

And she slumbered and writhed in her soft nest, dreamed she smelled blood and was chasing her prey.

When consciousness returned, she didn't know how long she had been out. Fatigue overwhelmed her the moment she attempted to lift her head off the sheet or move a limb. Haze drifted before her eyes. Fatigue weighed her down, an exhaustion heavier than she had ever experienced. Sheba was still there, but something told Sheila that time had passed, that Sheba had stayed away for a while. The room had no windows. Nobody, at least not Sheila, could determine if it turned light outside, but Sheila felt time was ticking, ticking, ticking.

She *sensed* Sheba inside, her movements through veins, through thoughts. The image of the saliva dripping from her long, pointed teeth remained crystal clear to her inner eyes. Body crouched, pulled itself into a fetal position. She felt so *dirty,* so thoroughly raped that she wanted to close herself off from the world, but Sheba didn't even allow that. Sheba's presence was totally and utterly irresistible and all encompassing.

Eyes remained open and she couldn't close them. Dully, unmoving she stared at Sheba while she took Wynette and Rod, too, drank from them, and left them, too alone on the bed.

Sheba pulled away, the satisfied glow visible in her eyes. She dried blood from her jaw, licking it from her hand.

– I have marked you now. More blood flooded her jaw and neck. She didn't dry it off. – Made you a part of myself, an extension of my own being. There's no escape for you anywhere, now. I can feel you wherever you go. Soon I'll make you mine completely, utterly, bind you to me for all time.

She stepped away from Rod, turning her head for a moment, looking affectionately at him.

– You, my boy are an unexpected bonus. She scratched his neck. He whimpered in his despair. – You'll be my angel of death, my confidante.

Then she pulled back and seemed to be dissolving, vanishing into the shadows and the darkness.

Later. Thoughts stumbled in Sheila's mind. She wondered if Sheba was truly gone, or if she watched them from the shadows, having her sport. Or if she had to leave because of the daylight. It might weaken her, visibly, even if it didn't touch her directly, even if she, herself couldn't see it. She wouldn't want them to see her… weakness.

That stray, stumble of thought should have brought triumph, joy, but it didn't. It brought nothing. Nothing more, nothing less.

Later.

Time shrank. The Sun moved across the sky. The pale, dirty Sun. So lethal to the woman waiting in the shadows. Flashes before Sheila's inner eye. Sunlight on naked skin. Smoke, even fire. Flash. An initiation, bodies writhing and twisting in ecstasy. Blood devoured, blood mixed. Screams echoing between ancient walls, ceilings, skies. Of pain, of ecstasy, of Life, of Death.

There was no time in here. No watches, no candles shrinking. Just the slow, painful beating of hearts.

Everything had happened so fast. A scientist would probably have called it a series of paradigm shifts… or something. An irritated pull in the chain. It tightened instantly and the throat tightened, too. She could no longer decide if she wanted time to move fast or slow. Her heart beat towards the moment Sheba, the Goddess would return. Fingers touched the chain, caressing it, tightening around the metal, pulling it, pulling hard. Fingers hurt. Everything hurt. The human being turned constantly in bed. Nightmarish images kept haunting her. The condition sort of reminded her of a hangover. One knew one had to get up, but also knew that then the pain would come in full. A hangover was basically in the head, though, in the mind. Here the poison made every cell in the body hurt. No… it didn't hurt. It was *pain,* on an indescribable, fundamental level.

Eyes could see. Sheila Watts stared at the ceiling. Blind eyes. But Sheila could see. See the pattern, the infinite number of patterns in a way she never had before. The bed sheet was torn to shreds. She had done it, without really registering it had happened, without pushing herself. She pulled the chain again.

And again and again. She fought herself up on her knees. It was easy. She felt, knew she was strong, much stronger than before. But the chain, thick and smooth slipped in her grip. She pulled, throwing herself backwards. Stood on her knees, gasping for air. Stared at the brick mortar loosening from the wall. The fine layer of dust floating in the air around her. So much of it. She coughed.

Smiled.

Predatory.

Did she just imagine she glimpsed her fangs flashing in the smooth wall's surface?

The image changed then, turned to the snarl of Sheba's smile.

Sheila held hard around the chain. Her knuckles turned white. She threw herself backwards, landing, throwing herself backwards again. And again. There was a loud crack. Her neck breaking. She stretched on the floor. The chain was unbroken. But it wasn't connected to the wall anymore. She breathed and breathed. Blinked. She wasn't imagining anything. This wasn't any of Sheba's cruel games. True. Real.

The others rested unmoving in their beds.

She attempted to stand up. Failed. She strived to crawl. That worked, slowly, painfully. She stopped. Looked at the door. Looked back.

– Pull the chains, she whispered. – Free yourselves, please.

She kept crawling on her knees. The door seemed ever further off, the further she crawled. A shaky hand reached for the handle, missed, and fell back to the floor. Breathing, taking a short break, breathing, feeding herself with the torrid air. She pushed her body, her back at the door, using that as a lever to get up, and she reached out with a shaky hand. Fingers clutched the handle. She let the arm fall and the weight of her body pushed open the door.

The great hall seemed infinite. The road ahead eternal. No daylight here either. No windows, not even narrow chinks. With its bloody chinks, the large door, the gate was the only thing she could see. Sheba could stand right behind her now, and she wouldn't see it. Sense it, but not see.

All kinds of thoughts tumbled through her head. She wouldn't think about it, wouldn't think them. They came anyway, unbidden, unwanted. She fought herself up on her knees, the sore knees again, pushed down the golden handle. The door opened. She rolled outside. Daylight bathed her, so very bright. She cried out, pressing her hands at the flowing eyes. She remained there, for a long time. She finally got on her feet. Took one step forward, then another. Stumbled down the stairs, completely normal stairs. Everything seemed normal from the outside. She watched carefully the naked skin on her arm. There was no smoke, no fire. She looked up. It was raining. The raindrops fell into her sore eyes. She started *moving*. Ever faster walk, until she was running. Holding feverishly around the remains of her clothes still clinging to her body, carrying the chain in her hands. Postponed the thought of what was behind her. All her thoughts concentrated on what was ahead. She didn't really think at all. Instinct fueled her, like a compass whirling at the center of a magnetic storm. Something fueled her. Not anything like what was seen as consciousness, but something else, something more. If a physician had examined her, he would have claimed she was unconscious, where she walked and avoided colliding with people, cars and poles on her predestined path.

She didn't care about the people. They were just ghosts, stumbling on their predestined path.

Rain poured. Water was hot before it hit the ground. The droplets jumped snarling back in the air. Rivers like waterfalls flowed into the sewer. Steam drifted meter high above the road and sidewalk. The ground had yet to cool down after the white-hot day. This flood after a dry and hot sunny afternoon shouldn't surprise anybody living here. This happened often in London during the summer. There was a period of torrential rain and ten minutes later the street was just as dry as it had been before the deluge.

The woman stumbling out of the Camden Town Underground Station had long since turned soaking wet. She didn't seem to notice, but just kept moving blindly forward. Every time she put a foot down showed how unsteady she was. The few who studied her closely also realized quickly that something had to be wrong with her vision. She often collided with poles and corners. Something was wrong with her. The eyes had a strange frozen quality, and her entire behavior more than struck a weird chord. They hurried on. It wasn't worth caring about caring.

She stumbled across the street. It seemed like the sheerest miracle she wasn't hit by a passing car. The sound of the angry horns drowned in the torrential rain. People couldn't fathom how she could possibly fail to notice or react, but the face remained impassive, and she continued on her predestined course - forward. It dawned on those who followed her with more than a passing interest that she was half naked, and that she was probably headed somewhere. Something seemingly being confirmed almost instantly, since she was headed straight for the Green Rose. Perhaps it was a coincidence that her course led her to the door and not the wall, but it was no use anyway. The door was locked. She knocked on it, hit it with her fist one, two, three times, before collapsing, slipping down the smooth surface, until she crouched there, on the sidewalk. Rain kept pouring, and she kept crawling. Felt her way forward, stared ahead with blind eyes. While crawling, crawling and crawling, until there was no more room to crawl.

CHAPTER ELEVEN

She woke to the sound of music. She couldn't tell if it was the music that had awakened her, or if the dark, haunting sounds had merely eased her transition from darkness to shadow.

The song sounded completely different compared to that on the viddisc. Much more intense, far more… haunting. It cut through her. The lyrics didn't seem like mere lyrics anymore, but like words pushed into her. The lyrics, the music, the greater than the sum of the parts impression, recreated reality in her surroundings. Sheila Watts shuddered.

She laid on her back in a bed, dry. Dry hair, a mildly sweating, but dry body. The weakness penetrated her limbs. Every move cost her. She sought out her throat, touching it carefully, anxiously. The collar, the chain had been removed. She sought further, until she found the two marks, punctuations in the transition between neck and shoulder. Swollen skin itching and thudding against her fingertips. She tensed and released an involuntarily moan of sudden pain.

Real. No dream.

Shudder turned to shakes. She wanted to crouch into a fetal position and stay there, stay like that forever, but couldn't move. Slowly the shakes stopped, and she laid still, staring at the ceiling.

The music had stopped. She couldn't tell whether or not it had happened before or after her outcry.

There were no lamps, no source of light within the room. What little light there was crawled through the open door. Recognition hit her like a pain in the stomach. She laid in *his* bed. The very thought made her tingle.

Evan strolled into the room. Relaxed walk, relaxed facial expression. Relaxed.

– How did I end up here? Voice was hoarse, more like a whisper than normal talk.

– By knocking on the door, he grinned. – Knocking quite decisively, I might add.

– And I woke up to your wonderful music and singing, she said pointedly. – You're better than ever, far better than when you first recorded your songs.

– Thanks…

He halted a few steps from the door, a somewhat «safe» distance from her. She didn't need any confirmation, but she got it anyway, by looking at him. Guilt, relief, everything flowed through him, expressed in the expressive face.

– I should have known, she said weakly. – In spite of all the possible pitfalls of denial, all the attempts throughout history to turn it into a myth. You're a bit too pale, even compared to the rest of us subterranean half-lives.

He didn't comment on her words. Not in words. But he kept staring, kept surveying her.

– I've made some food, he told her.

– Food…? She realized he stood there holding a tray. – But can I…

He put the tray in her lap. She could finally move, and she sat up in the bed, looking down at her body. He had dressed her in a white gown. She looked carefully at the sandwiches. Her stomach made two abrupt turns just by her looking, a fundamental unnatural reaction.

– Eat, he bade her.

And she did. Stretched out a hand at the closest lovely sandwich and put it in her mouth, chewing carefully, apprehensively. The next one was far more inviting. She realized how hungry, how empty she was. She wolfed down everything on the tray without thinking thrice about it.

– I love sandwiches, really juicy sandwiches, and I've hardly tasted anything better than yours in my entire life. You're a Champ, an unsung champion.

– I've had long practice.

It dawned on her what his funny remark entailed. The apprehensive look reappeared in her eyes. Fear lurked in its depth, terrifying and paralyzing.

– Why did you come here? he asked quietly.

– I've already told you why, she replied. – I trust you.

He didn't comment on that either, but sat down on a stool he had brought, in this room so lacking in furniture. He attempted to make her feel better.

– What is it like? she asked whimpering.

– A lot of the legends are pure bullshit, he said. – Only a few things are the way we've heard. The sunlight, the bloodlust, immortality, immortal youth… I haven't aged visibly since it happened.

She turned over on her side, didn't want to look at him, desperately didn't want him to read her. Every second felt like an eternity. Was that how it was like? Did time slow to a crawl?

Suddenly vomit erupted from her mouth, without warning, without her noticing it moving up through her throat. He was there instantly with a bucket, the bucket she hadn't noticed he had brought.

She remained in her spot a long time, before speaking, with a raspy, sore voice.

– I want you to be the one doing it, I want you to b-bite me.

– NO! He rose abruptly, very abruptly. – Absolutely not.

She heard the naked anguish in his voice, the violent unrest.

What had been Sheila Watts pulled into fetal position, frozen.

– She did it, she finally said. – She bit me.

– How many times? Only one?

She nodded.

– I believe so, I don't know really. We, our thoughts, our bodies were like putty in her hands.

He met her with silence, unbearable silence.

– Will I… Change?

He waited a bit before he managed to speak.

– Probably not. Your immune system will probably kill off the attack in a day or two.

Probably.

She looked at him with sore, red eyes.

– I saw it, she said aggressively. – I fucking experienced it. I saw her sink her teeth into you, saw you wag your tail for what she had to offer.

Flashes of blood, flashes of teeth, in a room filled with smoke and sweat.

– It was voluntarily on my part. I wanted what she could give me, wanted it very much.

He disappeared for a while. She hardly noticed his disappearance, his return. Not until he pushed another tray of sandwiches at her.

– I don't want it, can't even stand the sight of it. Please…

– *Eat!*

And so she did.

And a few minutes later she threw up again.

Was it her imagination or did some nourishment remain in her stomach?

She slumbered then. Even the horrible desperation faded, the fear that she wouldn't awaken, wouldn't awaken as herself. Her surroundings, close and far continued to haunt her.

She sat upright in the bed, had done so a while, eating her third supply of wonderful sandwiches.

– It's just like a hangover, she said with a cracked laughter.

Except for the fact that she continued to feel stronger, brighter than she usually did. She saw better, heard better, felt pain stronger.

She put the tray on the floor, pushed the blanket off and rose from the bed. Everything was swaying, but she stood straight. Sweat poured and she started stinking virtually instantly. But she stood somewhat straight.

– Do you have a jacket or something? The gown is great, but hardly the correct dress code where I'm headed.

– You shouldn't leave, he said tightly. – She will hunt you.

– And this is a sanctuary? She said mockingly.

He held his tongue.

– Don't say more. I've been through sufficiently many personal paradigm-shifts to last a lifetime the last few nights. I know what I'm doing.

She noticed that he glanced outside, glanced at the infinitely weak ray of light spreading from the open door and into the room. She noted that he didn't stand as straight as he usually did.

– Don't worry, I'll close the door on my way out.

She left and closed the door. He remained there. She imagined she saw him drag himself to the bed and lay down on it, uncovered. Out there, in the huge room, covering the entire floor, she felt bathed in light. While looking through the remains of her clothes, she found, incredibly enough her wallet and badge. He had procured new, practical clothes. They fit her perfectly. He had considerable practice in this, too, she gathered, in measuring measures.

The mirror, the woman in the mirror stared back at her, at the stranger. She walked down the stairs to the bar, as she clothed herself in the last few pieces of clothes, the comfortable jacket. The door closed behind her.

Claudette waited downstairs, staring angrily at her. Sheila walked by her, without saying a word, without anything even resembling a look.

– You will return, will be crawling on your knees, the woman screamed to her back.

Outside. The traffic moved slowly down the street, roaring and cutting. It cut into her, shaking her innards. The morning rush traffic did its usual imitation of a snail. She crossed the street in a few steps, running before she knew it. She ran across the street to the underground station, covering her eyes. Vomited violently and painfully before stumbling inside the station, down the escalator, down and into the lovely darkness. Earlier she had irritated herself over the considerable lack of working bulbs. Now she was overwhelmed by a completely irrational emotion of gratitude towards the people responsible for the maintenance.

The pale sun, daylight, just on its way to its strongest level (so limited these days) almost struck her to the ground, as she exited the St. Paul tube station. She grabbed a pair of sunglasses from a kiosk after walking several blocks with a hand covering her eyes. The vendors threatening attitude vanished like smoke the moment she pushed her badge into his face.

Very conscious about what it did to her she chose the longer street route to the physician's apartment, avoided the tunnel below street level, holding out the pain, the unpleasantness.

Two police blockades stopped her on her way. One outside the physician's house and another further down the street. The same explain away explanations, the same procedures to hide the truth. The present policemen probably didn't know who lay gutted before them. Though they knew that they had laid here for a while, and that the murders and the murdered wore The Faceless' mark, and that they had been gutted to warn, to terrify.

Further down the street the many bodies had been removed, but the presence of influential persons grew steadily to something huge and infectious. Something had happened, happened again, something new and terrifying and Unknown.

Watts didn't identify herself, but kept to the background for a while, before pulling away completely, backing off into the nothingness.

She searched for a while, for the palace. She attempted to use her memory, her instinct, in vain. Everything looked the same here, just a lot of old Roman style buildings indistinguishable from each other. And she had been half beside herself, half Gone the day before, while stumbling through these streets.

The food smell from a restaurant distracted her, Her stomach rumbled. She went there and ordered a steak in a very aggressive manner. Perhaps they recognized her from TV, in spite of her not looking like the painted, over-the-top doll, because she didn't show her badge this time, and no one demanded money from her. She still felt the nausea, forced herself to eat with delight, enjoy the meal. Afterwards she sat still, looking out of the window, in the hope of something clicking. A direction, an address, anything. It didn't. When she had puked out her guts in the toilet once more, she more than sensed that something remained. The light outside didn't feel so strong anymore, in spite of this being the middle of the day.

But there was no way she could be certain, now, was it?

And she hated the insecurity, the uncertainty.

Feeling pronouncedly… disconnected, she wandered around virtually aimlessly the rest of the day. Not tired, not sore, only what drove her on, making her able to put one foot in front of the other. During the twilight, when crossing the Plaza, passing the rotating sign, she felt the shaking stop, the shivering within and without dwindling.

She noticed it even before she entered the premises, how activity had markedly increased. A frenetic activity resembling, smelling of panic, and even one more pronounced than two nights ago. Two nights ago, she had been on her way away from this place. No matter what she did, whatever happened she kept returning.

– What has happened? she asked the desk sergeant.

– Nothing much, he said, in a low tone of voice exposing his underlying nervousness. – Anthony Johnson keeps acting up, that's all I *know*. He and Ferrie are creating a lot of hell for the guys looking after them.

– What about the other three?

– They're somewhat… mellow, I guess. Colton is voicing his demand to speak with a superior every half an hour, that's all.

Flashes returned with a vengeance, of The Beast chasing and mutilating and killing in the night. A creature without eyes, blood, thought and humanity.

– I need access to storage.

Her resolve only increased as she saw his astonishment and met his gaze with her stare, her insane glee.

– To *The Storage?*

She nodded impatiently.

– You know I can't grant you access there without authorization, he tried.

Nice try, she gave him her best grin. She just looked at him. He swallowed hard and rose from his chair, tore a set of keys from its knob on the wall and staggered behind her over the floor. Another civil servant instantly took his place.

Everybody looked at them, at her. She pretended they didn't exist. To her they didn't.

The basement surrounded a human being, clutching it, filling it with rotten, stiff humidity. The sergeant walked in front now, turning his head every second or so, staring nervously at her. She returned his stare with a merciful nod.

«The Storage» was never used, had never been used as far as the sergeant and Watts knew, men they had been given a certain insight in its content, what situations that had to arise for it to actually be used. Watts figured such a Force Majeure was about to arise in London right now, and she wanted to be the first sticking her hand into the cookie's jar.

He found his three keys. She found her one.

– In case you're wondering, she offered offhand, – I can tell you that both the retina scanning, and the spit analysis will probably work after your death. At least if I act quickly.

That took care of his remaining resistance. She pushed her key into the hole and turned it. He, grasping for the mercy she had offered him sucked at his finger before sticking it into the machine, and he allowed himself to be scanned in the eye. There was a hum. He turned the three keys one by one, and the door, the heavy door slid open. They went inside. The door closed behind them. This wasn't meant to be an exit and they would be forced to take another way out.

– Funny, isn't it? She grinned. – We on the higher levels don't have to identify ourselves, but there's always an advantage to have a poor sergeant to blame, now, isn't it…

Suddenly he stopped and dropped to his knees. His entire body was shaking, almost shaking apart. She had overdone it a bit, scared him out of his wits. He was, after all just a simple civil servant.

– You pathetic worm, she said in contempt.

The need to kill and mutilate almost turned overwhelming then.

She pressed on. The dog rose and hurried after her.

His fear, his dog-like obedience was useful, of course. Both his assistance when she carefully and thoughtfully picked the necessary and crucial equipment, and because there wasn't any fight left in him.

Weapons, equipment, deadly and destructive were piled up everywhere, on all the countless shelves, row by row. Flashes of metal, black and oiled blinded her. There were gadgets and special «useful» equipment, tools she had thought she would never consider using, but now knew could mean the difference between life and death.

She started arming herself, buckling up, building the «armor».

Everything consisted of light and easily maneuverable parts. Armor for attack, not merely protection, something that wouldn't have helped her. A manifold of concealed and visible weapons. She studied the result in the mirror. Clothed herself in the long coat, made giggling a pirouette, and terrified the poor sergeant further. She drew a gun, pointing it at his forehead, returning it to its confines inside the coat, all in one, fluid move, pulled forth the grenade launcher, pulled forth the shotgun. A shotgun not a shotgun. She nodded to herself.

The outer world awaited her, once more turning to life. She awaited it. The door to the inner closed. They found themselves in a corridor twenty, thirty steps from the entrance on the ground floor.

– An excellent execution of service, she excused the man, did it with a merciful nod.

He hurried off, back to his safe, shitty life. She stood there breathing, taking in the surroundings, exploring the new world welcoming her.

He was nothing. He would forever remain nothing. And she… she was Everything.

The ruckus began. A penetrating sound cutting through life and limbs.

– What the hell, a man close by exclaimed. – That's the intruder alert.

– Is nothing sacred anymore? She grinned at him, exposing her fangs.

Then the lights went out. Pandemonium instantly erupted all over the place. People ran back and forth in their confusion and fear. Watts fell after being pushed by several parties there in the darkness. She crawled swiftly to the nearest wall, temporarily removing herself from the maelstrom, and put on the infrared glasses. The world remained Chaos, remained vortex of panic and mindless ruckus, but she was finally able to see in the dark. She ran towards the internment section on the first floor with all the speed she was able to muster (and she was able to muster a lot).

The lights returned. Not even the entity invading this place had any chance of destroying the main power supply, and the first, second and third back up generators simultaneously. Just the fact that he (it) had been able to do what he (it) had done told her a lot.

She stopped abruptly by the base of the stairs. Three officers had been thrown at the floor in a random pattern. They and their blood, and their guts. They had deep cuts in the belly and torso. Perhaps they would survive. Everyone moved. Watts kept moving. She tore off her glasses, wasted time in securing them inside the coat, before further speeding up her run. A sound and she turned fast and murderously, drawing her shotgun. Standing face to face with a young patrolman, with his own weapon directed at her. She recognized him. But she kept him covered. This in spite of her taking it for granted that this bundle of nerves didn't present any danger to her. Except that he could blow her head off at any time, in sheer expression of shaky nerves.

– Watts, Sheila, she recited. – Service number xYz15336835, Inspector, Special Branch.

She hardly heard his stuttering recitation, signaled to him to follow her, advancing the long ascent up the stairs, passing the first floor, reaching the second. Other officers and patrolmen ran after her up the stairs. She signaled to them, too, taking charge, as she was turning a corner, running down the second floor corridor.

A considerable contingent outside a very specific internment room cocked their guns when she and her spontaneous platoon appeared. These were experienced and professional people, but nervousness surrounded them like a valve.

Something had happened. She stopped, raising her arms above her head.

– Watts, Sheila…

– There's no need for that, Inspector. I recognize you.

He wasn't scared exactly, but visibly uncomfortable. She lowered her arms.

Two rooms beyond the honor guard, thick walls. One entrance only. No windows. She saw Johnson, Ferrie, Shaw, Williams and Colton. A reunion of old acquaintances, of times long gone.

Colton sat on a chair, unshaven, roughed up hair, off any rack.

Johnson crouched on the couch.

– He w-was here, he stuttered. – I h-heard him.

– We all heard him, Ferrie confirmed, completely relaxed.

Watts turned to the operational super.

– Play the tape. The man nodded to a subordinate.

The voice not exactly belonging to Dominic Colby wasn't any less horrible as a recording.

«Six little Indians walked on a road...
One Indian got hit by a stone in the head,
and then there were only five Indians left».

– We heard him, but never saw him, the operational super reported. – We weren't fooled into leaving our positions.

Watts looked down the long, narrow corridor on both sides. Not even a creature such as the one they were faced with could attack this local stronghold, in this bright light, without jeopardizing personal security. He was vulnerable.

Or he had been satisfied playing with his designated victims this time, prolonging the torture. Because that was what it was, had been from the first, flickering glimpse of the monster. To say he carried out psychological warfare against them was a way too mild expression. It worked. To the bone. Beyond any physical reality.

They all knew, now, if they hadn't before, that they would never could never feel safe anywhere.

Sheila knew, too. The walls seemed to bulge and stretch before her eyes.

– I have to PEE, Johnson cried. – I have one hell of a BAD stomach, do you hear me? Is there no decent food around her? Is there no SERVICE at this hotel, this excellent establishment?

He was cracking up, in more ways than one.

– To be confined here, is the worst part of it, Ferrie raged. – Waiting, waiting for him coming closer and closer. He will come, he will come.

More servicemen arrived. Every one of them was checked almost to the point of a security clearance, even more than they had already been. Slowly, but surely things returned to normal, or what passed as normal.

Kathy Williams rose from her chair, where she had been sitting for so very long, without moving. She stared at Watts and directed her entire attention at her.

– We've heard what happened, she insisted. – We've heard that certain… parties failed to stop it. Let us out of here, we can be useful.

Everybody froze. In spite of her not mentioning The Faceless, The Unmentionable directly, the rumor of them having been massacred, slaughtered en masse and that they were all dead, dead, dead had not yet completely surfaced.

– To mop the floor, perhaps, Watts cried mockingly.

The entire watch erupted in laughter and the mood turned a little lighter.

Williams spoke for Colton. Everybody knew that, so he shouldn't lose face. Watts knew how his mind worked: That he could still save the remains of this «fiasco».

But there was a naked, almost completely exposed vulnerability in Williams' face, the look she sent Watts, making Watts feel this hot, pleasant glow inside.

The expanded watch split in two. Johnson was accompanied by a number of guards that could undeniably be seen in a comical light. Could.

The toilet. A huge, naked room. A monster whopper of a room. Thick walls, no windows. The toilet itself had been placed at the center of the room. Not an ant could get near it without being spotted. And stamped on. Door was closed, leaving the poor sucker to relieve his need in «peace». Watts demonstratively closed the door. But in her mind of minds, she saw how the creature appeared from cracks and the smallest of openings, with a demonic grin, proceeding to cut poor Johnson in pieces.

Chief of operations opened the door. He opened it fairly often, peaking inside.

– Yes, I'm still here, Johnson cried in a clear nasal voice.

Ninety seconds later the séance reoccurred.

– YES, I'M STILL HERE, Johnson cried in a clear, nasal voice.

– Isn't this great fun? A guard turned to Watts, as if seeking permission to laugh.

– Extremely so, Watts confirmed.

He smiled in unlimited gratitude.

It dawned on Sheila that she was the last. The last Faceless. A pleasant heat shot through her.

– I'm taking a shower, she informed the super. – Don't hesitate to disrupt my peace if something happens.

– As you wish, Madam, he declared, «at ease,» like a soldier.

He had seen too many movies.

The shower room resembled the toilet to the point of copycatting (and it was). The shower itself was placed on a pedestal at its mathematical center.

All dirt, all shit flowed from her aching body. The water ran into a series of small pipes, impossible to crawl through (she added in her mind). Everything here spotlighted English thoroughness, at its most thorough. Sheila laughed to herself.

But every time she was forced to close her eyes because of too much water, too much soap the dream visions appeared, of a sleek, deadly shadow closing, closing, closing, closing in on her.

On a huge tombstone it said:

THIRTEEN OF THIRTEEN

– *I knew that my little Sheila would think of the number thirteen...*

She touched her lips and instantly felt the soreness. The red fluid was slowly cleaned from her fingertips, disappearing down the pipes. She had bit herself.

Some of the blood ended up in her mouth, salty and sweet. She sucked on her lips, sucked, until she tasted the iron in her throat. Wet eyes widened. She made a fist, in a determined, controlled manner, one single time, a short while, before leaving the chamber and stepping over the floor to the mirror. She couldn't remember having turned off the water.

Sheila Watts stared into the mirror, at the indistinct form in there.

In frantic hand moves she attempted to remove, to dry the humidity covering the smooth surface. With every stroke a thin line disappeared, until everything returned to its previous, milky surface, as if she had made no effort at all. Face looked like a mask, changing to resemble a puzzle, where everything pulled together and fell apart in a constant, ever changing flowing stream.

She dressed in yet another set of clothes, dry and pleasant… and new. Refitted the equipment. Tied the hair in a simple, single braid. Rejoined the watch outside.

Their shitty nerves still surrounded them like a blanket. One was quite simply *not used to* the alarm sounding in this house. It happened frequently otherwise all over the town, of course, but not here. It had subsided physically some time ago. Watts couldn't recall the moment it had been turned off, but it didn't sound now. It had subsided physically, but continued to ring within people's minds. The alarm and the ghostlike voice. She had studied them when the recording had been replayed. One tiny sound from nowhere then, and they would have lost it completely.

He waited out there. They waited out there. Beyond the protective walls. Seconds passed, minutes passed without anything happening.

– It seems like…

The person speaking up never got to complete the sentence. The lights went out once more. The alarm started up again.

Sheila put on the infrared glasses in one single move. In the next heartbeat she simultaneously lit two flares, and threw them in opposite directions down the corridor. It lit up like a christmas tree and not even the smallest shadow could hide anywhere, could sneak up on them now. She looked at the ceiling, the floor, the walls. Nothing. She turned in one direction. Before the next thudding heartbeat, she had turned 180 degrees. The guards followed her lead at first. They looked at her for leadership, for any direction to watch, to go. But something… happened then. She noticed something, in their eyes, from their viewpoint. She saw through their eyes, saw herself… disappearing, fading into the background, into the shadows. And she felt both proud and scared. It wasn't enough, wasn't sufficient.

The lights returned. It blinked once, before seemingly flooding the entire complex. The loud alarm stopped roaring and silence reigned everywhere. The calming voice sounded through the com-link:

– *The grid has collapsed in major parts of the city. The last breakdown didn't originate here in the building.*

There were visible signs of relief.

– Never thought I would be happy about another one of those fucking power failures, a female constable exclaimed.

Sheila looked at the wet dogs inside the room, the «volunteer» prisoners. She blinked.

She, like others turned to see Anthony Johnson run down the corridor. There was no one chasing him, even though it surely looked that way. He held a gun to his head. The gun, the arm shook violently. A finger curled around the trigger.

Watts instantly signaled to half of the watch to remain. The other half she made to follow her.

They ran without raising their guns. Johnson, a wreck of a man stopped by the corner, just a few steps from the stairs.

– DON'T MOVE, he cried in a desperate, wailing howl. – I'll pull the trigger.

– Don't be silly, Anthony, Watts told him irritably. – He can't reach you here, unless you let him. He tried, but failed.

– He's coming. HE'S COMING!

He turned away once more and started running, turning the corner. Watts suddenly turned very anxious. She attempted to shoot the hysterical man in a leg, but missed. *Satan!* She reached the corner just in time to witness how he threw himself over the banister, as he was descending all the way down the open path, the open airways to the ground floor. When she finally reached the stairs and was able to see in a straight line down, admire the view, he crouched crushed and dead and still on the smooth, polished floor down there. She observed people reaching him, examining him, shaking their head, a confirmation she didn't need. The Hunter had taken home another prey.

He didn't even have to touch it physically. He had touched it, terrified it to death, crushed all the juice from it, until nothing but a shell remained.

One second, two did she allow herself to lean over the banister, a moment or two too long, before turning, with all senses on guard, all muscles tense. Nobody there. If he was a policeman or tied to the police in any capacity, if he had been before starting his rampage… She hurried back. Everything looked calm, was calm, relatively speaking. Through her inner eye she had seen a body nailed to a wall, cut open, mutilated. She stared hard at all the guards, didn't care about etiquette or whether or not they took offence. Nothing. They were visibly shaken. She saw nothing there of he she was hunting. She knew he could hide as much as he wanted behind a nice exterior. He couldn't hide from her that way, not anymore.

The four remaining, Warren Ferrie, Tiberius Shaw, Kathy Williams and Joseph Colton sat there somewhat relaxed, resigned to their fate on the same spot she had previously seen them.

The flares were still burning. In a strange way it seemed to make the place darker. Sparks and embers and white glowing fire cast long shadows. She looked down the corridor, towards the opposite side of where she had come from. There were stairs there, too, to the more central, administrative parts of the building. Even better guarded, even more hurdles for an intruder. Emerson, among others held court there. She grinned ironically. Something started within her then. She experienced the quiver as alien at first, before she sensed it growing to something familiar and terrible. Her feet, seemingly acting of their own accord, steered her down the corridor. She went alone. A sign from her held the others in place. First, she went all the way, the milelong stretch to the stairs, a flamethrower in one hand, the shotgun in the other. She couldn't recall actually having pulled it from her humid coat. Nobody here. Nothing. No presence. He had a way of… zeroing himself, making himself neutral in any given surroundings, she knew that. But not to her, not while she carried what she carried in her bloodstream. She returned to the… the scene of the flare. She looked at the wall, looked at the message above the light.

EIGHT OF THIRTEEN

– It isn't BLOOD, you asshole, she shouted. – You're cheating. You didn't dare come back here to collect true *paint*.

And the shout echoed through the building, even in its most civilized and lit places, and the human creeps trembled.

She returned to the nervous guard, taking quick, decisive steps.

– I don't want to be disturbed, she enlightened them. – If anybody attempts to do so you will use all means at your disposal to keep it from happening. If you do let anybody in, anybody, I assure you you'll regret it, regret it deeply.

She walked in to the four and closed the door behind her. They heard her turning all locks, activate all bolts.

Sheila Watts stood there, glaring at the four, and they shrank from her stare.

– I want to know everything you know, every minor detail. If I find you have withheld anything, anything at all from me, I'll kill you.

There was no hesitation, merely servile obedience.

– We roughed up a man, Colton said in a hollow voice.

– What a startling revelation…

– We approached him in the backyard of The Green Rose and beat him to a pulp. He showed up at the Camden Branch morgue stone cold. We didn't fucking kill him, but gave him a beating.

– We're professionals, Williams insisted. – We know the difference between a «softening» and an execution, damn it.

Sheila could have confirmed that to them. According to the examiner the guy had been dead before the beating began. She had no intention of sharing that information with them, though.

– Someone is evidently convinced we did it, Colton kept on it. – It was shortly thereafter everything started, whatever it was.

– Who was he? Watts inquired.

– We have certainly spent enough of our time afterwards wondering about that, he glared at her.

– WHO? She slapped him brutally in the face. The sound made Williams jump.

– WE DON'T KNOW! He shouted desperately. – Certainly an Untouchable. We never managed to trace his ID.

She pulled back a bit, as the cold smile turned hot and rusty.

– So, you finally fucked with the wrong person, she stated, sort of to herself, laughing softly.

They would have preferred her coming at them with stinging sarcasm.

– I can get you out of here, she said distantly, mercilessly. – What do you say?

– Yes! Williams exclaimed. The others nodded eagerly. – Yes!

– I will get you out of here. Sheila spoke with the remote half smile. – I am Chief. I give the orders, you obey. My slightest whim, get it? You're of less worth than ants I can crush under my heel, if I'm not pleased with your performance, if I'm not *pleased,* do you understand?

They nodded, dully, bowing their heads, desperate.

– Do you understand? She slapped Williams.

– Y-yes.

– Good!

Another tour through the inner world, through the storage. They had never been through here before and their eyes shone brightly and dully. She had them eating of her hand. They belonged to her, now, being merely extensions of her being and not individuals. They loaded themselves with weapons and equipment without thinking, without knowing. They followed her blindly, into the night.

Outside everything had turned cold, turned blue. She had never quite seen, experienced the night like this before. The feeling burned and intoxicated her.

The very streets seemed to change, to pale, to fade around her… into sets of pieces and illusions. And that was exactly right, the exactly right perception. They were so very far from the real life of the Human Beings.

A ghost led the four, led them by their noses. They followed it so accurately, so blindly that they were slowly, but surely turning into ghosts themselves. They followed their leader, the best hunter of the hunt. She danced, and they danced in her footsteps, down streets and invisible paths.

How far had they strayed from the relative safety of the camp? She imagined that if she turned her head, she would still see the familiar territory behind her, still see the characteristic signpost turning. She stopped. Something told her that they didn't have to stray any further. She looked at her watch. Temptation rose to unbearable heights. She couldn't tell how long time had passed since the fall of this night, this darkness. Not long. Longer than seconds. Shorter than years. She didn't know the time, not for the life of her. She didn't care, but concentrated on her senses that were all screaming at her… as she imagined she was able to glimpse the faint light of the sunset in the southwest. Just a few short days ago she would have rejected even the notion of such an overactive imagination. She knew better, now. Time slowed to a crawl, flowed as it willed. The sea went its own way occasionally. Other times one had to set the course oneself.

She stopped. Again? Listening with her head tilted, her face frozen in intense concentration. And she heard the quick steps, the long intermissions from one to another.

– He's using the *roofs,* she stated. – More easily than most people use the streets.

And she saw him, in a whirl of movement, of power, before he vanished once more… If he had even, ever been there.

– But… Ferrie opened his mouth briefly, before closing it abruptly.

– Yes, Watts confirmed. – The gap between certain rooftops is indeed vast.

She glared insanely at him, at them.

– Did you hear that? Williams jumped. – Did you all *hear* that?

Sheila heard it, heard the sounds from the streets and alleys around them. She heard steps, feet move softly over the tarmac and sidewalk.

Then she saw them, saw them a second or two before the others couldn't avoid seeing them. The three of them didn't hide, really. There was a lot of room, a lot of tarmac between them and Sheila's group. But it wouldn't last, it wouldn't last. Sheila remembered the physician (the dead physician) in her apartment, the speed in which she had moved, and she remembered Sheba, demolishing The Faceless before most of them could move. Watts looked at the approaching trio, two of them whom she knew so well. What bothered her more than anything was the smile. It looked the same on all three. She would remember the smile forever.

– You left, sweet one, Wynette sang to her. – We have come to fetch you, to take you home.

The song was so beautiful, so mesmerizing that Sheila felt a lump in her throat. She saw tears flow down Tiberius Shaw's cheeks.

– I was right, Sheila, doll, Rod said. – I was right all along. It's all so wonderful. You will enjoy it. Enjoy it so very much. I know you will.

His eyes were deep, black pools of oil, flowing and boiling, cold and silent. She could see it even from this far away, hear his raspy voice as if he was standing right there, at her side. And he was. She felt her own breathing, heard how her heart started beating faster.

– FIRE, she shouted at her loyal subjects. – Blow them away.

Already finely attuned to her moods, her voice they obeyed instantly. She shot Rod first, deliberately. The potent shotgun load hit him in the chest and pushed him back at the wall. His recovery was virtually instantaneous. He moved to the side and forward like the wind. She fired the rocket launcher, aiming ahead of him, of them as they advanced in a frightening speed. Taking their cue from her, so did Colton, Williams, Shaw and Ferrie. Wynette was caught between explosions. The ground shook, as the deadly fire lit up the streets. Rod was thrown to the side. His entire left arm was missing. He kept advancing, his entire face transformed into a snarl. It happened so incredibly fast, but to Watts it seemed to go in slow motion. There was a pain in her arm. She realized she had cut herself on a weapon. She kept firing. Williams shot Rod in the chest. He fell and rose again. All four fired grenades at the ground in front of him. He dissolved into nothing, and this nothing did not rise again. The cameraman and Wynette, what was left of them writhed on the tarmac. The man dissolved slowly, until there was no more than smoke and mirrors left of him. Wynette had one leg and much of her upper left side missing, but she kept striving, kept attempting to rise and the snarling beast there before them hardly had a resemblance to the pleasant looking television reporter they were all, in various ways familiar with. They could observe how skin and flesh and limbs and tissue were regrowing on the spot. Watts shot her once, twice, thrice emptying her shotgun at her. The others did so, too. Finally, everything boiled down to a smoking black spot just a few steps away from them.

– This isn't real, Ferrie mumbled. – It's a trick, you fuckers, just a trick. You think you can SCARE me with this shit, do you? It isn't real, not real, not real

And he turned and ran, howling, into the night.

– Come back, you idiot, Colton cried after him, to no avail.

Sheila felt her heartbeat, felt the air wheeze in and out of her lungs. She forced herself to stay on guard, amazed about how calm, detached she really was. The cold, hard spot inside grew, and she welcomed it, welcomed the emerging savage beast, ready to take on anything. Shaw looked at her, and in his eyes, she saw the heat of unrestrained adulation. Colton's eyes were bright with fear and respect. In Williams she read a distinct doglike admiration. It would all do. Everything would do.

No one approached them. No one cried out. No one appeared. The street fires kept rising and showed no sign of abating. They walked through streets of fire, and no one dared approach them. There were sirens, but none growing any closer.

There was a kind of relaxation, but no calm, not compared to the drive keeping her going. The city was in turmoil - again. Everything had been shaken loose and continued to deteriorate, to fall apart. The glue holding everything together had lost its potency some time ago and no one knew what to do. Chaos ruled the streets. She sensed it in every step she took, every time her feet touched the ground.

It flowed through her veins.

Finally, the sirens grew louder. The police cars and men «hurried» to the scene, as if their lives depended on it.

And it did.

The four shadows pulled further back, leaving the stage to the humans, the rabbits. Sheila stretched out her arms, as she danced through the streets, as if she owned them.

And she did.

– I'm sooo in the mood, she sang aloud.

The others looked at her, as if she was mad.

And I am.

She knew her behavior was totally uncharacteristically of a faceless. But they were dead, and she was alive. She danced faster until she stopped, her eyes frozen at her charges.

– We've vanquished enemies, she told them. – There's reason to celebrate.

They laughed a bit then, as if she had told them something they didn't know. The rock-hard lump of fear in their throat loosened a bit, but didn't dissolve, didn't fade completely. It never would. She led them away, further from what they had known, down streets and blocks, down below the bottom of the soul they hadn't admitted they had. They didn't deserve it, but she did it anyway. They were useful to her. That was sufficient, for now.

She fumbled with the key in her pocket, pulled it up and free. A key. Not a keycard. Something strange these days. Before them was a door, a perfectly ordinary door, in an ordinary street. A bit dusty, perhaps even a bit dustier than most streets these days, but not excessively so.

The metal slid between metal. She turned the key, and she sensed something click, something open, in metal, in flesh. The quarters were adequate, perhaps even more so than those Colton and bunch had enjoyed in their heyday, but it didn't really seem important anymore. A room, like everything wasn't really a room, or a street or a police station, but a state of mind. The walls bulged and changed, but she didn't feel threatened.

Not anymore.

Sheila Watts sat down on a chair. It… squeaked, as if it was about to give under her weight. She laughed scornfully at it.

There were many beds here, in these rooms, many empty beds, screaming to be filled.

– What happened? Kathy asked weakly. – To them?

– Sheba did, Watts replied. – She killed them all, rolled over them like they were nothing to her. And they were not. If we're going to survive, we must make ourselves better than they ever were.

– Sheba? Colton asked sharply.

– Yes, she's one of the creatures of the night roaming the party scene of our proud city, though most of the others, the pretenders don't truly know her.

– I know of her, Colton said.

– Is she… Kathy struggled to find words. – Is it she?

– No. A headshake. – It's a male. I'm pretty sure about that. And I'm even more certain that it's not Sheba. It isn't her style leaving trophies of her work, not like that. She's just Here. She will always be here, and we have to deal with that, too.

Something moved inside and she felt the pain. She rose abruptly. The others didn't follow her as she left the premises, and went outside, as if they knew she didn't want them to.

The outside was crisp, sharp air. The dust and the heavy poison ever lingering still made her want to cough all the time. She placed herself in the middle of the street, waiting. When she turned Sheba stood there, not fully ten steps away.

– My salutations, the woman, the ghoul said. – You are at least as resourceful, as dangerous, as cruel as I knew you would be.

Sheila already had the gun brought forth, but she didn't raise it.

– Your ingenious method won't work on me, you know, Sheba told her.

Sheila nodded, slowly. Sheba smiled. The ancient, serene mask was transformed into a very human expression. It was an absolutely terrifying sight.

– My poor children, Sheba said, shaking her head. – They're so vulnerable, particularly in the first, critical nights after the transformation. They feel like they can take on the world. And they can't really. Not then.

She started walking, even though that wasn't anywhere near the correct word to describe what she did. Pacing was a bit more accurate, but nowhere close. No word could describe it. It was so fast, so agile that Sheila couldn't keep up with it, couldn't keep it in her sight, so she didn't try.

– But they aren't important. They never were.

Sheba didn't come closer, but Sheila felt it like she did, like she touched her cheek, like her fangs penetrated her neck. Her neck hurt.

– It's the Blood. The Blood hurts. It will fade. Pain always does.

The imposing figure stopped, and it looked at her.

– You're the important one, my dear, sweet savage Hunter.

The smile embraced Sheila, sucking her in.

– I can complete what I started, right now, start the completion of your education.

– W-why g-give me a choice? Sheila finally managed to speak, and she hated the sound of her own voice.

– Isn't that obvious, my dear? You escaped. You freed yourself from my clutches, my reign. You've earned your freedom, your right to roam, free of my rule.

– You're talking about rules… rules of… engagement?

Sheba laughed delighted.

– My, my, aren't you clever… You're *such* a bright child.

Sheila Watts felt the appreciation as a physical heat in her flesh.

– So, what do you say? You do hunger for my dark touch, I know that. You're all so very transparent to me. Will you roam with me, through centuries, through millennia, over land and beyond seas?

– Was that the choice you gave *him?*

– Yes. It came out very matter of fact. – And he was quite eager, I assure you.

– N-no… feeling nausea, and all sweaty and horrible, Sheila repeated it firmer: – No!

– As you wish. And the female creature didn't walk, but faded into the night, as her voice was heard from far away, from close by. – We will meet again, my bright child.

Sheila started walking, returned to the compound. She half expected to find three mangled bodies there, but all three of them were whole and hearty, if such a description could fit them at all. They walked and talked and even breathed. She dried her forehead with a sleeve, then with the other sleeve.

– You're completely drenched, Kathy Williams told her.

– Sheba paid me a visit, Sheila said straight out. – She just wanted to chat, though.

– Chat? Colton looked befuddled at her.

Sheila didn't say more. She just looked calmly at them.

They made the necessary mental leaps. They weren't stupid. The looks they sent her weren't unsympathetic. They knew now, knew it very well, how it felt to be scared.

There was food here, lots of it. Some servants obviously put it here, filled the fridge. The faceless didn't forage, didn't scout the local groceries. It was very much like some tribe, Sheila ventured, giving praise to the gods. They placed the offering on the altar, and left. They didn't see it being removed, but when they returned the following morning, it was Gone. And they praised the gods for not taking them instead.

Watts sat down and ate, they all did. She still had the strange taste in her mouth, still tasted all food like it was a piece of heaven. The Blood in her veins still made her feel better, more astute. But it was fading, fading.

Silenced reigned and it felt good. They sat there, eating, lost in their own thoughts.

She couldn't identify the sound at first. There was a lot of repetition, like the humming of angry bees.

– My cell phone, she said dumbfounded. – I thought I had relieved myself of that damn thing.

A hand reached down in a pocket for it, pulling it out. The four all had a distant look in their eyes. No one looked at the others. She pushed the reply button. Everything turned quiet.

CHAPTER TWELVE

The Westminster Cathedral was huge. One could hardly see the ceiling. There were several rooms, though no actual walls separated them. It was an enormous hall, resembling a field, a field set in stone.

There were small lights burning everywhere. Several of the policemen were Catholics and they had lit most of the candles, the candles for the dead. Sheila caught them crossing themselves several times. She wasn't really there. Neither was Colton, Williams or Shaw. The policemen saw them, but didn't truly interact with them, even though they did reply to questions, to interrogation. A cold draft visited the field, the field of stone, and almost blew out the candles.

Warren Ferrie hung on the cross. His neck was torn apart in front, the shirt on his chest soaked in blood. Apart from that he seemed remarkably undamaged compared to the other victims.

– He came here looking for solace, looking for protection. The priest started his litany once more. He had repeated it more than a few times since Sheila's arrival here. – He said these walls could protect him, but they couldn't really. When the spirit of vengeance came charging there was nothing these walls could do.

Watts walked to the altar. It was smeared in blood.

– The perpetrator, before nailing the victim to the cross evidently smeared the altar with the body.

The new, very fresh-meat chief examiner spoke in a whisper, but it was all useless, as all sounds were enhanced in here. When silence reigned, as it did now, a whisper in one end could be heard in the other.

On the floor, a floor evidently slightly tilted, close to the altar there was writing. The letters were thick and elaborate:

NINE OF THIRTEEN

– Hello, Sheila, Sheila mumbled.

There weren't any more bystanders, well-known figures or people on their way up or journalists around. The murders had become too weird, too gruesome. There wasn't any publicity value in it anymore. At best it showcased incompetent cops. At worst a government completely incapable of dealing with the situation, and implicit: Of dealing with anything.

Even the present cops were torn between fear of getting themselves killed and fear of disgrace. Status meant that much.

A pervasive mood filled the cathedral completely. Nobody wanted to look at each other, but occasionally, suddenly there could be a sound, and everybody froze, baring weapons, turning rapidly and staring with wide-open eyes at the shadows on the floor, in the corners. Candles just didn't do it. And there were a few here, who had been at the police station during the «electricity failure», too. They knew that even burning electrical lights were insufficient, wouldn't actually do the trick, knew that Shadow ruled the world.

Ferrie, or whatever remained of him was finally taken down. His face wasn't exactly frozen in fear, but in a kind of panicked resignation that scared the brains out of the bravest soul. He had died a broken man, given in like a prey before the predator.

Life had left him way before it had actually done so. And that was the truly scary part. When they all looked at him, they saw a mirror. They saw themselves.

Watts registered a certain commotion by the main entrance. Not really a commotion, in terms of being noticeable to most, but a disturbance, a ripple in reality. She saw, long before the others, Evan Shelby approaching, walking silently towards them through the center of the great hall. Surprisingly enough no one attempted to fire at him, a very wise choice. They would have been dead in an instant. She took one look at him, at his eyes and realized that he had… had just fed. He confirmed it by nodding imperceptibly. To others, not to her.

– I didn't know you were a Catholic, he said, flashing the not so impressive version of his fangs.

– I was, she said lightly, she swallowed hard. – I even said the evening prayer until I was five.

She imagined she could remember the fully extended version, as glimpses in her nightmares, like pointed spears penetrating her gut.

– I didn't know you guys could even enter a church, she joked lightly, swallowing hard.

– Ferrie thought that, too. Shelby nodded. – He made quite a mistake there, don't you think?

Did the others actually hear the words? Did they even know Evan was present?

Evan… An overwhelming heat assaulted her. His very presence made her breathe rapidly and her knees turn to rubber.

At that moment he didn't hold himself back at all, baring all his insides.

– Are you finishing up here?

– Yes, she said. – I'll be with you in a moment.

– I'll be waiting outside.

The ghost, the spirit vanished down the aisles. And then it was seen no more. Long before it could possibly reach the entrance, the very visible entrance ahead.

Watts looked at Ferrie, Ferrie's remains again, before the stiff body was taken away. She didn't really listen to the new examiner. There was no need to know the details anymore. He didn't know what he was talking about anyway, as he merely recited the facts, saw it all in technical terms. It was just a job to him. He had no real understanding of Death, of Life.

She walked alone outside. The other three didn't follow her. They knew her wishes, her moods beyond the need for her to convey anything verbally. She had that much control over them, all the control in the world at the tip of her little finger.

The Blood in her veins moved, what was left of it. She knew he was still here. Williams, Colton and Shaw had followed her. She discovered that merely as an afterthought. They followed her ten steps behind. She hadn't consciously signaled them, but they were very astute to her wishes, and she discovered that she didn't mind. And she didn't care if they saw her with him anyway.

There he was. She saw him in a glimpse just before he disappeared around the next corner. And the next. She increased her own speed.
He could easily ditch her if he so wanted, she was fully aware of that. Irritation and determination warred within her. And there were flashes of fear. It was impossible for her to actually know to whom she was giving chase. It didn't have to be Evan, but could just as well be… the other… if another there was.

He stood there under the streetlight, waiting for her, taking her hand as she breathlessly caught up with him, leading her away.

They caught the underground north. Her three shadows, Sheila's three shadows sat silently in another part of the coach. There were other people as well, ghostlike in the shifting, often failing light of the coach, of the tunnels outside. There were frequent, unscheduled stops between stations. Sometimes the engine just died. Sometimes there were other, less identifiable reasons. To Sheila they kept moving anyway. Her surroundings passed by her in a rush of air, of indistinct materials and creatures. It wasn't real, wasn't real. Reality stung her like a giant wasp. She felt its sting, sensing its poison entering her, sensing Death coming. She studied him, first from the corner of her eyes, then directly, openly, turning her head, staring at him with huge, frozen eyes.

The night moved around them, as they moved through it. She couldn't really remember leaving the Camden tube station. The four of them, following his lead didn't move towards The Green Rose, but in the opposite direction, heading down Camden High Street. They passed the smaller Inverness Street Market close to the tube station, heading further down towards the Camden Lock. She didn't look at anything but him. It was impossible to know if the other three were still there, somewhere behind them. She hadn't heard them or seen them since long before the train had finally stopped. The image of them bleeding, stretched out on the sidewalk, on a wall assaulted her violently. It caused her little or no distress.

Straight lines were bending. Everything straightened, like a branch unbending after someone had released it from a grip. Reality shifted and changed in a heartbeat.

She could hear the huge Camden Lock Market from far away. Sounds carried far in the fog, in mists of Time and Shadow. Suddenly she found herself there, walking beside him, walking like he did, sliding in and out of shadows, like he did, and she felt pride.

– I met Sheba, she said. – She… visited me.

He didn't say anything, didn't offer anything but the slightest nod.

– She implied something about «Rules of Engagement». Is it true? Am I… safe?

– No! He shook his head. – Those informal rules do exist, and Sheba is quite traditionally inclined, but it's just a whim from her side. She could just as easily decide they don't apply to her, and she would be right. They don't truly apply to anyone.

– Rules and laws are all like that, she nodded to him, giving him a smile and the fire in her eyes.

She walked beside him, between the flashing and flashy lights. The tents and houses existed side by side. The exclusive and the mundane only divided by feet or inches, by thin tent walls or brick walls. Everything living, pulsating in the same boiling cauldron.

They closed in on a cluster of tables on an extended corner. Most hadn't been taken, but they remained empty, nonetheless. She recognized «Smiling Franzz» Herbert from the police archive. His army of bodyguards surrounded him, virtually embraced him. The cluster of bodies parted instantly in honor of Evan Shelby and his entourage. Herbert smiled his famous smile, but Sheila saw easily that it didn't have its usual extraordinary quality. Something was amiss.

He was nothing but a shadow. They were all nothing but shadows bathed in the glory of the sun, the giant moon by their side.

– I haven't seen you before, she said to him, to the sun, the giant moon.

– I can’t believe how I can have missed you, but I haven’t truly looked. Perhaps I still don’t.

Shelby looked at Herbert, staring straight through him. He didn’t say anything, any vocal words.

– The pressure has let up a little, Herbert said in a rusty voice. – At least in appearance. There’s no overt action anymore, but the forces are gathering, I can tell you that much. I feel it in my bones.

Shelby nodded.

– Keep up the pretence, he ordered.

Herbert nodded, his eyes glossy, the admiration clear in their depths.

– Nice to meetya, Inspector, he greeted her.

Then he and his bruisers were gone. They were good. She saw them go, but was willing to bet that very few others did.

Just like that they disappeared. People listening in wouldn’t have any fucking idea of what had been going on. Perhaps they would scratch their head and wonder a bit, but nothing more. Soon they would be on their way once more, completely clueless.

– That was some performance, she told Evan, giving praise with a taint of mockery in her voice.

They had hit the streets again. Lights turned dimmer, turned distant.

– Why did you show me this? She asked harshly.

– I wanted to.

He didn’t look at her, but he looked at her, and she felt like she wasn’t really there, but somewhere deep within his being, drowning. Her voice sounded very, very far away when she replied.

– I… understand.

They stood still (but were still moving) outside the tube station. She saw no other people around them. There were creatures moving, hardly more than statues with the speed of turtles. It didn’t rain. Droplets of water hung in the hair, in the moist air, the air thick of boiling blood, of icy spikes.

– Bite me, she insisted

– No, he said tight-lipped. His lips usually so bloodless, now so full.

The face usually so sunken. Now positively radiant.

– Bite me…

She whispered, pushing herself close to him. She snuggled her head against his neck and pushed her lips against his, kissing him.

He didn’t return the kiss.

– I love you, she breathed.

He grabbed a passing man and sank his fangs, his terrible fangs into the man's neck. He fed while he walked. She froze. There were the loud, sucking sounds. The sight of blood flowing from his jaw, turning it bright, glowing red. The prey resisted with sounds, with withering arms, but it was like nothing to him. She continued to walk, to move, but she froze. All blood left her face. He threw the man away like he was nothing, like a discarded husk.

– Do you still love me? He snarled

He's losing control, she thought.

Perhaps he had for a long time. Perhaps he, to this point had been better at hiding it.

– How can I not? She whispered. – You're a god in a man's clothing.

She staggered back, frozen by her own admission. Shame and longing fought inside her.

He left her then, left her alone. One moment he was there, then he was Gone. She stumbled and would have fallen, if not the wall, the rock-hard wall had been there to catch her. She leaned against it, leaned hard. Sheila Watts stood like that for a long time, without opening her eyes, and she died a thousand times.

She found herself outside the tube station again, the hole of the underground sweeping her in, sucking her in.

They came to her, the three of them. Their faces were very clear to her, as they separated from the darkness. She sensed their scorn, their fear and their triumph. She ignored it.

Evan Shelby raced through the night, running to something, as well as from it.

He didn't really feel like he was moving anymore. He experienced movement like a rush of air, that's all. Each time his feet touched the ground it could just as well be air. He walked into a street, experiencing its beginning. A blink later he found himself at its end, fading and appearing to people he passed. On a roof he surveyed the town below, the ashes far below. As below, so above. He held a man in his grip, a big powerful built man hanging from a grip, keeping him from falling to the far below street.

– I want you to take a message to your boss, he told him.

– A message? The man's lips shivered, his jaw and his entire body shook in horror. – Sure, man, anything. Give it to me, I'll take it to him personally.

– I know you will.

Evan opened his hand, releasing his grip. The man fell screaming to the ground far below. His heavyset body hit the tarmac with a thump. Bones

broke and the entire internal system was crushed to a pulp in a moment.
And he knew everything was recorded. Every sound, every image, every scream.

Evan moved through the hotel corridor on his way down. Occasionally there would be men and women with guns guarding a given floor, guarding the elevators. He avoided them easily on his way down, as he had on his way up. Occasionally he would be registered on the monitors, but only as a blur, a rush of wind. He emerged from the main entrance, immersing himself in the night. He could feel himself breathe.

As he moved away, he pulled a cell phone from his pocket. He activated it with a few, easy pushes with his fingers. Usually, he kept away from such things. This toy had been gathering dust in his top drawer for months. Now it moved and glowed, and people were watching. They watched his every move. After satellite surveillance became useless a decade ago the cell phones had been one of the few remaining ways for the government to keep track of people beyond the street video surveillance. What they didn't realize was that it could work the other way around as well, for people who wanted to be seen, when they wanted to be seen.

He stood at the top of the arch at Marble Arch, surveying the park, with its lights and shadows. Somebody had lit fires somewhere in there. The police had given up keeping order in this area a long time ago. It was described as a hotbed of insurrection and crime, a headquarters of all the «wild elements of the city». All bullshit, of course, but it was, like the areas where the Dirty lived off limits for most people, and even for the police, except for the occasional show of force, when they ventured into it like an army on the warpath.

The phone rang. He had expected it. It didn't startle him, like it used to. He said hello in the most relaxed manner.

– *We're speaking to Evan Shelby, I trust?* The voice on the other end of the microwave bath inquired.

– Speaking, he replied. No more than that.

– *We've been instructed to set up a meeting of possible mutual benefit.*

– You know what? He said pleasantly. – That sounds like a very intriguing proposition.

The «conversation» ended. He had had quite a few similar during his long life, and they didn't truly faze him anymore. He threw away the phone, threw it far into the darkness, the shadow of the park, and jumped off the arch. People saw it, also those on the safer side of the monument, frequenting the heavily fortified Oxford Street and Edgware Road, but they had grown quite jaded concerning the unexpected and insane lately and didn't react with too much horror. He landed softly on the almost dissolved and uneven tarmac, and proceeded to walk from there virtually uninterrupted by the landing, a landing making the ground shake.

He hardly used the Tube anymore. Not just because he detested being watched by the people jerking off in front of s monitor screens, but most of all because he didn't need to anymore. He walked by a house, observing a girl touching the keypad numbers, opening the door to her apartment, passing there, penetrating deeper on the line between light and darkness.

There was a dance here, he realized. He stretched out a hand, touching it, and he danced it. More even, than he had done in the whiskey and go-go bar so long ago. So much had happened since then. He had changed, grown so much.

He approached a woman on the street head on, not caring if she saw him, wanting her to see, see it all. He held her suspended in the air with one arm, and it was like holding a feather.

– I've become the wind, he told her, – and tell me, pray tell, who can touch the wind?

She couldn't reply. He had taken away her ability to speak, to move, except in the smallest of gestures. The fear was present in her face. He could easily see it, as he lowered her a bit, as he sank his dripping fangs into her skin.

The residential area in Hampton and surroundings had been a nice, desired home for a long time, and it stayed that way still. Even though it was as riddled with pollution as everywhere else it remained a favored post card subject. A little retouching here, a little image enhancement there and everything in the picture made people want to live there. And when they arrived, to sample the place, with the train to Hampton Court, for instance, even feeling the sting of disappointment they still wanted to live there. It was better than anywhere else they had been visiting a reasonable distance within London's expanded city limits.

Tonight, citizens and visitors alike would feel different, though. There was a substance in the air of fear and excitement that did indeed threaten to scare them out of their wits. Some of the people arriving at the train station from Waterloo took the same train back, without really knowing why. People still having cars at the parking lot this late at night were tempted to let them remain and call for a cab. Some gave in to the temptation, the irresistible pull. The others broke into a run, opened the doors to their vehicles and rushed off on screaming tires.

The message from Evan Shelby to Superintendent Lloyd Emerson and his men had been quite precise:

«Take the 2.02 train to Hampton Court. You may search the train for bombs, but neither you nor any of your men must under any circumstances arrive at the parking lot from elsewhere. This will be taken as a serious breach of conduct».

The Superintendent left the train surrounded by a considerable number of his closest associates. A few of the men were cops. Others clearly weren't. They moved very similar, though, as if they all were made from the same model, mold. The group, moving as one didn't have to go far. The parking lot was just a few steps from the front of the train, opposite the small station building.

Emerson looked at the deserted parking lot. He saw a few cars, but no people.

Mist hung over the place, heavy and cold. Even the ever-hotter nights couldn't change that.

– I've always hated mist, one of the men mumbled.

Several of the men looked uneasily at each other. They were certainly not unapprised of current events.

Emerson looked sharply at them, as if he could practically sense their very action.

And perhaps he could.

– We're early, he mumbled, after a short glance at his watch. – God bless us, the train has actually arrived ahead of schedule. God bless English trains…

The men refrained from pointing out, no matter how much they might have wanted to, that the rail companies, in a desperate cooperative, unprecedented move the previous year had decided to make the schedule so roomy that it would be virtually impossible for a train not blown up to arrive late.

And trains were not generally blown up these days. A lot of other things were set to blow, but not trains.

The assembly walked down the short staircase and proceeded to the center of the open space. Suddenly a man stood there in front of them, just a short distance away, surrounded by mist. Several of the massively numbered entourage almost fired at him, but being professionals they caught themselves in time. It would have turned into a bloodbath, and they knew it. It was visible, enshrined in every single part of their features.

– Where are your guards, Shelby? Emerson wondered aloud.

– That doesn't really matter, does it? Shelby grinned and stretched out his arms, indicating the entire general area. – The only thing you need to know is that they're *here*. Like a tremble in the earth, a whisper in the wind, blood flowing through veins.

– Jesus, one of Emerson's tight men exclaimed. – I *heard* you were crazy.

Emerson waved him off.

– There has been a bit strained… competition between us lately, some misunderstandings, the Superintendent said jovially. – I called this meeting to clear up things.

– Okay, Shelby nodded. – That sounds reasonable. Let's hear it.

Emerson paused a bit before starting. He was an actor, after all, on the stage of cutthroats in the modern city.

– Restraint, he began, coughing a bit. – Restraint is the first order of the day.

Shelby looked at him. He didn't comment.

– You know: Emerson kept at it. – Traffic rules and all that? In an intersection you shouldn't necessarily insist on pushing forward no matter how right you are. If everybody did that there would be a massive number of crashes…

– And there are, Shelby said, non-commentarial.

– Precisely my point. Emerson lifted his right hand in a dramatic gesture. – The idea is, for all parties involved to pull back now and then, and let go of their god given rights, and everything would proceed smoother. Compromises don't necessarily signify defeat, but rather a practical way of interacting. No profit, in at least two meanings of the word can be made without it.

Shelby clapped his hands slowly and deliberately.

– Well-made points by the honorable Superintendent, he said mockingly, humorously.

Emerson bowed eloquently.

– Well, I certainly try, he said modestly.

Everybody laughed, Emerson and Shelby loudest of all. The laughter seemed to fade and vanish in the surrounding mist, leaving nothing but Night.

The absurd theater, the well-rehearsed performance went on for a while longer, but it was mostly pleasantries. The important words had already been spoken. The meeting of people ended as it had begun, in the mist, and only the mist remained.

Emerson and the men turned to return the few steps to the station, where a train was just approaching.

– You know, Shelby… Emerson raised a hand and turned back for a moment.

He stopped. His men turned. They all stopped. Shelby had disappeared, vanished like smoke… or mist, like he had never really been there at all.

The train that was never late arrived at the end station once more, to promptly reverse its engine, and return to the glittering inner city. And the visitors returned with it.

No one said a word there in the coach. There were no other occupants. They all waited for the boss to say something, but he didn't. He just looked at them all. He hardly took his eyes of them, not any of them.

Emerson's «evil eye», already famous gained an entire new level of reputation this night.

The Green Rose was filled with people. Tonight, he had been forced to set the tables tighter. It had either been that or rejecting people at the entrance.

Evan Shelby gazed at his world, his domain. He played with a band, the old-fashioned way, in the flesh in a provisional corner stage deep inside the house. In fact, it was like he wasn't in the house at all, but back in his birthplace on the American west coast, a place, if not forever denied him (not him), then very far away these days. He could smell the ocean, the trees in a forest he had run through once. He couldn't even recall which, what its name was or had been, but he yet remembered it in detailed clarity. There was a deer running away from the human, even though it was just a little boy running joyfully through the dark of the forest.

And he returned to the barroom in San Francisco, where naked girls and a mad, drunken magician fought for the guests' attention. It should have been an easy contest… and it was. The naked girls doing their erotically charged dance should easily have been the winners, but they weren't. It returned to him in flashes, in ways it hadn't for generations. He returned to it, the place where he had thrown all caution to the wind.

And there was a Storm.

The blond, dark-skinned powerful woman spoke to him. She sang to him. He wanted her to.

– There's pain in you, like it is in him, she told him, Sheba told him, nodding towards the dancing, drunken magician on the stage. – But methinks yours is even a bit more delicious to behold.

Claudette had just been to the john. He met her in the intersection between the back exit hall, and the guestrooms. The guestrooms were filled to the brim tonight. People came and went as they pleased, and no one bothered locking any door. Naked bodies shook and were soaked in sweat as they clashed and parted. The scream in the air ripped into him, turning sound to heat.

– Hi, she greeted him, her eyes markedly dilated, her speech slurred.

Everything had happened so fast tonight. It usually was like that for him, an ordinary lifetime being akin to yesterday, but tonight had been like a rush of wind, a blink of an eye.

– Hi, she greeted him huskily, in a very good mood, – I heard there was very good news tonight.

She kissed him on the lips, pushing against him, smelling heavily of sex juices. Her scent assaulted him and made his sensitive nose twitch. Her being assaulted all his senses. And he had himself to thank. He had removed her inhibitions… the same night he had let go of his own.

– Perhaps, he shrugged. – It remains to be seen.

He removed the scarf around her neck, and started to touch the red, swollen marks there. She started shaking in fear and desire.

And he fell on her. And he tasted her blood. It spread through his body like wildfire. He wanted more. He wanted it all. But he pulled back. Her eyes stayed glossy, her breathing shallow, but he could hear her heartbeat like a roaring waterfall in spring, something he hadn't experienced for many years, but now was as close as it has ever been. He had pulled back in time. She would live. He let go of her, leaving her on a chair in the hall. Tears were flowing from her eyes, into a face flooded in joy.

A bit later that night he sat in a chair, relaxing in front of a computer screen, typing on a keyboard. He was making lyrics, making music, something he hadn't done for ages. The night moved and shifted around him. There was no light, but he could easily see, see the shadows. The fire, the fire in the air danced and flowed.

Some time later he had moved to another keyboard, a playing keyboard. The music spread through the large apartment, to the bar below, to the streets outside. People heard it, through their ears, beyond ears and they shuddered in the hot night.

And he did, too.

What he carried inside had always scared him, always intrigued him.

CHAPTER THIRTEEN

When Sheila woke up it was morning, and the day had turned dark gray once more. Her bright vision of it had faded, and she felt just a slight echo of the nausea haunting her the day before. The blood no longer moved in her veins. The sun had returned to being no more than a badly working lamp in the sky. She felt each step as she walked across the floor. It wasn't like she hardly touched it, like it had been the previous nights. The day brought not clarity, but lethargy and confusion. She stood before the mirror, the full-length mirror in the strange, impersonal apartment reserved for her at the police station, naked and cold. There was no terror anymore, only pain, dull and faint. The night dreams couldn't touch her in the light of day. She touched herself. Flesh felt like paper, dead and still. She dressed slowly, automatically. Her eyes, her shining eyes her grandmother had called them before she died, stared at nothing.

She moved easily, casually, could still do that, as the morning stiffness loosened in body and mind. Her morning exercise started slowly, deliberately. Movement through air, across floor. Sweat poured from her skin and she welcomed it, welcomed the sweet aching pain from straining muscles. She showered, cleaned herself up. Pleased, she looked at the smiling bitch in the mirror. She rubbed her body with a towel, rubbed it until it was pink and flushed.

With the towel covering her upper body she opened the door and walked down the hall, to another bedroom. She virtually kicked in the door, as she pushed it open with both her hand and foot.

– RISE AND SHINE, ASSHOLES, she shouted.

On the three used beds Colton, Williams and Shaw jumped out of their good skin, and screaming, half in terror, half in rage, they had their weapons pointed at her in less than a second. Not good, but not bad either. She nodded, not dissatisfied.

– Get up, she said flatly. – We have a lot of work ahead of us.

– No rest for the wicked, huh? Shaw grinned, as he lowered his gun

She liked him. Or she would have, if the circumstances had been different. She nodded once and left the room.

Williams didn't lower her gun. She kept it at the doorway Watts had just left, staring at it with rigid eyes.

Sheila dressed, slowly, very deliberately. Not only covering her body in clothes, but in weapons as well. Not only dressing her body, but her mind as well. She considered cutting off most of her hair, even all of it, but decided against it, putting down the scissors, picking up the brush, brushing it with fast, furious moves. When she and her three minor shadows stepped off the lighttrain inside the Thatcher Center, in the area of town once called Docklands she still remembered vividly the sight of herself in the mirror, so indistinct and foggy she could hardly make herself out from the general background.

There were crowds of people here. There always were. But these days a subdued mood haunted the gatherers, the shoppers and the sellers, all selling themselves. Sheila and her brood moved through it all, truly like a hot knife slicing butter. They were not there. They were not like ghosts. They were ghosts, not walking, but flowing across the polished, dirty floor. She heard the murmur, the whispering awe and fear, even though she neither heard nor saw any sign that the four of them were even noticed.

A girl stood close to the giant window, staring at the pale disk there on the cityscape background. A statue, a doll, with no more life than a piece of rock. Her eyes at the back of her head were huge and black, staring at Sheila, making her shudder like a leaf in the storm.

They walked to the wardrobe area. No one attempted to stop them. The guards stared at nothing but nothing.

The door to the wardrobe wasn't locked. No doors here were locked. No one not belonging here ever went inside. She stopped at the room's center, sensing Williams closing the door behind them all. She didn't see it. She did hear the door being closed, of course. But she didn't actually see who did it. She knew.

The room was basically the same. It hadn't changed since her last visit. The cleaning lady had been here, but the room was virtually untouched. Sheila walked to the chair, mirror and shelf in the corner, the face-painting place. There was hardly any presence here at all. Not really more of Wynette Richards than the cleaning lady.

– What are we really doing here? Williams asked sourly.

– Oh, I don't know. Sheila grinned. – Perhaps I'm just retracing my own steps, attempting to get a grip?

She went through the drawers throughout the room, ever more impatient.

In an obscure drawer close to the floor, by the television set she found it, a bright, shining electronic keycard. Any key, opening locks, was hard to come by these days. So, everybody kept several spares, at work, at home, at any place they might or might not venture during a given period of their lives.

The evening arrived quickly, the day being just a glimpse in the eternal gray. The fire protuberances from the burning of excessive amounts of oil and faulty equipment reached far and high above the futuristic pyramids along the Docklands trail. The other passengers looked away or generally avoided even a casual glance. Sheila looked straight at it, at the dirty fire. Or perhaps at the fire, the only thing that could never be dirty. She saw it burn, burn in Space. Not the Sun or a star. A relatively small fire burning in the void. It was alive, speaking to her, as if a living thing. It had eyes, and a mouth and nose. She approached it, and her wings withered and died. A cold breeze blew through the train as it shook from another quake, another ruptured gas line somewhere. If one was prone to look out of the window (and one was not) one could see the new seabed below, visibly see it shake and crack. She shook, as if awakening from a dream.

She walked past the outer checkpoints without even flashing any ID this time. Nothing happened. People didn't even seem to notice them. They were ghosts and shadows walking on air. Nothing prevented their quick intrusion to the inner circle condos, where the final hurdle remained. The small group entered the gigantic hall. The three others might feel small, but she didn't. The reception hall hadn't truly changed, but she had.

– We are going to Wynette Richards' apartment, she enlightened the man behind the counter, the same man she had been partly appeasing such a short while ago.

He shrank under her ruthless scrutiny. And she knew he would never speak about this, hardly even allowing himself to remember it in his conscious memory.

– You will look through the tapes at the end of the day, and see nothing, hear nothing and speak nothing. Pray that I am right. I know you wouldn't want to sense us one more time.

She smiled and he backed away. It was the most terrifying smile he had ever seen. He could call security at any time, he knew that, but he also knew, beyond doubt that they would see no one but him here.

– Yes, she nodded. – Tell of the shadows. Tell that they are and will always be.

They walked alone, without escort into the seemingly abandoned construct. From their point of view, it was as if there wasn't and had never been humans here. The paintings on the wall, the dust on the floor, it all seemed dead, without the most remote signs of life. They walked on. Watts heard no sound as they touched the floor with their feet. They didn't walk across the polished surface, they slid on it, moving in a flowing forward motion.

– It's still there, she mumbled, feeling her limbs, sensing the fire inside.

– … still here. It has always been here.

She didn't see the three behind her. She still knew their exact position. If she wanted to kill them, she knew where to direct her guns, throw her knives.

Sheila Watts stopped. She turned toward her underlings, her brood, directing a fixed stare at them.

– We're hunting a savage, one chasing through the streets as if it was a jungle. It is a jungle. If you look carefully, you can even see the trees, feel the pressure of the damp heat on your skin.

Williams looked at her, her eyes empty, like the jungle, like the trees they passed on their way.

Wynette's lush apartment was empty, abandoned. No people remained. The furniture and all the amenities were still here, though. Sheila threw herself on the bed, the bed covered in silk, closing her eyes one tiny moment before opening them once more, and rising.

– This isn't real, she told the three. – It's just a mirage in the desert, and just as healthy.

They left, taking even less with them than they had brought, leaving even more of themselves behind.

No one had seen them come. No one saw them leave.

– We're not ghosts, she told them. – The rest of the poor fuckers are.

And without looking at them she saw they were listening. When she had first met what had then been Colton's group, she had been the student. Now, she was the teacher. And she smiled.

They headed for the lightrail station with fast, decisive steps. There was fog. There was ever fog these days, thick smog making her throat itch and burn. The phone in her pocket rang. It called to her like bells on a Sunday morning. She stopped and froze, before she fumbled the phone out of her pocket and replied. She didn't hear the sound of her own voice as she replied, or what she said. Time had stopped and space distorted itself all around her.

– *I can sense the blood moving,* she heard. And it was him.

This was him. Of that there was no doubt. The voice from the old cemetery, easily able to imitate any voice on Earth.

– Ev-van, she stuttered.

It sounded exactly like him. And she knew Evan's voice so much better than she had ever known that of Dominic Colby.

– The tiny ogre has grown up, become big, but has it truly? Is it still tiny inside?

– WHAT DO YOU WANT? She screamed at him with a voice hoarse

and coarse.

Suddenly she was once more covered in sweat, and she stank, as if she had not washed for days. This in spite that she knew for a fact that she had showered this morning.

But it had been hours ago, and now the night had come.

– *Events have been set in motion that cannot be stopped. Tiny ogres should crawl back into hiding and stay there.*

– What the fuck are you talking about? She asked, suddenly deadly calm.

– *There are no terrorists in this country... sir,* she heard.

And she heard her own voice. This time she did turn cold, as cold as the voice. She let the arm holding the phone fall, well before she actually heard the beeping tone, the signal that the connection had been broken. The lighttrain station fifty steps away blew up in an intense blast of elemental fire. The explosion rocked the ground they stood on, causing their teeth to rattle in their dry mouth.

She turned to them, her three companions, her partners in crime, while the flames remained sky high in the smog behind her.

– Looks like the nine-zero-two departure has been cancelled, she said calm as death.

Dust settled slowly behind her. The fire kept burning.

– I knew it wasn't you, she told Evan Shelby an unimaginable long timespan later. – There wasn't a shred of compassion left in that voice, as if he, she or it has thrown away everything making he, she or it human.

– I knew it wasn't you, he echoed, in an exact imitation of her voice.

– I can be wrong, of course, she stared pointedly, enraged at him. – I hardly know you, after all, and I don't know much of what you've been doing the last seventy-five years or so…

She could hear the faint sound of car engines outside, as the day's last remaining cars moved snail-like down Camden High Street. Williams, Shaw and Colby were standing behind her. They always were.

– It seems like It has singled me out, she said exasperated, – and I have no idea why.

– Why shouldn't he single you out? The question is whether or not you're a random piece in the game, one of convenience and opportunity or deliberately chosen, a queen or a pawn.

– So, there *is* a game, she flared, stepping closer to him, clearly excited. – What kind?

She looked into his eyes, forced herself to stare directly at the pain, the death.

– I don't know, he replied.

She patted his cheek, touched his skin briefly with wet lips.

– So, what am I, in your humble opinion?

– A bit of both, I suppose.

And that was that. She pulled away from him.

– Thanks, she said, as she, as they left him. – Thanks for nothing

– You handled him brilliantly, Kathy told her later, on the underground train, speaking with shiny eyes.

Kathy had been a woman. Now she was hardly more than a girl, admiring an adult role model, a dog wagging her tail for the strongest in the pack. Sheila didn't even dignify her with a look of reply, and that, she knew, made the other woman admire her even more.

– I especially enjoyed your seventy-five-year comment. Shaw laughed out aloud. – That one was truly priceless.

She looked at him, at them all, without looking. They didn't understand. They had watched a lot of what was happening, but still they refused to see.

Back at the Yard. Hidden files and records were no problem to her anymore. She just asked for any given password, and it was given to her. The four of them went through report after report, until Sheila got fed up and walked away, leaving it alone. Wherever the truth was hidden, it wasn't here. She hadn't expected it either, but had felt a certain need to have it confirmed.

The day had been short, like pieces and cuts. She remembered it like moments from a life, nothing more, and thus the night continued, fragmented, gray, lost. There were no moments stretching beyond seconds, Time could be 10.02, and then seconds later it was 10.45. Sheila found herself looking into mirrors, and she looked at the shadows, she looked a lot. She went several times to Superintendent Emerson's office, but he wasn't in tonight. The place looked completely deserted, as if it hadn't been used for days. She imagined she saw cobwebs in the corners. Suspicion rattled her like spiders. Something was happening. Something was clearly happening, something she was not privy to. Shaking her head she left again, and didn't return.

The headquarters, she easily saw, remained in a state of high, increasingly high alert, as if the tons of arms, of visible and invisible guards were seemingly insufficient to the task… whatever task there was. When she returned to what passed for her temporary office these days, she found a well-dressed man eagerly awaiting her return. She recognized him immediately as Parker's driver and servant.

She recognized once more the murmur in her ears, rising to a roar, ever rising, to a crescendo of sound. Not now, but soon. Soon.

– Mister Parker desires your presence at the Mansion for dinner tonight, Miss Watts, he said formally.

The well-dressed monkey was afraid of her, like everybody was, now. He didn't show it in his outward manner, but she saw straight through him.

– Then I guess you've come to fetch me, then?

– Yes, Miss Watts.

– I'll be ready in a few minutes, she dismissed him.

She stood before the mirror, dressing up. The dress was dark gray, revealing and bold. She chose one of her stiff, specially prepared coats, and started fitting all the weapons inside of it. It looked like a coat, it smelled like a coat, but it was really armor, an armor coated in black velvet. She brushed, made her hair again, a ponytail in the neck, hair coating her brow in front. The light curls flowed down her back as fire in the twilight. She perfumed herself. Hands seemed to move by themselves, performing the routine operation. She did so with an ironic twist of her mouth.

The driver waited, holding open the door to the Rolls Royce, a statue, nothing more than a function, a stiff mask of indifference. She sat in the seat, covered in velvet, as the car moved through the streets of London, through a carefully selected and guarded route. She looked at it all through the one-way glass, pretending to be windows. She saw riot police being out in full force, and she saw groups of people, finally giving voice to their discontent, their fear, their rage, desperate for assurances, demanding it, from any authority, any person in high places. Everything was unraveling, like carefully placed cargo on a boat traversing stormy seas. Once one barrel was put back in place, another started moving. And another. And another. There were Dirty even in the finer parts of town now. They were chased away, but they returned. There was nothing, absolutely nothing for them elsewhere anymore. They behaved nicely, having learned their lesson, and those who had were allowed to stay, for a while, performing their dance of servitude and hailing, before returning to their dank, hollow homes, to their place in the scheme of things.

There were now two new, heavily fortified gates far from the actual property they had to pass through. The guards knew the car, knew the driver, but they made him open the trunk and the doors anyway. She saw, she sensed how they froze when discovering her inside, realizing who she was. She grinned wolfishly to them, and they pulled back, like sheep before the slaughter. They stood still, like sheep before the slaughter.

They passed the old gate, even more fortified. Sheila hardly recognized the surroundings from the first time she had visited, changed as it was, beyond recognition. There was no control there, though. The guards stood still, with their guns and stiff uniforms. The gate opened as the car approached, closed the moment the car passed through. The car stopped before the entrance of an eloquent, luxurious mansion. There were lights everywhere. Every corner was lit. Except around the car. Around the car was Shadow.

The driver opened the door for her, and she stepped outside, on the red carpet and line of servants. One wanted to take her coat.

– I'll hold on to it, thank you, she grinned.

Around the woman was Shadow, and it sparked and stretched as she moved through the wide portal, into the house. The car once more turned into a car, and nothing more, as the shadow moved through the front chambers into the holy grail, the inner circle. The woman heard music, hardly music at all, forever stale, forever horribly even. Music to fall asleep, not to awaken. A man sat in front of a piano, playing like a puppet, not a human being. The orchestra hardly moved at all, except for the essentials to produce sound.

A puppet led Sheila Watts to her chair. She carefully removed her coat and sat down. She didn't look around, treating the dinner table guests with the contempt they deserved.

– Ah, Sheila, Johnston Parker said from his place at the end of the table. – Welcome. Glad you could come.

– Happy to be here, Johnston, she replied, grinning some more.

There were whispers and low exchange of words, fear and loathing, as if they were looking at a wild animal.

And they were.

She looked at all the sweet dolls, the pampered bitches, shaking her head.

So lost, she thought. I'm so lost.

These suckers had never been outside, never seen anything other than their sheltered life, not like she had. She envied them.

She realized she was sipping. She emptied each glass the moment it was put in front of her, and the world was drowned in a pleasant haze. The three-course dinner started. There was no signal she could discern from Parker, but everybody seemed ready when the plates were put before them.

Good little puppets. She couldn't tell whether or not she said that aloud.

Suddenly she wanted to, to get a reaction, any reaction out of them, any proof they were still human.

The alcohol slowly paralyzed the body, but something strange happened. Her mind cleared. Many experienced it that way, she knew that. Just as she knew that this was real. Conversation picked up as the eating and drinking progressed. The silence in the room easily overwhelmed the buzz of voices. A slight turning of the head, a blinking with the eyes and it was gone. Braindead talk turned even more braindead. It was more like a buzz than any real conversation, and Sheila had never bothered to listen to it.

– I've heard the natives are restless these days, one said.

– They're always restless, another stated.

They called them natives in high profile parties such as these. In closed company they, too, called them Dirty, the most common name.

– I heard they trashed a soup kitchen yesterday. They got a lot of nerve.

Sheila turned off. She turned off twice.

The main course was served. Or the second main course. Sheila couldn't tell which. She giggled hysterically. Nobody seemed to notice. Silence settled for a while, settled for her. It wasn't safe here, she knew that, but she chose to choose a low-keyed awareness anyway.

– I don't understand what has been happening in the city recently, a woman suddenly exclaimed. – I don't recognize it lately. Everything has become strange, strange and alien, if you know what I mean.

The buzz quieted for a moment. Somebody had actually broken the unwritten law, and actually said something of consequence.

– Nothing that dramatic, Sheila stated, her speech slightly slurred. – It has just turned stranger, more alien, too much for you not to notice, that's all…

Parker turned towards her, with the same sharp ember intact in his eyes.

– Yes, what is loose in our proud city, Sheila?

– What has always been here, she replied softly, without slurring the slightest. – The wild, untamed, savage humanity.

He nodded. And a selected lot of the other present Gentlemen and Ladies nodded, too. The same people that had studied Sheila since her arrival.

Sheila studied herself, pinched her hand a bit under the table. It, the very skin itself seemed as sleepy as a jaw after being anesthetized by a dentist. She wondered if she was ready now if something happened, if her body could react in any circumstance, if her will could make the body react, no matter its condition. She had done it before, she knew that, but she wondered if she could keep doing it, again and again and again. Images came to her, of chains on a wall, how the dust loosened from that wall, in her moment of total helplessness, total despair.

They danced. He led. She followed.

– Where is home, she whimpered. – I've searched for it my entire life, without even coming close.

– I'll take you home, he assured her.

– I'm drunk, she complained, giggling. – I don't think I've ever been this drunk, been this blitzed before. It's frigging strange, that's what it is.

– Please follow me, he insisted.

She did, after discretely saving her coat from the chair, her heavy, heavy coat.

It was misty inside the smaller room. At least she saw it that way. The men and women sitting there were indistinctive to her, dissolving. She didn't dare look at her hands or herself in a mirror. She kept looking at the floor, constantly gazing, locking her eyes at the assembly in front of her.

– You all know about Sheila, I gather, Parker said. – Which we've heard so many good things about lately.

Nods and mumblings across the room. Some sat by the long table. Some in sofas and chairs along the walls. She nodded and mumbled, and smiled brightly in return.

– Sheila is a survivor, Parker said.

A funny image assaulted Sheila then. Her pulling out her arsenal from her coat, annihilating everyone in the room. She giggled hysterically.

They took it for bravery, for contempt, and it sat well with them. They saw a completely different Sheila then she herself saw.

She saw straight through them, their plots, their games, their pretence, including in that their pretence of mastery. She snarled at them.

Johnston took her arm, leading her to an even smaller group within the group on a sofa in the inner circle of the room. He sat down. She sat down in the available seat beside him.

The ladies and gentlemen of the room drank their port, ate their well-prepared sandwiches. They reminded her of people in old pictures and movies, depicting colonial Britain, perhaps even a tad more ridiculous. Their fangs and claws were dulled, but they still killed and mutilated, through their proxies.

– You grew up in Camden Town, didn't you, Sheila, a woman said. – In rooms where there was no glass in the windows?

None of them introduced themselves to her or told her their name. She was beneath that honor, yet.

– Yes, there was already summer all the time, Sheila shrugged. – No need for any glass.

Laughter. Polite, merciful.

– I was caught stealing when I was eight, and was placed in a catholic orphanage. Almost all the children there were enrolled in public service classes, one way or another. My… eagerness was noted early by the… teachers, I guess.

She spoke. She spoke a lot, about nothing and everything, about things in the past, about things past. She didn't look at her watch. There was no need for that. She had long since learned to measure time without artificial means.

– I must say I find you very articulate… for one with such a… rough education, a red-faced man grumbled.

– My experience is that such is often the case, sir, she hummed happily.

Let them believe they controlled her, she respected them, feared them, vaunted their position, their place in society. Let them believe everything.

– What do you think of the weather forecasts? Sheila, the woman asked her casually.

– What weather forecasts, madam? Sheila countered grinning.

There was laughter, polite, controlled, only slightly beyond what was considered proper.

– How do you see the supply situation develop in the coming months?

They prodded her, interrogated her, looking for cracks. It was something, in which they had long practice. Sheila had expected that. But there was something… something beneath that. She realized they were prodding her for something specific.

Slowly, only slowly a sense of unease started to creep inside her. Of something beyond the nausea she had felt since the beginning.

– It isn't an immediate problem, she shrugged. – The number of suppliers, even independent suppliers is fairly constant. Some may be taken out, but others quickly take their place. As long as there is production, I see no immediate need for concern. There are a lot of long-term *problems*, but I trust you're aware of them?

With that pointer it stopped.

She mingled, not remembering much about it until she returned to Parker.

– You did good, he praised her.

– I was merely repeating the official line, she shrugged. – It hasn't changed much since they beat it into us at the orphanage.

– I haven't had the opportunity to say this to you before, but I'm sorry about what happened to Wynette, he offered sympathetically.

– Thank you, she whispered.

He touched her cheek, catching a tear.

– You saw her body, didn't you? he said, casually again.

– Yes, she nodded, – I saw her body.

– It must have been hard on you. I understand you were old friends.

– We left the orphanage together.

Her voice was even, completely even. There wasn't even a hint of emotion in it.

– She was a good friend, he said. – She wanted what was best for you.

– Yes, she replied. – She did.

They walked some. The others dissolved around them, fading away like smoke. She discovered they had retreated into a smaller, inner chamber. There were no windows here, no contact whatsoever with the outside world.

The flames in the fireplace reached for her, danced in the twilight of the closed-off room.

– I've wanted to tell you, for a long time, how you have impressed me.

He took her hand, pulling her to him. She let him. He kissed her on the lips, passionate and demanding.

– I don't see the Superintendent here, today, she said casually.

– No, Parker replied, a bit taken aback, – he has business elsewhere.

She wondered if there was a slight hesitation before the last word, but suddenly she found it didn't matter.

The sense of unease suddenly turned overwhelming.

They were out in the other room again. The ghosts turned solid, fading in, fading out.

I must go now, she told them.

She dismissed them. Not the other way around. They looked amazed and pleased at her.

– Sure, dear, you run along, the front woman said. – We will see you again at a later occasion, I trust?

– Count on it. Sheila flashed a smile, exposing her fangs and claws.

She kissed Parker softly on the cheek.

– I've had a lovely time. We must do it again sometime.

He mumbled something, or she didn't catch his words. No matter, suddenly she had it… whatever it was. She hurried through the hallway. The car waited for her outside. Everything slipped away. The car faded around her. She stood in a street somewhere, tense and rigid.

Her cell phone rang.

– You should see this. She heard Gordon Tyler's voice. She didn't know whether or not it was truly Tyler or the monster tyrannizing the streets of

London, and she no longer cared.

She broke the connection, and started running. The underground station was close by, just minutes away from Camden Town. Minutes, but it surely felt like hours. Every touch the train made with the rail below felt like a slow beating of a heart. Her heart, though, hammered like a stone.

Already far below, at Camden Town Station, before the escalator she had smelled the smoke in the air, and something far beyond thought, even intuition told her what transpired. She hurried up the escalator, ran all the way up. They exited the station, the four of them and saw, saw it all instantly. The enormous fire lit up the streets and thick soup of night miles away.

The Green Rose was burning. Like a hungry beast the flames consumed the Rose, leaving nothing but ashes, nothing but thorns.

Nobody attempted to put out the main fire. A few of the buildings close-by had also caught fire. Hoses of water were directed at them, and it seemed to have the desired effect.

Sheila remained on the spot she had stopped, unable to move. The implication, significance of what had just been revealed wasn't lost on her.

– Holy Mother of God. She crossed herself voluntarily, involuntarily, deeply shaken.

CHAPTER FOURTEEN

The carnage started that very night and continued unabated the next and all following.

The entire building was filled with bloody, mangled corpses. They hung from the ceiling like trophies and had been thrown all over the floors and furniture and everywhere. The blood from the bodies on the higher floors had coagulated further than on those further down, as if whatever had done this first had sneaked all the way up, beyond the countless guards protecting the head honcho, offing the said head honcho, and then proceeded to leave the building, leaving an entire churchyard of victims behind.

The man at the top sat in his chair. What was left of him, that is. Half his head was gone. No one ever found the other part. His upper body was almost cut in two. Pieces were found all over the considerably sized office.

– This is the third, the third tonight.

Gordon Tyler in more than an advanced state of confusion and horror wagged back and forth in the room, and in the building in general. Sheila and bunch studied it all in a good-humored way. No one seemed to notice them, as if they were outside time and space, undetectable to all. People spoke as if they weren't there, behaved as if no one stood just a few steps away.

– The guys used swords. Tyler shook his head. – What in the world is the world coming to these days?

– No bite-marks. The new examiner spoke to no one in particular. – I haven't looked at everybody yet, but so far everybody has died of being hit by incredibly powerful sword-strokes. If I didn't know better, I would have said a gorilla did this. The guy who did this must have an extremely powerful build, that's for sure.

He sounded totally gone, like a little boy lost.

They were all lost.

There was a… presence, an all-consuming presence in the room, in the building, in the streets outside, pervasive, rattling bones, freezing flesh.

– It will take days, just to clean this up, a police officer swore. – What a mess.

He didn't fool anybody.

– The world has changed, Watts told them. – You better get used to it, for your own sake.

They heard her. They gave no overt indication of it, but they heard.

There was a whisper in the wind. Merely the smallest shadow seemed enormous, like it could literally hide anything.

– It's night, Shaw said. – Night on Earth.

Everyone else faded around the four. They were alone, walking through a desolate, remote landscape. Buildings, previously cozy little huts where one sought safety, now looked like ruins, remnants of a time long gone. Human beings stumbled through this landscape, pale, broken figures, into the twilight.

– This is the Grand Waste, the shattered lands, spoken about in so many human legends. There were said to be gates, portals to this place people could step through, images of the future Earth, the battleground of the gods.

Everything happened so fast. The streets rushed at her. She rushed through the streets. Her phone rang. She stopped. They all stopped.

– Yes?

She heard an anonymously sounding voice and nothing but. Sheila nodded a bit, before breaking the connection.

– What is it? Colton demanded.

– That was the desk Sergeant at the Yard, Sheila replied absentmindedly. – Almost every officer has left the building. Superintendent Emerson has sealed himself off at his home, using his impressive arsenal of automated and computer-enhanced weapon-systems to fire at everybody even remotely approaching.

The three of them looked at her, a bit nonplussed.

– So, what's the big deal? Williams shrugged.

– He isn't merely doing some target practice. Watts shook her head in amazement. – He and his loyal guardsmen are firing at *everybody*, including the growing number of constables gathering outside the property. In short: He has gone apeshit on us.

– Another one with sunstroke. Shaw shook his head. – What *is* happening to the world?

There were choppers in the air, a lot of choppers, suddenly, shockingly. One landed just a few steps away from the quartet in the darkened street, picking them up. And the flight of mechanical birds dominated the pale London night sky. The one thousand and one rotors cutting holes in the very air, revealing a reality of nothing beyond. Sheila looked at the city below, its streets, its houses, its many rooms. She had seen it many times from the air, walked endlessly through the streets, visited its rooms. She could no longer tell if she had ever truly looked at it before.

Emerson lived in Chelsea, an old distinctive area, one still relatively untouched by the various upheavals of recent years. Many distinctive citizens lived in Chelsea. Which, undoubtedly served to explain the almost hysterical presence of London's finest this night. A considerable part already looked like a war zone, growing worse by the minute. Forces from the army and police had surrounded a cluster of blocks with a circle of tanks and armament. Explosions rocked the ground, shaking the chopper as they landed, followed by an eerie silence as they crossed the street. The flashes of the explosions still blinded them, like echoes thrown back and forth between mountains.

A hastily assembled command center covered an entire street a few blocks away from the real action. Presumably a safe distance away, but Sheila still saw blood on the ground. Everybody was sweating, sweating profusely. She recognized two other Superintendents by a switchboard up ahead.

– BE REASONABLE, she heard, – WE HAVE PULLED BACK FOR THE MOMENT SO WE CAN DISCUSS THIS RATIONALLY. PLEASE THROW AWAY YOUR WEAPONS AND GIVE YOURSELF UP.

– NO WAY. Another hysterical voice, not belonging to Emerson. – THERE IS NO WAY WE WILL ALLOW ANYONE TO COME CLOSE. WE WILL MAKE SWISS CHEESE OF ANYONE ATTEMPTING TO CROSS THE LINE.

Where the line was wasn't instantly evident, even though the heap of bodies in the broad circle around the extended Emerson estate gave a pretty decent indication.

– They're frightened beyond their wits, a voice croaked. – They're actually scared to death.

No one argued with him. They just shook their head.

– How many are there inside? Superintendent Ashley asked a subordinate.

– Hundreds, sir. Possibly slightly above one thousand.

Ashley shook his head. His eyes were glazed. He showed clear signs of shock.

– What a mess. He shook his head. – What an awful mess.

Resolve, and the first signs of anger, swiftly increasing anger showed in the narrow chinks of eyes.

He grabbed a microphone.

– THIS IS YOUR LAST CHANGE. GIVE YOURSELF UP NOW, OR WE WILL USE EVERY MEANS AT OUR DISPOSAL TO RESOLVE THE SITUATION.

– GO FUCK YOURSELF, HAROLD, was the only, gleeful reply.
Then, once more and briefly, silence reigned.
The tanks were brought forward. The shooting started virtually instantly, without any discernible transition. The target was bombarded from all sides. The remaining buildings within the not so distinct circle were blown to bits. Then the charge began in earnest. There were still defenders left, as incredible as it seemed. They fired and fired and fired, until they, themselves were shot dead. Video cameras recorded everything. There weren't that many left of the recording-devices after all the shooting, but more than enough to give everybody behind the line a graphic impression of what happened.
– They gotta be Muslims, Ashley mumbled between two heavy salvos. – Yeah, that gotta be it. They've all converted the last twenty-four hours and decided to become martyrs, to get their fill of virgins in heaven.
It was a massacre, and when it was over, when the death-dance ended the bodies laid in heaps, bricks, blood and flesh mixed into something unrecognizable. People still alive were shot, were filled with bullets. Sheila Watts stared at the monitors, stared at the insanity. Smoke cleared, fog drifted. The red haze slowly returned to the sunder-shot bricks and mortar, creating a layer of red dust on the ground. The last, few shots were fired. Their echoes faded slowly, so very slowly. The sound hurt. It shattered bones and rattled flesh. Superintendent Ashley stared at the monitors for a long time, until finally crouching in his chair, vomiting over himself and all over the provisional office. The sour stink of vomit mixed with the sweet one of blood.
– Superintendent... There was a voice coming through the speakers, hoarse and full of anguish.
– Yes? Ashley replied, so hoarse that his voice was hardly more than a whisper.
– It's Superintendent Emerson, sir. He's still alive.
– How can he be? Ashley shook his head, almost enraged.
– He's inside a bomb shelter, sir. We can see him on the monitors. The shelter is virtually unscathed, sir. Superintendent Emerson is grinning, sir. Grinning widely. He's laughing. The speakers are still working, sir.
– Of course, they're WORKING, you idiot, Ashley shouted into his microphone. – It's good and well-proven old British technology. It can take a direct hit from whatever bomb is sent at it.
He relented a bit then, looking embarrassed around him.
– Come, Watts told her three followers, and they did.
She grabbed a remote hands-free set, and they were on their way. They

walked to the center of the storm, through a landscape even weirder than what they had been used to the last couple of days. There were ruins. Sometimes there were remains of a ceiling above, sometimes not. She was able to see Emerson on her cell phone display, inside the bomb shelter. Its interior looked more like an office than any shelter she had ever seen.

– Please come out, sir, one of policemen implored Emerson.

– You come out from there this second Lloyd, Ashley shrieked, – or we will be forced TO GO IN. AND YOU WON'T LIKE THAT. OF THAT I CAN ASSURE YOU.

– You won't come in, Emerson shrieked, just as loud. – I have a *bomb* here, do you understand? You'll be SORRY!

He virtually jumped up and down in his excitement in there. The surveillance equipment showed him from all sides. His sweaty front. His completely soaked back. His once white shirt was colored gray and black, and variations of pale colors. The face was clearly visible even in the occasional shadow in the room. They were able to see every corner, every piece of floor, walls and ceiling. Emerson was alone.

– Don't come NEAR me, DON'T COME CLOSER, and stop W-WATCHING ME.

He evidently knew every single camera's position. He pulled forth a gun and during the short span of a few well-directed shots he had vanquished them all.

– And to think he was a paragon of calm, just yesterday. Williams giggled, more than a bit hysterical herself.

It was too much, all of this. It was all too much.

– It's an… it's an atomic bomb, s-sir, they heard an aide whisper to Ashley.

They kept moving on, kept moving frozen limbs.

Another command center materialized closer to the smaller, the nail point center stage. Equipment moved with men or men moved with the equipment, closing in on the absolutely desperate man at the center of tonight's activity.

The four shadows reached the shelter. It was clearly visible in the ruins, exposed by the bombing, but as good as unscathed. Ugly and huge as most houses. There was one door, resembling one leading into a bank vault.

– This is the only door, the sergeant in charge said to no one in particular. – As far as we know. We have the building plans right here.

Sheila looked at the papers. As stated, they revealed one single door, into a labyrinth of passageways and hideouts, a very intricate setup.

– Be reasonable, Lloyd, the chief negotiator opened up the conversation. – Let's calmly discuss your grievances, whatever they are.

– My… grievances? Emerson let out a bark of a sentence, accompanied by an absolutely hysterical laughter.

The chief negotiator, a seasoned veteran immediately shook his head.

– He has completely, utterly gone fishing.

– YOU'RE WRONG, Emerson yelled. – NO FISH IN HERE, NO, SIR.

The chief negotiator turned off the microphones, directing his attention towards Ashley.

– My recommendation is delaying tactics, sir. As it stands, we have no other options. This is a highly volatile situation. He may trigger the bomb just for the heck of it or he may do so because of heightened stress. We must get him to calm down. It's imperative that we calm him down. We're looking at a long, exhausting *battle* here, sir.

Ashley nodded, and nodded again.

– Do so. Let's gut that son of a bitch like a pig.

Ashley sounded and looked very similar to a cliché of an urban gang leader black man just then.

The chief negotiator prepared himself, rubbing his knuckles against each other, stretching his muscles. Sheila and bunch could hear his bones move.

– Okay, Lloyd, he said. – Why don't we have a relaxed, civil conversation?

There was a long break. Everybody looked at each other, ready to shake their head.

– Okay, Axel, why don't we? There was a voice, silent as the grave.

Sheila suddenly stood rigid on her spot.

– I must get inside! She spoke fast and furry to the Sergeant. – Is there no way to get inside?

He shook his head.

– Not unless you know a secret entrance or something.

She immediately got to it. The other three, too. They started pushing and prodding. She sensed the cold metal against her skin, hot and acid-like, burning her fingers.

It was no use.

– What about the sewers? She asked close to the Sergeant.

– They're bombed to smithereens, he said to the air.

Watts walked back and forth in frustration.

– Please, let us in, Lloyd, the chief negotiator uttered, in what was more desperation than any real hope of accomplishing anything.

There was a long break of silence, where no one moved.
– Enter then, of your own free will…
A click, and the door slid open, from ajar to fully revealing the black hole inside.
Everybody looked incredulously at each other.
The four moved in, with drawn guns. Everybody else remained on the outside. Nobody followed them. They entered a world of passageways and elaborate labyrinths.
– Emerson was really paranoid, Watts mumbled.
– Raving paranoid is more like it, Colton snorted.
She noticed how the other three, even though they kept moving forward froze in their tracks, and she also knew why.
The floor was wet. Probably from leaking pipes somewhere. It would be amazing if the shelter hadn't taken some damage.
It could just as well be from the city's generally higher water level, of course. She didn't bother to check whether or not the water was salt. And neither did her brood.
They moved like a unit, through tunnels, from corner to corner. A kind of translucent light brightened their path. Put there to benefit the surveillance, no doubt. Everything was quiet. Someone stepped in a pool occasionally, inevitably and made a splash. Otherwise, the place was eerie and silent. Watts half expected the entire London police force to join them inside, but they didn't. They were on their own.
There was no obvious change, nothing telling them that this was it, but they found themselves in front of a door. It was slightly ajar. Watts signed to her, and Williams pushed it fully open. They entered the room two and two, in fast and deadly moves, ready for anything.
They saw mist, floating in several layers, levels of air. There was light coming from somewhere, even though they couldn't say from where. They saw a massive office desk at the center of the room. A body sat in the chair. On one side of the table was placed the bomb, a small, innocent-looking sphere, so far developed from its first, primitive forefathers and mothers, connected to a laptop. Sheila instantly noticed the setup had been made inert. One of the wires had been disconnected. On the screen blinked two words:

NOT VIABLE

As they watched those words changed, metamorphosed… into one.

EVERYONE

On the other side of the table, in a continuance of the very deliberate setup someone had placed Lloyd Emerson's head. It had been torn from its socket and threads of skin on the desk easily matched those missing on the body in the chair. The head's eyes were open and stared at everybody coming through the door.

– No blood, Colton noticed, cold as ice. – No blood anywhere.

Sheila found the two punctuation marks on the neck without truly looking. She moved constantly with her weapons raised in front of her, turning and twisting towards whatever might charge. There was no one else in the room. Nothing else. No lockers, almost no furniture, except the desk and the chair, and some other, virtually transparent stuff. It was… empty. She stared at the doorway, the only way out of here, the only way in. Nothing left, nothing approached. She slowly lowered her arms, her muscles staying tight as drums.

– Not much hide and seek material in here, Shaw whistled.

– So short a time, she mumbled, – and he has made mincemeat out of everyone.

She led them back out. She didn't really think it would be any trouble, but still she stayed on guard. After a while, retracing their own steps they emerged through the opening they had entered such a short while ago. They emerged. Tons of soldiers and police stormed in.

The four just kept walking. They walked through the inner ring and approached the command center. People met them outside the tent.

– What happened tonight, Inspector? Superintendent Ashley attempted to return some authority to his voice.

– I haven't the foggiest idea, Superintendent, Inspector Watts replied.

– He seems to have… suddenly skipped several levels of *grievances,* obviously on his way to the very top. Shaw's voice had an unbelievably light quality.

– Impatient bastard, isn't he? Williams giggled. She giggled all the time these days.

They walked past everybody, without bothering to stop for a second.

Things kept moving fast. Nobody could claim that the city's fathers and mothers didn't know how to act when it was merited. They came to her. She played pool with Cotton, Shaw and Williams in the special relaxation quarters at the Yard. Parker led them. She also recognized most of the others.

– We want you to be *the* new Superintendent he stated. – Everybody knows you're the only one even close to ending this.

– I accept. She smiled infinitely sweet to him.

She cocked her brow, once more asking herself how many nights had passed since that special night she had stepped out of Camden Town

Station, and started on her new path.

She didn't remember.

– I would like to be alone, now. She ordered them out with a wave of her voice.

And they all left, all the most powerful men and women in the city.

She entered what had been Emerson office, which now belonged to her. Cotton, Shaw and Williams entered it with her, but she was alone.

– We're gonna remake this town, she told them. – We're gonna turn it downside up.

Superintendent Watts pushed a button on her desk, summoning her subordinates, those who had been above her such a short time ago, who now were below her. They filed towards her, past her, hating her, fearing her, offering their dishonest congratulations.

– I want you to call in all the reserves, she ordered them. – Absolutely all of them, do you understand. Keep up our presence on our streets, but establish a revolving system where everybody is brought to the station for evaluation.

Silence greeted her words. They wanted to speak. They wanted it so badly that saliva dried in their mouth and their limbs froze from lack of gel. Her words were one thing. Their true meaning something vastly different.

– What evaluation? One finally worked up enough courage to speak.

– Untraditional, she enlightened him, them. – Untraditional and harsh. Very harsh.

They backed away from her, unable to look into the ice-cold eyes.

She studied them all, as they arrived, as they looked nervously to all sides, as everything organized itself during just a few, short hours. So easy, so very easy.

They were placed in small rooms, usually used as interrogation rooms, ten and ten together. She watched them all on monitors, studied them all as they stood straight, as if they were soldiers. They shook visibly when the key was turned in the lock. The interrogation rooms were cleaned fairly often. But remains of blood and skin remained, and the locked-in men and women glanced nervously at it, at each other.

– Look forward, Watts ordered them over the intercom.

They obeyed instantly, the mild, relaxed voice freezing them more effectively than any scream.

– You're such obedient, attentive little children. I love you all…

The rooms were humid and hot, even more so, she suspected, than the city outside. She showered once again, having long since lost count over how many times she had done that the last month. The humidity and the rapid perspiration would make her hair greasy in a matter of hours. And that was in what could be described as currently ideal circumstances. She looked at the men and women standing straight inside the greenhouse that was the holding cells. They stood still, looking straight forward. Sweat poured from their skin. They got it in their eyes, and it stung. They blinked to keep it from their eyes, but that only made it hurt more. Eventually they stopped sweating. A man ran to the door, and started hammering at it.

– WATER, he shouted. – GIVE ME WATER.

There was no response. He almost collapsed there, in front of the door, but finally he nodded, getting the point, making his way back the few steps to the center of the cell, to his designated place in the line.

Ten people stood straight in a cell, without moving, under the ruthless scrutiny of the lamp above. It burned their skin, burned their eyes. Their arms hung. Unable to lift them, unable to move a finger, unable to even blink, they just stood there, frozen, like statues, and wax poured from their pale skin.

A man had to take one step to the side, suddenly losing his footing. In the helpless, useless attempt to regain his balance he finally fell, fell like a felled tree to the floor. Unable to move his arms to protect himself, he just went straight down, the head hitting the floor with a dump sound. The others imagined they heard his ribs break, too, but they couldn't be sure, could no longer be certain of anything.

The cell door opened. Uniformed cops, colleagues entered the room, fetched the living dead thing on the floor. And then they were nine.

Watts sat behind her desk, enjoying her meal, studying the huge monitor screen in front of her. The office was cool, air-conditioned, pleasant. She exhaled with a satisfied sigh. The three waited for her just outside the door, sat there, on wooden chairs, desperately attempting rest, their appearance considerably more haggard. They rose as one, without her having to signal them. They easily fell in behind her, like they were born to it.

Now, everybody noticed the quartet, as they made their return to the basement. People either stared blindly in front of them, or averted their gaze. The four opened the first cell door and walked inside.

– Good morning, officers of the court, she greeted them.

– GOOD MORNING, MADAM! they replied.

– That will do, that will do… She nodded pleased.

She walked to the first in line, a woman.

– Who are you? Superintendent Watts asked her.
– Adams, Jennifer, number 328fng, Madam.
– That is the correct reply, Watts nodded. – At least I'm presuming it is.
Williams nodded, consulting the electronic screen in her hand
Watts slapped the woman on her cheek with her flat right hand. Jennifer Adams looked at her in horror. A mark started appearing on her inflamed skin. Watts slapped her again, still with her right hand, but on the other cheek and using her knuckle side this time. Adams' head was like thrown aside.
– Are you a good girl, Jennifer? Watts asked flatly.
– Y-yes, Miss Watts, the woman replied. She had trouble speaking, her mouth already swollen. – YES!
Watts started using her left hand. One more slap on each cheek. Adams' legs started shaking, but she managed to stay on her feet. Watts walked to number two in the line, a big bruiser of a man. She didn't say anything, just looked at him.
– Lockhart, Thomas, number 467wsd, MADAM.
Watts didn't wait for Williams' nod this time, but slapped him the moment he had completed the sentence. Right, left. Blood flowed from Lockhart's mouth.
– Are you a good boy, Thomas?
– I'm not a boy, he stated, with hard eyes.
She struck him in the abdomen. He gasped and went down on his knees.
– ARE YOU A GOOD BOY, THOMAS?
– Yes, Miss Watts, he gasped. – YES!
– On your feet, Thomas, the good boy, she ordered softly.
He fought himself up. His legs were shaking, but he did remain on his feet. He stared straight ahead, at a point on the wall. She grabbed him around the jaw, locked it in her grip.
– Look at me, she said softly.
After a short resistance he did. She released the jaw, giving him a dazzling smile.
– Kiss my hand, Thomas.
With doglike servility he obeyed.
– Good boy. She patted his cheek.
Her hand, turned wet by his tears fell slowly, until it once more rested on her hip. She walked further down the line, two fast steps to number four, giving him a singing and sudden slap. Number three just stood there, his eyes glazed, his legs shaking nervously. She returned to him when she had finished, sort of, with number four.

There was a female, number eight in line. She stood there, gritting her teeth, a determined look in her eyes.

– Antonia Logan, Madam. Number 728ksh, MADAM!

Sheila didn't look at Williams.

– That's wrong, she stated.

Antonia Logan looked astonished at her.

– Wrong? But…

– YOU DON'T SPEAK BACK TO ME, ROBERTA!

– But my name is not, Roberta, the girl said in tortured anguish.

– YOUR NAME IS ROBERTA, AND THAT'S ALL YOU ARE FOR NOW. I WILL TELL WHEN YOU ARE MORE, IS THAT CLEAR?

– No, the girl whispered, a tear dropping from her left eye. – NO!

Watts slapped her, slapped her hard. Tears flooded the girl's face, and she dropped to her knees. She screamed in her anguish, and collapsed there, totally out of it, shaking uncontrollably, her face rolling from side to side.

– Get her out, she said to no one in particular. – Get poor Roberta out of here.

The door opened, and two officers came and dragged the totally unresponsive woman away.

– That's just the way it is, Sheila shrugged. – Some people's grasp of reality is tenuous at best. When it's challenged everything just fall apart.

There was a shocked, beyond shocked expression in all the dull eyes before her.

She worked herself down the line, even though she took detours, and seemingly at random gave some her special attention. And when she had given all of them her attention once… she started all over again. Time began and ended, and began again. It dragged on, and each breath seemed to last forever. Sweat hissed as it hit the cold floor. Everything just slipped away for the people lined up before the acid touch that was Sheila Watts.

Number five stood there, sweating profusely in her presence.

– WHO ARE YOU? She shouted.

– Grant, Stephen, number 284ekd, MADAM, he replied weakly

– WHAT DO YOU WANT?

– To SERVE, to…

He took one step to the side, in order to keep his balance, but the right foot gave way under him, and he fell to the floor. He remained there, hardly conscious. His eyes flickered and swam, and he seemed unable to focus.

– Get this bag of shit out of here, she said to no one in particular.

The door opened, and the two officers reappeared and took «the bag of shit» away.

– He will never advance, she declared. – He will never do anything else than brushing other people's teeth.

She stopped before a woman, one who was now number five.

– Do you *understand,* Edith Fallon?

– YES, MADAM! Fallon declared, standing straight, with a feverish look in her eyes.

Watts slapped her once. She slapped her twice. Blood flowed freely from her mouth now. A mark just under her left eye had started swelling. A dull, foggy expression dominated her face.

The slaps were lighter now, but they hurt perhaps more, because of the swellings, and because every one of them more than anything hurt inside, hurt their imagined pride.

– You love my affectionate caresses, don't you? she said to no one in particular. – All of you?

– YES, MADAM!

She looked at them, stared them all down. Everybody looked away or down. They had lost count of how many signs of affection she had granted them. She had lost count. They all had the indistinct look in their eyes, as if they had not slept for days. Sheila knew that look well.

– You don't, Michael Crawford, number 242jas? she said softly, stopping in front of him. – You didn't reply?

– NO, MADAM, he replied, with eyes hard as glass.

– You don't love my affectionate caresses? She teased him, a honeyed voice cutting and molesting.

– NO, MADAM! Absolutely not, MADAM!

She slapped him again. The first time she did hit his face, but the second time, he parried her blow. She attempted to hit him in the chest, but he parried that, too.

Then she kicked his legs away from under him, and he fell hard on the floor. She kicked him in the ribs. He screamed and turned limp. Tears started to flow from his swollen eyes.

– You love me, don't you? She grinned to him.

– NO, he screamed, he *howled.* – DAMN YOU! How can you do this? How can you…

He started sobbing in boundless frustration and anger. She straightened slowly, stepping away from him.

– This is s NO way to treat a human being, n-no w-way at all.

He attempted to stop the tears from flowing, but they kept coming. He crouched there shaking, with his fists in curls. Watts smiled to him.

– Congratulations, she told him, – you've won the big price.
And she read understanding in his eyes, in all their eyes.
– The rest of you may leave, now. Her command cut them like a razorblade. – Report to your duty officer immediately.
They looked at the kneeling, sobbing man on the floor, both with pity and envy, unable to tell which was which.
She looked down on him, when all the rest had left.
– You will be the cannon fodder, she told him. – You will be first in line to die.
And she left him, there on the floor. She and the three in her company walked out and closed, locked the door behind them.
– You three take over the legwork in the next three cells, she said grinning, holding up her bloody hands. – It takes its toll, this, on vulnerable skin. We'll keep taking turns, of course.
They did. And the screams kept rising from the holding cells throughout the night. Sheila went to bed, eventually. She held up her hands. They were mildly disfigured, swollen. She curled them into fists, curled them hard. Pain riddled her frozen features. She kept curling the hands, as she stood before the mirror, as she went to bed, and far into sleep.
She showered the next morning, and had breakfast, accompanied by her honor guard. Williams was very pale, and had the most expressionless face Sheila had ever seen. The milky white skin seemed almost translucent. Eyes were like glass. There was no expression there, none at all. There was nothing there, nothing at all. She moved, she breathed, and reacted to commands, to directions, but aside from that Sheila doubted there was anybody home, anybody at all. The woman's hands were clearly swollen, but there was no pain in her face when she reached for the bread, the butter, the milk.
No pain at all.
– So, what's next on the agenda? Shaw grinned cheerfully at Superintendent Watts.
She stared at him, and there was fear in his eyes.
– Yesterday was merely the first step, she said in a relaxed manner. – The ordeal is just beginning for our young charges.
They were all thrown on the floor, at the hard concrete, at the center of a much bigger, badly lit room, a gathering of wretched men and women. Watts, with Shaw, Colton and Williams in tow waited for them there. Watts with a bottle of water and a glass in her hands. She filled the glass to the brim and bent down to the closest of her creatures, feeding it the water. He drank greedily, a beyond grateful look in his eyes. She filled the

glass and walked to the next in line. To everyone in line. No words were spoken.

– You're my Chosen, she finally said, – My weapons, my shadows. Welcome to my court.

– On your feet, Williams commanded them, snapped at them. – Ready yourself.

They stood there, frozen under her command, ready to do her bidding.

– Undress, Watts said. – I want you to be naked in my presence.

They obeyed. Obeyed without a notable hesitation. Her words registered instantly, undistorted in their mind. She walked among them, studying them with her icy stare, and they shivered in her presence.

– Humanity is at a crossroads, she told them. – What we do in the very near future will determine our course for generations ahead. Many say the hunters are dying off, but that's hearsay, and quite simply not true. The hunters are not dying off. They've only slept, slept through the long winter day. They're returning, now, with the coming of the new age. *We* are returning.

Even more lights were turned off, to the point of everyone being merely indistinct shapes, almost impossible to spot in the shimmering air.

– The enemy moves in the dark, the ghostly voice admonished them. – A creature without skin, bones, eyes and soul. To be anymore than a tasty snack to it you have to be shadows yourself… and even that isn't sufficient. You must be hunters. You must smell the dark, taste its blood in your gut, and be ready to become dark, become blood. These are the words of the hunter. Heed them well.

She attacked, from a shockingly different direction from where they thought her voice had been coming from. They turned, feeling like they moved under water. She knocked two down before the attack had even truly begun. And two more before the fifth managed to raise his guard. She decked him, and four or five more before she stopped.

– That was slow, she said matter of fact, no discernible animosity or scorn in her voice. – Do you think I moved fast now? I could have killed you all before you could blink. I would have, you know, if I didn't see a glimmer of hope in you, a glimpse of the potential hidden within.

They sat on the floor. They glanced at the chairs and table far away, but made no attempt to get to it. She fed them with pieces of meat, sandwiches and cheese, easily noticing the hurt in their eyes.

– To be treated as humans, you must *be* human, she replied in response to their silent accusation. – This is your world. This room. This is your cage. You hold the key to your locks in your hand. All you have to do is to turn that key, to be that key, and you will no longer be your own jailer, your own cage.

They saw weapons in the room, lots of them, but made no attempt to reach for them or even acknowledge their existence.

– That's right, Shaw told them. – You don't need weapons. You are weapons. You become what you think, what you *do*.

– The world has become so big, a female moaned, – so dark.

– That's right, Chloe. It has become big, become dark once more. And we can become human beings once more.

– What is your number, Chloe? Shaw asked her.

She looked at him in confusion.

– I don't remember.

There was a moment she looked fearful at Sheila, begging her with the wet eyes.

– That's good, Sheila said.

And a bright smile transformed Chloe's face.

All the lights went out. Suddenly all the lights went out.

All sound faded. Sheila felt it, felt its waves surrounding her. She formed the word «wait» with her lips, and knew that Colton, Shaw and Williams could see it, could hear her. There was a sound somewhere, of wind touching the floor, walls and ceiling, as it closed in on the four human beings at the center of the dank room.

«Wait», Sheila spoke. «Wait».

She was Shadow, now, and could feel the other, enormous Shadow approach. There was nothing her eyes could see, nothing her ears could hear, but something completely beyond eyes and ears, and perhaps even flesh.

But she didn't believe that.

She reached for the club-like prod she had stuck under her clothes, pulled it out with a mighty shout.

– NOW!

The four of them pulled the strings, and four glowing suns, illuminating everything, reducing all shadow to a minimum suddenly lit the room. She threw the true light flare at the floor, the moment Colton, Shaw and Williams did the same, drawing her shotgun the moment they drew theirs. To the others present, the naked recruits it was like everything happened in distorted time, neither slow nor fast. Sheila swept the room with burning eyes, eyes drowning in fluid. The light was so bright after all the darkness.

And then, for the first time she saw it. An indistinct figure, moving so fast that it was hardly visible, raced against them. Its tears of blood flowing because of the sudden, bright light, showing that it was vulnerable, that it was human. It had already reached the table and the chairs. The four of them fired as one. All shots hit the target. It was pushed back as if by a mighty sledgehammer. Blackened blood shot from its body and into the air like rays of shadow in the intense light. Turning into a pool by the time it hit the floor it spread as if being alive across the concrete. A scream, a… shriek totally beyond description filled the room, and paralyzed minds. She could see the man's face, a bundle of black hair covered most of it, but she could see it, through the fog in her eyes, like a puzzle, distorted, even with all the pieces in place. The blood boiled and died there on the floor, cut off from its life-giving body. The figure kept moving. They fired again, and again. They did hit him, they did miss him. Some of the hails hit the recruits. Shaw hit the beast straight in the chest, point blank. The beast grabbed him with its claws and drew him close. Sheila kept firing, while staring transfixed at it all. Shaw was hit, too. It was as if he, Shaw, too, was completely unaffected by the lead tearing his body to pieces. He had one stake in each hand. Sheila knew it was one of iron, one of wood. He pushed the two stakes into what stood snarling in front of him, holding him in his iron grip, pushed them deep into the chest, the heart. Shaw's face was as torn, as distorted as that of his enemy. Two bloody fangs appeared, long as knives, the way Sheila imagined it anyway, burying themselves in Shaw's neck. She saw it drink his blood, saw a terrible glow lit its eyes.

And then they were both gone. She caught a glimpse of a shadow exiting through one of the doors. No more than that.

The flares still flared. They would flare for a long time.

– GRAB WEAPONS, she shouted to the nude women and men in the room. – We'll chase it now, chase it when it's vulnerable.

She lit another flare. She ran, she gave chase, sensing Colton and Williams right behind her, and a crowd of breathing, scared and angry human beings behind them again.

They stopped. She stopped. Just on the spot where one way turned left, further inside the building, where one way turned right, further out of the building, the fortress of human oppression.

Tiberius Shaw hung upside down, on the tall wall, above the door. A rope, fastened on the wall somewhere had been tied around his feet. He had been gutted from groin to head. Bowels had been distributed unevenly throughout the floor. His face frozen in a mask of death and unbound fear and rage. There was no blood anywhere. Some remains on

blackened skin, that was all. Except for that… not a single drop…
Except for the message on the wall:

TEN OF THIRTEEN

It was written in haste, hardly the height of penmanship. Her face turned into a grinning snarl.

– You're getting sloppy, she shouted, – careless. We will get you.

She was sweating, and there was a look of profound insanity in her eyes. She didn't turn towards them, but kept staring at the body on the wall.

– Well, she said slowly, making a deliberate shrug, burying the pain deep inside, – this wasn't quite the demonstration I had in mind, but it will have to do, won't it?

CHAPTER FIFTEEN

Daybreak. Sheila stands there sweating, before the window, staring blindly at the light, wondering if it's reaching her, reaching her at all. The window is new, and swept clean of dust, of dirt. So, she ordered, so it is. Her entire office has been swept. Sheila Watts is weary. She can feel the crumbling of her bones, the disintegrating of her blood. She can smell the cleaning fluid in her itchy nose, hear her small army breathe behind her.

– I saw It drink his blood, a woman finally said frosty, a while later. – I saw it, and I will never forget it.

– Good, Watts told her, nodded, told them all. – You know, now, you all know much more of what the world is about.

Sheila sat in her chair, turned towards her soldiers. She shook her head, as if it rested there with its luring eyes between her knees.

– So close, she said. – I can almost touch it, touch something…

And the insane glee in her eyes was strangely comforting to the others assembled in the bright, shadowy room.

– There is but one, last recourse left to us, she said to the remaining two, standing there in front of them. – We must find its hiding place, find it during the day and drag it out in the sun, and hope that *that* will destroy it.

The three of them were in her office, as the day dawned outside, as the rays of fire burned them.

Sometimes the crowd of other, younger men and women were present, sometimes not. Reality kept shifting and turning, turning back and forth on itself.

Williams and Colton nodded. Colton had thrown up. Williams looked serene, like a doll.

– We will turn every stone, search every corner and cranny, demolish every building. And we must prepare… for another night, for two, three, four…

They left. They all left. She was alone. She fell down in the deep chair behind her. For a long while she sat with her arms on the table. Her hands were shaking, shaking badly. She imagined she was back in the closet in the old, derelict hospital, hiding in darkness, in plain view, and that the monster came for her. She hit the table once, twice, thrice… screaming in pain and rage. The last time felt like her hand had been severed from the arm.

She waited. No one entered the room, disturbing her, daring to disturb her.

She rose, holding out her swollen hand. It was steady. Calm like water. The surface was calm. Inside she was a raging storm. In the mirror she could see it. Images flashed before her eyes, of last night repeating itself endlessly. She joined the patrols in the streets, all the uniformed men and women of London Town, joined them as they filled the streets, filled every house, every cellar, every attic, every dark room. She joined them as they ventured into the sewers. Everything down there had surely drowned ages ago. They kept sticking sticks in shallow water.

There was an ancient, derelict building they walked through, reminding her of Sheba's lair. Except it couldn't be. It was just ruins, remains of what had been.

There were sounds in the shadows, sending shivers down her spine. But nothing more. Nothing… *conclusive*.

– I can FEEL the Hunger in my gut, taste the blood in my mouth, she cried. – You're not the only one.

The hours passed, the few hours of daylight, of twilight, and then darkness once more swept the land, as knives flaying the skin.

The chopper was huge, even by normal Metropolitan police standards. It had eight millimeter machine guns and rockets on each side. A bird of prey. One of the few remaining in the world.

– Inside, quickly, she barked, – we're already running late.

They all cast nervous glances behind and to the sides, as they loaded gear and themselves into the chopper.

Well inside, she scrutinized them all, even the two pilots, before closing the door with a bang.

– Take us up, she shouted.

The pilot had already started the engines. Once the door was sealed the noise faded to hardly more than a soft background growl. This had been the very latest in technology some years back, and the cabin was virtually soundproof. Even the metal's vibrations were reduced to a soft hum. So, everybody heard the Superintendent's shout very well.

– Take us up, she said, softly, now, – take us as far up as possible, and stay there. Keep looking for… hostiles. Any craft… or anything attempting to approach, blow them out of the sky.

No one added anything to that. There was no need.

The copilot and Watts both studied the ground and air through the windows, through the monitors, and the most sophisticated tracking equipment ever devised, as the bird of prey rose from the roof of the New Scotland Yard building and into the night's poison mist. London vanished from visible sight almost instantly. Just the illuminated dirty soup remained.

– If you spot a heat signature moving fast down there…

– Yes? The copilot swallowed hard.

– Fire at will, the Superintendent said. – Use every possible arsenal at your disposal. Those are your orders.

The human-made machine continued its flight across the nightmare of the London night. She saw it, through the monitor she carried on her arm. It was like it was much bigger, a screen making her believe she was the one flying out there, through the mist, through the light and the shadow.

It was hard to sleep. All lights were turned off, and silence descended on the assembly. They were tired, to the point of exhaustion. They were too tired to sleep. Sheila could hardly close her eyes. The lids were frozen in place, and she caught herself wondering if she would be able to sleep with her eyes open.

There was sound, though not very loud. The low background noise that no insulation could ever stop invaded them. There was movement, constantly, as if on a train, and occasionally the train encountered an abrupt turn.

She just drifted away. She knew this, because she was the last being awake.

A man screamed, screamed his lungs out.

– It's HERE! He shouted, waving his gun around, pointing it everywhere, with eyes hard as glass.

– Everybody sits still, Watts ordered. – Nobody moves a muscle without me saying so.

Sleepy, weary eyes looked around, looked at him. He looked around. He saw nothing, no movement.

– I SAW IT, he whispered aloud, gasping for breath. – I saw the glowing mist penetrate the hull.

– It was just a dream, Watts said. – Nothing but a dream.

But her words sounded empty, even to herself. And as everybody lay down once more and relaxed somehow, they suddenly found themselves with an irresistible urge to look behind them. And below, above, and everywhere. The strange, muted light in the chopper became a threat, not a valve on strained nerves.

– What *was* that, l-last night? One of the newly recruited ghosts asked with his lips blue of cold. – What did we s-see?

– A wild beast, she replied, she shivered. – One feeling neither pain nor remorse, one born to hunt and kill. Resilient to the point of invulnerability it stalks the night, feeding on blood and fear. Power without guilt.

Her words resonated within them, turning and probing and growing, and it pleased her.

– Sleep now. We will stalk it tomorrow. Tomorrow, we will become the hunters, and it our prey. Sleep.

And there was no more sleeping that night, not even a slumber. They awoke to the early morning light. It flickered on, on the screen on her arm. Awoke dog-tired and with an exhaustion that just wouldn't leave them.

– Here. She handed each of them one pill. – Swallow it. Collect spittle in your mouth and swallow.

– What is it? One of the recruits asked.

– Industrially produced amphetamine, she shrugged. – Among the best stuff ever seized by the narcotics division.

The use of illegal substances had exploded in the twenty-first century, in all social layers. The police and the army had never been able to stop it, only somewhat control its flow. Now, the last vestige of control had flown out the window.

She swallowed. Most of the others did, too.

– My mouth is d-dry, a woman stuttered.

– Lick your palate, Watts admonished.

There was obedience and soon an intense expression of relief in the woman's face.

Sheila sensed it fairly soon, the gooseflesh running up and down the arm, the sense of extreme awareness creeping into her.

– This will keep us going for quite a while, she said. – Be aware of the extreme mood swings when it stops working, though. We can do it two, maybe three turns before we must stop.

The day brought not release. But an unending series of dark alleys and houses. They walked up dark stairs, down into misty cellars.

The sun rose. It didn't rise in the sky, but in the soup of clouds and dust, which went for the sky these days. There were probably not that many clouds, because the sun was clearly visible most of the time through the thick layer of poison blanketing the city. It cast no more than pale, almost invisible shadows.

– It's getting worse, Sheila heard someone mumble. – I swear it's getting worse. This isn't even air anymore, but pure smoke, impossible to breathe.

She heard the familiar choir of coughing, from the frightened crowds forced to leave their homes and offices in the middle of the day, without their protection, naked and vulnerable in their thin clothes. Some of them hadn't been out in the sun for years, and tears ran down their cheeks.

But none of them suffered any truly adverse side effects. Nothing dramatic but the fear and terror.

– The sun's deadly rays won't kill you, she enlightened them. – Not this fast. The sun's deadly rays don't even officially exist. And let's not forget: This is a national security issue.

They didn't exactly appreciate her wit. She didn't care, but grinned wolfishly to them, and they pulled back, timid and terrified.

The group walked through the darkest of hallways. There was light there, but nothing direct, nothing even resembling sunlight. Sheila could feel the drug inside her, enhancing any emotion, any random thought. She observed all the moving eyes, and it made her own nerves even shittier.

A guy fired his machinegun, an expression of absolute terror vivid in his face. She held up her hand. No one else fired. There was a scream, the sound of someone hitting the floor. They all moved at the target, in a prearranged pattern, drilled during hours and hours of intense teaching, both in the academy and later.

There was a body, unmoving and silent behind the wall. She pushed it around with her foot. It was a lurker, a homeless, clothed in shreds. There was hardly any blood, as if it had just shriveled inside of him a long time ago. His face was drawn and old. He had been alive, sort of, a few seconds ago, but looked more like a zombie than anything living.

– False alarm, she shrugged.

Strangely enough, as she had kind of expected and hoped for, the sound of her voice calmed them all down a bit, a little bit.

They sat down inside one of the dark hallways, relaxing, not relaxing.

– I can't close my eyes, one said. She couldn't tell if it was male or female. – I'm tired as dogshit, but I can't close my eyes.

– As stated, she told them. – The drug is a drug. It isn't a miracle cure for fatigue. It puts it off for a while, a little while.

It wasn't a mind-altering substance, she knew that, but she still imagined she imagined the walls move, and steps loud as thunder moving in on them.

They fed. They ate, fed like beasts, there by the stairs.

This building might have been like a modern castle just ten, fifteen years ago. Now it was just a ruin. There was a hole in the ceiling somewhere, because there was a kind of twilight upstairs somewhere, but when they went up continuing their search, it was nowhere to be found.

Everybody stared at the dark. It followed them wherever they went.

The sun set in the western sky. Air darkened all around her. The last dirty bright clouds faded from view, and only the city's artificial light remained.

They rushed to the helicopter, heart beating, cold water in their eyes, already late and in a hurry, hurry, hurry.

– It's true, a boy said aloud. – They can't hunt at day. That's one thing we have working for us… right… if it's true.

They stared at the chopper door, opening so very, very slowly, stared back at the hangar door, at the shadows created by the dying Sun.

She couldn't recall them actually entering the chopper. She sensed the closing of doors, the ascension into the dirty twilight, into preliminary safety.

As the drug stopped working some people started crying on the spot. Tears flowed, and there was no stopping them.

Goddess, she was tired. She closed her eyes, and suddenly, terrifyingly she was unable to reopen them. There was sleep. She was certain of it. But even so she could see the room, all its details, hear all its sounds, sense the sweat and moves from the people around her.

A hunter never sleeps, she thought. She said it aloud, but no one heard.

– We should get away from here, Williams said abruptly. – Either leave for good or give ourselves time to recuperate and plan our next move.

Watts nodded weary.

– You're right, of course. A retreat is the only sane options. Let this city drown, drown in flames and water.

She saw the relief, the shame in everybody's eyes.

The chopper tilted slightly. It was turning. She was certain of it. Attuned as she was to them all, she saw worry in the others' eyes.

She heard the voice from the cockpit, the hellpit. The others did, too.

– «Four little Indians walked on a road...

One Indian got bit by a snake in the leg,

and then there were only three Indians left».

– It isn't him, she said instantly. – It is him.

She calmed them all, calmed their raging waters. They stared at the cockpit door in fear and rattling nerves. She didn't, but walked to it in a calm, detached manner, her gun drawn. She opened the heavy door, as if it was nothing. She immediately recognized the pilot, that it was indeed the pilot. She spotted the copilot, dead as a duck on the floor.

– ONE LITTLE SNAKE GOT HIS HEAD SQUASHED UNDER A HEEL, she countered. – AND THEN THERE WAS NO SNAKE ANYMORE.

There was a hiss, surrounding them like air, just as if it was the night itself hissing. Sheila shivered. She knew no one else inside the chopper could see it or sense it.

– So, you're running away? The pilot turned and smiled, moving his lips and nothing more. – What a disappointment.

The pilot wasn't there anymore. *He* was.

– I've turned this bird around, he said teasingly. – What are you going to do? He's the only one who can fly this technological wonder.

She raised the gun in a fast, fluid movement and shot him, shot the pilot in the head. He fell to the floor, dead as nails. The chopper rocked and tilted to the side. There was a loud, deep, wailing bass sound from the engine. She grabbed a handle in the ceiling with one hand, the body with another, pulling it back. She jumped into the seat and struck a big red square starting to flash immediately:

AUTOPILOT

The bird stabilized. The wailing faded. Watts breathed out, breathed in, calming herself, slowly, painfully. She turned to Williams and Colton, approaching her from behind, staring at them. Their eyes were still their own.

– Take a good hard look at everybody. If they do anything funny, waste them. If I do anything funny waste me.

They nodded, and she imagined she saw a glimpse of actual compassion in their eyes.

She looked down at the dead nail.

– You felt that, FUCKER, didn't you? I *know* you did!

– Nothing funny yet. She heard humor in Williams' voice.

And that was Williams. Watts had learned to recognize the nuances and inflections in the beast's voice, no matter what voice he had.

Watts and Colton stared at each other, clenching their guns, nodding slowly.

– Either he can only take the unaware or he has chosen not to take us. Watts spoke in a highly accentuated, enraged voice. – I don't give a fuck. We're «safe» for the moment.

Things calmed down. Things calmed down again. Raw nerves relaxed somewhat, never off the edge. There was the sound of crying from a few in the back. Desperate, horrible sobs.

Concentrating on the indecipherable instrument panel in front of her she had a glimpse of understanding, a glimmer of hope. She was sweating, her hands shaking, but she managed to go through the motions, do what was necessary.

– We're on a preprogrammed course back to base. That isn't an option, right?

– No, Colton replied.

– Okay, she nodded, staring at him. – Then I'm going to disengage the autopilot and *land* this thing.

He nodded. Both smiled, smiles completely without warmth, a detached, ironic humor.

– NONE OF YOU GUYS BACK THERE HAVE ANY FLIGHT TRAINING, RIGHT?

There were no takers.

She grabbed the stick, breathing in and breathing out a few times… and then she hit the button.

Concentrating, sweating already she held the stick steady. The chopper continued at its course. She looked at the map on the instrument panel.

– We're still in the north, she mumbled.

The little turn of the head was enough to tilt the stick the necessary millimeters. The chopper started turning, seemingly by itself. She attempted to get control back by twisting it the opposite way, and she obviously twisted it too far, overcompensated.

– We're going down, she said relaxed and in a very matter of fact manner.

She pushed the stick slightly forward. The buildings down there turned clearly visible on the monitor, the foggy windows. She spotted a broad street. Her hand seemed to move on its own volition. The chopper turned… and tilted violently. She was almost thrown out of the seat. Colton hit the wall hard. She strapped herself in. It took three try-outs, but finally the belt pushed comfortably, uncomfortably against her body. She recognized the street instantly… Camden High Street. She giggled. What an irony. She had come home.

There was a high-pitched sound as she finally and utterly lost control over the machine. She realized a bit detached that they were between buildings. They hit the ground hard. Metal grinded, flesh broke. She felt pain somewhere, didn't know where.

Broken glass, metal shards everywhere. She looked at herself in a window mirror, one still miraculously whole. There was blood in her face. A piece of metal buried in her arm. She moved, made the first attempt to rise from the seat. The pain instantly doubled. There was smoke, but not much. That brought little comfort. She knew everything could blow any minute. She rose, crying out enraged. Colton crouched on the floor. He moved. She left the cockpit, walking through the back to the exit. There was death here, blind eyes staring at nothing. People moved and moaned, alive. She pushed the button that was supposed to open the door. It slid open effortlessly, with just minor sounds of sand in the machinery. The chopper had tilted about 45 degrees. It wasn't far down to the ground. She jumped. She landed. Dust whirled in the air. There was no additional pain.

Dust and dirt floated in the air. The street she stumbled through was silent. No lights were lit behind the heavy curtains. There were no signs of life anywhere. The stink of ashes still hung heavily in the air there, as she walked down Camden High Street, the ruins of The Green Rose a black, repugnant emptiness in the night. Electricity was gone again. Only the lights of the city reflected in the dust above «brightened» the streets. It started raining. She hardly noticed the drops hitting her.

– EVAN SHELBY, she shouted. – EVAN SHELBY THE THIRD OR THE FIRST. COME OUT AND PLAY, WHEREVER YOU ARE.

There was nothing, not even an echo, just the emptiness of a dead, desolate place. Not even the transparent ghosts usually traversing these places. No cars. Nothing moved. There was a christmas tree on display in a window, but there were no lights.

She passed Inverness Street Market. There was nothing, except shadows. She looked around, constantly moved her eyes, her head. Nothing or no one moved. She could no longer see the chopper. There was still smoke rising from it, mixing with the poisonous air. Across the street from the Inverness Market there were more tents. Most were torn, with big holes. The tables had been crushed by their own weight. Not even dust moved here. The rain made everything quiet and still.

There were sounds somewhere, lights somewhere, in this street dead and still. She walked further down the street, looking in every window, every broken window, derelict room. Signs with half faded writing remained above various doors. There had been shops here once, a somewhat thriving community, but now all that was gone. She stared through a broken window, through shards of glass and dust, and she spotted a shadow of a light. A glimpse of fangs, of a snarl, a face. Head turned, and turned again, turned back, turned back again. The door was ajar. She pushed it fully open and walked inside, walked right through the outer room, to the room within. Lights were sparse here, in the room within the room, only a few candles burning darkly. There were four creatures sitting by a table, two women, two men. They moved, and suddenly they were on their feet, facing her, smiling to her, their fangs very visible. She held her hands well away from her body, deliberately displaying a passive mode, like a prey before the predator, standing her ground, meeting the glaring eyes. The room was fairly large, but she knew they could cover the distance between them and her before she could blink a second time. But she knew she could draw her gun even faster than that.

– I have a gun, she said. – Please believe me when I say it could easily kill even you.

One of the women stared at her, the cold glow in her eyes a mesmerizing quality threatening to drown Sheila in its wave. She shook her head, clearing her head, making a deliberate telltale sign, a move towards the inside of her coat. The glow faded.

– You're disturbing our peace, the woman said. – Tell us why we shouldn't tear your limbs from your body.

– I'm not here for you, she said calmly, with just the slightest quiver in her voice. – I'm here for James Evan Shelby the first, the first and only.

– We heard you the first time, the other woman said, flashing her fangs. – Are you sure it's him you're after?

– Yes, Sheila said, shivering. – I'm sure.

– He isn't here. Leave now. You're his. He will deal with you.

– You're afraid of him, she grinned, couldn't help herself, easily seeing the anger in their glow.

She pulled back, attempting to look in every direction simultaneously. When she looked back the four were gone. She returned to the street, to the wet drizzle from the gray city ceiling.

He waited for her outside. Trees and their branches whispered behind the sidewalk fences. There was no wind.

Dark alleys cut her as she passed them, dark and foreboding.

She saw him, an unmoving shadow in the rain, between the alleys and the gray, the broken streetlights. She froze, pulling a weapon, fast as lightning from its confines.

– This is a special gun, she cried. – It shoots pellets filled with a highly combustible agent, designed to explode upon impact. It will penetrate the skin, and blow you up from within. Can even you guys survive that?

There was no reply. She couldn't even be completely certain he was aware of her presence, or if he cared. She lowered her weapon, walking towards him, walking to him.

– I knew you would come, she said.

He had been there all the time. The itch in her back, the tear in her eye.

– You have done well, he cried, – You have roused every night stalker for miles and miles.

His voice was not a voice. Just vibrations in the air and the rain. His lips didn't move. She could see them clearly, see the red, smell the rust.

– Is that what you're calling yourselves?

– No, not really. He shrugged. – I just made it up on the spot.

The shadow reached her, she didn't know from where, illuminating the dark night.

– Your training of them won't help, he told her. – The only reason your methods were any use, any at all was because those you killed were new, nebulous, vulnerable.

– I knew that. I just wanted to leave something behind, something alive.

– You have, he told her, suddenly, unexpectedly. – You have shown them how to face true adversity, how to fight faced with the impossible. They know, now, what they will never forget.

– I am a pawn, she said. – I was a pawn.

– It's true. True power can never be given, only taken.

And then he moved. His lips moved, and his soft voice was like thunder in her ears.

– Come with me, the voice whispered. – It is time.

She shivered, sudden and total, all over her body, within her Core.

– I could make you come, he said, – but I won't do that.

He didn't say the final words. He didn't have to.

She looked back, one final time, far up the street, the many yesterdays away, where she had left the others, leaving them forever.

They walked through the gloomy rain. She followed him inside somewhere, through a door opening by itself, and it was still raining. Everything around her dissolved, except the sight of him in front of her. Everything dissolved and recreated itself. They walked through a long, dark hall. She realized that it was, that it wasn't the same place the two of them had visited in the more central parts of town, the lair, the lair of...

But also a place where powerful men and women in town visited. Not the casual spot, where she had encountered the four, an eternity of minutes ago. There were whispers. A door opened. There was light, so bright. They walked through a crowd of people. Evan ignored them, but she couldn't. She saw one woman with fangs snarl at her, smiling enigmatically, not hiding herself at all. This place was different. Everything was more open. Or perhaps everything had opened up lately, as the roar of water could be heard everywhere. Sheila imagined she heard it, flowing, penetrating everyone and everything.

Lights were sparse here, only a few candles burning darkly. Flashes of shadow and fire. Sheila froze. She burned.

– Passion is a fire, he said.

And he did turn. And she did look up, into his bottomless well.

– Then let me burn, she replied.

And they walked.

Dissolution and recreation. She blinked and mist brought her elsewhere, totally into the wretched night.

The candles hardly burned, casting their soft light across the table, across the room.

One smaller room, an apartment of sorts, a table, two chairs and a bed, a large bed, covered in black satin. She shivered visibly.

– This is a sort of an emergency solution, he said.

– It isn't that bad. She smiled radiantly at him.

Her expression turned somber, desolate.

– All your beautiful things gone, she whimpered. – I'm so sorry.

– They were just things, he said.

He really looked like a night stalker just then, poised, in front of her, dressed in his dark clothes.

– Would you like to change? He offered. – Change into something more comfortable?

– Yes, she replied. – Yes, I would. Thank you.

– There's a room, an adjacent apartment over there. He nodded, and she spotted a dark, half opened door. – You may hear… sounds from down the hall, but don't worry, you won't be disturbed.

His flashing smile disturbed her. She stood before the mirror, in a bathroom of sorts. Old walls, old floor. She studied herself, the assault outfit, the protective gear, the guns, and technological equipment while she drew it from its confines, putting it away on the table before her. It turned out to be quite a mound. She smiled to the mirror image, exposing her canines, flashing a smile.

She loosened the tightly bound hair, letting it flow down her back and on the shoulders. Fingers, hands, arms undressed her in slow, deliberate movements. Eventually she stood before the mirror image, nude, revealing her battered, scarred body. The wounds on the head and arm had stopped bleeding. Distracted she realized that the metal piece was still buried in her skin, sticking out like a bone or a finger in the wrong place. She looked towards the shower. Over the back of a chair hung a dress, a dress black, velvet and beautiful. She showered. Water cascaded down her sore skin. She couldn't tell how long she remained there, in the moist, hot place. There was a memory of her turning off the water, but she didn't know whether or not it was real. She heard sounds, sucking sounds. Snarls in the night. She dried herself with a large, soft, rough towel. There was a first aid kit in the drawer, the first place she looked. She grabbed the metal piece, biting her lower lip… pulling it out. A minor sound escaped her, that was all. She cleaned that, and the head wound. There was some blood, but not as much as she had feared. She bandaged the wounds, without overdoing it. The headband looked like a headband, like an ornament. She grabbed the velvet dress from the chair and slipped it over her head. Even though she had lost weight recently… It fit perfectly.

He stood by the table, pulling out the chair the moment she entered the room. There was a bottle in his hand, of wine, of life's water. He still dressed in the same clothes, but now there was a difference, a qualitative… change. He looked even more like what he was.

– Berlinger 67… with a twist, he said. – I have saved it for a very special occasion.

Dark fire consuming the ebony candles flickered on the table. There were no plates, only two glasses. He opened the bottle and filled the glasses. Ruby fluid filled them to the brim.

– You look lovely, my dear. He bowed.

– Thank you, good sir. She curtseyed deep before him, as he took her hand, eloquently leading her to the chair.

She sat down. They both sat down. She observed him lift his glass, his ruby wine and drink.

– Here, have some.

She accepted the glass, tasted carefully its content. It was cold, frozen, like wine, but it was blood.

– I want this, she stated. – I want this more than anything.

And she drank. And she felt something then, an irritation as the spiced wine flowed down her throat.

– One last thing, he said.

– Yes…?

– No more sunsets, he said. – No more sandwiches. Even the shadows of the day will be deadly to you.

– I… understand, she said slowly, deliberately. – I'm ready, ready to pay the price. I can live with that. I can thrive.

– We must sate the Hunger, she told me, and she was right. We may hold it at bay for a while, but eventually we must give in. That's one difference between us and other humans. They may bury it deep within themselves, deny their most fundamental urges, but we can't.

– I don't want to.

– Neither will I. Not anymore. You taught me to free myself, and now I don't want to go back. I lived so long without emotion, without passion, but now it's back. I learned, relearned it from you. I threw away, wasted three generations. I didn't realize, until you showed me, that we don't stop being human, but are on the contrary becoming more a human being than we ever were.

– I'm glad, she said.

There was laughter from down the hallway, the hallways, shrieking and passionate vocalizations, and… they were both right.

– Humanity has, from its very beginning strived to live beyond good and evil, she stated slowly, deliberately. – It has usually gone down the tubes. We always end up choosing one alternative, always falling on one cliff of the Abyss. We lose every time.

– I think that's more than a correct observation.

He lifted his glass, in one, final salute.

– This isn't truly necessary, is it? She lifted her glass, lifted hers, too.

– It makes everything a bit more… pleasant.

– Thank you, she whispered.

There was a slight feeling of discomfort, and she moved on the chair. She opened and closed her mouth without a sound. An echo returning to her with a vengeance. She bit her lip again, tasting the blood.

– Black suites you, he grinned. – You look very lovely.

– Thank you, she whispered.

– You look ravishing.

She looked sharply at him.

– You killed Emerson, I know you did.

– What makes you say that? He flashed a smile, exposing his fangs, always there now, when he didn't hold himself back anymore.

– Because the *other* would never have bothered with cutting off the head.

– I disintegrated him. He shrugged. – I've never wanted anything more than I did in that very moment. I wanted his complete destruction. I wanted to make sure he never returned to life.

He looked at her, burying his daggers, his daggers of shadow deep within her.

– I started on the ground floor of his organization and worked my way up. I took everyone actively involved and slaughtered them all. I even took some passively actively involved. There's a big, black hole now where Lloyd Emerson and his works used to reside.

Ice, his voice was ice.

Shadows moved in the room, on its walls, its floor, its ceiling, its shifting air.

She rose. He did, too. She felt the cloth cling to her skin, noticed in meticulous detail how her thighs turned from moist to wet. He remained in place by his chair. She wanted to go to him, but couldn't move a limb. Her hand moved, grabbing the collarbone of the dress, pushing it aside, pushing it off her shoulder, totally exposing her neck, smiling slightly as she stayed in contact with his eyes.

– You can do with me what you want, My Lord…

She observed how he reached out a hand, how she felt the mesmerizing touch of his eyes. Everything turned in her. She gasped. He stood still. She knew he did. He filled her vision. And then it was too late, too late for regrets, too late for everything. She was nothing but a buzz, a tiny hum within herself, as she filled herself to the brim, as she floated into his embrace, whimpering at his first touch.

He kissed her. It hurt then and as she fiercely returned the kiss. She writhed close to him. Her nipples were free, hardening beyond words. He undressed, too. She felt his nipples against her skin, as hers pushed again his.

– I thought you would be cold, she whispered, – but you're not. You're warm, so warm…

She looked down, seeing his huge, erected cock. And as she watched, it grew even bigger. She cried out, involuntarily, with all her heart, as they embraced, as the fire burned them.

The floor moved, the house itself moved, she knew it did. They walked. She knew they did, even though she couldn't feel the floor under her feet. She sensed his hands on her body, his lips kissing her shoulder. There was still apprehension, as she imagined she felt the sharp pain of his fangs and it didn't come. Anticipation rode her. She wanted him. I want you. I want you. I want

She gasped, as she breathed, breathed the world.

He touched her weakness, touched her strength, and she shook in passion, in desire, as his claws touched her, as her claws raked his skin, his hard and soft skin.

She fell on the bed, still standing, gasping, her body shaking in throbs of savage passion.

They were in bed, fucking. The blade was hardening within her, above her, cutting deep, the blade of fire. She screamed in ecstasy, in fear, knowing fully well that this was merely the beginning, the threshold, the first step on the way up, the way down. The fire, minor as it was already, moved violently in her veins. He fucked her from behind, holding onto her hair, holding her body upright close to his own. In a distant, distant part of herself she noticed that her head wound had started bleeding again. His tongue moved over skin, drinking every last drop, perhaps advantageous, holding his raging need somewhat in check, delaying it, as his heart and hers beat harder and harder, closer and closer to be in complete tandem, harmony. His thrusts were wild, savage, but still he kept himself reined in. He had to. She sensed his rage, his passion, his raving, building need. He sensed her expectation, and it almost drove him mad.

She cried out. Carnal lust ravaged her, and she gasped, moving below him, like a wild animal coupling in the forest.

And then

And then…

She felt the glow, soft bodies turning rigid, saw his fangs grow further, as she turned her head violently from side to side, as words turned meaningless. Joy and pain mingled instantly, transforming into something else, something greater.

– I give you… he gasped. – I give you the gift of Life, one kiss before dying.

His head moved in a swift, virtually invisible bending forward, sinking his fangs into the soft skin between the neck and the shoulder. Blood instantly flowed down her back, painting it red, dripping on the black satin, painting it red. The loud sucking sounds filled the room. Hot fluid flowed into her, into him. Heat lost her. She lost heat, lost everything. Life left her. Thought left her. Numbness started spreading in the body. At the limbs first. Movement slowed down, and then stopped. She gasped for breath. He turned her, lowering her down on the bed. She rested there on her back, looking up at his misty, bloody, content face, the pale glow in his eyes.

– Now, it's up to you, he said.

She understood and tried to move, tried desperately, but nothing happened. She was dying. Every breath shorter, less than the previous. Hands were dead, feet were dead, body was dying.

He made a scratch on his wrist. Blood started flowing from it, down on her unmoving, oh, so useless body. Everything turned black, turned dead.

Her body jerked upright. Sensitive hands, sensitive as a flower grabbed his outstretched hand. A hungry mouth buried itself in the wrist wound, and she started sucking, sucking greedily.

She gasped, had to stop momentarily as the visions began, as blinding shadows filled the dark. She saw it, in flashes. He had experimented on another girl, turning her. It had been a success. He had seen her in the street as she opened the door to her apartment. And that was that. He had simply walked into her apartment, hushed her, making her turn rigid in fear and lust. «Hush», he had told her, and descended on her. The girl grew a set of fangs, becoming a creature of the night. But he cared nothing for her. Sheila felt his emotions or lack of it, as they were her own. But he cared for her. There was no doubt about that. She shuddered and stretched as he moved over her, her mouth and hands glued to his.

Eyes opened wide, opened so wide that they burst.

Flashes filled her. Emotions, memories filled her completely. James Evan Shelby, looking exactly as he did now, walked into the Whiskey and Go-Go Bar an eternity ago… yesterday, where dancing, nude girls warred with the players on the stage for the people's attention. Surprisingly enough it was a draw. Evan felt alive, felt the excitement all around him, felt the glow burning his skin. This was a time of Change, of transition, and everything was up for grabs. Clothes, customs and desires had changed virtually over night. The Sixties, a wild, desperate intermezzo in human history.

He saw her, and she noticed him that very moment.

– There's pain in you, like it is in him, she told him, Sheba told him, sometimes later, nodding towards the dancing, drunken magician on the stage. – But methinks yours is even a bit more delicious to behold.

The drunken magician sang, cried his despair and life over the yet unsuspecting audience.

> The man is dead
> A walking dead
> A ghost breathing
> The wind is bringing
> Fake rot and all bad things
> The child is dying
> Breath by breath
> The man is dead

The room dissolved and recreated itself. Evan and Sheba were alone in a room filled with shadows.

– I want this, Evan said desperately. – *Please!*
– How badly do you want this? The velvet voice sang to him.
– More than anything in the world, he solemnly swore.
– And that's also how much you must want it, she told him.
It was days later. The Hunger was a pain in his gut, overwhelming everything else. He resisted it, resisted it with all the might he could muster. Life beat in all the veins passing him, and he resisted its lure. He resisted it desperately.
Pain raged within him, overwhelming and terrifying, as it became him, everything he was. He had resisted the urge for so long, not only days, but centuries, and now the reckoning was here.
Flashing forward some more. Evan sat on the floor in the middle of a room, a slaughterhouse, staring at Sheba with shock, bewilderment, horror… and wild joy, everything evident in his expression, his deadly, bloody pale face.
Dead people, too many to be counted covered the floor all over the room, the large room, the large room in shadow. The bodies had been mangled as if a wild beast had ravaged them.
– This is what happens, she told him, – when you're trying to be something you are not.
And there were flashes of Pyramids, of Sheba walking its halls. And the buildings weren't for the dead at all, but for the living, for the firedrinkers, the shadows breathing fire in the night. Sheba was called to it, descending its many stairs filled with anticipation and boundless apprehension, called to the shadowy creature behind the throne. And she was Changed, and she moved her Shadow through the millennia, through the sands of time.
Sheila fell back on the bed, fell on her back on the bed, the black, black hole of the bed. Not a hair moved, not a muscle twitched. Sheila Watts breathed her last, gasped her last, and died. Open eyes stared at nothing.
And the dreams came. Vivid, haunting images of a creature stalking the night, a being without skin, eyes and soul.
And the city itself crumbled under its terrible power.
And then there were no more dreams, only the deep, black hole she(ila) fell into, and nothing and no one moved.

CHAPTER SIXTEEN

She opened her eyes, staring at the ceiling. She looked at herself from the side, at her nude body lying still on the bed. The once so dark room had turned brighter, to the point of hurting her eyes. There were no tears, though, no blinking, only the cold, unblinking stare. She sat up in the bed. Straight up. No distracting moves. It was more like a flow than actual normal movement, the way she dimly recalled it. She rose, flowed from the bed, effortlessly across the floor. Before being conscious of the thought of wanting to flow to the mirror she was there. Stopping, but not really stopping, more like retardation, like temporarily slowing down, moving, not moving in front of the mirror. She studied her mirror image, studied herself, absolutely, totally fascinated. The eyes had changed. Green eyes had turned deep green, like a blade of grass, like the deepest of forests. She drowned in her shining eyes. The facial features had seemingly changed, stretched, until becoming unfamiliar, but trait-by-trait the face might not have changed at all. She opened her mouth, and the fangs protruded from the snout her mouth had become. And now there were real fangs. Not the pretence humanity had struggled with for so long. She turned again, taking in the room around her, her surroundings. The room had changed, to a point that it was no longer the same room. There was noise and sounds from the outside. Her hearing had grown so accurate that she was able to identify direction and distance in just a tiny moment of time. She heard her own breathing, but she was willing to bet no one else could.

– Am I dead? She asked the air.

She stopped a bit, nodding to herself, as she moved her tongue, researched her new, strange mouth, its new pointed teeth. Her speech was slurred. It was hard to speak with the fangs fully grown.

– Do you feel dead? He replied.

She felt him, felt the blood move in her veins.

– No, she pondered. – I feel alive, more alive than I have ever felt.

She turned towards the doorway, and he was no longer there. She couldn't say for certain if he had ever been.

The phantasm, in the mirror and not, had blood all over her. All of it coagulated and turned to rust. Centuries, she knew, might have passed in the outside world. She touched her neck. It was a bit tender, but there was no wound there, no bite-mark. She removed the bandages around the head and the arm. There were no marks, not even scars. No marks, or blemishes on her entire body.

She showered again. Another strange experience. It was as if the drops fell in slow motion, that she could avoid them all, if she put any effort into it. She dried fast and didn't really need the towel. It was still pleasant, though, the rubbing of her now immensely sensitive skin. She wondered what pain would feel like, now. Fear passed her briefly.

– You're still vulnerable, Sheba told her. – It will take nights of feeding until you're truly immortal.

– I know, Sheila nodded. – I will take care of it.

– I know you will, dear. I know you will…

Sheba had been sitting in the chair, just now. Sheba had touched her on the cheek. Now, she was gone.

She opened a closet. There were velvet dresses there, all clean and smelling good, good, good. She sniffed them all before choosing one, before letting it slip over her head, rest on her body.

– Why don't I feel any Hunger? She wondered.

– You're a newborn, Sheba told her. – You don't need to feed for hours.

– What about the woman in the apartment, the physician? She wondered

– Nobody turned her. She was brought thirsty into the world.

The newborn heard the howls from below, the clink of glasses meeting. She listened to the flow of water from outside. It moved like blood, but as if through hardened veins. Her feet hardly touched the floor as she moved, moved across the room like the wind. She laughed giddily, darkly, and even the laugher felt strange. Outside, in the hall people passed by, but they didn't seem to notice her, not even those with flashing fangs. She moved out in the hall. She saw lovers stumble to a room, and she saw shadows move, flashing condescending smiles at the baby girl attempting to walk. There was no one here. Everything was quiet, except for the constant background noise in her ears, in her blood.

She remained in front of the mirror as he stumbled into the room.

Sheila Watts recognized him, somewhat, in a haze of clarity.

– I heard what happened, Johnston Parker said. – My people tracked you to this place.

Four men accompanied him. They checked out the room, and the adjacent rooms with drawn weapons and a professional, calm demeanor.

– Thank you, she said, – that's kind of you.

Sudden saliva in her mouth made it even harder to speak.

He stepped closer, one or two uncertain moves.

– Jesus Christ, what has happened to you?

He was Here, she knew that. In flesh and blood.

– I have become Shadow, she grinned, – become Mist.

Feel the Hunger, Evan said inside her. Smell the blood.

There was a contraction somewhere in her gut, and she crouched slightly. Saliva flowed in her mouth, dripped from her fangs. She felt a sense of panic grip her.

– Get out of here, NOW.

She didn't shout, but to her, her voice was filled to the brim with anxiety.

He shook his head in irritation, dismissing her words, her warning.

– Come with me, he said in his compelling voice, the voice she had thought to be so compelling. – I'll take you home.

She turned, and he saw her fangs. He saw the creature's demonic face and its deep, mesmerizing eyes.

– I am home.

The vein on his neck beat, beat, beat, smelling so nice, nice, nice. She smiled to him.

– It's okay, he said, backing off. – I'm going. I think you're right. I should be going.

He was no longer the strong, confident man she had known, but a child, afraid of the dark. And that was how he had always been.

– It's too late, she sang to him, – it's too late…

The other men didn't notice anything. She didn't have to do anything to them, to lull them into a haze of indifference, of false confidence. They saw nothing, and thus they sensed nothing. Their reality didn't cover the true reality.

He tried to run, but to her he wasn't. To her he hardly moved at all. She was over him in a flash. As he was drowning in her smile, her hum. He had hardly more than half turned, when she pulled close to him, slipped into his humid, blood-red embrace.

– Let's go into the other room, she whispered. – Get some privacy.

– Privacy, he nodded, nodded feverishly.

The four bodyguards supposed to guard his life with their own, just smiled and nodded.

Do I want to do this? She wondered. Does it even matter anymore?

Suddenly she was hungry, did feel the Hunger, and she couldn't believe Sheba had told the truth when she had stated that it would be worse in a few hours.

– Make the men leave, she told him. – I want us to be alone. I want to be alone with you. I don't want us to be disturbed.

He nodded.

– You guys get downstairs, he cried. – We'll catch up.

She heard them leave, heard the rustle of leaves of their boots moving over the floor, down the stone stairs, as she brushed aside his collar.

– Catch up, she whispered. He smiled to her.

She bit through the soft skin, to the life below.

And Life

Filled

Her.

She sucked greedily, insatiable, sucked him dry. He tried to scream, but it was just a weak moan, hardly audible. Her vision flickered, He turned rigid, as the last drops of Life were sucked out of him. She observed from outside herself, from deep inside the fire fade in his eyes. She gasped and released the body, the soon to be lifeless husk, and he fell to the floor, gasping his last breaths. He died, and her heart thundered in her chest. His spirit, everything he was vanished in the blinking of an eye.

And Life

Exploded

In her.

And then there was *pain,* like a hot poker in the gut. It was like every spot in the air turned alive around her, like she became every spot of air, every possible angle in the entire room, as if she became the entire room. She felt the Glow, the heat and cold spreading to everything, transforming her.

She cried in pain, as she changed further, as her body strengthened itself further, as she let go of the old, as her senses spiked at impossible angles, as if everything turned itself inside out, and finally was right.

And her tears, they were blood.

There was just a bit of blood around her jaw and on her cheeks. She swept it off in swift, relaxed, sensuous movements. The skin was like a firm, smooth, milky surface. The predator stared at herself in the misty mirror, flashing her fangs, her fangs gleaming in ivory and ruby. She was fully aware of the fact that she could appear normal by an act of will, but she didn't want to. This was what she was, now.

This is who we are.

– There is no need to drain the prey totally every time, Sheba told her.

Sheila turned, and this time there was truly Sheba in the doorway, looking so different, experienced through an enhanced consciousness.

– It's natural to do so the very first time, but later it is rather wasteful. We do indulge ourselves rather often, though. That's our nature.

– Thank you for your advice, Sheila slurred. – Why have you come?

Sheba smiled, radiant and full.

– I always enjoy seeing the newborn taking its first, hesitant steps. And you're such a delight, my dear. I always knew you would be.

Her presence was still overwhelming, in fact even more so, now, when Sheila saw her for what she truly was, for the first time. The impulse, the urge to kneel before her, in a shaking heap of joy was strong, but the newborn resisted it, resisted it with all her newfound might.

– I notice your Master isn't here, to rein you in…

More joy, more fear ran through her.

– Maybe he stayed away, deliberately, to allow me to take my first steps on my own.

– Maybe… That sentimental fool…

Sheba shrugged, smiling some more.

– But I'm rather pleased with him these days. I think he's coming around.

Queen Sheba faded away, and the newborn didn't see her go.

Sheila went downstairs, down broad stairs made of rock, painted in blood. She saw it, saw the ghost of all the red. Smoke and mist were thick in the room. Her sinister smile was painted on her face as the snarls and passion in the room greeted her, welcomed the new wolf in the pack. There were those who greeted her and those who attempted to subvert her. She denied them. It wasn't hard. Nothing was hard. She had become Night, become Shadow. Night welcomed her. The woman, one of the four from earlier tonight, from tonight, long ago, touched her cheek, touched it tenderly, before smiling, took a little blood, tasted a little blood from her cheek, before pulling back. Others, not drinkers, not night stalkers, the socialites, and men of power in society attracted to these places looked at the blood-covered woman in horror, and with strange smiles, both repulsed and attracted. The four bodyguards looked at her. She smiled to them. They pulled back. She wanted them to be scared, and they were sore afraid. Sheila walked outside, through the bright shadow tunnel. It was raining like thunder. She heard a crow squeak somewhere. She looked down startled. Water reached her to the knees.

– It's the fucking wall, a man cried. – It's leaking again.

– Leaking a *lot,* another belched.

People were running back and forth, or at least trying to, in the river the street had become. Some were already floating, being carried off by the second by second increasing current.

One of the bodyguards followed her outside. She moved at him. There were small cracks of thunder as he fired. She felt the sharp pain as the burning lead penetrated her skin, her soft skin. A hand grabbed his throat.

Another his gun, tore it from his weak hands.

– You ruined my dress, she wailed, like a little girl.

She looked down at herself. There was a little blood, a lot of blood flowing from the punctures on her belly, before they closed. Her skin repaired itself, as if the wounds had never been there at all.

– Don't fret about it, she told him, comforted him, kissing him several times softly on his cheeks, smothering him in kisses, in a predatory expectation. – I have quite a few left.

She sank her teeth in him. He was huge, and had a lot of blood in his powerful frame. He fought against her with all his power, nothing more than a child in her hands. The rain turned hot as it hit her, turning to vapor, turning to mist. She sucked and swallowed, sucked and swallowed. It took time, wasn't instantaneous. It just felt that way, as life flowed down her throat, and swelled within her. People saw her, saw what happened, and as they struggled to get away, they lost their footing, and were swept off their feet by the tide.

Strong hands shaking, as the rapture hit her, let go of the man. He fell into the river, and was gone from her presence, gone from sight, gone from mind.

She crouched, as she felt the current, both inside, and in the river surrounding her, felt mountains rise and fall. She gasped, as a radiant smile transformed her face, and the current led her away.

A woman with long, fair hair hunted the empty streets, moving so fast and in such a way she was hardly more than a revenant to the few poor souls that had dared venture outside tonight. Sometimes, in the coal dark gray her face was like painted in white, other moments like cloaked in Shadow. The human female felt their fear, their blood, the blood they would hardly acknowledge, felt it all flow through hardened veins. The heart they denied beat like thunder in their chest.

She moved, and she hardly felt she was moving at all. The world moved, and she moved with it. The old construction site stopped before her. Old buildings reeking of age, moved around her. The tiny rats stood still around her, as they desperately attempted to run, to flee, from the beast hunting them. She stopped them, stopped them all, with a thought, with a wave of her hand. The grown female briefly looked back, at herself, days ago, long ago, and could hardly even acknowledge that she had felt intimidated by these sweet creatures.

They stood still, still as statues, as she moved among them. She touched a boy, a girl, under the jaw.

- You're mine, now, she snarled, she told them gently. – You're all mine.

My servants.

The children nodded, as they looked up at her, looked at the beast in their midst with respect and subservience.

- Your eagerness pleases me, she said. – It fills me with joy.

There was no more smacking of lips, no more patronizing snarls from them. She was the snarl, now, the cry in the wilderness, and the beloved small beasts knew it, knew it in their hearts of hearts. They knew power, had always known it, and now, as they faced it, truly faced it, for the very first time in their young life, they were devoured by the deep, deep abyss below their feet.

She lifted up the girl, bit her, sucking just a bit, before putting her back down. They came to her, then. They all came to her, filed past her, offered themselves without choice, and she accepted them, took them as hers as she willed.

- You wear my mark, now. I will always know you, know your taste, your scent.

The beast laughed at them, dismissing them. A breath of wind, and she was gone.

The human female doubled back, returned to where she had come, but she took her time, covering vast distances. There was so much. The world was so much.

She stood on a rooftop, on a fake chimney, sitting on her heels, in perfect balance. There was no longer a matter of balance. The word itself had become meaningless. She walked a tightrope from roof to roof, and it was as if she walked on flat ground. The beast happily grinning, exposing her bloody fangs laughed thrillingly, as she jumped up and down on the rope. She sensed how it gave and then tightened below her. The blood she had consumed was still being consumed in her system, burning on a low flame, slowly, slowly, bittersweet fading. She cried out, howled happily, giddily. And long before she was empty, she would feed again. She knew that. And anticipation coursed through her.

Unaware of where she was going, really, she let herself be led, wherever she went, led never more. She stopped outside Camden Lock Market, suddenly hundred miles further down the street, listening. The night turned silent, and she heard the sound of someone stepping on a piece of glass, as distinctive, as identifiable as if she had always known that particular sound (and she had).

There were birds on a roof somewhere. They sang to her. There was the heavy scent of seawater. In the air, not in the river by her feet.

She moved, moved again, and this time she was like the wind.

The birds, all the birds rose from the roof.

And she saw Johnston. Except she knew it wasn't Johnston. His features were similar, but even if they had been identical, it wouldn't have been Johnston.

He moved in on two miserable creatures uselessly running. They stopped, finally, drawing their guns, drawing more guns, emptying one, throwing it away, drawing another, until there was no more left. He wasn't even hit when the firing pin hit the last empty chamber. Kathy Williams and Joseph Colton crouched there by the lock. Buildings around looked indistinct, misty. Sheila didn't see them. She moved. Just as the hunter charged the two wet figures, she blocked his path and pushed him back.

There was silence. He rose, fairly slowly.

– You were the man, the stiff in the morgue.

Charles Parker grinned, and he used his entire, impressive rows of teeth to do it. He practically snarled at her, as if he had completely lost his ability to smile.

The man she had, to this moment only spotted in glimpses, in snarls, in the heat of the hunt, she now saw fully, for the first time.

– You did choose the Change, didn't you, Sheila? I knew you would.

The voice certainly not belonging to Dominic Colby was like a knife cutting through butter, now, unrestrained as it was, reaching her undistorted.

She didn't speak. Her reply was a proud stance.

– You would protect… that?

She looked at the two, the two wet dogs, baring her bloody fangs, observing the shock in their eyes, looked hard at them, feeling nothing.

– I mean you would probably not be able to stop me, but I am curious…

He was right. He had fed like a tornado all over town the last week, and she merely twice. And it didn't matter anyway. She stepped aside.

Colton belched, cried out in absolute misery, and fell to his knees. Charles Parker was over him in a flash, but taking his time, savoring the moment. He lifted up the powerful built man like he was a feather, sinking his fangs into the thick neck. A wailing sound erupted from Colton. He felt it, felt it all, all the pain. There was no valve covering his thoughts, dulling the horrible pain of having life sucked out of you. Charles held on to him, massacred him, tore him to shreds, until nothing but pieces remained. The remains of the huge, heavy body hit the ground, lying still.

Kathy Williams stood there, still and silent. Sheila probed her eyes, attempting to find anything and didn't. She had left the building. There was nobody home.

Parker stood there. His eyes, his entire posture a storm of dark fire. Sheila experienced it all, took it all in, feeling marvelous. He looked at Kathy, the frozen husk, shaking his head.

– She's already dead. I don't need to kill her twice.

Sheila just stood there. She waited.

– There's still one left, he said calmly.

There was movement around them. She saw Evan approach. He took his time, but in less than a heartbeat, he was by her side, gently touching her shoulder.

There were people passing by in the street, in High Street. They couldn't really fathom what they saw. Some ran, some remained curious. There were policemen with guns. They stood their ground, though on shaky legs. Hands shivered around their weapons. Sheila recognized some of them as her people.

– Are you okay? he asked.

– I feel the storm, she replied. – I am the storm. I'm right as rain.

He nodded, smiling, unable to hide his relief.

– Nobody ever understood me before, she said softly, – understood my deeper nature, but you do. You do.

She sought to him, sought close to his burning body, heard him swallow hard, and knew it was all right. A rage, a peaceful rage settled within her. She kissed him, kissed him hard, and he returned it, more unrestrained than she had ever seen him, and she gasped in delight. Their teeth, their ivory touched and clinked. They tasted each other's blood, and felt its glow, its burning glow. It was nothing visible, but something seething inside.

He didn't hold her. She took one step back, smiling sweetly to him.

– Wow, she whispered, she grinned. – And what a delight, what delightful delight…

They stood there, taking it in, taking it all in, and they wanted more.

– JAMES

They looked up, heard the discord, the echo in the night, heard the voice from the other side of the ravine, the Abyss making the ground shake, shaking the air itself.

- IT'S TIME, JAMES

They saw her, as she floated towards them, as she greeted them with her blood, all her regal composure.

Sheba placed herself on the other side of the lock's «river».

– All my current children gathered for the family photograph, she said. –

Isn't that sweet.

– I've asked you this before, Sheba, Evan said, with more than a stint of anger in his voice. – What are you after? *What do you want?*

– Isn't that the wrong question to ask? She grinned teasingly.

Then she took one step forward, revealing everything to them, revealing the shadow creature from the halls of ancient Egypt. It was as if the Earth cracked open, and revealed everything, revealed nothing. They saw her, and they cringed in her exalted presence.

– I want my family in my court, she said softly. – Is that too much to ask? My other children are long gone or they're on the other side of the planet. I've waited more than half a century for you to come along. Now, granted, that's no more than a night for me, but I think I've been patient, been lenient. You've finally seen the light. There's no reason for you to resist anymore. None at all.

– You're not completely wrong, he said. – There's no Law, only the need, the Hunger and Death…and Life chasing through the eternal Night.

She smiled in triumph.

– But you're wrong on a couple of counts. Yes, I've embraced the beast inside, but not your version of it. The point is: You haven't. You cling to the civilized ways like glue. Perhaps you're wrong about yourself, too, I don't know. But I know one thing…

Parker looked at him, crouching in position, in defense, in offense, suddenly realizing something. He hadn't looked so good, a hateful, scared look in his eyes. But now there was only anticipation.

– You're wrong about me!

And unbridled rage.

Parker charged the female with a mighty, chilling snarl. Unbelievably enough taken off guard she was unable to completely ward off his attack. They tumbled into the water, the artificial river

He thought there were three against one, Sheila thought.

The savagery of Charles Parker cut into Sheba in ways she had never before experienced. She, too, howled in rage, throwing him off her, howling in pain, for the first time in millennia. Evan jumped at her then, using all he had of fangs and claws to cut into her. Parker returned. Blood flowed from his open wounds, wounds closing before he reached the ancient Egyptian woman.

And he was right.

There was a cruel, horrible standstill, as the two men bit into the taller female figure, as she tore them up, and blood and pieces of skin flowed like water. Without really thinking, considering anything, Sheila joined them. The two males held Sheba. Sheila bit into her neck, grabbing hold of the powerful body from behind, holding on with everything she had. Sheba's blood flowed into her mouth. There was a shadow swelling in her, fireworks behind her eyes. A clawed hand cut Sheila from neck to groin. She cried out and fell backward. Pain shot through her. *Pain.* She howled. The water, the current pulled her away. But then, seemingly by itself one of her hands grabbed the concrete, the naked concrete, without anywhere to easily hold on to. But she did. Held on. Easily. Her claws penetrating the hard surface like it would skin. She looked thunderstruck down on her body, at her flesh. There was a huge, gaping hole, a scar deep and broad as a dried river, a river of blood partly hiding the exposed, torn organs and innards.

Snarls and growls and howls filled the air completely. She saw it all, experienced everything, from all sides.

She rose once more, feeling the strength in her limbs, the blood flow through the heated veins.

– I feel strong, she said amazed, and then crying out with a voice yet drowning in the thunder. – I AM STRONG!

The thunder of her voice echoed through the streets, through eternity.

She watched, as her ghastly wound healed itself and completely closed in seconds.

Evan and Charles bit into Sheba's neck from two sides. For the first time in millennia Sheba SCREAMED, a shrill sound, completely devoid of humanity, penetrating everybody watching and within the slightest hearing range. One of humanity's oldest legends was brought to life once more, utterly and totally undeniable. The spectators stood there like statues, unable to move a finger.

Sheba pushed Charles away, but she couldn't get rid of Evan. He hung on, standing his ground. Sheila attacked again, sinking her teeth into her enemy's neck, Sheba's blood flowing like wildfire in her veins. The visions started. She watched Charles and Sheba on the balcony of the luxury resort by the Thames River. Johnston was inside, with a host of guests and dignitaries. The pain is just temporary, Sheba wooed him, biting into his neck, forcing herself at him, with will and physical strength. The Joy is eternal. Charles stared in shock at the night, at the passing river, feeling himself grow weaker, feeling himself surrender, and then… unable to tell where he got the strength from, he tore himself free, biting into Sheba's cheek, taking a huge, blood-filled chunk of it with him… as he threw himself off the balcony, and into the muddy, dark river, the river Styx, its current taking him, breaking his heart in pieces.

Sheba… howled, in despair, in fear, as the tree of them held onto her, tearing into her flesh, sucking out all her blood, her immortal blood. She waved her arms, kicked with her feet. White-hot light blinded Sheila, as ancient blood flooded her body, her soul, not just the relatively small amount needed during a Turning, but a lot of what made the ancient creature in their grip what it was. Waving arms, kicking feet slowed down. Sheila realized it was happening, that it was indeed actually, unbelievably happening, and raw, savage triumph swelled within her. The wolves bit into the lion and wouldn't let go. Sheba moaned, a long, distorted cry of despair, as her body turned limp, as life left her. The moan turned into a death rattle. There was no more blood. The three of them held on, kept sucking. The ancient creature was dying, but she didn't die. There was the feeling of drinking, drinking Power, incredible Power… There was no Glow, no sense of finality. Eyes stared at them, in boundless hatred, slowly, so slowly fading. Breathing stopped. Evan stopped the other two, pushing them away. He threw Sheba at the ground. She didn't move. She attempted to speak, but there were only distorted, guttural sounds.

He stepped on her neck, stepped hard once, twice, separating the head from the body.

The body lay still. The head rolled a bit, before lying still, too.

Once vibrant eyes were dead, cold.

– BUILD A FIRE, he shouted. – BUILD TWO FIRES, UNDER THE ROOF, far from each other.

Charles looked hesitant. Sheila halted when she saw the worry in his eyes.

The onlookers started moving, slowly, as if being asleep. Sheila couldn't tell if Evan controlled them, controlled them all, if he was powerful enough for that, now. They scrounged for wood, inside the old, derelict buildings without walls. There were at least twenty of them, hurrying like rats back and forth over the floor. Sheila saw them all like fire. She kept gasping, as her body, as all their bodies changed further under the onslaught of the totality of the Mother's blood.

– Sheba lived in the past, Evan said harshly. – *We* don't. That's where she was wrong. She wanted to recreate ancient Egypt. She wouldn't let go.

Sheila felt the force rise within her, felt it engulf her like a beast, a snarling beast, and she knew that she, too, had been wrong. Sheba wasn't the one waiting in the shadows. *She* was! She moved her arms, embracing her surroundings, studying the people scurrying around her, the prey. The Shadow shone in her eyes, rose from her body, virtually turning solid, tangible. She laughed in euphoria, a dark, ominous laughter.

She had sunk far below the deep hole. There wasn't the emptiness there, the expected and feared emptiness, but fulfillment. A fulfillment she couldn't possibly have imaged existed.

In the three seconds, the three days she had slept she had learned thc truth about what she was. She was Life and Fire, the Beast in the forest, a Power beyond anything today's world had to offer.

Evan put the unmoving body on one heap, the head on the other. He pulled back and someone lit the fire.

The Fire rose under the shaky roof, blinding her.

The body twitched, before once more lying still, before catching fire, being engulfed in fire.

The crowd cried out in boundless shock. Sheila stared blindly as the figure started moving, as it rose, as it stumbled towards the outside, the rain. Impossibly enough there was a scream, a scream of rage, from the headless body. And nothing from the head, the burning skull. Sheila felt the fire, felt her own skin ooze and burn, even at this distance.

Evan grabbed a huge, half rotted beam, swung it at the fire creature, pushed it back at the fire. It fell, and kept burning. Finally, it lay still and remained still, as it turned to ashes, and disintegrated before their eyes.

The head, the burning skull, was no more.

And then she felt it, they all felt the Glow, as mist rose from the fire and swept the area, immersing the three standing there. They all gasped, as the energy ravaged them, as it made them grow even more.

It was done. There were only embers remaining. Sheila sensed them pulse and spark within her.

Charles Parker took one, two three steps forward, turning towards the crowd, a hand raised to a fist.

Sheila sensed, imagined how he attacked the crowd, how he tore them all apart, and they did, too. He made them sense it, made them see and experience it all.

– The hunters didn't die out, he shouted. – They were just hibernating, waiting for the day when the world was once more theirs. And now it is. Live with it, all of you, if you know what's best for you. Civilization's day is done. Now the long Night is here, and you all better learn. You've all lived your lives like in a dream. Now you better wake up, before someone make you wake up. These are my words to you. Heed them well… or *perish.*

He stood before them, a man no longer holding any emotion, any notion, any impulse back.

When he turned to the two holding hands, the two shadows mingling, he was somewhat calmer, but there was no rest in his eyes.

– I'll see you two around, he said. Nothing more.

Sheila couldn't tell whether or not he smiled or if it was just a twitch at the corner of his mouth.

They saw him leave. He walked off, slowly, as slowly as he was able to.

She did no more than look at the crowd, and they were gone, even more afraid of the night than before. Hopefully a few of them would see the light, embrace their Shadow… for their own sake.

Kathy didn't run. She remained. Sheila realized she had stood on her spot the entire time. The statue spoke, and its voice was thin and loud. It hurt Sheila's ears, the now so very sensitive ears.

– Please, Kathy said. – I want to be one of you, and I want you to do it, to be m-my Maker.

Sheila looked at Evan, a thin smile on her lips, her rusty lips.

– Is that the correct colloquial? She jested.

– It is as good as any I've heard, he grinned.

His grin was Deep, his grin was Scary. She liked that. She loved that.

– I'm not sure I can do it, she said. – Not yet.

– You can't. Evan shook his head. – In spite of having a lot of Sheba's blood in your veins. You aren't yet «set». Not now, and probably not in months.

She turned to Kathy.

– I will do it, she said softly. – In the meantime, we need someone who can protect us, protect us in our sleep.

– With my life, Kathy swore.

Sheila stepped close to Kathy, biting her, sucking the small amount of life, of fire.

It was done. Kathy looked at her, filled with love.

– You need time, as well, Sheila said to her. – To find yourself, to find the deep within and bring it out.

Sheila and Evan turned and left. Kathy remained. Sheila had to call to her.

– Come with us, she called, and the child did.

They returned to the hideout, briefly. The current continued to increase in strength. Kathy strived to keep up with them, with their ridiculously slow pace.

– Do you think the dam has fallen, fallen down?

– No. He shook his head. – Not yet. There's just a hole in it. But it will eventually rupture completely. It will collapse soon. There's merely a matter of time.

He turned to Kathy, flashing his fangs.

– What do you think of Wales?

– Wales sounds great, she said dreamingly. – I've always wanted to go there.

Sheila saw it, its tall mountains, and deep valleys.

They returned to the house, the room of smoke and mirrors. Half of the guests ran in panic from the place, but the other half, mostly those with fangs and claws, remained and quite enjoyed themselves. Evan and Sheila walked out on the dance floor, and they danced.

This is dance, Sheila thought. This is wild. This is Life.

In one way it was as if their feet didn't touch the floor at all. Each step felt that light. But each time Sheila touched the floor, she felt it, felt it like never before.

It felt like soft ground. It felt like hard rock. Under their whirling feet. She noticed her body move through the air, noticed as the air brushed against her skin hairs.

This dance ended. The dance continued… Forever. She sensed the others' eyes on her. They saw, smelled the blood on her clothes. On him. More than that. The boiling blood within her, within him overwhelmed them. They knew. She sensed rage, envy, fear and respect. And in a few also joy. Everything within herself.

In the room of shadows Sheila picked a few velvet dresses, the pellet gun from the inventory, the one with the explosive charge, a lot of pellets, and hardly anything else.

They packed each their rucksack, a few items, a few kilos of necessities, nothing more.

– We're leaving Atlantis, she said. – Atlantis is sinking. In a hundred, a thousand years it will be just another myth. But we won't be. We'll see the mountains fall and rise, rise and fall.

She saw it, saw them wander through the gray, the endless gray until there was gray no more, and everything had once again turned green and lush. Perhaps they would walk, walk and run in the night. Perhaps they would travel in a wagon, pulled by horses or bulls, as they hunted, fed and lived. It didn't matter.

They had time.

Amos Keppler
1992-10-31 – 2004-07-07
199th Night 12059
In the fourth year in the time of the Twilight Storm
Amazing. I never thought I would complete this one.

Printed version 2010-09-24
276th Night 12065
In the tenth year in the time of the Twilight Storm.

Other published and upcoming novels and books by **Amos Keppler** from **Midnight Fire Media**:

Your Own Fate

From The Book of Fate:

In the Book of Fate there is everything. Every incident, all times, everything that has been, that is, that will ever be, everything that might be, everything that could have been.

But who is writing it? Who is penning it? Who is turning page by page, too many to be counted, blowing in the wind? Does it perhaps write itself, with a pen moving across the yellow sheets? Or is it a hand moving the pen, one unseen, one stretching back into the past, back to the time before everything was created, creating itself from nothing?

Timothy Joyce is an enigma, a man without a past, appearing from nowhere, to go on a rampage in an astonished world.

Jeremy Zahn is hunting Timothy Joyce. It seems like he has always been hunting him, from old London, from the island of angels, where it is said they met for the first time, to the city of angels, California, the new world.

Here, on this shaky ground, following confrontations spanning the globe, its time and space the two will fight for the last time.

And the world is watching, its people shivering in their frozen hearts.

ISBN 978-82-91693-05-7

The Defenseless

The two rivers meet and join in the city of Denver, becoming one...

The two dark brothers, growing up with their sister Linda in a mundane, average suburb, a place well entrenched in modern United States and the world, have since their moment of birth been at odds with the world... and with each other.

Mike and Ted Cousin are not who they are. There is a mystery here, one of birth and upbringing, one of fate. Violence and death, blood and fire follow them all the days of their lives. The fire is resting somewhere inside... waiting for the Spark.

Their parents know something, but are not telling it. The policeman Mark Stewart and their aunt Trudy do, too. Everybody knows something, pieces of the whole, but nobody knows the whole truth, nobody telling it.

The ancient power is returning to the world, a world massively suffering from physical and spiritual poison, on the brink of collapse and a collective tailspin suicide run without its like in human history.

Magick is returning from its long exile. Thus begins the story of the wild beasts rising from their ashes.

The Spark is struck, horrible and terrifying.

First book of ten in the Janus Clan series: Ten stories of the wild man in the modern world, forty years of wandering, before the Phoenix is rising from its ashes.

ISBN 978-82-91693-08-8

Complete Poems 1989 - 2003

Venture into existence with Amos Keppler, into the rainbow, of red and green, shadow and pitch black. Experience Life through ShadowWalker's many senses.

That's all, folks.

Contains eight collections of poems, the first 291.

The Green Rose 1989 – 1993, 1995
Cry of the Jester 1993
Poems of the Hot Wind 1994 to 1996
Travels And Revels, Life and Magick, Tales from Hell and Beyond - Aleister Crowley 1995
The Infinity Cycle 1995 - 1998
Chronicles of Our Dreams 1998 - 2001
Diary of a Traveling Man 2002
TheBeautifulExcitingWorldinPieces January to August 2003

Also included are author's remarks and background material.

For sale February 28, 2011